THE
HOUSE
AT
PHANTOM
PARK

First published in the UK in 2022 by Head of Zeus
This paperback edition first published in 2023 by Head of Zeus,
part of Bloomsbury Publishing Plc

9 7 5 3 1 2 4 6 8

A catalogue record for this book is available from the British Library.

ISBN (PB): 9781801104005
ISBN (E): 9781801104012

Cover design: Ben Prior

Printed and bound in Great Britain by
CPI Group (UK) Ltd, Croydon CR0 4YY

MIX
Paper | Supporting
responsible forestry
FSC® C171272

Head of Zeus
5–8 Hardwick Street
London EC1R 4RG

WWW.HEADOFZEUS.COM

THE
HOUSE
AT
PHANTOM
PARK

GRAHAM MASTERTON

An Aries Book

For my friend Michael Halperin... with best wishes.
He has the power!

The scream was so shrill and so agonised and it carried on for so long that Alex dropped his iPad on to the bed and ran out into the corridor.

It sounded as if it were coming from the floor below, so he hurried along to the stairwell. By the time he reached it, though, the screaming had abruptly stopped. He stood holding on to the banister rail and looking downwards, his heart beating hard, but there was no sign of anybody down there.

'Hallo?' he called out. 'Hallo? Do you need any help? Hallo?'

He waited, listening, but there was no answer, so he made his way down the creaking oak stairs to the second-floor landing. The hospital was utterly silent now, and gloomy, although three thin shafts of sunlight were shining down the stairwell, with specks of dust floating in them.

'Hallo?' he called out again, but only once, because the sound of his own voice was an unsettling reminder that he was supposed to be the only person here. The hospital had been abandoned for over two years now, although beds had been left in many of the wards and private rooms. Some of the beds were still covered by stained and wrinkled sheets. On some lay pillows that were still dented by the heads of the last patients who had rested on them.

Alex walked along the corridor labelled Wellington Wing. There were eight doors on either side, some of them open. The oak floor had been laid over with speckled green linoleum, but it still squeaked when he trod on it. At the far end of the corridor there was a stained-glass window with the crest of the Carver family, whose house this had been before it was requisitioned as a military hospital. A white bull, standing upright. It had a ring through its nose, but it was wearing a zucchetto skullcap and dressed in a white robe like the Pope.

Alex peered into one room after another. Apart from their beds, and their bedside cabinets, and three or four drip stands, they were empty.

He reached the end of the corridor and turned around. Who the hell had been screaming? He was sure he hadn't imagined it. It was possible that there were squatters in the hospital, and that they had screamed to frighten him away. But it was doubtful that they would have guessed why he was here, measuring the building for its conversion into luxury retirement homes.

He walked back to the landing. He wondered if he should search the whole building, but that would take at least half an hour, and he had to complete his measurement of the upper floor before it started to get dark. The electrical supply was still cut off and wouldn't be restored until next week, at the earliest.

He had started to mount the stairs when he was sure he heard a door being closed. It sounded as if it had come from somewhere along the corridor on the opposite side of the landing, the Montgomery Wing. That led to a ward with multiple beds that had once been the Carvers' library.

He hesitated. A strong autumn breeze was blowing outside, and every room in the hospital was draughty, so it was likely that the door had simply closed by itself. But even if some illegal occupant had closed it, was it really his job to confront them? He was a surveyor, for Christ's sake, not a PCSO.

He took a step upwards, and then another, holding on to the banister rail. He was about to take a third step when he heard groaning. It was the groaning of somebody in both pain and despair, and it went on and on, and grew louder and louder, and increasingly desperate. There was no doubt that it was coming from the Montgomery Wing.

Oh, shit, thought Alex. *There's somebody here and they've been badly injured. The least I can do is find out where they are and how seriously they've been hurt, and call an ambulance if they need it.*

He went back downstairs, walked along the corridor, and opened up the double doors of the Montgomery Wing ward. The last of the orange sunlight was shining in because there were three tall French windows along the left-hand side of the ward, each of them giving out on to a balcony and a view of the woods that surrounded the hospital grounds. The trees were waving frantically in the wind as if they were warning him from a distance to be careful.

There were eight beds in the ward, all along the right-hand wall. None of them had sheets or blankets or pillows, and only one of them had a drip stand next to it, forlornly bent.

The groaning continued, sometimes low and wavering, but then rising higher until it was nearing a scream. Yet there was nobody there – not that Alex could see, anyway. He made his way slowly along the line of beds, ducking his head down to look underneath each of them in turn. The groaning grew even louder and more tortured as he approached the last bed. It was empty, but the mattress appeared to be depressed in the middle as if somebody were lying on it, and he thought he saw the depressions move, as if they were rolling themselves from side to side in agony.

For a few seconds, Alex stared at the bed, both baffled and frightened. The groaning dropped down to its lowest pitch, more like grumbling than groaning, and then it suddenly rose to a triumphant scream. The mattress springs suddenly scrunched, and Alex felt two powerful hands seize the lapels of his jacket. He was pulled violently off his feet and tipped face first on to the bed.

He had no time to fight back. As soon as he sprawled on the mattress, he was gripped between the legs by a pain so intense that he felt as if he had fallen on to a train track and straddled an electric rail – a pain that blinded him and deafened him and made him scream so loudly he thought he had torn the lining of his throat to bloody shreds.

He pitched on to the floor, knocking his head against the drip stand so that it fell on top of him with a clatter. He thrashed and kicked and screamed but the pain was relentless, and if anything it grew more and more unbearable.

He lay there and went on screaming. Outside the French windows, cumulus clouds piled up from the west and covered the sinking sun, and the ward rapidly grew darker and darker. And still the pain went on, no matter how Alex screamed, and sobbed, and groaned, and begged for somebody to put him out of his suffering.

Nobody came, and as the hours passed, he lapsed into silence, his eyes closed, wondering how such pain could even exist.

In the darkest hours of the night, he thought he could hear men's voices, although he couldn't make out what they were saying to each other. He called out two or three times, but nobody answered. And still the pain went on.

2

'Look, his car's here,' said Lilian, as David turned into the forecourt of St Philomena's. 'I can't understand why he hasn't been answering me.'

'Maybe there's no signal,' said David.

'He didn't have any problem calling me when he first arrived. He said he was making good progress and hoped to have the whole top floor measured before it got too dark. He's usually *so* reliable. He measured up that Kingswood golf club conversion in two days flat.'

Lilian climbed out of the car and straightened her skirt. She had put on three or four pounds this week and the waistband was slightly too tight for her. She had sworn that she would stop eating bread but she had been late home every night and instead of soup or salad she had ended up making herself sandwiches. She wished that she had put on her Spanx.

David shaded his eyes with his hand. 'Is that him up there?'

'Where?'

'Up there, on the top floor. I thought I saw him looking out of that window next to the ivy. Well, I saw somebody's face, anyway. But he's gone now.'

'Perhaps you're right and there's simply no signal. Let's go in and see how he's getting on.'

They crunched across the shingle forecourt to the pillared porch. Lilian was more excited about St Philomena's than any other development she had taken on. The former military hospital was an imposing brown-brick house in the Jacobean style, with latticed windows and elaborately decorated chimneys. It was surrounded by eighty acres of woodland on the North Downs of Surrey and she knew she could convert it into a stunning residential complex that would sell for millions.

Before she stepped up into the porch, she stopped for a moment and looked around, listening to the soft rustling of the trees all around the house. She had never felt so contented and fulfilled.

'He's only gone and left the bloody door wide open,' said David.

Lilian turned around. 'He must have got my message after all, and he's expecting us.'

'Not very security conscious. Any bugger could stroll in, couldn't they, and help themselves to whatever they want?'

'What could they steal? Old hospital beds? I wish they would. It would save us the expense of having them all carted away.'

They entered the hallway with its oak panelling and its faded purple carpet. It smelled of oak, and faintly of antiseptic too. Most of the pictures had been removed, but a portrait of St Philomena's previous owner, Sir Edmond Carver, still hung beside the staircase. He had a drooping grey moustache, and bags under his eyes, so that he looked ineffably weary, as if life had beaten him down, for all of his wealth, and for all of his achievements as a banker and a great philanthropist.

'Alex!' called David. 'We've arrived, mate! Where are you?'

There was no answer, so he called out again.

'Alex! Are you upstairs?'

Still no answer. David turned to Lilian, with one eyebrow raised, and now he was beginning to looked worried.

'I was sure I saw him up at that window. But maybe it wasn't him. I hope it wasn't some squatter.'

'Even if it was, what's happened to Alex?'

'I'd best go up and see if he's there, hadn't I?' said David, almost as if he was hoping that Lilian would tell him not to bother.

'All right,' said Lilian. 'I'll take a look down here. Perhaps he's measuring the cellars and that's why he hasn't heard us.'

'What if that *was* a squatter I saw?'

'Then give me a shout. We can always call the police if we have to.'

David reluctantly began to mount the staircase, while Lilian went through to the huge, high-ceilinged drawing room. The only furniture remaining was a single spoonback armchair, pushed into a corner, and all the curtains had been taken down. The carpet had been rolled up, and the parquet floor was strewn with grit and cigarette butts and lumps of plaster. Somebody had abandoned a wheeled walking frame in the sandstone fireplace.

A dusty mirror was still hanging over the mantelpiece, and Lilian caught sight of herself crossing towards it. In a room as vast as this, she appeared to have shrunk, like a character in *Alice Through the Looking-Glass*. She went closer to the mirror, stood on tiptoe and peered up at herself, and she was pleased to see that she didn't look as chubby as she felt.

She fluffed up her sharply cut brunette bob and pouted her bright scarlet lips. Her face was round, and she might have a little suggestion of a double chin, but in the happy early days of their marriage her ex-husband, Tim, had always told her how much he loved her chestnut-coloured eyes, 'like shiny conkers', and her snubby little nose. 'Ski-jump nose', he had called it. But that was before he had lost his job as a reward manager for Price Waterhouse and turned to drink and started to shout at her and hit her and blame her for everything that had gone wrong in his life.

Today she was wearing a black Hugo Boss business suit. She always wore black suits to work because she thought they gave her more authority, and they took attention away from her figure – or at least, she thought they did.

She walked over to the French windows and looked out into the overgrown garden. She had already chosen a site for the tenants' swimming pool and an elegant veranda with an Italian-style stone balustrade all around it.

She was still staring out of the window when she heard a clattering noise from the direction of the kitchens. She turned around, listening. There was a long moment of utter silence, and then she was sure she could hear someone softly and repeatedly crying out, 'Ah – ah – *ahhh!*'

She walked quickly back out to the hallway.

'Hallo?' she called out. 'Is there anybody there?'

There was silence.

'David? Have you found any sign of Alex yet?'

Still more silence.

She hurried along the corridor that led to the kitchens. Although the kitchen walls were still tiled with olive-green Victorian tiles, all the original stoves had been removed when St Philomena's was converted into a hospital and replaced with what had then been modern Aga ovens. The oak dresser had remained, though, and two of its top drawers were hanging open, and six or seven kitchen knives were scattered across the red-tiled floor.

Lilian stooped to pick some of them up, but as she did so she heard another breathy 'Ahhh' from the scullery.

'Is somebody *there*?' she demanded, trying to sound as schoolmistressy as possible. 'I hope you realise that this is a private building, and that you're trespassing!'

There was no reply, so she dropped the knives back into the cutlery drawer, slammed it shut, and went through to the scullery. That had hardly changed at all from Victorian times, with a deep cast-iron sink and two mahogany draining boards, although one of the lower cupboards had been removed to install a dishwasher.

To Lilian's bewilderment, there was nobody there. She went right down to the end of the scullery, up to the back door that led out to the garden, and tried the handle. The key was still in it, but it was locked.

There was a tall cupboard door beside her, and she opened that up, but there was nothing inside it except an old-fashioned mop and bucket and a broom with most of its bristles missing.

Perhaps the 'ahhh' sound had been the hospital's old plumbing, or the wind blowing under the scullery door. But that dresser drawer couldn't have opened by itself, and how had all those knives tumbled out?

Lilian waited for a few moments, in case there *was* somebody in the kitchen, and somehow they had managed to hide, perhaps by curling themselves up inside one of the ovens, although she didn't have the nerve to open up either of the oven doors to find out. In any case, she told herself, they would have to be a contortionist.

She listened, but she heard no more breathy cries, so

she walked back along the corridor to the entrance hall. She glanced back over her shoulder when she reached the staircase, in case she was being followed.

'David?' she called, still looking behind her. 'Have you found Alex yet?'

It was then that she heard an appalling scream coming from somewhere upstairs. It was the scream of somebody in unbearable pain, and the last time Lilian had heard anything like it was when her neighbour's pet Labrador had been crushed under the wheels of a bus.

'David! Who's that? What's happening up there, David?'

'I don't know!' David shouted back. 'It's coming from one of the wards! Second floor! I'm going there now!'

'Wait for me!' Lilian told him, and she started to climb the stairs. All the time the screaming continued, wavering up and down in desperation, as if the screamer were singing the chorus in some bloodthirsty opera like *Bluebeard's Castle*, in which half the cast were being stabbed to death.

David was waiting on the second-floor landing. He was staring at her in sheer horror.

'I think it's coming from that room along there!' he told her, raising his voice so that she could hear him over the screaming. 'The Montgomery Wing.'

Without a word, Lilian stalked along the corridor with David following her. She pushed open the doors that led into the Montgomery Wing and the screaming in here was piercing. When she walked into the centre of the ward, she saw at once where it was coming from. Alex was down at the far end, lying on the floor on his back, his head and shoulders out of sight under one of the beds, kicking his legs. He had soaked his grey trousers, and soiled them too, by the look of it.

Lilian hurried up to him and knelt down on the floor beside him. 'David – help me to pull him out.'

Even though Alex was kicking so violently, they managed to grasp his ankles and drag him out from under the bed. His blue eyes were bloodshot and bulging, and though he was looking at them directly, it appeared that he couldn't see them, or else he was suffering such agony that he was blinded to every other sense except his pain. He had chewed his lips so ferociously that they were hanging in rags, and his chin and his neck were smothered in blood.

He kept on kicking his legs, so hard that he kicked off one of his shoes. Not only that, he was repeatedly beating his chest with his fists, really hard, as if he were punishing himself for feeling such torture, or trying to make sure that his heart kept beating.

'Alex! It's Lilian! Alex! What happened?'

Alex shook his head violently from side to side, but he didn't answer. He stuck his tongue out from between his lips, and Lilian could see that he had bitten the end off that too. As he screamed, bubbles of blood poured out of the sides of his mouth and dripped down on to the floor.

Lilian stood up, took out her phone and prodded out 999. When the emergency operator answered, she had to walk over to the French windows and stick one finger in her ear so that she could hear her over Alex's screaming.

'Ambulance please, St Philomena's Hospital in Downlea. We're on the second floor, in the Montgomery Wing. It's a man in his thirties, Alex Fowler, and he's in terrible pain. I don't know why. I can't see any sign of injury. But just listen.'

She kept the line open, but she went back and knelt down beside Alex again, placing her left hand over his forehead to try and calm him down. He felt chilled, and sweaty.

After three or four minutes, he stopped screaming, and let out a gargling sound. Lilian was afraid that his heart might have stopped, but he kept on shivering and shaking and snuffling, as if he were so exhausted that despite his agony he had fallen asleep, but was still feeling it in his dreams.

3

As soon as Moses sat down at the kitchen table, Grace said, 'My God, Mo. What's the matter? Have you been having that nightmare again?'

Moses nodded. 'I thought I was all over it. But it came back last night, and it was worser and clearer than ever. I might just as well have been there all over again. That was why I went and slept in the spare room.'

'I thought it was because I was making you too hot.'

Moses covered his face with his hands. 'I can never seem to shake it off. I thought all them sessions with Dr Walmsley would help me to forget it. They did for a while. But last night – I was *back* there, Grace. I was back there in Kajaki, with all the heat and the dust and the smell, and Corporal Simons lying there in front of me.'

Grace came around the table and laid her hand on his shoulder, as if she were giving him benediction.

He looked up at her and said, 'I tell you, I am going to be seeing Corporal Simons lying there in front of me till the day I die.'

Grace kissed the top of his bald head. 'The best therapy I can give you right now is a strong cup of tea. And some breakfast. I was going to make some akara and akamu.'

'I don't know if I could eat anything at all, honey. That nightmare made me feel sick to my stomach.'

'Oh, you say that now, but you wait till the middle of the morning, after you've been out there gardening. You'll be back in here saying you're starving and I'll be halfway through the ironing.'

She went back across the kitchen, switched on the kettle for his tea, and then lit the gas under her frying pan so that she could start to sauté the akara, the fritters that she had made with black-eyed beans and Scotch bonnet peppers. She would serve them with akamu, which was fermented maize custard. After instant Indomie chicken noodles and eggs, this was Moses' favourite breakfast.

'Don't forget you're picking up Lewis and Daraja from school this afternoon,' said Grace, as she set down his plate in front of him, with a china bowl of akamu on the side for dipping.

'No, I have not forgotten. They always cheer me up. Did Blessing say when they was coming back?'

'He doesn't know yet. It won't be too late.'

Moses had his mouth full of akara when his phone rang. He took it out of his shirt pocket and frowned at the unfamiliar number.

'Hallo?'

'Is that Captain Moses Akinyemi?'

'Yes, but retired now. Retired for ten years.'

'This is Robert Wells. I'm the clinical lead at the emergency department at St Helier Hospital in Sutton.'

'Oh, yes? How can I help you?'

'I'm sorry to trouble you, but a patient has been admitted this morning suffering from acute pain. I've had to classify it for the time being as chronic dysaesthesia, because we can find absolutely no sign of what might be causing it – either external or internal. There's no injury or inflammation of his coeliac plexus and I've just been given the results of his CT scan and that's a hundred per cent clear. No aneurysms, no swelling, no tumours. Nothing.'

Moses slowly finished chewing his akara and swallowed it. 'Like I say, sir, I retired from the Army Medical Corps ten years ago, so I don't know why you are calling on me. I was a front-line military medic, so I never came across any case like the one you're describing. All the personnel that I treated were suffering from bullet wounds or massive trauma from roadside explosive devices.'

'I'm aware of that, Captain Akinyemi. But despite the fact that our patient's pain is almost unbearable, he has managed in his few brief moments of lucidity to tell us his name – and to give us *your* name, too. He says you saved his life and that you will know more than anybody else why he is feeling such pain. We contacted the RAMC headquarters in Camberley and they were able to give us your number.'

'*I* saved his life? When? How? What did he say his name was?'

'Terence Simons.'

Moses looked across the kitchen at Grace, who was drying the dishes. She was mouthing '*Who is it?*' at him. He flapped his hand to indicate that he would tell her later.

'I did once treat a casualty by the name of Simons, out in Afghanistan. Corporal Simons, although I never knew his first name. And, yes, I probably did save his life. But that was way back in 2013. And the injuries he sustained – believe me, the only word for them was catastrophic. If your patient has no signs of physical disability, he cannot be the same Simons, no way. The Simons I treated lost both his legs and half of his left arm, and he was blinded in one eye.'

'In that case, we're definitely not talking about the same man,' said Dr Wells. 'Are you absolutely sure you've never treated any other patient called Simons?'

'I guess I may have done. It was a long time ago, and I cannot remember every casualty I treated. There was dozens of them, and most of them, I never got to find out their names. Their uniforms was all bloody and torn and the medical emergency response teams used to arrive in their Chinooks and whisk them away before they came to – that is, if they ever *did* come to.'

'Well, I'll tell you what,' said Dr Wells. 'I can have a picture taken of this chap, and email it to you. Perhaps that might jog your memory. It's just that he's suffering such excruciating pain and apart from pumping him full of oxymorphone we can't think of any other way of relieving it.'

'All right. Okay. Send it to me and I will see if I recognise him.'

He laid down his phone on the table, staring at it as if he were afraid it might explode.

'What's wrong?' asked Grace. 'Who was that?'

'A doctor from St Helier. He says they have a patient who knows me. A patient called Simons.'

'Not *Corporal* Simons?'

Moses pushed away his plate. 'I'm sorry, Grace. I cannot eat any more. This has put me off completely.'

'Not *Corporal* Simons, Moses! It can't be!'

Moses went to sit in the living room and Grace brought in his mug of Nigerian tea made with cocoa and milk.

'Drink it before it goes cold. You need something to keep up your strength.'

On the window sill, next to a picture of their wedding day, stood a framed photograph of Moses at Camp Bastion, along with some of the other members of his medical team. He was wearing combat fatigues, with his little monkey-head mascot hanging from his lapel. The monkey head was a juju charm that his mother had given him to protect him from harm.

He couldn't take his eyes off the photograph. Although he knew that Grace was right, and that the patient who had been admitted to St Helier couldn't possibly be the same Corporal Simons who he had treated by the roadside in Kajaki, he was still filled with a sense of dread – the same dark sense of dread he had always felt when he climbed into a Mastiff protected patrol vehicle to be driven to a forward operational base.

His tour in Afghanistan would never leave him, especially the sight of Corporal Simons lying up against a rocky slope with both legs blown off, his left eye hanging out, and his left forearm ripped into rags. His legs didn't even look like legs, because the explosion had smothered them in blood and dust. It had also driven earth, dust and animal excrement into the soggy gaping cavity of his groin.

Despite his appalling injuries, he had looked up at Moses with his remaining eye and actually smiled at him.

'Was that an IED?' he had asked. 'I didn't hear nothing.'

Moses' phone warbled. He picked it up and saw the photograph that Dr Wells had sent him by messenger. It showed a pale-faced, thirtyish man with a mole on his upper lip and a short businesslike haircut. He was frowning as if he were working out a particularly knotty maths problem, but Moses could tell from experience that he was trying to concentrate on anything else except his unbearable pain.

Moses had never seen him before in his life, and apart from that he looked too young to have served in Afghanistan. He called Dr Wells back.

'No, doctor. I do not recognise this man. Not at all.'

'You're sure? He's been saying your name over and over.'

'I have never seen him. I am sure about that. And since he has no sign of any serious injury, no combat scars, why would I have treated him? From his age, I question if he was ever in the military at the same time that I was – that is, if he was ever in the military at all.'

'I'm finding this extremely hard to understand, Captain Akinyemi. It's not as if you have a common name, or a name that's particularly easy to pronounce. I can't think how or where he could have picked it up from, or why he's so sure that it was *you* who saved his life.'

'I am sorry that I cannot help you more. All I can hope is that you are able to find a way to relieve this patient's suffering.'

Dr Wells paused for a moment. Then he said, 'I realise that this is asking an awful lot of you, but do you think you could possibly come to the hospital and see him in person? He is so insistent that you are the only person who can help to relieve his pain.'

'I do not know what possible good I could do. Especially since I do not know him.'

'Well, it's up to you. But we would cover your expenses… your taxi fare, if necessary, and any other costs you might incur. To be honest with you, I've completely run out of ideas, and even if there's only the slimmest of chances that you could give him some respite, I think it's worth a shot.'

Moses took a deep breath. Would Afghanistan ever give him any peace? But although he was retired, he was still a professional medic, and a professional doctor had asked him for assistance.

He covered his phone with his hand, and said to Grace, 'He wants me to go to St Helier and see this man.'

'Don't. Not if it is going to upset you.'

'I have to. How can I refuse him?'

Grace shook her head. 'Well, go if you think you have to. But I won't forgive you if you wake up in the night screaming and sweating, the way you used to.'

When Moses arrived at St Helier Hospital, it had just begun to rain. The hospital was a huge collection of white concrete buildings in the 1930s modernist style, the largest hospital in Surrey, and Moses himself had been born here. The last time he had visited was when their older son Isaac had nearly died of a heroin overdose. He thought that if he could be haunted by any other place apart from Camp Bastion, this was it.

Dr Wells was waiting for him in the emergency department. He was built like Falstaff, with rounded shoulders and a white lab coat that was almost bursting its buttons. He had a high wave of white hair and heavy spectacles that looked as if they might drop off the end of his nose at any moment. Two nurses were standing either side of him: a slender male nurse with tightly pursed lips, who looked as if he were Korean or Chinese, and a red-headed young woman with freckles all over her face, carrying a tablet.

The emergency department all around them was clamorous. At lunchtime, a serious traffic accident on the A217 had involved a school bus and a concrete mixer truck, and several children had been badly injured. Nurses were hurrying left and right, and porters were wheeling trolleys with squeaking wheels along the corridors, while anxious-looking parents were gathered in the waiting area.

'We've moved our man upstairs,' said Dr Wells. 'He started screaming again and he didn't stop, even when we sedated him, so we've isolated him where he can't distress the other patients. Especially the little ones.'

He led Moses to the lifts and pressed the button for the second floor.

'I have to say that I have never come across a case like this before, not in all my thirty-five years. Of course, I've had to treat many instances of psychosomatic pain, usually caused by emotional stress. Stomach cramps, migraines, that kind of thing. But this patient is wracked with agonising pain from head to foot and there seems to be no reason for it, either physical or psychological.'

'When was he admitted?'

'This morning, around half past eight. He's a surveyor who works for a development company. Apparently, he was measuring the building that used to be St Philomena's Hospital in Downlea. His colleagues discovered him in one of the wards, and as far as they knew he had been lying there in agony all night.'

'You said that his name is Terence Simons.'

'That is what he insists on calling himself,' the red-headed nurse put in, in a strong Mancunian accent. She lifted up her tablet, prodded at it, and then she said, 'His colleagues told us that his real name is Alex Fowler. He's thirty-four, single, and he lives with his mother in Dorking.'

They stepped out of the lift and began to walk along the corridor.

'You have checked his medical history?' asked Moses.

'Of course. He suffered the usual childhood illnesses like

chickenpox and measles, but apart from occasional episodes of eczema, he's always been reasonably healthy.'

They turned a corner, and the red-headed nurse raised one hand to her ear. 'Listen up! He's gone quiet for now. Let's pray he doesn't start that screaming again!'

They reached the last door at the end of the corridor and she opened it up. It was gloomy inside, because a bottle-green blind had been pulled down over the window. Alex was lying flat on his back in a spotted hospital gown, without a pillow, and without a sheet or a blanket to cover him, although bumpers were attached to both sides of his bed to prevent him from rolling off on to the floor. A black student nurse was sitting in the far corner of the room, and when Moses and Dr Wells and the two other nurses came in, she stood up.

Dr Wells went over to Alex's bed and peered at him over his spectacles. 'Well, well,' he said. 'You're awake. And you've managed to stop screaming. How are you feeling? Any better?'

'No,' said Alex in a croaking voice, his eyes flicking left and right as if he was worried that somebody malevolent was creeping up on him, and he was in imminent danger of being attacked.

'I sang him a song,' said the student nurse. 'After a while he just stopped.'

'Perhaps I ought to try that myself,' said Dr Wells. 'What did you sing him?'

'"Nothing Compares 2 U".'

'Oh. Can't say I know that one. You'll have to teach it to me. Are you still feeling just as much pain, Terence?'

Alex nodded, and snuffled. Moses could see that he was gripping the sheet beneath him tightly with both hands.

'I've brought somebody to see you, Terence. Let's see if you recognise him.'

Dr Wells stepped to one side and beckoned Moses to come up to Alex's bedside. Moses said nothing, but Alex's eyes stopped flicking from side to side and he stared at Moses in what appeared to be utter disbelief.

'Captain Akenyemi,' he croaked. 'You found him!'

'Are you sure it's him?' asked Dr Wells.

'Of course – of course I'm sure! Captain Akenyemi saved my life! I'd be dead now, if it wasn't for Captain Akenyemi! I'd be six feet under!'

'I do not know why you think that,' said Moses. 'I do not remember you at all. In fact, I am sure that I have never seen you before.'

'You saved my life! How can you say that when you saved my life? Corporal Simons, how could you forget me? I was blown to buggery and you saved my life!'

Alex attempted to sit up, but Moses could see that as soon as he did so, he was lanced right through by unbearable pain. He let out a harsh, high, seagull-like scream and dropped back flat on the bed, shivering and sniffling and kicking his heels in agony.

All Moses could do was shake his head. 'I have no idea what you could do to stop him from hurting like this. You say you have given him oxymorphone. If that does not work, I do not know what will.'

'You saved me before,' gasped Alex. 'Why can't you save me now?'

'Because you are not the same man,' said Moses, leaning over the bumper.

'What?'

'Corporal Simons was blown up by a roadside bomb. He suffered from devastating injuries. He lost both his legs. You – there is nothing at all wrong with you, so far as the medical team here can tell. I simply cannot understand why you think that you are Corporal Simons, and how you know my name. Perhaps you have read about me in a newspaper article, or seen a documentary on TV.'

'You saved my life,' Alex whispered. 'I can't forget it. I was lying by the road and you came and you knelt down next to me, and I can remember that monkey's head you had pinned to your body armour. It was grinning at me, that monkey's head, and that was when I was sure that I was going to make it.'

Moses stared at him. 'You remember my monkey's head?'

Alex pursed his lips tightly together and nodded, and then he let out another scream so piercing that Moses clamped his hands over his ears.

Dr Wells patted Moses on the back to indicate that they should leave. He beckoned to his nurses, too, and they all filed out into the corridor. The red-headed nurse closed the door.

'I cannot believe that he knew about my *biri layya*, my monkey charm,' said Moses. 'How could he know about that unless he had seen me in Afghanistan? That was the only time I wore it.'

'He's a mystery all right,' said Dr Wells. 'I'm beginning to think that he might be suffering from some unusual variety of complex regional pain syndrome – what we used to call RSD.'

'But RSD,' said Moses, 'that's usually caused by the sympathetic nervous system continuing to react to an injury or a stroke long after the pain should have worn off. Yet you say this man shows no sign of any physical injuries, and his brain scan was clear.'

Dr Wells shrugged. 'We'll have to dig deeper to find out why he's hurting so badly. I'll be ordering an MRI, a bone scan and a thermography test. In the meantime, though, I'm considering giving him a large bolus of ketamine and midazolam, to induce a coma. We can't allow him to go on suffering like this.'

Moses went back to the door and peered in through the oval window. Alex was still writhing around on the bed and screaming. The black nurse was standing over him, and it looked as if she were singing, although Moses couldn't hear her.

'I still cannot understand how he can know who I am, and how he knew about my monkey charm. He scares me. Do you think I am overreacting? Some of the things I saw in Afghanistan, I cannot describe to you how terrible they were. Now this man has brought them all back.'

Dr Wells said, 'Why don't you come down to the canteen and I'll buy you a cup of coffee? It's the least I can do.'

Moses gave him a bitter smile. 'It is very kind of you, doctor. But all the coffee in the world could never make me forget the sight of men blown inside out.'

4

It was still raining, a misty drizzle, and the low clouds were as ruffled and grey as pigeon feathers. Lilian and David drove to the Cock Inn, a country pub just under a mile away from St Philomena's, and ordered Cornish pasties and two glasses of red wine. They said very little to each other as they sat by the window eating their lunch. Lilian was scrolling through her phone most of the time. She had arranged with Billings Chartered Surveyors in Crawley to send them up a replacement for Alex Fowler, and he was due to arrive at three o'clock.

She called St Helier Hospital, too, but they had no news about Alex's condition. Then she called Tim, her ex-husband, because she wanted to pick up some cookery books that she had left behind in their flat when they separated. It sounded as if Tim had a woman friend with him, and he sounded drunk, too, because he kept laughing and saying in a slurry voice, 'Get off!'

'Are you all right?' asked David, when she finally put down her phone.

'Why shouldn't I be?'

'Well, if you don't mind my saying so, you've got that face on.'

'What face?'

'That face you put on when somebody gets up your nose.'

'You know I always want everything to go like clockwork. And Alex falling ill like that – of course I feel sorry for him – but it's put us at least two days behind. I was hoping to be able to hold a presentation for potential investors next Wednesday. Thank God I haven't sent out the invitations yet.'

David was about to say something, but decided not to. He knew that Lilian wasn't nearly as hard-nosed as she pretended to be. None of the five women who worked for Downland Developments could afford to be sympathetic or sentimental or to show any sign that they were offended by blue jokes or sexist banter. It was a company that still lived in the 1960s, in which 'woke' was what you did after sleeping, hopefully with a 'dolly-bird'.

They rewarded their women well, though. Soon after he had started the company, the owner, Roger French, had cottoned on that women had far more organisational ability than men, and could see that his luxury housing developments were always completed on time and almost always under budget. 'Good housekeeping' is what he called it. Roger French was on his fourth marriage.

'Come on,' said Lilian at last, wiping her mouth and crumpling up her napkin. 'Back to the grindstone. We need to take photographs of the gardens so we can get some estimates for landscaping.'

'In this weather?'

'Gardeners work in the rain, there's no reason why we can't.'

'Good thing I brought my wellies then.'

They drove back to St Philomena's, but as they were turning into the hospital entrance, they found that the narrow driveway was blocked by a man in a cumbersome electric wheelchair. He was draped in a shiny black waterproof cape with only his pale face visible, and a monstrous black umbrella was attached to the back of his seat.

David gestured for him to move out of the way, but he stared back at them as if he didn't understand what they wanted him to do. The windscreen wipers squeaked monotonously backwards and forwards and Lilian had the uneasy feeling that this man was obstructing the driveway on purpose.

She climbed out of the car and went up to him. The drizzle prickled against her face.

'Excuse me, but we need to get up to the hospital. Would you mind backing up a bit, where it's wider, or pulling over to the side?'

The man looked up at her with eyes like two milky marbles. He had a hooked nose and the left side of his top lip was curled upwards, baring his snaggly teeth. He reminded Lilian of Mr Punch, from the seaside puppet show.

'What d'you want to go up there for?' he asked her.

'We have business there. Now, if you don't mind. We have a lot to do and we're in something of a hurry.'

'What kind of business?'

'I don't really think that's relevant. But if you must know, I represent the new owners. So if you'll just kindly move.'

'Nobody owns that hospital. Nobody – excepting my friends that live there.'

'I'm sorry, but it's vacant at the moment, and we really need to get on.'

'My old Army pals live there. What do you think I'm doing here? I've just been up to see them.'

Oh God, thought Lilian. Mentally disturbed as well as disabled. If he refuses to move we'll be forced to push him out of the way, and then there's the risk that he'll accuse us of assaulting him, and that sort of publicity is the last thing that Downland needs. 'Greedy property moguls force disabled veteran into hawthorn hedge.'

'*Please*,' she said, clasping her hands together. 'I'm asking you as nicely as I know how – please will you move out of the way and let us pass.'

'You don't want to be going up there anyhow,' the man retorted. 'Not by yourself. I'd be scared shitless if I was you. They might be my friends but they're no friends to nobody else. What they might do to you, well – it don't bear thinking about.'

David had climbed out of the car now, and he had been listening.

'There's nobody there, mate. The hospital's empty. Everybody moved out years ago. I know you probably have memories, but that's all they are.'

The man shifted underneath his crinkly waterproof cape and Lilian had the impression that he was severely lopsided, as if he had only one leg, or that his pelvis was askew.

'You go up there,' he told them. 'You'll find out.'

'We've already been up there. The place is deserted.'

At that moment, a middle-aged woman in a long brown riding coat and noisy wellington boots came storming up the driveway.

'Frank!' she snapped. 'Are you causing trouble again, Frank?'

'I'm giving these nice people some cautionary words, that's all,' the man called back.

'I'll give *you* some cautionary words, you perpetual nuisance!' she told him. 'Come on, get yourself moving back to the house or you won't be allowed out again!'

'I was only warning them, that's all.'

'I'll give *you* a warning!'

The man started up his electric wheelchair and hummed off down the driveway. He disappeared around the corner and the last Lilian saw of him was the large black mushroom of his umbrella.

'Sorry about that,' said the woman in the riding coat. 'He was two years in St Philomena's after he was wounded in Afghanistan and he can't stay away from the place.'

'He said that all his friends were still there,' said Lilian.

'Yes. And he really believes it. He's had therapy, but it hasn't shaken his belief in that, not one iota.'

'Perhaps when we develop it into luxury flats he'll come to realise that those days are over,' said Lilian.

'Oh, that's who you are! Good luck, then. It's such a beautiful old building it's been sad to see it neglected. My name's Marion Crosby, by the way. I run a small hospice for five former patients, just down the road in Downlea. Frank's the only one who's mobile, but he's always causing one sort of ruckus or another. The last time he was throwing lumps of horse manure at some poor woman because her horse had done its droppings in the road, right in front of him. Anyway – I'd better go and see that he's heading straight back and not annoying anyone else.'

Marion Crosby left them and they climbed back into the car and drove up to St Philomena's. The rain was easing off now, and a sickly sun was trying to peer through the clouds.

Lilian said, 'We can start off by taking pictures in the formal garden right outside the drawing room. That's going to be the focus of the whole development – you know, with fountains and seats and rose beds. That's why we're going to call it Philomena Park.'

They walked up to the porch and Lilian was disturbed to

see that the front door was wide open, as it had been when they arrived here earlier that morning.

'I'm sure I closed it properly,' she said. 'Don't tell me that Frank fellow has a key.'

'I can check with that whatshername, that Marion Crosby. But in any case we'll be having all the locks changed, won't we?'

'I'm not even sure we'll be keeping this door. I know it's original, but I can visualise one with a stained-glass panel in it. Art nouveau style, with trees and a setting sun.'

David looked around the driveway. 'No sign of our new surveyor yet.'

They entered the hallway. Lilian stopped and called out, 'Hallo? Is there anybody here? Hallo?'

They listened for a few moments, but there was no response. Lilian went into the drawing room, crossed over to the French windows, unlocked them and opened them. Outside, the formal gardens were damp and weedy and overgrown, with creepers snaking their way across the shingle pathways and twining themselves around a stone cherub who was standing in the middle of a dried-up fountain, looking infinitely sad.

'We'll have to find ourselves a really creative landscape gardener. An up-to-date Capability Brown. Creative, but classic.'

'I can do classic,' said a man's voice, off to her left.

Lilian turned around, startled. A tall man with tousled brown hair was stepping out of the alcove beside the French windows. He was wearing a long tan leather jerkin and corduroy trousers and green rubber boots.

'Excuse me, but what are you doing here?' Lilian demanded. 'This is no longer government property. It's private.'

'Really?' the man replied. 'Nobody told me that.'

'Well, I'm telling you now. You'll have to leave.'

'But I'm the gardener. I've been the gardener here for the last ten years.'

'I'm sorry, but I'm very surprised nobody informed you that the hospital was being closed and sold for development.'

'Sold?'

'Yes. *Sold*. And that meant that any contracts connected with it were automatically terminated. Housekeepers, cooks, window cleaners, maintenance staff. Gardeners, too, presumably.'

Lilian looked around. 'By the look of it, though, you haven't exactly been overexerting yourself. Have you been doing any actual gardening, or have you just been standing around watching the weeds grow?'

The man stepped forward, and as he did so the sun suddenly came out and lit up his face, as if they were having a supernatural visitation from a saint. He was handsome, in a dark, Nordic way, with grey, deep-set eyes and heavy eyebrows, and a strong cleft chin.

'I've been waiting on instructions,' he said flatly, as if that explained everything.

'You can't stay here, I'm afraid. If you leave me your name and phone number we might be able to find some gardening work for you later on, when we start our development, but we have no use for you just at the moment.'

The man stared at her in the way that men stare at women they find irresistibly attractive. His eyes really were the most extraordinary grey, like the sea on a thundery day.

'Martin Slater,' he told her.

'And your phone number?'

'You won't need a phone number. I'm always here. You only have to call me.'

'I think I've explained to you, Mr Slater, you can't remain here on these premises. Whatever arrangement you had to tend the gardens for St Philomena's, that expired when the hospital was closed. It's a question of security and also insurance. If you were involved in any kind of accident while you were here, and we had allowed you to stay, then we would be liable.'

Martin Slater smiled and closed his eyes for a moment, as if he were thinking of another time. It was then that David came out of the French windows and saw him, and said, 'Who's this, then?'

'He says he was employed by St Philomena's as a gardener.'

'So why's he here? Come to ask for his old job back?'

'It seems like it. That's why you're here, isn't it, Mr Slater?'

Martin Slater opened his eyes. 'I never went. I never will.'

David made a screwy-emoji face and silently mouthed the word '*nutter*'. Then he held up his camera and said, 'Shall we take a few snaps? Might as well, while the sun's out.'

'Yes. Mr Slater, you'll have to forgive us,' said Lilian. 'We have a great deal of work to be getting on with. Perhaps we can talk some other time about taking you on.'

'You have... a very special look about you,' Martin Slater told her.

'All right. Thank you. I'll be in touch. Not that you've told me *how* to get in touch.'

Martin Slater touched his fingertips to his lips and blew her a kiss. Then he turned away and walked off, making his way through the overgrown garden before crossing the sloping meadow beyond it and disappearing among the trees.

'Who the fish fingers was that?' asked David, watching him go.

'Don't ask me. This place seems to be a magnet for weirdos.

Now, do you think we can take some pictures? This garden first, then that playing field there at the side. That's where we'll put in the swimming pool. Then we can go round to the tennis courts.'

5

They had almost finished taking pictures of the tennis courts when a white Mini drew up outside the front of the hospital, its tyres crunching on the shingle.

'Ah – our replacement surveyor,' said Lilian. She opened the door in the fence around the tennis court and walked across the driveway to greet him.

Except that it wasn't a 'him'. The door of the Mini opened and a young blonde woman climbed out. She looked early-thirtyish, pretty in a rather Julie Christie way, with a high messy bun and a fringe that came right down to her eyebrows. She was wearing a tight pink sweater and a tight grey skirt.

'Lilian Chesterfield?' she asked, as she opened up the Mini's boot.

'That's right. Are you from Billings Surveyors?'

The young woman lugged out a heavy black briefcase and an iPad. 'Yes. Sorry I took so long to get here. There were roadworks all round Gatwick Airport and the traffic was practically at a standstill.'

'I was expecting Charlie Thorndyke.'

'Oh! I am Charlie Thorndyke! Charl-*ene* Thorndyke, actually. But everybody calls me Charlie.'

'I see,' said Lilian. She was a little irritated that Dennis Billings hadn't told her their replacement surveyor would be female. 'I suppose you know that Alex has been taken seriously ill.'

'Yes, of course. Dennis told me all about it. Have you had any more news?'

'None so far, I'm afraid. Come along inside and I'll show you how far he'd managed to measure up before he collapsed. He was in agony, poor chap. I've never seen anything like it. Oh – this is David, by the way. David Barton. David, this is Charlie.'

'Hi, David.'

David raised his hand in greeting and his face lit up like a sixth-former with a sexy new geography teacher. 'Hi, Charlie.'

Lilian and David led Charlie into the hospital hallway. Charlie stopped at the foot of the staircase and sniffed. 'Oak,' she said. 'And chlorohexidine, unless I'm mistaken. And a very faint mushroomy smell. There's dry rot somewhere in this building.'

'You've got a nose and a half,' said David. 'I'm impressed.'

'You know what we're planning to do here?' Lilian asked her.

'Oh, yes. I saw your development schematics when you first asked Dennis to carry out a survey. I have a copy on my iPad, too, for reference. All you have to do is show me where Alex got up to, and I'll crack on from there.'

They took Charlie upstairs to the third-floor bedroom where Alex had first heard the screaming from the Montgomery Wing. His iPad was lying on the bed where he had dropped it.

Charlie sniffed again. 'This place still has a hospital atmosphere, doesn't it? You could almost believe that the wards are still full of patients. And I don't just mean the smell of antiseptic.'

She paused, and turned around. 'It's like the whole

building's holding its breath, hoping that nothing terrible's about to happen. Can you sense that? It's actually caused by static. It can build up, static, when a building's left empty for any lengthy period of time.'

As if to illustrate what she felt, they heard a door closing, somewhere downstairs.

'There's nobody else here, is there?' she asked.

'It's only the draught,' said David. 'It makes whistling noises too. You know – in case you get worried that there's a ghost wolf-whistling at you.'

From the way Charlie glanced over at David, it was clear she didn't appreciate that kind of humour. Lilian thought that, half-hidden by her fringe, her eyes had a slightly wounded look about them, as if most of her experiences with men had been either unfunny or hurtful.

'I'll be giving you a full report on the ventilation,' she said. 'And of course any dry rot that I happen to find.'

'Right. We'll leave you to it, then.'

They left Charlie in the bedroom and made their way downstairs.

'Not exactly a bundle of laughs, is she?' said David, as they went back outside to the tennis courts to finish off their photographs. 'Nice figure, though. I wouldn't say no to giving her a bit of a survey.'

They took half a dozen more pictures of the gardens, but then it started to rain again, and so they retreated inside.

'Now what?' asked David, looking at his watch.

'Come on, David, there's a lot more for us to do yet. I need you to chase up *all* those construction companies who haven't yet put in their provisional tenders. There's five of them we're still waiting to hear from. And call our architects, too, to find out how far they've got with planning permission.'

It had been Lilian's idea to make Philomena Park more attractive to wealthy potential buyers by building an extension to one side of the existing house, with a gymnasium and a sauna and a reception room for holding social events, such as dances and political get-togethers and book launches.

While David sat down on a window sill in the drawing room and started tapping away on his laptop, Lilian circled slowly around the ground floor. She was making notes of those original Jacobean-style features that she thought were worth preserving, to give the development character and class. The doorway that led to the kitchens was flanked with fluted pillars, and two cherubs with trumpets were perched on the architrave, although the left wing of one of the cherubs had been chipped off, and the other had lost his nose.

As she was walking past the open kitchen door, she heard another metallic clatter, much louder than the sound of falling knives that she had heard before.

She stopped, and listened, and then she heard that gasping again.

'Ah – ahh – *ahhhhh!*' This time, though, whoever was gasping sounded even more distressed. In fact, they sounded agonised. '*Aaahhhhhhh!*'

This time, she didn't call out, but walked quickly into the kitchen in the hope of catching the intruder by surprise. She found that the top drawers of the oak dresser were hanging open, and this time the floor was scattered not only with knives but with tongs and skewers and spatulas.

Apart from that, a ten-inch carving knife was sticking upright in the kitchen table. She could have sworn that it was still shuddering.

'Who's there?' Lilian demanded, although she was frightened now, and she felt as if her skin was shrinking. 'Come on, show yourself! Where are you?'

This time, she opened all the oven doors, but inside they were cold and empty. She went back into the scullery, but again she found that the back door was locked and that the cleaning cupboard still contained nothing more than that mop and bucket and that sad-looking broom.

She returned to the kitchen. She felt utterly bewildered. If she had heard nothing more than those gasping cries of pain, she could have convinced herself that her imagination had been tricked by the hospital's atmosphere. As Charlie had said, there was a palpable tension in the building that was caused by static electricity, while the ill-fitting doors and century-old plumbing were constantly whistling and groaning.

But her imagination could never have pulled two drawers out of the dresser and thrown all that cutlery on to the floor; and her imagination could never have stuck a carving knife into the middle of the kitchen table.

She went back into the hallway and called David. He called back, 'Won't be a mo!' But she snapped, '*Now*, David!' and he appeared in the drawing-room doorway, with his phone still pressed against his ear.

'Who are you talking to?'

'Smith and Boyd. The contractors.'

'Tell them you'll ring back.'

'Gordon. Sorry, I'll have to call you later. Something's come up.'

David ended his call and followed Lilian into the kitchen. She stood beside the kitchen table and said, '*There*. What do you make of that?'

'I don't know. What am I supposed to make of it? It's a knife.'

'And all these knives and spatulas and stuff, all over the floor.'

David shook his head, mystified.

'David – you and me and Charlie, we're the only people in the building, and Charlie's right upstairs on the third floor. I heard all this cutlery falling on to the floor and I thought I heard somebody moaning. But when I came in here to see who it was, there was nobody here. This is the second time this has happened.'

'Perhaps they dodged out the back when they heard you coming.'

'The door's locked on the inside, David. And there's no other way out. There's nowhere that anyone could have gone without me seeing them. I've even looked in the ovens.'

David frowned up at the ceiling as if he thought there might be a trapdoor in it.

'And look—' Lilian persisted. 'Why did they empty out these two drawers, all over the floor? And why did they stick this knife into the table?'

'And you say this has happened before? When?'

'This morning, just before we heard Alex screaming. After all that drama, I didn't really think it was worth mentioning. I thought the noises I heard could have been anything – the cistern filling up, or something like that. And maybe the cutlery was left lying on the floor from the time when the hospital closed down.'

David bit his lip, looking around the kitchen and then leaning sideways to take a look into the scullery.

'There's nobody in there, either,' Lilian told him.

'Maybe it's a poltergeist. I mean, you do read about

them, don't you? And I've seen videos on Twitter of objects mysteriously flying around on their own. Even a wheelie bin once. Right up in the air it was, this wheelie bin, fifty feet up, spinning around like a top.'

'David, I don't believe in poltergeists. I don't believe in *any* of that supernatural twaddle. There has to be a logical explanation for what happened here.'

'Well, yes. Maybe Charlie was right. I mean, she said she sensed something here, didn't she? Maybe it *is* static. It can make people's hair stand on end, can't it, static? This building's been empty for a long time, hasn't it? Like, years. Who's to say that enough static couldn't have built up until it was strong enough to pull all this metal cutlery out of its drawers?'

'What, and stick a knife into the middle of a table?'

David shrugged. 'Don't ask me. Stranger things have happened.'

Lilian looked at the carving knife but made no move to touch it or pull it out. If all this disturbance hadn't been caused by some scientific phenomenon, then it must have been caused by an intruder, and there was a possibility that they had left fingerprints or DNA on the handle.

In fact, she was almost sure this was the work of somebody who was trying to frighten them, or prank them at the very least, although how they had managed to slip out of the kitchen without her seeing them she couldn't imagine.

'I don't know, David. Perhaps there's a secret passageway hidden behind the walls. Let's go and see what Charlie thinks. She's a surveyor. She could measure the walls and see if they match up. I'd like to see how she's getting on, anyway.'

Although two large lifts were installed in the hospital, one at each end, there was still no power, so they had to climb up the stairs again. Lilian wondered if Roger French had paid the utility company. He was notoriously tight with money. She had learned in her first month at Downland Developments that whenever he invited his staff out for a drink, he would invariably say that he had forgotten his wallet.

They walked along the third-floor corridor to the bedroom where they had left Charlie, but she must have completed her measurements in there, because there was no sign of her.

'Charlie!' Lilian called out, but there was no answer. She called again, 'Charlie, where are you?' But there was still no response.

'Maybe she's packed it in for the day,' said David.

Lilian went to the window and looked down to the driveway. 'Her car's still there.'

'Charl-*ee*!' shouted David. 'You're not playing hide-and-seek, are you?'

Silence. Not even the draught sighing under the doors.

'God, this place is beginning to give me the creeps,' said Lilian. 'She must be up here somewhere. You didn't hear her come downstairs, did you?'

They walked along the corridor, opening one door after another and looking inside. Most of the rooms were empty, although two or three of them still had beds, and chairs, and wardrobes. In one of them, a tailor's dummy was standing close to the window, draped in a sheet. It gave Lilian a split-second scare, and she clapped her hand against her chest. David saw what had frightened her and couldn't help grinning.

'*Wooo!* Couldn't get any spookier, could it?'

'Shut up, David. We just need to find Charlie.'

At the end of the corridor, the door to the last bedroom was half open. It was dark inside because the dusty brown hessian curtains were drawn together. All Lilian could see was a single bed with several blankets neatly folded on top of it, and a white wickerwork armchair that had tipped over on to its back.

She went over to the window to open the curtains. As she came around the end of the bed, she was shocked to find Charlie lying sideways on the floor, her arms straight down by her sides. Her legs were straight, too, and she was staring unblinkingly at the skirting board.

'David! She's here! It looks like she's fainted or had a fit or something!'

Lilian dragged the bed to one side so that she had enough room to kneel down.

'Charlie? It's Lilian. What's happened? Can you speak? What's happened to you, Charlie?'

She gently turned Charlie on to her back. Charlie was breathing, although each breath was a panicky little squeak. She looked up at Lilian, opening and closing her mouth in desperation, but she couldn't fill her lungs with enough air to say anything.

'David, call an ambulance! Tell them it's an emergency! Then go outside and wait for them!'

Lilian turned back to Charlie. 'Do you think you can manage to get up? You'd be much more comfortable lying on the bed.'

Charlie simply stared at her, expressionless. Lilian took hold of her right arm and tried to lift it, so that she could hook it around her own shoulders and heave Charlie on to her feet. But her arm was completely rigid, clamped down by her side, and her elbow refused to bend. Her left arm was the same, locked into position, immovable.

Lilian sat back on her heels, wondering how on earth she was going to pick Charlie up from the floor and lift her on to the bed. Maybe if she managed to sit her up first. She leaned over her, so that their faces were only an inch apart. She forced her hands down behind Charlie's back and attempted to raise her up towards her, into a sitting position.

She strained as hard as she could, but Charlie's spine simply wouldn't bend. It was like trying to lift a marble statue. What was worse, Charlie showed no reaction whatsoever. She didn't speak, she didn't nod, she didn't shake her head. She didn't even blink. She kept on panting, but that was the only indication that she was still alive.

Lilian's eyes filled with tears of frustration, and she gave up. Instead, she took hold of Charlie's stick-like fingers and held them tight, hoping that this would give her reassurance that she wasn't going to be left here alone, paralysed and helpless.

Rain sprinkled against the window. Lilian kept her ears open for the sound of an ambulance siren, but all she could hear was Charlie panting. After a while, though, she thought she could hear that gasping again, the same gasping she had heard downstairs in the kitchen.

'Ah! Ah! *Ahh!*' High and desolate, like a man crying out in pain. '*Aaahhhh!*' It sounded as if it were coming from the second floor, just below them.

She let go of Charlie's fingers, stood up and went to the door. The corridor outside was empty, and the gasping had stopped.

She stood in the doorway, listening. She was sure now that somebody was doing their best to scare them into cancelling this development. Somebody who would stop at nothing to make them believe that St Philomena's was haunted. Staring down that deserted corridor, hearing Charlie struggling for breath, she made up her mind that she was going to find out who it was, and make them pay for what they were doing.

The ambulance arrived outside without a siren, but she heard it crunching on the shingle. The next thing she knew, David and the paramedics were clattering upstairs.

'She's in here!' she called out. 'I've tried to get her up off the floor but I couldn't move her! She's totally paralysed!'

She stepped back to allow the paramedics into the bedroom. David came up to her with a frown.

'Are you okay?' he asked her, and it was only then that she realised her cheeks were still wet with tears.

'No, David, I'm not,' she told him, pulling out her handkerchief and dabbing her face. 'I'm frustrated, and I'm angry. I'm angry as all hell.'

6

At eleven o'clock the next morning, Moses was out in the garden, raking the grass, when Grace came out of the kitchen door to tell him that Dr Wells was on the phone again.

He came inside, tugging off his gardening gloves.

'Dr Wells?'

'Yes, Captain Akinyemi, I'm sorry to bother you again, but Alex Fowler has been calling out for you. Not just once or twice, but repeatedly. Every three or four minutes, in fact, over and over. He's been driving my nursing staff to distraction.'

'I wish I knew what I could do for him, Dr Wells, but I have no idea. I thought you were going to put him into a coma.'

'That's the reason I'm calling you. Last night he wouldn't stop screaming so I administered enough ketamine and midazolam to put him out for a month. He stopped screaming but he kept on calling your name. I've never had a patient who can remain even half conscious after a combined dosage of that strength.'

'Do you want me to come and see him again?'

'If that's possible. The last time, it seemed to give him some sense of relief.'

'What about all those tests you were going to give him? Did they show up anything unusual?'

'Nothing. His MRI scan was clear, and there was no

indication of reflex sympathetic dystrophy or chronic regional pain syndrome. The only conclusion I can come to is that his pain exists nowhere else but inside his mind.'

'It could be. I have read about people suffering from imaginary pain, but I cannot say that I have ever come across any actual cases of it myself.'

'But if it's imaginary, don't you see, that might well be to our advantage. Even if you can't make him realise that he's delusional, and that he never served in the Army, perhaps you can convince him that you successfully treated his injuries out in Afghanistan and because of that he should no longer be suffering any long-term pain.'

'If you really think that it will help,' said Moses. He could see Grace standing behind the sofa, staring at him fiercely and silently mouthing '*What?*'

'I really don't have a clue if you can help him or not,' Dr Wells admitted. 'But if we give him any more sedatives they could very well prove fatal, and if we can't induce a coma then I have absolutely no idea what else we can do to relieve his pain.'

'Very well. I will come if you want me to. I have been gardening so give me half an hour to take a shower.'

'I'm very grateful to you, Captain Akinyemi. And I know that my nursing staff will be grateful, too. More than I can possibly tell you.'

When Moses arrived at St Helier, Dr Wells was waiting for him in reception. He looked tired and worried, and he had fastened the wrong buttons of his lab coat so that it was lopsided.

'He's stopped screaming for now,' he told Moses, as he led

him over to the lift. 'He's still very much conscious, however, and he keeps repeating that he's in terrible agony – in between asking for you, that is. The inexplicable thing is that he's experiencing the PTSD of Corporal Terence Simons, even though he never knew him. How can you treat a patient for a traumatic experience that he never had?'

They started to walk along the upstairs corridor. 'Do you think it might be helpful if we could contact Corporal Simons?' asked Moses. 'Perhaps if Alex Fowler saw him in the flesh, so to speak, he might realise that it wasn't him.'

'I thought of that. The hospital secretary contacted the Combat Stress charity for me, and they had Corporal Simons on their books. Unfortunately, he passed away eighteen months ago.'

Moses stopped where he was. 'He is *dead*?'

Somehow, this news disturbed him even more than knowing that Corporal Simons was still alive. Since he was dead, how did he keep appearing in his dreams? Hadn't his spirit at last found peace, either in heaven or whatever afterlife he might have believed in? Unless his spirit was now possessing Alex Fowler, like the demon that possessed the girl in *The Exorcist*.

'I'm sorry,' said Dr Wells. 'I should have told you before.'

'No, it is just that it— It brings back memories, that's all.'

They were about to continue down the corridor when they heard a trolley behind them, and a porter called out, 'Excuse me, gents! Coming through!'

Moses and Dr Wells stepped back against the wall so that the porter could push the trolley past them. A young woman with tangled blonde hair was lying on it, covered up to the neck with a pale-green blanket. As she was wheeled past, she stared at Moses and suddenly jerked her head up, opening and closing her mouth like a goldfish.

'*Murrrggghh!*' she groaned.

The porter turned to Moses and Dr Wells, pulling a face that was half amused and half sympathetic, and carried on pushing. But the young woman was straining to keep her head lifted and continued to stare at Moses, and as she was wheeled away she screamed out, '*Murrrgggh – ingghh – us!*'

'Wait!' said Moses. He caught up with the porter, catching hold of his shoulder to stop him. Then he went up to the young woman and said, '*What* did you say?'

She dropped her head back down and whispered, '*Min.*'

'Is that it?' said the porter. 'I'm supposed to be down to X-ray after this and I'm running late already.'

'Please, just a moment,' Moses asked him. 'Take a few breaths, darling, and try again.'

The young woman licked her lips, staring at Moses in frustration. She panted four or five times, and then she closed her eyes and said, '*Mingus.*'

Moses turned back to Dr Wells. 'How could she know that? How in the name of God could she know that?'

'I'm sorry. How could she know what?'

'In Afghanistan, in Camp Bastion, that was my nickname – Mingus. They used to think that I looked like Charlie Mingus – you know, the jazz piano player. In those days I had a head full of hair.'

Dr Wells came up to the trolley and picked up the emergency department admission form.

'Charlene Thorndyke, thirty-two years old. Admitted yesterday afternoon at fifteen thirty-five suffering from tetraplegia. Preliminary tests show no indication of physical trauma or stroke or transient ischemic attack. Neither is there any indication of paralysis caused by infection or toxic substance, or any rare condition such as Guillain-Barré syndrome.

'It's conceivable that we might be looking at a case of conversion disorder. We had a young man here only about a month ago who was partially paralysed because of mental stress. It may be worth getting in touch with her GP to see if she has had any treatment for psychological problems.

'Of course, complete immobility can also be a symptom of catatonic schizophrenia. Patients can either freeze in some unlikely posture or else they can become wildly hyperactive. But it is extremely rare.'

He leafed over the admission form and read quickly what was written on the second sheet. 'My God,' he said. 'It says here that she was found by her business colleagues at what used to be St Philomena's Hospital, at Downlea.'

'*What?* But that is where Alex Fowler was found.'

'Exactly. She was carrying out a survey, just like him. It says in the notes here that she was discovered lying on the floor totally paralysed and although she was still breathing she was unable to speak and explain what had happened to her.'

'I cannot believe this,' said Moses. 'I mean, this is like, *crazy*! There is Alex Fowler saying that he can remember me treating him after he was blown up by a roadside bomb. He even says he saw my monkey-head mascot. And now this young woman can remember my nickname from Helmand Province. How can this be possible? I have never seen neither of them, never before.'

Charlie had closed her eyes now, but she seemed to be breathing more steadily. It was then that the lift door at the far end of the corridor opened with a *ping!* and another doctor came hurrying along the corridor, a middle-aged woman with grey short-cropped hair and an expression on her face like an angry bull terrier.

'Honestly!' she snapped. 'That Aarif Shamsi thinks I can pull rabbits out of hats!'

'Aarif Shamsi is our chief finance officer,' Dr Wells told Moses, in a sideways murmur. 'He's a great believer in health care, particularly when it comes to the health of his accounts books.'

'What are you dawdling around here for?' the woman doctor asked the porter. 'I need to put this patient on a potassium drip as soon as possible.'

'Dr Morton, this is Captain Moses Akinyemi. He's the man that our screaming patient has been calling out for. He's been kind enough to come in this morning to see if his presence can calm our patient down. Captain Akinyemi, this is Dr Helen Morton.'

'Please, call me Moses,' said Moses.

Dr Morton gave him a cursory nod, and then she turned back to Dr Wells and said, 'My first tests indicate that Ms Thorndyke is hypokalemic, and that she's suffering from primary periodic paralysis. That's why I'm putting her on potassium. But PPP is so rare that I want to run a lot more tests to be absolutely sure.'

As she was wheeled away, Charlie opened her eyes again.

'*Mingus!*' she cried out, in the hoarsest of whispers. '*Mingus, help me!*'

The porter hesitated, but Dr Morton flapped her hand and said, 'Carry on, for goodness' sake! I'll be there right away!'

'"Mingus" was Captain Akinyemi's nickname when he was in the Army Medical Corps,' said Dr Wells. 'Somehow, she knows it, although we can't think how.'

'That's… strange,' said Dr Morton. 'But look, I must be getting on. I have five more patients waiting for me downstairs. I was hoping to finish by three to meet my daughter but it doesn't look as if there's any hope of that.'

'Perhaps we can drop in and see Ms Thorndyke after we've visited Alex Fowler. It would be interesting to find out how she knew the name "Mingus". It might even shed some light on her medical condition.'

'Really? I don't see how.'

'Well, for instance, she might have been out in Afghanistan, although Captain Akinyemi doesn't remember seeing her there, and while she was there she could have contracted some Afghani disease. Been bitten by a tick, for example.'

'Certainly, tick bites were always something to watch out for,' said Moses. 'The Kabul tick could give you Crimean-Congo haemorrhagic fever, CCHF, and that could lead to respiratory paralysis and kill you. But, you know, I very much doubt if it's that. CCHF usually affected its victims within two to seven days.'

'All right,' said Dr Morton. 'Call in and see her later if you want to. By that time, the potassium drip should have made it easier for her to speak to you. Let me know if she tells you anything helpful.'

Moses and Dr Wells watched her bustle off to catch up with Charlie on her trolley. Dr Wells shook his head and said, 'She's one of the best we've got, Helen Morton. She's even published a very well-received paper on various forms of catatonia. But she's worn down with overwork and she's chronically underpaid, like we all are.' He paused, and sniffed. 'It's a good thing we're all such saints.'

★ ★ ★

They entered Alex's room. It was just as gloomy as before, because the blind was still drawn down, and Alex was still lying on his bed between his two high bumpers, as if he were lying prematurely in his own coffin. He had stopped screaming, but he was shuddering from head to toe, and repeatedly whispering, 'It hurts, it hurts. Oh Jesus, it hurts.'

When Moses and Dr Wells came in, the nurse who was sitting in the corner stopped scrolling through her phone and stood up.

'Any change?' asked Dr Wells.

She shook her head. 'About half an hour ago he started screaming again, but only for four or five minutes, and then he stopped. All he does now is say the same thing, over and over and over. "It hurts, and where's Captain Ackin-somebody?"'

Moses went up to the bedside. Alex was holding both of his hands up in front of his chest like a begging puppy, and his eyes were squeezed tightly shut.

'It hurts, it hurts! Where's Captain Akenyemi? Where's Captain Akenyemi? *It hurts!*'

'Alex,' said Moses. Then, 'Alex, can you hear me?'

Alex's eyes stayed closed. Moses glanced across at Dr Wells, and then turned back to Alex and snapped out, 'Terence! *Corporal Simons!*'

Alex opened his eyes. He was still shuddering, but the expression on his face was one of surprise and huge relief.

'Captain Akenyemi! Captain Akenyemi! You came!'

'Yes, Terence. I am here. And I have come to put an end to your pain.'

'I can't believe it! You came! You can't imagine how much I'm hurting!'

'I can, Terence. I can. But in a few minutes, I promise

you, you will not be hurting any more. You were very badly injured, but that was a long time ago now. I treated all your wounds when you were blown up. I gave you painkillers. But since then, you have had many years to heal. You are whole again, and there is no reason for you to feel any more pain. Not in your body, and not in your mind.'

Alex carried on quaking, and he stared up at Moses, wild-eyed.

'You don't understand. I *haven't* healed. I'll never heal, not until I go back there.'

'What do you mean? Back to Afghanistan? How would that cure you?'

'You don't understand. Back to that place, back to that moment. Oh, Jesus, it hurts!'

'You mean the place where that IED went off? At the *moment* when it went off? You cannot go back in time.'

Moses hesitated for a moment, and then he said, 'On top of that, listen to me – you are *not* Corporal Simons. You were never in that place, not at that moment when that IED went off nor at any other time. Somehow you seem to believe that you are Corporal Simons, but your real name is Alex Fowler. Corporal Simons has passed away. Do you hear what I am telling you? Corporal Terence Simons is dead, so you cannot be him.'

'It hurts,' Alex whispered.

'You must try to get it into your head that you are Alex Fowler. You live in Dorking with your mother. You never knew Corporal Simons, and Corporal Simons is no longer alive.'

'Help me,' Alex croaked, lifting up both hands. 'Help me, Captain Akenyemi. Please. You don't know how much it hurts.'

At that moment, Dr Wells's pager beeped. He looked at the message on it, and said, 'I'm sorry, Captain Akenyemi – Moses. They want me urgently down in the emergency department.'

'That is okay, doctor,' Moses told him. 'I will stay here for a while and see if I can convince our friend here that he is not who he thinks he is.'

Dr Wells hesitated for a moment. 'Very well. But if you have to leave before I'm finished in the emergency department, why don't you drop in and see me again tomorrow?'

Dr Wells left the room. When he had gone, Moses leaned over the bumper at the side of Alex's bed and said, 'What makes you think that if you went back to that time and that place, it would put an end to your pain?'

Alex's eyes darted from side to side as if he were trying to think of some plausible explanation.

'You are not Corporal Simons,' Moses repeated. 'You were never injured in Afghanistan. I cannot think why you believe that.'

'I am, and I'm not,' Alex replied, although he spoke so softly that Moses could hardly hear him.

'You are, but you're not? Is that what you said? So you really do know that your name is Alex Fowler?'

Alex grunted, and then he started to laugh – a laugh that started off staccato and sarcastic, and then grew louder and more hysterical until it rose up into a harsh and terrible scream. He threw himself from one side of the bed to the other, thumping against the bumpers, kicking his legs and flailing his arms.

Moses tried to hold on to him, but he was thrashing too violently. The nurse put down her phone and hurried over to help, but even the two of them together were unable to keep him pinned down. He carried on rolling and bouncing and screaming until blood was spraying out of his mouth and spattering Moses' jacket.

The nurse pressed the emergency call button at the head of the bed. For the next three or four minutes they continued to wrestle with Alex, waiting for help to arrive, but nobody came.

'There must be some kind of incident on,' panted the nurse, struggling to keep her grip on Alex's left arm.

'Go and fetch Dr Wells!' said Moses. 'Or another doctor! Or anybody! He needs sedating! Go on – I can just about hold him down!'

The nurse hesitated, but then she ran out of the room, leaving the door open.

'Calm down!' Moses shouted, trying to make himself heard over Alex's screaming. Then, in the most commanding parade-ground bellow that he could manage, '*Corporal Simons!* At ease, Corporal Simons! *At ease!* And that's an order!'

Almost at once, with a moaning sound like a vacuum cleaner being switched off, Alex's screaming died in the back of his throat. He stopped struggling, although he continued to tremble.

Moses kept his hands pressed down against Alex's chest for a while, but when it was clear that he was not going to wrestle any more, he took his hands away and stood up straight. He was breathing hard, and he felt as if he had been in a fight.

Alex's eyes were closed again, although Moses could see his pupils flickering from side to side underneath his eyelids. His lips were chewed to rags and his chin was glossy with blood.

Scarlet drops were spotted all over his bed and his hospital gown, as well as Moses' jacket.

'Man,' said Moses. 'The state of you, my friend. The unholy state of you.'

He went to the doorway to see if anybody was coming to sedate Alex, but the corridor was deserted. He returned to the bedside, but when he looked down at Alex, he saw that his right eyelid had opened up. Strangely, though, his eye was glowing a dull yellow, like a citrine rather than an eyeball, and it appeared to have no pupil. His left eyelid remained closed.

Moses felt a creeping sensation all the way across his shoulders and down his spine. Right in front of him, Alex's entire face was beginning to glow like his eyes, and subtly to change. Underneath his gown, his body began to glow too, although the glow went no further down than his waist, as if he had no legs.

Moses opened and closed his mouth, but he was so unnerved by this apparition that his lungs were empty of air and his mind was empty of words.

'I'm his pain,' Alex whispered, although his voice had changed, and he seemed to have a Birmingham accent. 'I'm not Terence Simons. I'm his pain.'

Moses at last managed to snatch a breath. 'Somebody's coming to help you. They won't be long.'

'I'm his pain,' Alex repeated, but this time his voice sounded lascivious, as if he were enjoying the agony that he was going through. '*I'm his pain!*'

He was still glowing beneath his blanket, and to his horror Moses could see that his face had changed to the face that had haunted him in his nightmares for so many years since he had returned from Afghanistan. It was Corporal Simons, or a shimmering vision of Corporal Simons.

'You asked me what my name is? I'm his pain!'

With that, Alex arched his back in such an extreme curve that Moses heard his vertebrae crackle, and he pounded his fists against the mattress, as if he were trying to beat it into submission. Then he let out a harsh, piercing howl that went on and on, rising and falling, like a company of hungry wolves running through a forest.

Moses backed away, crossing two fingers and holding them up in front of him in a crucifix. He had never been religious, but faced with this glowing, baying apparition, the only protection he could think of calling on was the protection of Jesus Christ.

7

Shortly after five o'clock, David's wife, Linda, arrived in the family Picasso to take him to their daughter's school for parents' evening.

'Are you going to be all right here on your own?' David asked Lilian, as he stepped out on to the porch. 'We don't want anything spooky happening to you, not like Alex and Charlie.'

'I'm not staying long,' Lilian told him. 'I just want to take another look at the reception area and the billiard room. I'm still trying to decide if we should convert them into communal areas for the residents or whether they would be better as an additional apartment. They overlook the gardens, after all, so we could ask quite a premium price for them.'

'All right. But if you hear any screaming or any knives and forks being thrown around, get out of there sharpish. I'll give you a bell when I've finished at Dotty's school.'

He climbed into the Picasso and drove off. Lilian stood in the porch for a while before she went in. The sun was going down behind the tracery of trees that surrounded St Philomena's, and a murmuration of starlings was wheeling in an orange sky. She wasn't sure why, but she felt more lonely than she had in months, even lonelier than when she had first walked out on Tim.

After five and a half years of marriage, she had found Tim so dull and unadventurous and so lacking in passion that she had started to scream at him almost every day out of boredom and frustration. He had taken her abroad only once, to Spain, on a disastrous package holiday, and he spent every weekend playing golf, only to return in the evenings so drunk that he was unable to make love to her.

When she had left him, she believed she had enough drive and creativity to lead a fulfilling and interesting life on her own, and she had quickly made her mark at Downland Developments. But every night she still had to return to the silent and empty house that she was renting in a narrow back street in Epsom; and this evening there was something particularly sad and abandoned about the atmosphere at St Philomena's. It felt like a building that had lost all hope.

She went back inside. She wouldn't be able to stay longer than half an hour, because it was growing so dark. She could use her phone as a flashlight but it was down to 10 per cent charge and she didn't want to find herself completely out of touch.

She walked out of the hallway and along the corridor that led to the large reception area. She sniffed, and now she could recognise the mushroom smell of dry rot that Charlie had mentioned, as well as the faded chemical tang of antiseptics.

The reception area, too, had a sadness and a sense of abandonment. Originally, it had been used by the Carvers for parties and balls and other social occasions. During St Philomena's time as a hospital, convalescing servicemen had sat here, legless or armless or blind or stunned by stress. Their chairs were still here, as well as several wheelchairs, and out-of-date copies of the *Daily Express* were still lying on the floor where they had been dropped.

The ceilings were as high as in the drawing room, with two enormous crystal chandeliers that were now tangled with cobwebs. There were gilt-framed mirrors all around the walls, but they had been draped in sheets so that the wounded servicemen would be spared the sight of their own life-changing injuries.

Lilian weaved her way between the chairs to what had once been the billiard room. The billiard table had been sold to a pub in Esher, but there was still a score counter on the wall, as well as a dartboard.

She could see that if the main reception room were divided up into three bedrooms, a living room and a bathroom, this billiard room could make an attractive kitchen and dining area, especially if French windows were knocked through the right-hand wall to the garden. An apartment like this could easily fetch a million and a half, if not more.

Her phone warbled. She took it out and said, 'Hallo?'

There was no answer and she didn't recognise the number that was calling her. She had received numerous scam calls lately, mostly to tell her that her PayPal account had been compromised.

She was about to leave when she thought she heard somebody shouting. It sounded as if it were coming from somewhere upstairs, although it was so faint that she couldn't be sure. She went back through to the reception area, stopped and listened.

Yes, it was somebody shouting. Not just one person, either. It was more like three or four, or even more. And it was definitely coming from upstairs. The same mournful, repetitive cry from all of them, although it was too indistinct for her to be able to tell what they were calling out for.

She felt a deep sensation of unease, and she was tempted

to walk quickly out of the hospital and drive herself away as fast as she could. But her strong sense of practicality kept her where she was. This building belonged to Downland Developments, not to some random trespassers, and she was in charge of it.

Yet who were these people who were shouting out, and where had they come from? When she and David had looked into every room upstairs, they had seen nobody, so these people had either been hiding in the attic or some store cupboard, or else they had sneaked in through the front door while she was looking around the reception area and the billiard room.

But why were they shouting? They sounded desperate, but what could they possibly want?

Lilian the Pragmatist told her to go upstairs and find out what was wrong. But then she thought of Alex, screaming with pain, and of Charlie, totally paralysed. Supposing the people who were shouting were all in agony, or unable to move, how was she going to deal with them, all on her own? It would make more sense to call the emergency services.

She took out her phone but the screen was black and it was completely dead, even for a 999 call. She stood still for a few moments, listening to the shouts from upstairs, and then she thought: *No, I'm not going up there.* Supposing that's exactly what they want, whoever they are, and supposing I end up the same as Alex and Charlie?

Supposing it's only some elaborate hoax by protestors who don't want the hospital developed into a housing complex? There was at least one aggressive group of local residents who had lodged an appeal to the local council against Downland's proposal.

It was beginning to grow dark inside the hospital now,

and the shouting went on and on. It sounded like one word, repeated over and over again.

That's it, thought Lilian, *I'm going. I can drive to the Cock and use the phone there.* She hurried along to the hallway and up to the front door. When she tried the handle, though, she found that it wouldn't open. She jiggled it up and down several times, but the door still wouldn't budge. There was no key in the lock, and neither the top nor bottom bolts were fastened, so she couldn't understand why it was jammed.

All this time, the desperate shouting from upstairs continued, and now she was in the hallway she thought she could make out what they were saying.

'*Nurse! Nurse! Nurse!*'

I don't believe in ghosts and I don't believe in poltergeists. So that must be real people upstairs who are shouting out for a nurse. But there's no way that I can help them. They shouldn't be here anyway.

She gave the front door handle another forceful tug downwards, but it remained firmly closed.

Well, there are plenty of other doors. She made her way along the corridor into the kitchen, and then through to the scullery. The key was still in the back door that led out to the kitchen garden, but when she tried to turn it, it refused to move. She rattled the handle, but the door stayed shut.

She was beginning to feel panicky now. Why couldn't she open these doors? She practically ran through to the drawing room, across the gritty floor and up to the French windows. She could see the garden outside, and the pale moon that was peeping over the high alder hedge, like an elderly voyeur. But the handle that should have opened the French windows was locked solid, and even when she rammed her shoulder against them, the windows shuddered but remained obstinately closed.

There was another door that gave out on to an enclosed back yard and the storage sheds that had once been the Carver family stables. Lilian hurried through the hallway and the cloakroom behind it, where three or four raincoats and anoraks were still hanging limply on cast-iron pegs. But the door to the stable yard was stuck fast, too. Like the front door, neither of its bolts were drawn and it had no key in it, yet she shook it and kicked it, again and again, and all she could manage to do was crack one of its panels.

Right. As undignified as it was, she would have to climb out of one of the windows. She went back to the drawing room and tried the handle of the window on the right side of the fireplace. Again, stuck. The window on the left side couldn't be opened, either.

She went back to the kitchen and attempted to open the window behind the sink. The handle simply wouldn't move.

Now she was beginning to feel seriously frightened. She was trapped here in this hospital and she didn't know why. Did it have some security system that she wasn't aware of, some way that all the doors and windows could be locked, so that nobody could enter and nobody could leave? It didn't seem possible for a building of this age, and a building so large.

Or had somebody deliberately blocked every way out, in order to keep her imprisoned? Could it be those people upstairs, who were still calling out for a nurse?

She took several deep breaths to steady herself. There was only one way to find out. She went back out into the hallway and mounted the stairs. Fortunately, there was enough moonlight for her to be able to see where she was going, but she repeatedly snatched at the banister rail as she climbed up to the first floor. She didn't want to tumble down the stairs and injure herself now that she had no way of calling for help.

The shouting went on and on, and when she reached the first-floor landing she could tell that it was coming from the Wavell Wing, along the corridor off to her left.

'Nurse! Nurse! Please, nurse! Nurse!'

Come on, Lilian, if they're calling for a nurse they must be feeling really ill, and so they can't be that dangerous. And since when have you allowed any man to frighten you? Only your Uncle Maurice when you were twelve, trying to spy on you when you were taking a bath, and that unnaturally tall man who followed you all the way home from The Boogie Lounge in Epsom, one wintry night when you were nineteen.

She walked along the corridor to the double doors that led into the ward. One of them was half ajar, which was why she had been able to hear the shouting from down in the billiard room. And it was still continuing, strained and hopeless, as if the people who were shouting had no real expectation that anybody would ever come to help them.

She pushed the door wide open and went in. The windows on the left-hand side overlooked the gardens, so that the washed-out moonlight fell across the floor, although she could see that the moon would soon be swallowed up by a large bank of dark cloud.

As she entered the ward, the shouting became even more frantic.

'Nurse! Nurse! Nurse!'

They all sounded like men, although they were all hoarse and strained, and some of them were on the verge of hysteria.

Nine beds were lined up along the right-hand wall, with a further three at the far end. Most of them still had sheets on them, and four of them still had pillows. But although the shouting went on, every bed was empty. Lilian was the only person in the ward.

For several seconds, she didn't move. She could only stand there, listening. How on earth was it possible that she could hear all these desperate voices, and yet there was nobody here? She felt as if she were hearing an echo from the hospital's past, when injured servicemen were crying out in pain and despair. But they were long gone, those men, those who had managed to survive.

'Hallo?' she called out. 'Is there anybody there?'

The shouting faltered, and began to die down. The voices sounded like an audience settling down when the main attraction appears on the stage.

'Where are you?' Lilian demanded, stepping slowly forward, although her heart was beating so hard that it hurt. 'I can hear you but I can't see you!'

Now the shouting had died away completely, but she could hear a faint slithering sound, as well as a repetitive creaking. She walked along the row of beds, listening hard.

'Where are you? Are you hiding somehow? Tell me why I can't see you!'

The slithering and the creaking continued.

'Are you hiding behind the walls? Are you in some secret passage?'

She heard somebody whispering now, a soft conspiratorial whisper as if they were saying, *We've tricked her into coming here now, so what are we going to do next?*

'Where are you?' she repeated. 'Are you alive? Why can't I see you? Are you alive, or are you in heaven?'

She ducked her head down to look under the beds. Alex had been lying on the floor when they found him, after all. But all she could see was rubbish – crumpled newspapers and polystyrene cups and biscuit wrappers. Yet she could still hear those voices whispering, and she could still hear those slithering and creaking sounds.

She went right up to the end of one of the beds, and it was then that she could see what was causing those sounds. The sheets were twisting and untwisting themselves like a rope trick, and the mattress was bulging up and sinking down as if a heavy man were lying on it and tossing himself in agony from side to side. But there was no man there.

Lilian was frozen from head to foot with a mixture of disbelief and a sense of terror that she had never felt in her life before, ever. What she was witnessing was impossible, and yet she could see it with her eyes and hear it with her ears – Lilian the Pragmatic, Lilian the Sceptical. Lilian who had found it hard to accept that men had really gone to the Moon. Lilian who had resisted being vaccinated for Covid-19.

She took a step back from the end of the bed, but as she did so the air in the ward was split apart by the loudest and most hideous scream she had ever heard. At the same time, the bed in front of her was flooded with blood. It bubbled up in the middle of the mattress and soaked the sheets from one side of the bed to the other.

Lilian turned around and ran. She flung the door wide, sprinted along the corridor, and hurtled down the stairs. What was happening in this hospital was madness, and she was so frightened that she was whimpering.

She ran into the drawing room, crossing over to the corner where the single spoonback chair had been left against the wall. Perhaps she could hurl it through the French windows to burst them apart. She took hold of its arms and tried to pick it up, but it was solid oak, and she could manage to lift it only a little way off the floor before she had to drop it down again. She tried to push it, thinking she might use it as a battering ram, but its castors were rusted and locked solid.

She looked around, still mewling in the back of her throat. It was then she saw the poker in the fireplace, propped up against the abandoned wheelchair. It was at least a metre long, with a handle in the shape of a horse's head. She ran over and picked it up. It was iron, and really heavy, and she was sure she could use it to shatter one of the windows.

Grasping the poker in both hands, she hurried over to the French windows. She swung back the poker like a golfer, but before she could hit the glass, she caught sight of a figure outside in the garden, not more than three metres away, and she stopped in mid-strike. It was a man, and he was standing quite still, and although he was wearing a wide-brimmed black hat so that his face was in shadow, she could see by the glitter of his eyes that he was looking in at her. The moon was swallowed by the clouds, and it grew darker outside, but she recognised the sheen of his tan leather jerkin. He was Martin Slater, the gardener.

She dropped the poker on to the floor and took hold of one of the door handles. She shook it violently and shouted out, 'They won't open! I'm trying to get out but I can't!'

Martin Slater came up to the French windows.

'I can't get out!' she repeated. 'The doors aren't locked, but they simply won't open! None of the doors will open!'

Martin Slater reached out for one of the door handles and twisted it downwards. The French windows swung apart as easily as they had when Lilian had first opened them. She stepped outside on to the patio and stood beside him.

'There,' he said. 'They seem to be behaving themselves

now.' Even though she couldn't see his face, she could tell that he was amused. 'Maybe you were turning the handle the wrong way.'

'For goodness' sake, I'm not a complete idiot,' she retorted. She was trying hard not to sound upset, although her eyelashes were prickling with tears and the sudden fresh air was making her nose run. 'I do know how to open a door.'

'Yes, love. I'm sure you do. But they can be right tricky sometimes, in these old houses, doors. You only have to get a bit of grit in the lock cylinders, and then the spring pins get themselves all wodged up.'

'It's not the locks. I haven't been able to open *any* of the doors or *any* of the windows! And there have been people in the rooms upstairs. Trespassers, shouting and screaming, although I couldn't find them.'

'Trespassers? How did trespassers get in, if none of the doors and windows would open?'

'I have no idea. But they sounded as if they were up on the first floor, in the Wavell ward. They were calling out for a nurse. I could hear them quite clearly, but when I went up there, there was nobody there. There was nothing in the ward but empty beds.'

The moon reappeared, and Lilian could see that Martin Slater was staring at her with the kind of concerned yet remote expression that a vet gives to a suffering collie. There was something else about him, too, that unsettled her, apart from the way he had appeared out of nowhere and had easily opened the French windows that she had found impossible to budge. He had a smell about him, partly pleasant, as if he had been trimming a salvia bush, but partly acrid, like burned explosives. Maybe it was just his leather jerkin.

'Would you take a look up there for me?' she asked him. 'I just want to be sure that I wasn't having some kind of delusion.'

'If you want me to,' he said, and raised his eyes to the moon. 'You don't have the electric back yet, do you? But we should have enough light for a while yet.'

Lilian stepped back into the drawing room and Martin Slater followed her. They crossed the gloomy hallway and climbed the stairs to the first-floor landing. The hospital was silent now. No doors banging, no plumbing gurgling. Not even a whispering draught.

'The Wavell ward, you say?' asked Martin Slater.

'Yes. Like I say, it sounded like at least half a dozen men, all shouting out together for a nurse.'

Martin Slater led the way along the corridor and pushed open the doors that led into the ward. Lilian held back, fearful of who or what might be in there. But when Martin Slater went inside, he looked around, and then turned back to her and shook his head.

'You're right. There's nobody here. Just beds.'

Lilian cautiously entered the ward. There was one thing she needed to see, to find out whether she had been hallucinating or what she had witnessed was real. She walked along the row of beds until she came to the one that had bubbled with blood. Its mattress had been soaked through, but she saw that it was no longer wet and glossy and red, the way it had been when she had run in terror out of the ward, less than ten minutes ago. Now it was stained to a burnt umber colour, and crusted, and it was totally dry.

Somebody had suffered a massive haemorrhage on this bed, probably fatal, by the look of it, but not recently. Not since St Philomena's had been crowded with wounded soldiers.

Lilian stared at it, while the moonlight faded and then brightened again.

'I can't get my head round this. I swear to you that blood was literally *pouring* out of the middle of this mattress! It was like a fountain, and it was *fresh*! You can see that it's been drenched in blood at some time or another, but it's all dried up now. I mean, did I dream it, or what?

'I was wondering if I ought to call the police about it, but not now. They would only hold everything up while they carried out all their tests, and we're getting well behind schedule as it is.'

She paused, looking around. There was nowhere else in this ward that anybody could be hiding. No cupboards, and no doors to any other rooms.

'Do you know, I'm seriously beginning to wonder if someone's pulling a very nasty prank. Perhaps it's one of that miserable lot of conservationists. They've been trying their utmost to stop us from developing this hospital.'

Martin Slater didn't answer.

'You don't know of anybody who might set up a stunt like this, do you?' Lilian asked him. 'You've been gardening here for ten years, after all. You must know a lot of the locals.'

Martin Slater still didn't answer. Lilian turned around and saw to her surprise and consternation that he was no longer there, and that she had been talking to herself.

'Mr Slater!' she called out. 'Mr Slater!'

She hurried out of the ward and along the corridor to the stairwell. She stopped for a moment and listened for his footsteps on the stairs, but she could hear nothing.

Why had he walked out and left her on her own like that? He hadn't even said 'I'm off now' or 'goodbye'.

She ran back downstairs and across the hallway to the

front door, to see if it was still stuck shut. To her huge relief, it opened up without any difficulty at all. She left it open while she quickly went through to the drawing room to close the French windows. If there really had been trespassers or squatters inside the hospital this evening, she didn't want to make it easy for any more intruders to gain access. Apart from anything else, it could well compromise Downland's insurance. She was frightened, but she was still Practical Lilian.

She left the hospital, locking the front door behind her. Tomorrow, she would ask Sanjay from the office to join her and David in making a thorough search of the whole building, from the attics to the cellars.

Maybe it *is* my imagination, she thought, as she steered her Honda out of the hospital entrance and along the winding tree-lined lanes that led to Epsom racecourse. Maybe I've become too driven, and too compulsive. Maybe my brain is deliberately creating these frightening illusions to try and make me relax, and smell the roses, and enjoy my life more. Maybe it's a form of self-preservation.

But then again, maybe that screaming and that blood-boiling mattress and those twisting sheets – maybe they weren't a nightmare after all. And what about that agonised gasping and that cutlery scattered on the kitchen floor? Maybe there really is somebody lurking in the hospital – somebody who bears us raging ill will, and who will do anything to make us believe that we're going mad, so that we'll cancel our development and leave St Philomena's empty.

8

Moses arrived at St Philomena's shortly after eleven the next morning. He had phoned Downland the previous afternoon and asked them if it would be possible to talk to whoever was in charge of the hospital's development. They had given him Lilian's mobile number and when he had called her and told her about his experiences with Alex and Charlie, she had agreed to meet him.

A fine sparkling rain was falling when he parked outside the hospital building, and he lifted up the hood of his anorak as he hurried towards the porch. Lilian was waiting for him in the open doorway.

'Mr Akinyemi?'

'Please, call me Moses.'

Lilian led him into the hallway. David and Sanjay were standing by the staircase, talking about last night's premier league match between Tottenham and Manchester City. That morning, the three of them had spent over two hours searching the building from the attics down to the basements, opening every cupboard, looking under every bed, even pulling out drawers from the built-in storage units and checking inside the ovens again.

Lilian had cautiously approached the bed that she had seen

bubbling with blood. It was still stained dark brown, and the mattress was still as dry as a pastry crust.

She introduced Moses to David and Sanjay. Sanjay pressed his hands together as part of a *namaste* greeting, and David gave him an elbow bump.

'I've given David and Sanjay an idea of what you told me on the phone, Moses,' Lilian said. 'About Alex thinking he was one of the casualties you treated in Afghanistan, and about Charlie calling you by that nickname they gave you when you were out there.'

Moses said, 'I have no idea how you feel about this, and I know this sounds far-fetched, but I have been seriously wondering if we are not dealing with some kind of possession here. You know, a bit like *The Exorcist*.'

'Oh, come on,' said Lilian. 'I don't think any of us seriously believe in demons. But there's clearly something in this building that's left over from the days when it was a military hospital. Perhaps it's some kind of resonance. You know – like an echo.'

David nodded. 'It could be something like that. I mean, we've been through the whole bloody building top to bottom with a fine-tooth comb and there's definitely nobody hiding here.'

'No hidden loudspeakers, either, that could account for all that screaming you heard,' said Sanjay. 'So perhaps resonance, yes. My aunt in Kanpur told me that she had a room at the back of her house where she used to hear a woman sobbing, even though there was nobody there.'

Moses said, 'Somehow, in some way that I cannot understand, your Alex Fowler was reliving the experience of Corporal Terence Simons when he was blown up by a roadside bomb in Kajaki. For a moment I thought that he even *looked* like Corporal Simons, but that was probably my own stress playing tricks on me.'

'This is all so weird,' David put in. 'Maybe we ought to get a priest to sprinkle some holy water around, or something like that. Better still – why don't we demolish the whole bloody place and build some luxury apartments from scratch?'

'I kept telling Alex Fowler that he wasn't Corporal Simons,' said Moses. 'But before I left him, he kept insisting over and over again that, *no*, he wasn't the actual Corporal Simons himself. He was his pain.'

'His pain? What did he mean by that?'

'I have no idea. But it was obvious that he was in agony.'

Lilian thought for a moment, and then she said, 'There's a woman down the road who told us that she runs a hospice for five wounded veterans who used to be housed here. Maybe they can tell you a bit more. What was that woman's name, David? I'm terrible with names.'

'Crosby – Marion Crosby. I bet somebody at the Cock will know where she lives.'

'That's it, Marion Crosby. Why don't you go and talk to the men she's looking after?'

'Yes, I will,' said Moses. 'But before I do, would you have any objection if I took a look around here first? After what you have told me about that screaming and everything, and that bed covered in blood, it might help me if I got a feel of the place.'

'Of course. David – do you want to give Moses a guided tour? I have to call Roger and tell him that we've searched the whole building but we haven't found anything.'

Sanjay looked at his watch. 'I'd better be making tracks. I have a meeting with the Reigate planning department at half twelve.'

David said to Moses, 'Let's start at the top, on the third floor. That's where we found Charlie Thorndyke and that's where Alex left his iPad.'

They climbed the stairs and walked along the corridor to the bedroom where they had found Charlie lying on the floor. The hessian curtains were open and the wickerwork chair had been picked up and placed in the corner.

'She was lying right there, between the bed and the wall. And she was stiff as a board. We couldn't even bend her fingers.'

Moses looked around the room, trying to sense if there was anything in it that might remind him even remotely of Afghanistan. But this was an English hospital building, on a grey English day, with the rain sprinkling against the windows, and there was no heat, nor dust, nor dombura music with that hurried drumming that always sounded like a crowd of people in sandals running downstairs.

'Anything?' asked David.

Moses shook his head.

'I'll show you the other room then. We checked Alex's iPad and that was the last room he was measuring up. We actually found him in one of the wards on the floor below, although we don't have any idea why he might have stopped measuring in mid-measure and decided to go down there.'

Moses was walking out of the door when he thought he heard somebody whisper, close behind him. He stopped, and turned around. There was nobody there, and so he guessed it must have been the plumbing, or maybe a pigeon landing on the roof outside.

'You all right?' David called back, from along the corridor.

'Yes, I just thought—'

The whisper was repeated, so soft and sibilant that it was

barely audible. But this time Moses distinctly heard somebody saying '*Mingus*'.

He felt his wrists tingle, and he gave an involuntary shudder. He took a step back into the room, and looked all around it again. He even bent down sideways and looked under the bed.

'*Mingus*,' the whisperer repeated. He was certain of it.

David had come back to the open door now. 'Are you sure you're all right?'

'I am fine, thank you. But I swear I heard a voice.'

'A voice? Really? What was it saying?'

'I thought it was saying that nickname that Ms Chesterfield was telling you about, the one they called me in Afghanistan – Mingus.'

Both Moses and David stood still for over a minute, listening, but the whisperer stayed silent.

'Maybe I imagined it,' said Moses. 'I still suffer some flashbacks from my time in Helmand Province. When you have seen young men stepping on an IED, their legs and their arms blown off, that is not something that is easy to forget.'

'No, I suppose not. I think the worst thing I've ever seen is my window cleaner falling off his ladder and breaking his leg. His shinbone was sticking out, right through the leg of his dungarees.'

They walked back along the corridor to the room where Alex had dropped his iPad on the bed. Moses had an uncomfortable sensation that he was being followed, and twice he looked over his shoulder to make sure there was nobody there. He could almost feel that somebody was breathing against the back of his neck.

They entered the room and looked around. Apart from the bed where Alex had dropped his iPad, it was empty of furniture, although a picture was still hanging on the wall. It was a framed print of a woman in a purple cloak standing on the edge of a lake. She had her back turned, so it was impossible to tell what age she was. There was something floating in the middle of the lake, a log or a collection of weed. The picture was captioned *Lake of the Lost.*

Moses was still studying the picture when he thought he caught a movement out of the corner of his left eye. At first he thought it was nothing but David's shadow as he crossed in front of the doorway, but when he turned around he saw that David was standing by the window.

'Anything in here?' David asked him.

'I don't know. I don't think so, no.'

David raised one eyebrow. 'You don't sound terribly sure about that.'

'I thought I saw something moving. But, again – it's probably just my stress playing tricks on me.'

'What sort of something?'

'Like a shadow. Or a puff of smoke. Or somebody waving a black veil in the air.'

'You're beginning to give me the right creeps, you are!'

'Sorry, David. But I have been finding all this business very disturbing. I thought that my experiences in Afghanistan were long behind me. Now they seem to have caught up with me, and I cannot think how, or why.'

David gave Moses a reassuring pat on the shoulder. 'Come on,' he said. 'Let's go downstairs. I'll show you the ward where we found Alex. After that – well, it might be a good idea to call it a day, what do you think? Whatever's going on here, there doesn't seem to be any rational explanation for it. I mean, there probably is – there must be – but I'm damned if I can work out what it is.'

As they stepped out into the corridor, Moses took a last look back into the room, half expecting to see that flitting shadow again, but there was no sign of it. Only the empty rumpled bed and the raindrops sliding down the window. He guessed he must have imagined it, but at the same time he had the strangest feeling there was some presence in the room that was aware he had been there, and was watching him leave.

They went downstairs to the Montgomery Wing. Inside the ward, the eight beds were still standing in a line, and the bent drip stand still lay on the floor where Alex had knocked it over. Moses paced slowly down to the far end of the ward, looking at each bed in turn, while David went over to the French windows and stared out at the rain.

'Lilian told me that he was screaming when you found him.'

'Screaming? That's the understatement of the century. He was making so much noise you couldn't hear yourself think. He'd chewed his lips to rags and bitten the end of his tongue right off. He looked like he was wearing a red Covid mask.'

'All right,' said Moses. 'I think I have seen enough here. I will go now and find that Marion Crosby woman and see if the men she is taking care of can tell me anything.'

He walked back along the ward. A washed-out sunlight was beginning to shine through the clouds, so that he could see David's reflection in the French windows, as if a ghost of David were standing on the balcony outside. When David turned around, though, and started to walk towards the door, his reflection stayed where it was, still facing inward through the window.

Moses stopped and stared at it. He wished he hadn't left his glasses in his car, because his short-sightedness made it difficult for him to focus. The reflection resembled David, around the same height and with the same short haircut, but it didn't appear to be wearing a grey business suit, unlike David. Although it was translucent, so that he could clearly see the balcony railings and the distant line of trees through it, he could have sworn it was dressed in sandy-coloured battledress, the same as they used to wear when they were fighting in Helmand Province.

David said, 'What's wrong? You haven't heard another voice, have you?'

Moses pointed to the French windows behind him. 'Look. Am I hallucinating, or is that some kind of optical illusion?'

'What do you mean?'

'Does it look to you as if there is somebody standing outside there, on the balcony?'

David turned around and frowned at it. 'It's only my reflection.'

'To begin with, yes it was, but when you turned your back he did not turn around with you. He kept on staring in through the window. And not only that – I was sure for a moment that he was wearing Army fatigues.'

David went right back up to the window, so close that the tip of his nose was almost touching the glass.

'Hmph,' he grunted, half in amusement. 'I'm afraid it's only me. I'd recognise me anywhere. Sorry if I scared you!'

Moses approached him. He could now see that David was right. The reflection *was* him, and now it was wearing a suit just like his.

David unlocked the French windows and opened them wide. He didn't have to say 'Look, there's nobody out here', because there wasn't. Only a puddle filled with sodden cigarette butts, where the patients of Montgomery Wing must have come out for a surreptitious smoke.

'I must have been seeing things,' said Moses. 'But for a moment, you know—'

'Let's go find Lilian,' said David. 'Maybe she'll want to go along with you to visit this Marion Crosby.'

As they went back downstairs, Moses said, 'Here I am, hearing things that you yourself cannot hear and seeing things that you yourself cannot see.'

When they reached the ground floor, he turned to David and added, 'You must be thinking that I have a screw loose. Or maybe that I am suffering acute post-traumatic stress from my time in Afghanistan.'

'No, mate,' said David, shaking his head. 'I don't think that at all.'

'You are sure? I am beginning to doubt my own sanity.'

'Let's put it this way – I might have thought you were one pie short of a picnic if Lilian and me hadn't found Alex screaming blue murder, or Charlie lying on the floor as stiff as a fucking ironing board. And then there was all that cutlery that was scattered all over the kitchen floor. No, don't worry about it – when you say you heard something and you saw something, I believe you. It could well be that somebody's using all kinds of tricks to scare us into scrubbing this development. Either that, or it's that what's-its-name that Lilian was on about. That "resonance".'

'Perhaps the veterans that Marion Crosby is taking care of have an answer,' said Moses. 'If not, perhaps we should do what you suggested and call for a priest to hold an exorcism. Or knock the whole hospital down to the ground.'

9

They found Marion Crosby's hospice in a narrow hedge-lined lane called Tumber Street, about half a mile east of the hospital. The house was almost completely hidden from the lane behind a row of mountain ash trees, with a five-bar gate and a wooden signboard saying *Limani*, with a picture of an anchor carved into it.

Lilian and Moses went up to the front door and Lilian rang the doorbell. The house was large, with flint-covered walls and leaded windows, and had obviously been extended over the years, so that it was L-shaped. The porch was covered in ivy, which rustled in the rain.

Marion opened the door and looked at Lilian and Moses in surprise. She was wearing an apron and both her hands were dusted with flour.

'Oh!' she said. 'You haven't come about Frank, have you? He didn't do any damage when he was up at the hospital, did he?'

'No, no,' Lilian told her. 'I'm sorry we couldn't give you any notice but we didn't know how to contact you. We were wondering if it would be possible to have a bit of a chat with your veterans.'

Marion frowned. 'About...? Anything in particular? I'm afraid to say that none of them are very articulate.'

'About their experiences in Afghanistan,' said Moses. 'That is, if you think that it will not distress them too much.'

'Well, no, they talk about very little else most of the time. Especially Frank. But is there a reason you want to talk to them about it?'

'I'll be frank with you,' Lilian told her. 'We've had several disturbing incidents since we've come to St Philomena's to start our development. Two of our associates have been injured and we're trying to get to the bottom of what happened to them.'

'It is possible that these incidents are connected with what happened in Afghanistan,' said Moses. 'We have no idea how, but that is why we wish to speak with the men in your care.'

Marion hesitated. Lilian could tell that she was being defensive about her patients, almost motherly. After a few seconds, though, she nodded and said, 'All right. Come in. Three of them are sleeping but you should be able to talk to Michael and Frank. Excuse my floury hands. I'm right in the middle of baking some rolls.'

They stepped into the hallway, which was musty and dark, with an oil painting of a bearded cavalier on one wall, and a coat stand hung with long black raincoats, one of them hooded, so that it looked as if a tall priest was watching them from the corner.

Marion led them through to the day room. A wide casement window looked out over a garden crowded with rhododendrons and apple trees, and two men were sitting at a table by the window, playing draughts. A third man was fast asleep in a leather armchair, his mouth hanging open. His feet were sticking out from his grey tracksuit trousers and both were prosthetic, like two curved metal scoops, with pneumatic cylinders instead of heels.

'Frank – Michael,' said Marion. 'You have visitors.'

Michael looked around, and Frank took advantage of his momentary inattention to jump over one of his red draughts and capture it. Then Frank looked around, too, with those disturbingly milky eyes.

'Oh, it's you,' he said, when he saw Lilian. 'Not come to warn me off visiting my old mates, I hope?'

'No, I haven't. As a matter of fact, you're welcome to visit the hospital so long as you give me plenty of notice. It's a question of insurance. If anything should happen to you there, then my company would be liable.'

'I don't reckon anything's going to happen to *me* up there, love. If anything's going to happen to anybody, it's going to happen to you, or one of your lot. So far as my mates are concerned, that's their home now. Where else can they go?'

'That's right,' said Michael, in a Belfast accent. 'Where else can they go?'

Michael was broad-shouldered, with ginger hair and a wide face with an S-shaped broken nose. He had a slight cast in his pale-blue eyes, so it was difficult for Lilian to tell if he were looking at her directly or over her shoulder. She could see no physical impairment – no missing arms or legs – but the way in which he spoke was flat and expressionless, so that she suspected a brain injury.

'We wanted to ask you if anything unusual happened to you or your mates when you were wounded in Afghanistan – anything that struck you as strange,' said Moses.

'Half my bleeding hip was blown away,' said Frank. 'That struck me as strange, to say the least.'

'Of course. But what I mean by "strange" is... Did you ever have a detached feeling? How can I put it? A feeling that there was another person inside you who was not you?'

'"Another person inside me who wasn't me?" What d'you mean by that? I don't get it.'

'I get it,' Michael put in. 'I was shot in the lower back and when I woke up the pain was so bad I truly honestly believed that it was somebody else who was feeling it, and not me. It was like the pain was another person, a person made out of pain. And I still have that feeling sometimes, when my hydromorphone wears off.'

'Here…' said Marion, dragging over a chair. 'Why don't you both sit down?'

Moses helped her to place the chair next to Frank and Michael's table, and then he went across the room and brought over another.

'Frank,' said Lilian, 'you say that your Army mates are still inside St Philomena's. You can actually see them there?'

'I wouldn't say I could if I couldn't, would I?'

'No, I wasn't suggesting that. I just wanted to know *how* you could see them, because we can't.'

'You ain't got the nods, that's why.'

'What's "the nods"?'

'Night observation device,' said Moses. 'Goggles that allow you to see in almost total darkness. They make everything look green, but you can see people and things that you would never be able to see without them. They were standard issue for soldiers in Afghanistan.'

'But – Frank – you have some of these goggles?'

'Of course. Nice pair of AN/AVS-6s I managed to half-inch when I was invalided out. How could I see me mates if I didn't?'

'So you put on these goggles when you visit the hospital, and that's how you're able to see them? But otherwise, they're invisible?'

Frank rolled up his eyes as if he couldn't believe that Lilian was so slow on the uptake.

'So, all right. How many of them are there?'

'Fifteen, twenty maybe. It's not that easy to count them because they're always like milling around. There's quite a few in Wellington Wing, and about half a dozen in Montgomery Wing. Some in the upstairs bedrooms, too. Some of the worst cases.'

'There really are that many veterans still roaming around the hospital? Where do they hide during the day?'

'They don't *hide* nowhere, love. Don't you get it? That's their home.'

Lilian sat back. Her logical mind was refusing to accept that there was still about a score of Army casualties wandering around St Philomena's. Unless they were ghosts, and she simply didn't believe in ghosts.

Michael crowned one of his draughts. Then, without looking up, he said, 'You should tell her what we saw in Musa Qaleh, Frank.'

'I don't know. She probably won't believe that, either.'

'Go on, tell us,' Moses coaxed him. 'I saw action myself in Helmand Province, for nearly three years. I was a captain in the RAMC. Anything might help us to understand what is going on here at St Philomena's, even if you do not think that it is important.'

'You'll probably think it's a load of bull.'

'All the same,' said Moses. 'Pull up a sandbag and tell us.' That was the Army expression for somebody recounting a far-fetched experience.

Frank shrugged. 'It was 2012, the end of July. It was so bloody hot we could have fried eggs on our Foxhounds. We was all stressed and totally knackered. We hadn't had no sleep for two straight nights and we'd been ambushed during the day and lost one of our sergeants. Twilley, his name was. Really first-rate bloke. So to be honest with you, we was probably just seeing things.'

'Then again, Frank, maybe we *weren't* seeing things,' Michael interrupted in his expressionless voice, and still without raising his eyes from the draughtboard. 'I saw the same as you, and so did three or four other fellers. How was that possible, unless what we were seeing was really real?'

'Well, anyhow,' said Frank, 'we was camped for the night outside Musa Qaleh, which is a village on the banks of the Musaqara river. We'd been given a tip-off that a Terry on our most-wanted list was hiding out somewhere in the locality, and we'd been going door to door all afternoon looking for him. It ain't exactly a doddle looking for a target in Afghanistan when the only description you've been given is that he's wearing a beard and a *peraahan tunbaan* – just like every other geezer in Afghanistan, all fifteen million of them.'

'We pitched our tents opposite the cemetery,' Michael put in. 'It was the best position for keeping an eye on the road in both directions, north and south, and the ground was open in all directions, like, so that nobody could sneak up on us.'

'That's right,' said Frank. 'And there was half a moon that night, and not much in the way of clouds, so we could see all the way across the road to the cemetery. All these white gravestones with that scribbly writing on them. Dead spooky. Anyhow, I left me tent for a goodnight fag and I'd only been out there for five or six minutes when suddenly I caught sight of this geezer standing by one of the gravestones. All dressed in white, he was, but he had these red eyes. Glowing red eyes, like a couple of red-hot coals, and long black hair that was standing straight up on end like he'd stuck his fingers into an electric socket.

'I called Corporal Denman, who was standing not too far away talking to three other blokes, and he turned around and he saw him, too, this geezer in white. One of the blokes he was talking to was our interpreter, Ahmed, and Corporal Denman got him to shout out "who goes there?" in Pashto.'

'That was when *I* came out of my tent and saw the fellow for myself,' said Michael. 'And almost at once then we saw two or maybe three more fellows in white walking between the gravestones towards us. They all had those red glowing eyes and that black hair that was rising upwards like smoke.'

'They was challenged again, wasn't they? But none of them answered, so Corporal Denman told one of the troopers to fire a salvo into the air, to warn them off. That still didn't stop them. They just kept on coming and now they was crossing the road towards us. So Corporal Denman gave the order for the trooper to shoot them – shoot to kill, in case they was wearing suicide belts. So he did.

'When the rounds hit them their white robes went all flappy, but there wasn't no blood. Instead, their robes dropped on to the road and blew away, like they was sheets of newspaper, even though there wasn't that much wind. The geezers themselves, they blew away, too. They was twisting around like clouds of black smoke, then *poof!* they was gone, and you wouldn't think that nobody had never been there.'

'Frank,' said Michael, still without raising his eyes.

'What?'

'You're forgetting about Ahmed.'

'Oh, yes, well, that's the whole point of the story, really,' said Frank. 'Ahmed, our interpreter, he went doolally. I mean absolutely apeshit. He was waving his arms around and screaming his head off and when I asked him what was eating him he kept on gibbering about "dah-dahs" or something like that. Then he went haring off and we never saw him again, did we, Mike? Never saw hide nor hair of him, never again. Whatever they was, those "dah-dahs", they must have really scared the doo-doo out of him, that's all I can say.'

'But you never found out what they might have actually been?' asked Lilian.

'Never got the chance, love. Never got the chance. The reason I told you about them was because whatever they was, we never had nothing but bad luck after we saw them. Next morning, Mike here got hit in the back by a sniper. Then the same afternoon our Foxhound was hit by a rocket, which blew half me fucking hip off and killed three of our patrol. The other five was blown up by a roadside IED on their way back to base – two killed and three seriously wounded. Those three, they're still at St Philomena's.'

Lilian was silent for a while, thinking about what Frank had told her. Then she said, 'Do you think you could come with us up to the hospital and bring your night goggles with you so that *we* can see your old friends too?'

'Not today he can't,' Marion chipped in briskly. 'His physiotherapist will be here in an hour, and he usually has a long sleep afterwards.'

'Then tomorrow, perhaps? We really need to get to the bottom of what's been happening up there.'

'We'll see,' said Marion. 'I don't want him getting overstressed. The very fact that he can see his friends at all – well, I think that tells you a great deal about the seriousness of his condition.'

'All right,' said Lilian. 'If you give me your number, I'll call you tomorrow to see if we can arrange it. Frank – Michael – you've both been very helpful. Thank you.'

As she drove them back to St Philomena's, Lilian said, 'What did you make of all that, Moses? Do you think it made any kind of sense?'

'I have no idea, to be truthful. I heard dozens of stories about ghosts when I was in Afghanistan. There was one place called Observation Point Rock, which the British held for a while before the Americans took it over, and there were scores of reports that troopers had seen ghosts around there. I believe they even made a TV documentary about it.

'One of the ghosts was a little girl, apparently. Others showed up on infrared cameras but when they shone a white light in that direction there was nobody there. In spite of that, the Afghanis really believed in them.'

'Did you ever see any?'

'Me? No. Maybe as a medic I was too sceptical. When you have had to pick up the arms and legs of men who have been blown to pieces but are still alive and talking to you, it is hard to believe in spirits of any kind. Certainly I stopped believing in God.'

'Yet Frank insists that his mates are still roaming around the hospital, doesn't he? And all right, they may be nothing more than a figment of his imagination, but what about all the screaming and shouting that we've heard for ourselves, and all the weird things that we've seen? And worst of all – what about what's happened to poor Alex and Charlie? There has to be some explanation.'

'You do not believe in ghosts yourself, though?'

'No, of course I don't. I believe that once you're dead you're dead and you don't go walking around scaring people. I mean, when you think about it, why would a dead person do it? What would be the point?'

10

Before she locked up for the night at St Philomena's, Lilian stood at the foot of the staircase with her head bowed and one hand resting on the newel post and listened for nearly a minute. It was a minute's silence for the dead, but if the dead were still there, they remained silent themselves.

She crossed the forecourt, and as she opened the door of her car, she looked back to see if any candles or flashlights were flickering at any of the windows, or if any faces were looking out, but all the windows remained dark. No wounded soldiers. No ghosts with glowing red eyes and hair like smoke. No 'dah-dahs'.

She drove back to her small semi-detached Victorian house close to Epsom town centre. She drew the curtains and switched on the lights and then she went upstairs to change into a white roll-neck sweater and a tartan skirt.

Before she went out again, she looked at herself in the mirror beside the front door and asked herself, out loud, 'Well, Lilian? Do you believe in ghosts or not?'

Her reflection stared back at her with one eyebrow raised, but stayed silent, and she took that as confirmation that she remained a healthy sceptic. She didn't know what she would have done if her reflection had actually answered her.

She drove to the block of flats in Ewell, less than two miles away, where she used to live with Tim. His metallic green Mercedes was parked outside, as filthy as usual, and when she looked in the rear window she could see all the Big Mac boxes and crumpled copies of the *Racing Post* and other rubbish that he had probably just thrown over his shoulder from the driving seat.

Their flat was on the second floor, overlooking the garden. Inside, the television was playing so loudly that she had to press the doorbell three times before she saw the living-room door open and Tim's silhouette through the frosted glass.

'Who is it?' he called out.

'Who do you think? I've come to pick up those cookery books.'

'Oh. It's you,' he said, and opened the door. 'Right. Come in. Excuse the mess. Phyllis usually comes round to tidy up but she's gone down with something or other. Not Covid, I hope.'

Lilian stepped inside the hallway. Tim looked as untidy as the flat. He was a big man, two years away from his fiftieth birthday. His grey hair was wild and his once-handsome face was bloated and red and prickly with stubble. He was wearing a baggy purple sweater with a hole in the shoulder and sagging jeans. Lilian found it hard to believe that she had once thought he looked like Paul Newman's younger brother.

He smelled, too, of stale perspiration and cigarettes. But when she walked through to the living room she could smell something else as well. Estee Lauder's Bronze Goddess, if she wasn't mistaken. Bergamot, musk and coconut. And there was a woman's skinny red cardigan draped over the back of the sofa.

'It's not that Hannah, is it?' she asked.

'What? No, no! It was that Margaret from the estate

agents, that's all. She just came round to do her half-yearly inspection.'

'And left her cardigan behind?'

'Oh, come on, Lil! You're always so suspicious! I didn't notice it until she'd gone, and obviously she didn't either. I'll drop it round her office tomorrow if I get the chance.'

'Tim, I don't care who you see or what you do. All I want is my cookbooks.'

Tim pointed to a side table where about a dozen books were stacked up, well-worn recipe books by Gary Rhodes and Madhur Jaffrey and Ken Hom.

'You could have put them in a box for me. How am I supposed to carry them down to my car? Balance them on my head?'

'Oh, sorry. Didn't think.'

'You never do. You never did.'

'Hold on. I'll find you a couple of bags.'

He went into the kitchen and came back with two plastic carrier bags from Asda. While he was stowing the books into them, he said, 'I don't suppose you fancy going out for a drink tomorrow evening?'

'With you?'

'Well, of course with me. I know we're divorced now and everything, but I still miss you.'

'How many times have we been through this? I miss you too, but I miss the Tim that you used to be when we first got married – not the Tim you turned into.'

'I've changed, Lilian. I promise you that I've changed.'

'Not your underpants, by the smell of you. And have you looked at yourself in the mirror lately? There are smarter-looking men than you sleeping in cardboard boxes in the street.'

'It's been really difficult to find myself a new job. If you knew how many online interviews I've done. I'm all Zoomed out. The trouble is, the more senior you are, the less vacancies there are.'

'Fewer, not less.'

'God, you were always picking me up, weren't you? But I would still like to see if we could get back together. Even if it was only as friends to begin with.'

'No, Tim. When you started beating me, that was the end as far as I was concerned.'

'I swear to you, Lil! I swear on my life that I will never hit you again, ever!'

'You said that every time you hit me before. "Oh, sorry, darling, I'll never hurt you again!" So how do you expect me to believe you now? Now – do you think I could have my cookery books, please? I have a ton of things to do this evening, and I don't have the time to stay here and listen to a whole lot of empty promises.'

Tim handed her the two heavy bags full of books and she started to make her way towards the front door. As soon as she had stepped into the hallway, though, he came after her and seized the sleeve of her jacket, pulling her round.

'Tim – let go of me! It's no use. We're divorced and I'm glad we're divorced and there's no way in the world that I'm ever going back to being your punchbag. I mean it.'

'Lil, the fact is, I'm skint.'

Lilian stared up at him, trying to see in his face even a trace of the Tim that he used to be. The funny, confident Tim. The Tim who was always smart, always self-assured, and always protective. But she could see nothing of that now. His eyes were bloodshot, the skin between his eyebrows was dry and flaking, and he had cold sores on his lips. Now that he was standing so close to her, she could smell the stale alcohol on his breath.

'I said, let go of me.'

'You don't know how humiliating it is for me to have to ask you, Lil, but I haven't had a full-time job now in eleven months. I have a nine and a half thousand pound overdraft. I'm three months behind with the rent. Margaret from the estate agents was here, although I admit that's not her cardigan. She was here to warn me that if I don't settle my arrears by the end of this month, I'll be out on my ear. And when's the end of the month? Friday. So that means I've got three days and then I *will* be sleeping in a cardboard box in the street.'

'You beat me, Tim. That's why I divorced you. You beat me.'

'I've said I'm sorry, haven't I? How many more times do I have to apologise? I was under so much stress. I was drinking too much. I wasn't myself.'

'You're still drinking now. How can you afford that, with your nine and a half thousand pound overdraft?'

'I got myself an Ocean credit card. You know, one of those cards for people with bad credit ratings. But the spending limit on that is only fifteen hundred quid, and now I don't have enough credit left to buy a packet of fags, let alone a bottle of vodka.'

'Tim, will you open the door for me, please?'

Tim released his grip on her sleeve. 'Lil, I'm begging you. You're my last resort. I've already borrowed too much from my mum and from Netta. I can't ask them for any more.'

'I'm sorry, Tim, but the answer is no.'

'As soon as I get a job, I'll pay you back every penny. I swear on my life.'

'No, Tim, and it's not because I know that you'll never pay me back. It's because I don't want to have anything more to do with you, ever again. I don't hate you, because that would mean that I felt something for you, and I don't. I feel absolutely nothing.'

Tim looked down at her and his face was crumpled with misery. His eyes were crowded with tears and he was dribbling out of the corners of his mouth.

Lilian put down one of her bags of books and opened the front door.

'You need help, Tim. Alcoholics Anonymous or something like that. My giving you money isn't going to get you out of the hole that you've dug yourself into. In fact, it would probably make it worse, because you'd spend it all on drink.'

With that, she picked up her bag and walked off along the corridor towards the stairs. She didn't hear the front door close behind her, and she could only imagine that Tim was still standing there, with tears running down his cheeks and dribble dripping off his chin.

She hesitated at the top of the stairs, tempted for one fleeting moment to go back and tell him that, yes, she *would* help him after all, out of human charity, if not of love. But then she pictured the time he had slapped her so hard in the kitchen that she had stumbled backwards and hit the back of her head on the gas hob. She had needed six stitches for that contusion, and had to wear a woolly hat for more than a month until her hair had grown back.

She left the block of flats, dropped the cookery books into the boot of her car, and drove home. She felt angry with Tim for having asked her for money, guilty with herself for having refused him, but knowing that she had probably helped him more by saying no.

A van driver pulled out in front of her without making a signal. She blew her horn, and when she overtook him she put down her window and shouted out, 'You – *dunce*!'

The van driver shook his head as if he didn't understand what she meant.

While she was heating up a butter chicken curry in the microwave, she called St Helier Hospital to ask after Alex and Charlie.

Dr Wells and Dr Morton had both gone home, but the sister in charge told her that Alex had been put into a medically induced coma to relieve his unbearable pain, and that Charlie had been sedated to help her to sleep. Charlie would be undergoing more tests for her paralysis in the morning.

'Do you know long you'll be keeping Alex in a coma?'

'No idea, I'm afraid. We still don't know why he's suffering such terrible agony, and so we'll probably keep him under for as long as we safely can, until we find out how to relieve it. To be quite honest with you, one of the reasons that Dr Wells put him in an MIC was to stop him screaming. He was giving our nursing staff a nervous breakdown.'

11

The next morning, David had to take his daughter to the dentist so Lilian drove to St Philomena's on her own.

All she needed now to finalise her development plan for Philomena Park was accurate measurements of all the rooms in the hospital. Roger French had found her yet another surveyor, and he was due to arrive tomorrow morning.

The day was sunnier and warmer, because the wind had turned around to the south-west. Because of that, she could now hear the distant roar of traffic on the motorway three miles away, and the trees were rustling as if they were gossiping to each other. *She's back again, she doesn't give up, does she?*

She left the front door on the latch, in case the doors and windows locked themselves, as they had the day before yesterday; and when she walked through the hallway, she stopped for a moment at the foot of the staircase to listen.

The hospital was still silent. No doors closing by themselves. No cries for help. Not even the gurgle of antiquated plumbing. If Alex and Charlie had not both still been in hospital, she could almost have believed that she had dreamed all that screaming and crying and the bed that had billowed with blood.

She went through to the living room and sat down in the spoonback armchair, opening up her laptop so that she could run through her provisional plans and her estimated costings. Even though the final measurements had yet to be completed, she now had a fairly clear idea of how many luxury retirement apartments Philomena Park would be offering its residents, and how much Downland would be asking for them. Even a single-bedroom flat would cost £850,000.

She expected that they would clear a profit of at least thirty million once all the apartments had been sold, and she would be paid a very generous bonus. She might even be able to buy a house of her own, and give up renting.

When she had tried to drag the chair over to the French windows to break them open, she had turned the chair around so that it was facing the garden. After she had been tapping away at her laptop for about half an hour, her attention was caught by a flicker of movement among the trees on the opposite side of the lawn.

She looked up, frowning. At first she could see nothing but waving branches, and two pigeons that were strutting up and down and pecking at the grass. She was just about to return to her spreadsheet when she saw a tall, thin man making his way through the trees, followed by two other men, both of them equally thin. It was difficult to see them clearly, because they were weaving their way between the tree trunks, and they were dappled in shadows.

She laid her laptop carefully down on the floor and stood up. By the time she went over to the French windows the men had disappeared, but she opened the windows anyway and stepped outside. Now that St Philomena's was private property, the men were trespassing, and if they had anything to do with the conservationists who were trying to stop the hospital's development, then she was not going to hesitate to warn them to keep away.

She walked quickly across the sloping grass until she reached the trees. Then she stopped, trying to see if the men were still hiding behind the tree trunks, or if they had gone.

'Hallo?' she called out. There was no answer, so she ventured a few paces forward, among the trees. The pigeons were cooing, rusty-throated, and the leaves were whispering in the breeze, but that was all.

'Hallo? If you're still here, and you can hear me, I want you to know that this is private property now and that trespassers will be prosecuted!'

Again, there was no answer.

'And if any of you attempt to interfere any further with the development of this hospital – you can be quite sure that you'll be prosecuted too!'

'Quite right, too,' said a man's voice, close behind her.

She let out a startled '*oh!*' and turned around. Standing only three metres away was Martin Slater, with both hands pushed into the pockets of his leather jerkin and a quirky smile on his face.

'Mr Slater! You shouldn't creep up on people like that!' Lilian snapped at him, trying to sound crosser than she actually was.

'Sorry. But I saw you haring across the grass like a jill and I wondered what you were chasing after. Or who.'

'I saw some men walking through the trees. I wanted to warn them off, that's all.'

'I don't reckon they were anything to worry about. Probably greenkeepers from the golf club, taking a short cut through to the pub.'

'At this time of the morning? The pub won't even be open yet.'

Lilian heard twigs snapping among the trees and turned back to see if any of the men had reappeared.

'I don't care who they are. There's no public right of way through these grounds, even if there was before. So if you happen to see any more people taking a shortcut, I'd appreciate it if you told them that from now on, they'll just have to go the long way round.'

She could see nobody between the trees and so she turned back. To her bewilderment, Martin Slater had gone, and there was no sign of him. Either he had dodged behind the trees himself, and was taunting her by hiding, or else he was the fastest runner she had ever known.

She stood there, feeling a cold beetle-like sensation crawling up her back. The wind was blowing across the grass, so that it rippled in a long wave. This was the second time Martin Slater had vanished unexpectedly. Although she didn't believe in ghosts, he was beginning to remind her of the spirit of Peter Quint in *The Turn of the Screw*. Handsome, tall, and mocking – and dead.

This time, she didn't call out his name. But she heard more twigs crackle, and so she took a few steps further between the trees, looking left and right for any sign of him, or for the men she had seen walking through there.

She listened for almost a minute, with her fists clenched. No more snapping or crackling. Only the leaves whispering, *She's back, she's back, but she doesn't know what haunts these woods, or this hospital, and she never will.*

She had only just started to make her way back when she stumbled on something that was sticking out of the leaves, and if she hadn't reached out for the nearest tree she might have fallen over. She thought at first that she had tripped on a root, or a broken-off branch, but when she looked down she saw that it was a dirty white colour, with a knobbly end on it.

She kicked aside the leaves and then she realised what it was. A large bone, like a human leg bone.

She picked up a leafy twig and used it to brush away more dead leaves. It was then that she saw a curving bone half-buried in the soil, and when she scraped some of the soil away from it, she realised that it was part of a pelvis.

She went on scraping, more and more frantically, and gradually she revealed a spinal column, and a ribcage that was crushed like a broken basket. She uncovered three arm bones, too, and two triangular scapulas. She dug deeper and harder, but she could find no trace of a skull.

She stood up straight, breathing deeply. She had no way of knowing when this skeleton might have been buried here, but its bones had been blotched by the limestone soil and by the rotting leaves, so she guessed that it might have been lying here for some years.

No matter how long it had been here, though, she knew that now, at last, she would have to call the police.

She was halfway back across the grassy slope when David appeared out of the open French windows.

'Oh, there you are, Lilian! I was wondering where you'd got to!'

She was out of breath, so she didn't answer him until she reached the patio.

'I've found some bones. Some human remains.'

'What? You're joking, aren't you?'

'I wish I was. I thought I saw some men taking a short cut

through the woods, so I went to warn them that they were trespassing. That's when I found this skeleton, or part of a skeleton, anyway. It's buried in the ground. Not very deep. There was a leg bone sticking right up and I almost tripped over it.'

She paused to inhale, and then slowly exhale, to steady herself. 'I'm just going inside to call the police.'

'What does it look like? I mean, is it an adult, do you think, or a child?'

'Oh, from the size of the bones it must be an adult. But you can't tell whether it's a man or a woman. There's no clothing buried with it, or anything like that. And I couldn't find a skull.'

'Blimey. What do you think? Somebody at the hospital got murdered or something, and they wanted to cover it up?'

'David, I have absolutely no idea,' she said, stepping inside the drawing room. 'All I know is that this whole development seems to be cursed. Either it's cursed or somebody is doing their level best to wreck it. It wouldn't surprise me if those bones were deliberately planted there to hold things up.'

She picked her phone out of her bag and prodded out the number for Surrey Police.

'Yes. This isn't an emergency, but I'm at St Philomena's Hospital in Downlea, and I've found a human skeleton buried in the grounds. Well, yes, the hospital is closed, but it's been acquired by Downland Developments and I'm the project manager. Yes. Lilian Chesterfield. No.'

She waited while they found a detective to talk to her.

David said, 'I'm really surprised that Martin Slater hadn't come across it before. He's been gardening here for yonks, hasn't he? And if that leg bone was sticking right out, like you say—'

'Martin Slater was actually there, right before I found it, but then he disappeared. I don't know where he went to.'

'Oh – I passed him on the way here. He was walking past the pub. I gave him a wave but I don't think he saw me.'

Lilian lowered her phone and stared at him. 'He was walking past the pub? That must be – what – nearly a mile away. He couldn't have got that far in five minutes.'

'Well, it was him all right. He was wearing that leather waistcoat thing.'

'One minute he was standing right next to me and the next minute he was gone. But he would have had to sprint all the way to get from here to the Cock as quickly as that. I can't understand it. Was he running, when you saw him?'

David shook his head. 'Nope. He was strolling along like he had all the time in the world.'

'Hallo?' said a small voice from Lilian's phone.

'Oh, yes, hallo.'

'My name's Detective Inspector Barry Routledge. I understand you've disinterred some human remains.'

'Yes,' said Lilian, but all the time she was looking at David and the question that was burning between them was, how had Martin Slater gone so far, so fast?

'I gather you're at St Philomena's Hospital at Downlea. Is that right?' asked DI Routledge.

'That's right. I'm in charge of its redevelopment.'

'And you've found what looks like a human skeleton?'

'Yes. Most of a human skeleton, anyway.'

'Okay. Do you think you can take a photo of it for me, so I have some idea of what we're dealing with here? I'm in Reigate at the moment but I can come up and see you within the next hour or so. Take a photo, but please don't disturb it, will you? And make sure that nobody else does, either.'

Lilian lowered her phone again. 'I really can't believe this. It's all going from bad to worse to unbelievably terrible. I absolutely *dread* to think what we're going to find next.'

'Can I see the bones?' asked David.

'Yes, okay. But the detective said that they mustn't be disturbed.'

'Oh, great. He didn't worry about *us* being disturbed?'

They walked together down the slope to the trees. The wind blew Lilian's hair across her face and into her eyes.

'There,' she said, pointing to the pelvis and the broken ribcage that were sticking out of the leaf litter. She took out her phone and photographed them from three different angles.

David shook his head in disbelief. 'Bloody hell. Whoever it was, it looks like they've been crushed, doesn't it? That happened to a friend of my dad's once. He was working on a building site and a five-ton concrete block dropped on top of him. Dad said that when they lifted the block off of him, he was flat as a pancake. But I don't see how anything like that could have happened here – not among all these trees.'

They started to climb back up the slope. They were only halfway up when Lilian thought she saw a flicker of torchlight in one of the upstairs windows of the hospital. She stopped, and brushed the hair away from her eyes, and peered up at it. After only a few seconds a pale face appeared, and whoever it was seemed to be staring back down at her.

She gripped David's sleeve. 'Look – look up there! There's somebody up in Montgomery Wing!'

'Yes, I can see them,' said David. 'Don't worry – it's probably that replacement surveyor, and he's looking for us.'

He waved and called out, 'Hey! We're coming back inside! We'll meet you in the hallway!'

The face remained at the window, giving no sign that he had heard. And as they continued up the slope, another face appeared at the window next to it, equally pale. Then another, but this time in one of the windows of the floor above the Montgomery Wing. This face was black.

'It's not that Moses, is it?' asked David, leaning back to get a better look before they went in through the French windows.

'He didn't say that he was coming back,' said Lilian. 'Anyway, let's go up and see who's there, before they can get away. All this trespassing is beginning to drive me mad.'

They hurried through the drawing room, across the hallway, and mounted the stairs. By the time they reached the Montgomery Wing, Lilian was out of breath and her heart was beating hard, but she pushed the doors wide open and strode inside. David followed close behind her.

For the briefest moment, she imagined that she saw two men, standing by the windows. They both looked as if they were wearing combat fatigues, with blotchy camouflage patterns on them. But they vanished instantly, and she couldn't be sure that she hadn't been tricked by a pattern of sunlight and shadow.

'Nobody here,' said David, looking around. 'They must have scarpered as soon as they heard us coming up the stairs.'

'Scarpered to *where*, exactly? We've already seen that there's no other way out of here.'

'Maybe they went upstairs, where that black bloke was.'

'Well, let's go and take a look, shall we?'

They climbed up to the third floor. They went from room

to room, as they had done before, opening every door and looking inside. There was nobody there.

'We did see faces, didn't we? They weren't some kind of optical illusion?'

David didn't answer. He was drumming his fingers on the banister rail, staring down into the stairwell, and biting his lower lip.

'What?' said Lilian.

'I don't know. I'm not so sure I want to carry on working here in this hospital, to tell you the truth. I mean, there must be some kind of explanation for all this, but I'm damned if I know what it could be. And I don't want to end up like Alex, for Christ's sake, or Charlie.'

'So what are you telling me? You want to quit?'

David kept on staring down the stairwell. 'You probably think I'm a chicken, but something seriously scary's going on here, and even if it's nothing but activists playing silly buggers, like you said it might be, I've got my wife and my kids to think about, and if I was screaming my head off in agony, like Alex, or paralysed, like Charlie – how the hell would they be able to manage?'

'Come on, David. We can't give up now. What happened to Alex and Charlie, that could have been nothing more than a coincidence. People suffer from strokes, don't they, which paralyse them, and stress can cause people terrible pain. I've been googling all about it. There's no reason for you to think that anything like that is going to happen to you – or to me, for that matter.'

'But this gets more bonkers by the minute! We definitely saw faces at the windows, didn't we? But when we came looking, there was nobody there! Just like we've heard people calling out and there's nobody there! And now on top of everything else you've found a skeleton in the woods! I'll bet you didn't find anything on Google about skeletons in the woods, and how they got there!'

'David, there is no such thing as ghosts.'

David stared back at her. 'You really believe that? You really believe that this is all some kind of trick?'

'Yes. I have to believe it. What else could it be?'

David opened his mouth as if he were about to answer, but then turned away.

Somewhere downstairs, a door slammed.

12

Nurse Danjuma was texting her sister about her upcoming birthday party when Alex started to roll from side to side in his bed. At the same time, he started making a pathetic keening sound in the back of his throat, like an animal that has lost its young.

Nurse Danjuma put down her phone and went over to stand beside him. Dr Wells had told her he was so heavily sedated that it was unlikely he would regain consciousness for at least another eight hours, but his eyelids were flickering and he was intermittently slapping at the bumpers at the side of his bed.

'Mother,' he mumbled, and then he violently jerked.

Nurse Danjuma pressed the emergency call button. 'It's okay, Alex,' she told him. 'Just be calm.'

'Mother... I can see you! I can see you, Mother! What are you doing in the garden?'

He slapped the bumpers again, and now his eyes opened wide. He stared up at Nurse Danjuma but he didn't appear to be able to see her. The white gauze dressing on his chin where Dr Wells had treated his chewed-up lips made him look as if he had a goatee beard.

'It's starting to rain, Mother! You need to come inside!'

'Alex, do you know where you are?' Nurse Danjuma asked him. 'You're in hospital, Alex, not at home.'

'Mother, it's raining! You have to come inside!'

Suddenly, the continuous beeping of Alex's life support monitor was interrupted by a panicky *bip-bip-bip* of alarm signals. As soon as these stopped, they were followed by a steady, monotonous drone.

Looking over at the monitor screens, Nurse Danjuma could see that Alex's heartbeat had flatlined. He had stopped breathing and all his other vital signs were gradually shutting down. His blood pressure, his body temperature, his blood oxygen level.

She pressed the alarm button again. Then she pulled down the blanket covering his chest, lifted his gown, and picked up the pads of the bedside defibrillator. She shocked him once, so that he jolted, but his heartbeat continued to flatline, so she shocked him again.

He jolted a second time. He continued to stare at her, but blindly, and the monotonous droning went on and on.

The door opened and Dr Wells came bursting in, with one of his team close behind him, a young bearded Pakistani, Dr Janjua.

'I've shocked him twice,' Nurse Danjuma told them. 'He still hasn't responded.'

Dr Wells looked at the monitor and said, 'Shock him again.'

Nurse Danjuma waited for the defibrillator to power up, and then tried to start Alex's heart for a third time. Alex jumped as if a mule had kicked him, but the flatline went droning on.

'Again,' said Dr Wells.

Nurse Danjuma shocked Alex five more times. At last, Dr

Wells laid his hand on her arm and told her, 'That's enough, nurse. I'm afraid he's gone.'

As he said that, Alex soaked the bed with urine, and his bowels opened. The room began to fill with the rank smell of faeces.

'Oh, my God,' said Nurse Danjuma. 'And he is such a young man. Only a few minutes ago, he woke up and started to talk to his mother. He opened his eyes, although I don't know if he could see me.'

'He woke up? Are you serious? I gave him enough ketamine and midazolam to put a herd of elephants to sleep.'

'He was telling his mother to come in from the garden, because it was raining.'

'Do we have any idea yet what was causing him such pain?' asked Dr Janjua.

Dr Wells pulled a face. 'No idea at all. Physically, he had nothing whatsoever wrong with him. I can only assume that he was suffering from some rare psychological condition. He really believed that he was this soldier who had been seriously injured in Afghanistan, and that somehow he could feel this soldier's pain by proxy.'

'How could that happen?'

'I still haven't a clue. Perhaps he had read about this soldier in a newspaper article, or seen a documentary about him on TV, and become convinced for some reason that it was him. Now that he's passed away, I don't suppose we shall ever be able to find out.'

Alex's blue eyes were still wide open, although they had started to mist over. Dr Janjua looked down at him with professional curiosity but with obvious apprehension, too, as if he were afraid that Alex would suddenly come to life again and say, *Boo! Fooled you!*

'His next of kin will have to be informed,' said Dr Wells. 'I don't believe he was married, or had any children, but he lived with his mother, didn't he? We need to get permission to remove his brain for further examination.'

'There was no trace of him being on hallucinogenic drugs, or anything like that?'

'Nothing. Not even a trace of alcohol.'

Dr Wells went around the end of the bed to check Alex's life support monitor. He was only halfway there when he stopped and pressed his hand against his heart.

Dr Janjua frowned at him. 'Dr Wells? Are you all right?'

Dr Wells said nothing, but kept his hand against his heart. After a few moments he slowly sank to his knees.

'Dr Wells – what's wrong?'

It was then that Dr Wells opened his mouth wide and let out a scream. It was a harsh, agonised, wavering cry of despair, and Dr Janjua had not heard anything like it since he had treated an elderly man who had fallen under a Tube train.

Dr Wells dropped sideways on to the carpet and then rolled over on to his back, still screaming. He kicked his legs and humped his back up and down and pounded the floor with both fists. His eyes were bulging and his face was scarlet and his mouth was dragged down in pain.

Dr Janjua hurriedly knelt down on the floor beside him, trying to hold him still with one hand and tugging his tie loose with the other.

'Nurse! Fetch me thirty milligrams of oxycodone! Quick as you can!'

Dr Wells seized Dr Janjua's sleeves and shook him. 'My legs!' he panted. 'What's happened to my legs?'

'Nothing has happened to your legs, doctor. You're having some kind of an episode. Try to stay still.'

Dr Wells stared up at him for a split second as if he didn't recognise him, and then, abruptly, he started screaming again.

Nurse Danjuma handed Dr Janjua a hypodermic syringe. Normally, he never would have given an intramuscular injection through clothing, because of the risk of infection or of bending the needle or hitting a nerve, but Dr Wells was thrashing about too violently for them to attempt to take off his lab coat and his shirt.

Dr Janjua gripped his arm tightly and gave him the shot of oxycodone. After less than a minute his screaming became a series of shuddering gasps, and he began to relax, although he was still restlessly twitching and shifting himself from side to side.

Dr Janjua stood up. He looked over at Alex, whose face was as white as candlewax. Alex's eyes were still open, but his expression was peaceful, almost smug, like a man who has paid off all his debts.

At almost the same time, at the other side of the hospital, Charlie started to weep silently. Her eyes filled up with tears, which hovered in her eyelashes for a moment before she blinked, and then slid down on either side of her face on to her pillow.

At first she was alone. Nurse O'Grady had been sitting with her all morning, but Nurse O'Grady had taken a few minutes to go downstairs to fetch herself a cup of coffee and a KitKat chocolate biscuit, and before she went back inside, the disturbance at the opposite end of the corridor had caused her to hesitate to see what was going on.

Outside the room where Alex Fowler was being treated, she could make out Dr Morton and two of her team, as well as two male nurses and two orderlies. Then she saw a trolley being wheeled out, with somebody lying on it, covered by a sheet.

It was too far for her to go and ask what all the commotion was about, and she knew she shouldn't really have left Charlie unattended, so when one of the doctors turned around and caught sight of her, she pushed her way back through the door. She sat down beside the bed, prising the lid off her coffee and tearing the wrapper from her KitKat. It was only then that she noticed the glitter of tears in Charlie's eyes.

'Hey now, chuck, what's upsetting you?' she said, standing up again, and setting down her coffee cup and her biscuit on the bedside table. 'Is it any pain you're feeling there?'

Charlie looked up at her wildly and gave a little shake of her head.

Nurse O'Grady pulled a tissue out of the box and gently dabbed Charlie's eyes. 'You're not in pain, so what is it? Can you manage to tell me? Is it something emotional, like? Is there somebody you want me to call for?'

'They were telling us,' Charlie whispered, barely moving her lips.

'Who was telling you, love?'

'Those people. They were telling us to go.'

'What people are you talking about?'

'Those people in white. We thought we were seeing things, but we weren't.'

'Who do you mean? What people in white?'

Charlie stared up at her but didn't answer her. Instead, she started to moan and to rock herself from side to side. Nurse O'Grady took hold of her left arm and tried to restrain her, but Charlie kept on rocking, harder and harder, twisting her arm one way and then the other, as if she were trying to break free. Nurse O'Grady reached across and pressed the emergency button for help.

'Charlene, girl, you need to settle yourself down now!'

But Charlie began to throw herself even more wildly against the bars at the sides of her bed, ripping away the sticky pads that connected her chest to her heart monitor. She was panting now as if she had been running for miles, or was about to reach an orgasm.

'Jesus, will you keep yourself still!' Nurse O'Grady shouted at her. 'You're practically pulling my arm clean out of its socket!'

It was more than two minutes before the door opened and Dr Morton appeared. She was looking anxious and strained because she had only just left Dr Wells, who had been taken to intensive care. She had brought Dr Mark Latimer with her, one of the hospital's consultant neurologists, as well as two nurses.

Dr Morton had wanted Dr Latimer to see Charlie because he was a specialist in movement disorders, and had spent three years researching novel treatments for catatonia.

'Nurse O'Grady?' said Dr Morton. 'Nurse O'Grady – what on earth are you doing?'

Nurse O'Grady was tilted at an awkward angle over the rails at the side of Charlie's bed. She stayed in this position as Dr Morton and Dr Latimer and the two nurses entered the room, not turning around to greet them, and now she remained where she was, with her back to them, her head hanging down only two or three inches above Charlie's chest.

'Nurse O'Grady?'

Dr Morton laid her hand on Nurse O'Grady's shoulder,

and it was then that Nurse O'Grady fell stiffly backwards on to the floor, hitting her head against the leg of her chair. She was completely rigid, her hands held up as if she were appealing to the Lord to save her.

Both Dr Morton and Dr Latimer knelt down beside her. She was still breathing, and her eyes were open. Dr Morton pressed two fingertips against her carotid artery.

'Her pulse is normal.'

'But look,' said Dr Latimer, trying to bend her arm down. 'She's totally immobilised. Look – look at her fingers. They're like sticks. And look at her leg. I can't straighten her knee for love nor money.'

'Nurse O'Grady,' said Dr Morton, bending over her. 'Can you hear me, Nurse O'Grady? Can you speak at all? Can you tell me what happened to you?'

Nurse O'Grady made a gargling noise, and took in a breath as if she were about to speak, but before she could say anything one of the nurses called out, 'Dr Morton! Dr Morton – the patient here!'

'What about her?'

'She's gone, Dr Morton! She's passed away!'

Dr Morton grasped the side of the bed so that she could heave herself on to her feet. She looked down at Charlie and there was no question that the nurses were right. They had stuck back the electrodes from Charlie's cardiac monitor on to her chest, but the steady green line on the screen showed that she had no heartbeat. She had no other vital signs, either. She had stopped breathing and her eyes had already changed colour to a darker blue, as well as being tearful.

Dr Morton lifted Charlie's left wrist to feel her pulse, and instead of her arm being paralysed, as it had been before, it was floppy. Her right arm was the same. Her fingers and toes were all flexible and her knees could easily be bent upwards.

Dr Morton turned to Dr Latimer, who was massaging Nurse O'Grady's shoulders and neck.

'Can you believe this? Charlene Thorndyke was brought in because she was totally paralysed from head to toe. Now she's passed away and she's showing no signs of paralysis at all. But Nurse O'Grady here is paralysed, in exactly the same way that she was.'

'Well, you're right,' said Dr Latimer, kneading Nurse O'Grady's shoulders. 'Every muscle in her body is locked up tight.'

'But, listen,' said Dr Morton. 'I've only just come away from attending Bob Wells. He had a sudden attack of such acute pain that he couldn't stop screaming and he had to be sedated. Yet that was precisely the same condition that his patient Alex Fowler was suffering from, before *he* passed away.'

Dr Latimer continued to massage Nurse O'Grady's shoulder, but looked up at Dr Morton with his forehead furrowed, as if he were trying to work out a complex maths problem. 'Are you really suggesting that when these patients died, they passed their symptoms on to their carers? How is that possible?'

'I simply don't know, Mark. It seems like something out of a science-fiction story. The patients pass away but their condition lives on. It's not as though either of them was suffering from anything infectious – not as far as we know, anyway. Alex Fowler was experiencing the PTSD of a soldier who was seriously injured in Afghanistan – not even his own PTSD. Charlene Thorndyke was paralysed for no reason that we could account for at all.

'All they had in common was that they were both stricken by these conditions when they were working at St Philomena's Hospital in Downlea.'

'But that closed down ages ago, didn't it, St Philomena's?'

'Yes, but it's being developed into some kind of luxury residential complex and the two of them were working there. They're both surveyors, I believe.'

Dr Latimer stood up. 'Can one of you fetch a porter?' he asked the two nurses. 'Poor Nurse O'Grady needs to be taken to intensive care, and the quicker the better.'

He paused, and then he said, 'Maybe there's something at St Philomena's that affected them both. Some chemical, or gas leak. It certainly needs looking into. But you're right, Helen. It does seem like something out of a science-fiction story. Actually, more like a horror story, if you ask me.'

13

Lilian was on the phone to Roger French when two silver BMWs drew up outside St Philomena's. They were followed by a police car and two white vans with blue-and-yellow Battenberg stripes, one marked Forensic Services and the other marked Dog Section.

'I'm sorry, Roger, I'll have to go. The police have just shown up.'

'This effing hospital development, Lilian, for Christ's sake! It's been nothing but a pain in the arse from beginning to end! I don't know why you had to call the fuzz about that skeleton. If somebody was buried there, they probably were meant to be buried. It was a hospital, after all. You don't go calling the fuzz if you dig up some bones in a cemetery, do you?'

'Roger, I had to. It's not as if they were buried in a coffin.'

'I don't know. This delay is costing us thousands every day. And I mean *thousands*. And I'm seriously worried about the publicity, too. The police are going to tell the press and then we're going to see stories in the media about St Philomena's being a murder scene or something like that. You know yourself how hard it is to sell properties where people were murdered. That house in Gloucester where Fred and Rosemary West killed all those young girls, they had to demolish that and then they had to grind it completely down to dust, every last brick, so that some ghouls wouldn't come hunting for souvenirs.'

'Roger, I have to go. They're knocking at the door.'

'Has that replacement surveyor shown up yet?'

'Not yet. I'll let you know when he does. I'll call you later.'

Lilian opened the front door to find a tall, morose-looking man with a moustache standing in the porch, wearing a droopy brown raincoat. He was accompanied by two fresh-faced young detectives who looked like a pair of Saturday afternoon TV presenters. Behind them stood two forensic detectives in baggy white overalls – a bald man and a large woman with wiry red hair – as well as three uniformed officers, one of whom was holding the lead of a panting fox-red Labrador.

The man with the moustache held up his warrant card wallet.

'Detective Inspector Routledge. This is Detective Sergeant Woods and this is Detective Constable Merrick. You must be Ms Chesterfield.'

'That's right. Come through. The bones are in the woods at the back.'

'Thank you for the pictures, by the way, Ms Chesterfield. Most helpful. They made it clear that I needed to organise quite a substantial response.'

Lilian led the way through the drawing room and out through the French windows. As they all made their way down the slope towards the trees, David came hurrying across from the tennis courts to join them, and Lilian introduced him.

David ruffled the police dog's ears, but the dog shook its head and snarled at him. He laughed, and said, 'Don't know why, but dogs have never liked me. They can probably smell my cat on me.'

'Not a great cat lover, Quest,' said his handler. 'And he's very sensitive to atmosphere. Like this place. Got quite an atmosphere, hasn't it?'

'I'll tell you,' said David, 'this is the spookiest building I've ever worked in. I mean, I've known one or two that were old and creepy, but this one takes the biscuit, it really does.'

Lilian gave him a hard, meaningful stare. Discovering a skeleton among the trees was causing them enough delay, without telling the police about the faces they had seen at the windows, and the scattered cutlery, and all the wailing and crying and doors that refused to open.

'What exactly would you mean by "spooky"?' asked DI Routledge.

'The bones are just down here,' Lilian interrupted. 'I almost tripped over one of them, that's how I found them.'

But David carried on. 'Lilian and me, we've been wondering if it's all been some kind of elaborate hoax. There's an association of local people and they've made no secret of the fact that they don't want to see St Philomena's developed into luxury flats and a leisure centre. This building wasn't a hospital to start with, it was some rich family's private house, and it's listed. We reckon they could have been trying everything they can to scare us away.'

'So what have they been up to? They haven't been threatening, have they? I can give them a caution if they have.'

'No, but they've been hiding in the hospital and making all kinds of weird noises and chucking knives and forks around. You know – pretending to be ghosts and poltergeists. We've searched the place from top to bottom but we haven't been able to find them.'

Lilian shook her head but didn't say anything. She couldn't

believe that David was so blithely making her problems even more complicated than they were already.

'Well, let's take a gander at this skeleton first,' said DI Routledge. 'Then, if you like, we can have Quest here take a snuffle around the building. If there's anybody hiding there, believe me, Quest will sniff them out.'

They made their way through the trees to the place where the bones were half buried. The two forensic investigators crouched down beside them and carefully brushed the leaf mould away with their nitrile gloves. The bald man examined one of the leg bones and then he looked up and said, 'At a rough guess, Barry, I'd say they'd been here about ten or fifteen years. Maybe longer.' He spoke in a flat, bureaucratic tone, like a council official.

'Okay... so whoever this was, they were probably interred here when the hospital was still operational. I'll have to get in touch with Surrey Downs Heath and Care to see if they still have the hospital records on file. And with any luck I might be able to locate somebody who was here on the staff at the time. Somebody must know who this was, and why they weren't buried in a cemetery.'

The bald investigator picked up a rib and peered at it closely. 'In any case, we'll be running the usual radiometric tests, and maybe a BMD test, too, for bone-matter density. Hopefully those will tell us the age of the deceased, and their ethnicity, and quite a lot about their lifestyle, too. Like, how well nourished they were, that kind of thing.'

'These could well be the remains of somebody who once lived here when it was a private house,' put in the red-headed woman. 'Some people do like to be buried on their own property. And in the strangest places. What about that Major

Labelliere who was buried on Box Hill, upside down, because he said the whole world was topsy-turvy.'

'It's not a recent burial, though?' asked DI Routledge. 'We can't connect it with any current reports of mispers?'

'No. But I wouldn't rule out homicide. The way the ribcage has been crushed – you see how it curves inward? It looks as if it might have been done while the deceased was still alive, and while he or she still had internal organs. But we'll be doing plenty of measuring and scanning and we should be able to give you a conclusive answer on that, one way or another.'

While they were talking, the dog handler had been letting Quest snuffle around the trees, but eventually he came back. He was holding up a small gardening trowel.

'This is all we've found, and I reckon it's probably been here as long as these bones. Nobody's been through here recently, apart from Ms Chesterfield here.'

'*Really?*' Lilian frowned. 'The whole reason I came down here was because I saw at least three men taking a shortcut through the woods. This is private property now, and I wanted to warn them that they were trespassing.'

'Well, no, sorry, you must have imagined them. The only living things that have been through here lately are squirrels.'

'You're joking! I saw them quite clearly.'

The dog handler pulled a face. 'Sorry. Quest doesn't miss anything when it comes to the scents that people leave behind. Sweat, skin cells, toiletries – he can pick them all up out of the air, as well as the ground scent.'

'Are you absolutely sure?'

'No question, ma'am.'

The bald investigator stood up and smacked his hands

together. 'Right, we'll go and fetch our gear and then we'll crack on.'

Lilian stared into the trees. She was utterly dumbfounded by the dog handler's insistence that nobody had walked through the woods, at least not recently. She could still see their tall, attenuated figures in her mind's eye, like the Slender Man with two equally thin companions.

'While forensics set up shop, why don't we let Quest here have a run round the hospital?' said DI Routledge. 'Then we'll know for sure if some of the locals are playing silly buggers, or if there's another reason for all these disturbances.'

'These old buildings, I reckon they've got a life of their own,' put in DC Merrick. 'Me and my mate, we used to play in the old Dairy Crest milk depot in Epsom, after it was closed down, and one night I swear we heard milk bottles rattling and milkmen whistling, even when the place was deserted. We practically shat ourselves.'

'I don't believe in ghosts, as it happens,' said Lilian flatly.

'Neither do I,' said DI Routledge. 'And I've come across more than one incident when somebody was trying to scare the living daylights out of their neighbours or their relatives by making out that a property was haunted.'

'Oh, yes,' said DS Woods. 'Remember that bloke over in Brockham who kept climbing up on to his grandmother's roof and screaming down her chimney, so that she'd give up her bungalow and go into an old folks' home.'

DI Routledge shook his head in amusement. 'She wasn't as stupid as he thought. She bought a Guy Fawkes rocket and when he started screaming she lit it and sent it whizzing straight up the chimney! Almost blinded the stupid bastard, I can tell you.'

They had reached the hospital now, and Lilian led them

in through the French windows. Quest was already sniffing furiously, and straining at his lead.

'So where do you think these protestors might be hiding themselves?' asked the dog handler.

'Perhaps we should start off in the wards upstairs,' said Lilian. 'That's where we've been experiencing the most disturbances – people crying out for help, as if they were patients, and howling, and doors banging. And we've seen faces and figures, but they could very well have been tricks of the light, or optical illusions.'

'We could be talking about holograms,' said DS Woods. 'You can buy holographic projectors pretty cheaply these days, or even make your own. If you position your projector in the right place, you can make it look like there's somebody actually standing there, when there isn't.'

'That's right,' said DC Merrick. 'They've even put on whole concert tours with holograms of dead singers, haven't they? Elvis and Tupac and Whitney Houston. Come to that, I was down at the University of Sussex last month, and they showed me a hologram that you can hear and actually *feel*. That's really advanced stuff, of course, but here – some annoying twat could easily be using a thirty quid projector from Amazon.'

'But we've also had two people hurt,' David put in. 'Two of our surveyors, and they both had to be taken to hospital. One started screaming in pain, although there didn't seem to be any reason for it, and a woman surveyor, she was totally paralysed. Again, we couldn't think why.'

'You didn't report either of these incidents to the police?' asked DI Routledge.

'There didn't seem to be any need to,' said Lilian. 'There was no sign that anybody had hurt them.'

'But now you think there might be somebody hiding in the building, and they might have been responsible?'

'I just don't know. Both of them might have had underlying medical problems, and it was simply coincidence and bad luck that they both should have suffered them when they came here.'

They climbed up to the first floor, to the Wavell Wing, with Quest bounding up the stairs two and three at a time.

'I'll say one thing,' said DI Routledge, as they all walked along the corridor together, 'this place does have quite a spooky atmosphere, doesn't it? If you told me that you'd seen a real ghost here, I would almost believe you.'

David and DS Woods pushed open the double doors and they entered the Wavell ward. It was utterly silent inside, apart from Quest panting and his claws scrabbling on the grey vinyl floor. For a moment, they stood quite still, looking around, because all of them had been caught off guard by an inexplicable feeling of tension in the ward, as if they had walked in seconds before something catastrophic was about to happen, like a bomb going off.

'Hm,' said DI Routledge, pacing his way slowly down the line of beds. 'So it was in here that you thought you heard people crying out for help?'

'Yes,' Lilian told him. She was watching Quest sniffing his way along the walls and behind the curtains.

'But when you came to see who it was – there was nobody here?'

'No.'

DI Routledge had reached the bed with its mattress soaked crusty and brown. Lilian wondered if she ought to tell him that she had seen it bubbling with fresh blood – or thought she had, anyway – but then she decided to say nothing. She was beginning to think that her panic at being locked inside the hospital may have caused her to hallucinate; or maybe it had been a trick – a hologram, like the young detective had suggested.

Since those moments of sheer terror when she had found herself unable to open the doors or the windows, and heard all that begging and screaming, she had been trying to convince herself that there was a logical explanation for everything that had happened here, including Alex's agony and Charlie's paralysis.

There *had* to be a logical explanation, otherwise she would be forced to start questioning her own sanity. And if she couldn't find out who or what was causing these disturbances, there was a risk that Roger French would take her off this development, and might never give her a major project like Philomena Park, ever again. Her future career and her entire life would suddenly collapse underneath her. Her success at Downland had been all that had kept her together during her last months with Tim, and it was all she had now.

Quest was snuffling underneath the beds now. He had almost reached the bed that was caked with dried blood when he stopped, and lifted his head, and looked towards his handler. He appeared to be quivering, and his fur was ruffled.

'Go on, Questy, get on with it,' his handler coaxed him. 'It's not teatime yet.'

But Quest stayed where he was, still quivering, and he began to pant.

'Questy, pull your finger out and get on with it, will you?' his handler demanded. He turned to Lilian and said, 'He can be a greedy little so-and-so. If there was a trade union for dogs, he'd be their shop steward. He tries to blackmail me into giving him a biscuit by withdrawing his labour.'

But as soon as he had said that, Quest toppled sideways on to the floor, his eyes bulging and his legs rigid, and his shivering developed into a rapid, irregular trembling, as if he were suffering from distemper.

'Here, Questy, what's wrong, boy?' said his handler, and immediately dropped down on his knees beside him.

Quest rolled his eyes to look up at him, but then began to howl – a thin, plaintive cry that went on and on.

'He's hurting for some reason,' said his handler. 'Damn it – I'll bet he ate something while we were searching those woods. I noticed quite a few death-cap toadstools down there. I'd better get him to the vet, sharpish. If he doesn't get his stomach pumped, his liver could pack in and he could die.'

He heaved Quest up off the floor and started to carry him back towards the doors, with the dog's rigid legs sticking out, so that it looked as if he were carrying a coffee table. He made it less than halfway there. Quest suddenly jerked and jumped and tumbled out of his arms, hitting the floor with a heavy thump.

His handler knelt down again to pick him up, but he had lifted him only two or three inches off the floor when Quest screamed out like an agonised child. He gave a convulsive shudder, his head dropped sideways, and he hung lifeless in his handler's arms with his tongue lolling out.

There was a moment of silent shock. Then, 'Bloody hell,' breathed DC Merrick. 'The bloody thing's only gone and snuffed it.'

'What in the name of God could have done that?' said DI Routledge. 'That couldn't have been poisonous toadstools, could it?'

Quest's handler gently laid the Labrador on the floor and then stood up. His eyes were filled with tears. DS Woods and DC Merrick looked at each other with their eyebrows raised, and the three uniformed officers shuffled their feet uncomfortably.

'He's just died,' said Quest's handler, in bewilderment. 'I mean, he's just – *died*. I've never had a dog do that before. Even one that got shot.'

'Cummings, Rolle, help to carry that poor animal downstairs, will you?' said DI Routledge.

Two of the uniformed officers picked up Quest by his legs and carried his sagging body out of the ward doors, followed by his handler.

'Erm... what's the plan now, guv?' asked DS Woods.

DI Routledge looked around the ward, almost as if he were expecting somebody else to appear and explain what had happened to Quest.

'Well, since Ms Chesterfield and her colleagues have already searched the premises for intruders without any success, there's no point in us doing it without a dog. Let's go back down to the garden and see how forensics are getting on, and meanwhile I'll give Guildford a bell and see if they can send us another sniffer.'

DC Merrick walked next to Lilian back to the staircase.

'I can understand why this place gives you the heebie-jeebies,' he told her. 'But do you *really* believe it's some local action group?'

'That's the most likely explanation. Unless some bunch of idiots are simply doing it to frighten us. But then why would they? What would be the point?'

'I've got an open mind, me,' put in David, who was walking right behind them. 'My grandpa swore his house was haunted.

He said he used to hear somebody playing the ukulele in his attic, in the middle of the night.'

'The ghost of George Formby, probably,' said DI Routledge.

'Who's George Formby?' asked DS Woods.

'A music-hall singer and a film star. He was all the rage in the nineteen-forties. Some of his songs were a bit on the fruity side, though. Haven't you heard "When I'm Cleaning Windows"?'

DS Woods looked blank, and DI Routledge said, 'Never mind, Andy. Never mind.'

The two uniformed officers carried Quest's body outside and lifted him into the back of the Dog Section van. DI Routledge and his two detectives went back out of the French windows and down the slope to the woods, where the forensic investigators had put up a hexagonal blue tent. Lilian and David reluctantly followed them.

One flap of the tent was pegged up, so that they could see inside. The investigators had cleared away all the leaves and soil from the skeleton, and now they were taking multiple 3-D photographs of it.

The red-haired investigator came out of the tent, pulling down her face mask, tugging back her hood and wiping her forehead with the back of her hand. 'It's almost certainly a male, judging by the pelvis,' she said. 'You can tell by the shape of the pubic arch. Mickey Mouse shape in men, like two round ears. Wider in women.'

She was followed by her male colleague. Once he had removed his mask, he blew his nose loudly and then frowned at his handkerchief as if he were studying a blood sample.

'When do you think you'll be ready to take the remains up to Lambeth Road?' asked DI Routledge.

'This evening, if all goes well. It's a pity we couldn't find the skull, though. When it comes to identification, teeth are almost as good as a driver's licence. Better, in fact. You can forge a driver's licence but you can't forge your dental records.'

DI Routledge's phone warbled, and he turned his back on them and walked away to answer it.

'Okay,' they heard him say. Then, 'Yes. I get you. Okay.'

Once he had finished talking, he came back and said, 'The dog unit won't send another sniffer until their vet's carried out a full post-mortem on Quest. They're worried that there could be some kind of toxic substance in the building – some chemical that was left over from the days when St Philomena's was open as a hospital, or perhaps some poison put down deliberately by activists.'

'So what are we supposed to do now?' asked Lilian.

' Nothing – not before we know for sure what did for poor Quest. If it turns out to be a toxic substance, we may have to organise a full clean-up job before we can take another sniffer inside. Meanwhile, all I can ask you to do is to keep your eyes and ears open, and if there's any suggestion that there's somebody trespassing in the building or causing mischief, then you should let us know immediately.'

They all walked back up the slope and around to the front of the hospital. DI Routledge climbed into his car but put down the window so that he could speak to Lilian and David before he left.

'We'll put out some feelers and see if there's any local campaigners who might be out to give you grief. Believe me, I've dealt with this sort of troublemaker before. Crusties who sit down in the middle of motorways to hold up the traffic, all because they want the government to put double glazing in council houses and save the planet. Vegans who smash the windows of butchers' shops. Students who pull down the statues of slave traders. You name it.'

With that, he drove off, and the other police cars followed him. The Dog Section van had already left.

Lilian and David were crossing the driveway back to the porch when another car appeared, a red Fiat 500, and drew up next to them with a crunch of gravel. A white-haired woman put down her window and called out, 'Excuse me!'

'Yes?' said Lilian.

'I was passing earlier and I couldn't help noticing all the police cars. I was wondering what was going on.'

'I'm sorry, but I can't tell you.'

'There hasn't been any vandalism, has there? Nothing like that?'

'I'm not at liberty to say, I'm afraid. Not while the police are still looking into it.'

The white-haired woman opened her car door and climbed out. She was wrapped in a chocolate-brown cardigan with a shawl collar, matched with a brown tweed skirt, brown tights, and clumpy shoes. She reminded Lilian of the actress Judi Dench.

'It's just that I used to work here, when it was St Philomena's. I was in charge of the nursing staff. I was wondering if you'd been having the same sort of trouble that we did.'

'What trouble was that?'

'Well, nobody ever admitted it, not publicly, and it was kept strictly hush-hush. But it was the real reason St Philomena's was closed down.'

'I thought they closed it down because they opened up a better hospital up north.'

'Oh, they did, yes – that new military rehabilitation centre in Loughborough. It has a swimming pool and a sauna and a much better gym. But that wasn't the main reason they shut this place down.'

'So why was it closed?'

The white-haired woman looked around at the hospital building, and Lilian was sure that she saw her shudder.

'It was why the nursing staff stopped calling it St Philomena's. Just between ourselves, we started to call it St Phantom's.'

14

As soon as the white-haired woman had said, 'St Phantom's', all the trees around the driveway rustled and whispered, as if they were saying, *She's given away our secret*.

'Do you want to tell us about it?' asked Lilian.

At first, the white-haired woman didn't answer. She was still looking up at the hospital building as if she were expecting a face to appear at one of the windows.

After a few moments, though, she said, 'I'm not supposed to. An officer came down from the MoD on the day we moved the last patient out. He gathered all us nurses together and warned us that our contracts included a secrecy clause. We weren't allowed to disclose any information about the soldiers that we were treating here – their names, or their condition, or where they had been wounded, or even how many we were looking after. If we did, we could be prosecuted, and face a fine, or even go to jail.'

'Well, I will tell you this much,' said Lilian. 'Since we've been working here, we've been having some very disturbing incidents. I'm wondering if what you experienced was in any way similar. Especially since you started to call it "St Phantom's".'

The white-haired woman frowned, although she was

still looking up at the windows. 'When you say "disturbing incidents"…?'

'We've heard screaming, for a start,' David put in.

Lilian glanced at him in irritation, but he repeated, 'Screaming. Really loud screaming. You never heard anything like it.'

'All right, yes,' Lilian admitted. 'Screaming, and men crying out for help. But when we've gone to look for them, there's been nobody there.'

'Then there's what happened to Alex and Charlie,' David prompted her.

Lilian nodded. 'Alex and Charlie were two of our surveyors. They were both taken seriously ill while they were working here – Alex was in so much pain that *he* couldn't stop screaming, and Charlie – Charlene – she was totally paralysed.

'Not only that, we've heard voices, and seen people, even though the hospital was deserted. We've heard doors being slammed, and twice there were knives and forks scattered all over the kitchen floor.'

She paused, because the white-haired woman had turned towards her with an expression not of incredulity, but of sheer relief. She looked like a witness in a courtroom who has told a wildly fantastical story, but can see that the jury believes her.

'Did you experience anything similar?' Lilian asked her. 'Screaming, and doors banging – that kind of thing? Was that why you called it "St Phantom's"?'

'The screaming, yes – *yes*! That terrible, terrible screaming! And all those doors! But more than that. Some of my nurses were sure they saw men in the corridors at night, when all our patients were asleep. But if they were challenged, these men, they turned a corner or went through a doorway, or they simply disappeared.'

Lilian thought of the slender men she had seen walking through the trees, and the two figures in combat fatigues she had glimpsed for a split second in Mongtomery Wing.

'Why don't you come inside and tell me some more about it?' she said. 'Up until now, I've been assuming that all this screaming and suchlike is being done by local activists. There's a group who have been campaigning against us developing St Philomena's into an upmarket housing complex. But if all this kind of thing was happening while it was still a hospital – I mean, who would have been doing it back then, and why?'

The white-haired woman looked with obvious unease at the hospital's front door, which was still half ajar.

'I'm not sure. I saw some of those men myself. If they *were* men.'

'Then we can talk out here, if you'd rather.'

'No, no. I think I need to go inside. I need to convince myself that it was all our imagination – or *partly* our imagination, anyway. Perhaps it was nothing more than a kind of group hysteria. In any case, it wasn't the screaming that led to the MoD closing us down, or those men we saw walking around the corridors at night. The final straw was what happened to Doctor Cobb.'

'And what was that?' asked David.

'Let's go inside, and I'll tell you. It may be haunted, but I'll feel safer there. For some reason, I always have the feeling that I'm being followed, and watched. I don't suppose I am, but it's just an uncomfortable feeling.'

David opened the door wider, and the white-haired woman stepped warily into the hallway, with Lilian close behind her. She crossed to the foot of the staircase and then stopped, looking around her, with her left hand cupped to her ear and her eyes narrowed, listening hard.

'Can you hear something?' Lilian asked her.

'No. Not now. But sometimes, even when there wasn't any screaming or doors slamming, we could hear this faint monotonous warbling noise, like Arabian music.'

'Let's go into the drawing room,' said Lilian. 'Then we'll be able to see what the police forensic people are up to. This morning I came across some human bones buried in the woods there and they've come to examine them.'

'Human bones? My goodness. Do they have any idea whose bones they might be?'

Lilian shook her head. 'They think they might have been buried there for quite a long time, although they won't be sure until they've tested them back in their laboratory. By the way, my name's Lilian – Lilian Chesterfield, and I'm in charge of the new development here. This is my assistant, David Barton.'

'Brenda Wake,' said the white-haired woman. '*Sister* Brenda Wake, when I was here. I'm retired now, but I still help out at our local medical centre.'

They went through to the drawing room. Lilian and Brenda sat down on the window sill while David dragged over the spoonback chair.

'When you say "bones",' asked Brenda, 'was it a skeleton, or just a few bones?'

'A whole skeleton, apart from the skull.'

'My goodness. As if all that screaming wasn't enough, and what happened to your poor surveyors.'

'But what about this doctor?'

'Doctor Cobb? He was an orthopaedic consultant, and he used to visit about twice a month to treat those men who had suffered joint trauma. Hip displacement, that kind of thing. Very pleasant man. Quietly spoken, always polite. He made the men feel ten times better, even those who were going to be immobilised for the rest of their lives.'

Lilian was listening, but at the same time she was looking out of the French windows because she saw that the forensic investigators were slowly reversing their van down the path beside the grassy slope, towards the woods. They must have been preparing to pick up the bones and take them away to the police laboratory in Lambeth for more detailed examination.

'One afternoon,' Brenda was saying, 'I'll never forget the date because it was the day before Hallowe'en – Doctor Cobb was up on the third floor treating a young paratrooper. Derek Walker his name was, this young lad, and he always used to joke about his name, because he had suffered major trauma to both of his legs when his parachute failed to open properly at Musa Qaleh, and he didn't think he would ever be able to walk again. In fact, his legs were in such a state that Doctor Cobb was even considering double amputation.

'I was in the kitchen having a late lunch when I heard this really loud bump. A few seconds later, I heard one of my nurses calling me for help. I ran out into the hallway and there was Doctor Cobb lying on the floor. It looked as if he had fallen all the way down from the third floor. Both his legs were broken. Well, I say broken, but actually they were smashed.

'My nursing team took care of him while I went up to see if Derek was okay, and if he knew how Doctor Cobb had fallen.'

Brenda took a deep breath, her lips tightly pursed with emotion.

'And *did* he know?' asked Lilian.

'If he did, he couldn't tell me. He was dead – stone dead. He was lying face down on the floor as if he had rolled out of bed.'

'He was dead? Did you find out how he died?'

'They carried out a post-mortem at East Surrey Hospital but the result was inconclusive. Two days later, Doctor Cobb passed away too. He had hit his head very hard on the floor when he fell, and that had caused a massive bleed on his brain.

'I wasn't supposed to know about this, but a good friend of mine worked in the mortuary at East Surrey. She told me that the breaks in Doctor Cobb's legs were in every respect identical to the breaks in Derek Walker's legs. Right down to the last millimetre. They could have been the same legs.

'She also told me that the mortuary staff had been cautioned not to reveal this to anybody, especially not the media. If they did, they would immediately be dismissed.'

'So you shouldn't really be telling us about it?' said David.

'No, but there's not much they could do to me now. They can't sack me, because I'm retired. And I trust that you're not going to go to the media or post it on Twitter or anything like that. But I think about it almost every day, wondering who was screaming, and who those men were, and how Doctor Cobb's legs could have been broken in the same way as Derek Walker's, and how Derek Walker died. I don't want to go to my grave without ever finding out.'

'Did you know a veteran called Frank?' Lilian asked her. 'I don't know his surname but he has these funny whitish-looking eyes, and he said that half his hip had been blown off by a rocket. These days he's being looked after by a woman called Marion Crosby in a hospice not far from here, along with some other soldiers.'

'Oh, you must mean Frank Willard. Yes, of course I knew

him. And I know Marion, too. Lovely woman. Her husband lost his life in Afghanistan, and that's why she's so devoted to looking after those poor injured men.'

'Well, Frank keeps coming back to St Philomena's. He said that his comrades still live here. About fifteen to twenty of them, that's what he told us.'

Brenda raised her eyebrows. 'I really don't know. Frank was delusional, like a lot of those men who were wounded in Afghanistan. Those IEDs, they didn't only blow off their legs, they damaged them psychologically, too. They can't stop reliving the moments when those roadside bombs exploded, over and over again, and some of them feel that if only they could go back to those moments, they could escape unhurt, and have their legs back, and their whole life would be happy again. Or happier, anyhow. At least they wouldn't need prosthetic legs.'

'But you and your nurses saw some strange men here. Maybe they're the same men that Frank believes are his old Army friends. Maybe there's some kind of hidden basement here, which we haven't been able to find, and secret passageways. Maybe there are real squatters living here and they do all that screaming and slam all those doors to scare us away.'

'So how did they make one of your surveyors scream in agony, and paralyse the other one?'

'I have no idea, and I don't pretend to have any idea. But I don't believe in ghosts. Unless somebody proves it to me beyond a shadow of a doubt, I still think that we're being tricked, and by people who don't care if any of us gets badly hurt. You can give people injections that hurt them, can't you? And injections that paralyse them?'

'Yes, you can indeed,' said Brenda. 'Serotonins and some other substances can cause intense pain. And there are several chemicals can lead to paralysis, such as curare or tetrodotoxin or gelsemium, which is known as "heartbreak grass". Sir Arthur Conan Doyle almost killed himself by taking gelsemium. It didn't paralyse him but it gave him terrible diarrhoea.'

'Perhaps we should call in some thermal imaging company to give this whole hospital a going-over,' put in David. 'There's one that I used a couple of years ago when I was extending a house in Betchworth, and they found a whole bricked-up room that we hadn't known existed.'

'I don't know if Roger would agree to pay for it,' said Lilian. 'I can ask him. If we did find that there was a hidden room with people living in it, it would certainly be cheaper than cancelling this whole development.'

Brenda looked sceptical. 'Do you *really* believe there could be people living here in some secret hideaway?'

'I don't know what to believe, quite frankly,' said Lilian. 'I have never felt so confused in my life. And I have never felt so frightened, either. If it is real people, then it's incredibly scary, because they obviously wish us harm. And if it *isn't* – then what on earth are they, and what do they want?'

15

Moses arrived at St Helier shortly after midday. He felt tired and frayed, and he had a nagging headache behind his eyes. Yesterday's experience with Alex had given him nightmares about dogs howling and grinning death masks dancing around his bed, so that he had slept only fitfully. Grace had cooked him his favourite breakfast of noodles and eggs, but he had left most of it untouched.

'Moses – you have me really worried about you, darling,' she had said, scraping the bowlful of noodles into the kitchen bin.

Moses had put down his teacup. '*You* are worried about me? You cannot be half as worried about me as I am.'

He went up to the hospital receptionist and asked her to page Dr Wells for him, so that he would know that Moses had arrived.

'I'm sorry, sir. Dr Wells is unavailable.'

'Unavailable? He asked me to come and see him today. Cannot you tell him at least that I am here? I can wait, if it is necessary.'

'I'm afraid he's incapacitated. I don't know when he'll be well enough to see anybody.'

'He has been taken ill?'

'I'm afraid that's all I can tell you, sir. Is there anybody else you would like to talk to?'

'Dr Morton? Is she free?'

'Hold on. I'll see if I can find her for you.'

Moses had to wait in the relatives' room for nearly twenty minutes, but eventually Dr Morton appeared, carrying a thick folder under one arm and looking harassed. Moses stood up.

'Moses... sorry to have kept you waiting. I've had to take over two of Dr Wells's most serious cases.'

'The receptionist told me he has been taken ill.'

There was nobody else in the relatives' room. Dr Morton closed the door and said to Moses, 'Sit down. You've been involved with this from the start, so you need to know what's happened. Perhaps you can help.'

'So... please tell me. Dr Wells's condition – is it serious?'

'At the moment, we've put him into an induced coma. He was suffering unbearable pain, exactly like Alex Fowler. He was attending Alex Fowler when he was suddenly struck down, and according to the junior doctor who was with him at the time, he started to scream in exactly the same way that Alex Fowler screamed.

'The extraordinary thing is that Alex Fowler had just that minute passed away.'

'Alex Fowler has died?'

'I'm afraid so. But that isn't all. That woman who was also taken ill at St Philomena's, Charlene Thorndyke, she passed away yesterday, too, and the nurse who was caring for her was struck down with exactly the same paralysis that *she* was suffering from.

'When both patients died, their symptoms were immediately transferred to whoever was in the room with them.'

Moses stared at her. 'How can that be?'

'That's not the only question, is it? We still don't know why Alex Fowler was in such appalling pain and Charlene Thorndyke was totally paralysed. We hadn't finished all the tests on them that we were intending to carry out, but so far neither of them showed even the slightest indications of any physical injury or any neurological disorder.'

Moses stood up and walked over to the window. Outside, in the car park, a mother was trying to pick up her screaming toddler from the ground.

'I think… the answer to that question can only be found at St Philomena's,' he said.

'You could be right,' said Dr Morton. 'My colleague Dr Latimer certainly suspects that there's something strange going on there. But both deceased were sent away last night for post-mortem examinations, so we may know a little more about their condition in a few days' time.'

'Let us hope the post-mortems show up something that you have not been able to find already. All the same, I am going to go back to St Philomena's. Yesterday I went to talk to one of the former patients, along with Mrs Chesterfield, who is the lady in charge of its development. This man is quite sure that he can still see his old comrades there, roaming around the corridors. He has promised to come to the hospital with us so we can see them for ourselves.'

'You're not seriously suggesting that St Philomena's is haunted?'

'I do not know what to believe. Mrs Chesterfield suspects that a group of local protestors are trying to scare her away.'

'That sounds more likely. But let's you and me exchange email addresses. You can text me if you find out anything of interest at St Philomena's, and I can send you the post-mortem results as soon as I get them through.'

Moses watched the woman in the car park dragging her toddler over to her car and buckling him into his baby seat, still screaming.

'To be frank with you, Dr Morton, I am beginning to think that we will never know what caused Alex Fowler and Charlene Thorndyke to suffer the way they did, and to die. I saw some things when I was serving in Afghanistan that I still cannot fully understand. And you know as well as I do that the world of medicine still has many unexplained mysteries. The more we learn about viruses and other pathologies, the more we realise how little we know, and how much more we need to find out.'

Dr Morton had opened her file and was leafing through it, page by page, licking her thumb as she did so. Without looking up, she said, 'Yes, Moses, you're absolutely right. Perhaps we'll find out one day that there *are* ghosts, after all.'

Moses drove into the forecourt of St Philomena's just as the two forensic investigators were preparing to leave. They were standing in the porch talking to Lilian and David as Moses approached.

'We've removed all the bones that we've been able to locate,' the bald investigator was saying. 'However, we still have a considerable amount of work to do taking soil samples and searching a wider area in case we can manage to find the skull.'

'What is this?' asked Moses. 'What bones, if I may ask?'

Lilian said, 'I found a skeleton this morning, buried in the woods.'

'A skeleton? My God! Do you know whose skeleton it is?'

'Not yet, sir,' said the bald-headed investigator. 'We are

taking the remains to our laboratory for further tests and our colleagues will be checking their records for any notification of missing persons in this area. So you never know.'

He turned back to Lilian. 'We've taped that area off. Please stay well clear of it and make sure that everybody else does the same. Any new contamination will make our job that much harder.'

'Of course,' Lilian assured him, and the two investigators walked over to their van, climbed in and drove off.

'A skeleton?' said Moses. 'There is a saying in Nigeria, "*Sau daya, duk kasusuwa sun iya rawa*". It means "Once upon a time, all bones were able to dance".'

Lilian shook her head. 'It's probably nothing sinister. It could have been the remains of somebody who used to live here, when it was a private house. Except that there was no coffin, and no grave marker, which you would have expected, wouldn't you?'

They went into the hallway and through to the drawing room. Brenda Wake was still there, standing by the French windows making a phone call.

'Yes. I'll be back in about an hour. Don't worry. I can pick up some fish and chips.'

When she had finished, Lilian introduced her to Moses.

'When Brenda was working here, some of her nurses thought they saw figures walking around the corridors. But as soon as they tried to confront them, they disappeared.'

'As I said to Lilian earlier, it could have been mass hysteria,' said Brenda. 'In those days, the atmosphere here was incredibly fraught. Those young soldiers were coming back from Afghanistan in a terrible state, mentally. The nightmares that some of them were having, I can't tell you.'

'I would like to talk to you about that in a minute,' said

Moses. 'First, though, I am afraid that I have some very bad news. I have just come from St Helier. Both Alex Fowler and Charlene Thorndyke have passed away.'

Lilian stared at him, and pressed her hand against her heart. 'They're *dead*? Both of them?'

'I went there to see what progress they were making, and to talk to Dr Wells. It came as a great shock to me, too. But that is not all. What has happened is even worse than the two of them passing away.'

He explained how the symptoms that Alex and Charlie had been suffering appeared to have been transferred when they died to Dr Wells and Nurse O'Grady.

Lilian's heart began thumping hard and she felt breathless, as if she were going to faint. She reached out behind her for the window sill so that she could sit down. Brenda sat down next to her and took hold of her hand.

'Gracious me, I can't help thinking that's almost *exactly* what happened to Dr Cobb. The fractures in his legs were identical to Derek Walker's in every way.'

Brenda turned to Moses and told him how Dr Cobb had fallen from the third floor down to the hallway, shattering all the bones in his thighs and his shins, and how he had subsequently died.

'So what is going on here?' asked Moses. 'If it is protestors, how do they make such things happen? If it is not, then who? Or what?'

'I can't believe it's protestors,' said Brenda. 'As I was just saying to Lilian here, it could be some form of mass hysteria, and somehow it's stayed in the hospital after all the patients have left.'

Lilian said, 'Charlie felt that there was such an atmosphere here in this hospital you could almost cut it with a knife.'

'But how can that make one patient's symptoms be transferred to another?' asked Moses.

'Myself, I have no idea,' said Brenda. 'But I read about something similar happening once, in a mental institution in Delhi. It was closed down and converted into flats but almost everybody who moved into those flats went mad. They cut their pets' heads off or set themselves alight or threw themselves off the roof. In the end, so many residents committed suicide that they had to demolish the whole building.'

'Well, who knows?' said Moses. 'But whatever is causing it, we need to find out what it is, and as soon as we can. We owe it to those people who have died, and those people who are still suffering. I made a pledge when I joined the Army Medical Corps that I would devote myself to saving life and easing pain. I might be retired now, but I still keep that promise in my heart.'

'Let me call Marion Crosby, and see if she can bring this fellow Frank up here with his night-vision glasses,' said Lilian. 'Even if we don't get to see any of his old friends, at least that will eliminate one explanation.'

'But supposing we do see them? Then what?'

'God knows. Then *we* go mad and start jumping off the roof.'

16

It was dark by the time Marion Crosby brought Frank up to St Philomena's, and an owl was hooting in the trees as if it were trying to make them feel that they were in a ghost story.

David helped Marion to lift Frank's wheelchair out of the back of her estate car, and then to heave Frank himself out of the front passenger seat. Frank was clutching a black helmet in his lap, fitted with his night observation goggles.

They all went inside, with David bumping Frank's wheelchair over the front step. Now that it was beginning to grow dark earlier, David had brought the LED lantern that he used for camping with his family. It was stunningly bright, this lantern. It illuminated the hallway like an amateur stage play, with all their shadows stretching up behind them to the ceiling.

'So, where is it that your friends are hiding, Frank?' Lilian asked him.

'I told you before, love. They're not *hiding*. This is where they live!'

'All right, this is where they live. But where are they?'

'Upstairs, most of the time, in the wards, or the private rooms, but of course I can't get to see them up there because the lifts ain't working.'

'So how do you get to see them?'

'They come down to see me, once they know I'm here. They all come down to that big room with the chandeliers, the one we used to call the Social Room. Most of them come down, anyhow. Some of them have PTSD so bad they still don't know where the fuck they are, or even who they are.'

'But those who come down to see you...' asked Brenda. 'How do they know you're here?'

Frank reached into the breast pocket of his anorak and brought out an Echo harmonica. He blew a squeaky high-pitched chord on it, and then held it up. 'I play "If Tomorrow Never Comes", and down they come.'

'And you wear these goggles?' said Lilian, 'And that's how you can see them?'

'That's right, love. I'll give them a tootle on my harmonica, and once they've all mustered, I'll pass the nod around and you can have a butcher's for yourself.'

Lilian turned to Moses and David and Brenda. 'Do we think that we're all ready for this?'

Moses looked down at Frank. 'Just tell me this... is there any danger that your friends will harm any of us, in the same way that Alex and Charlene were harmed?'

'Yes,' said Lilian. 'You warned us about your friends being dangerous.'

'You're with me, so you don't have nothing to worry about,' said Frank. 'Besides, you've done nothing to them, have you? It's not like you're Terences or nothing.'

'But Alex and Charlene hadn't done anything to them either, had they?' said David.

'I can't account for what happened to them two, mate. It could have been anything what made them sick, do you know what I mean? Like, this used to be a hospital, right, and who knows what germs could still be lurking around?'

'I suppose it's possible that some viruses or some bacteria could have survived from that time,' said Brenda. 'They found that pithovirus in Russia, didn't they? They reckoned it was over thirty thousand years old, but it was still infectious.'

'Yes, but that was discovered in the ice in Siberia,' Moses retorted. 'This is a hospital building in Surrey.'

'Agreed. But I still think we have to consider that some kind of unfamiliar virus might have been brought here by one of the casualties from Afghanistan, or elsewhere in the Middle East. And supposing it was, it might have been able to stay alive much longer in a cooler climate. Viruses are highly adaptable, as you know. Look at all the variants of Covid. I mean, some of them are—'

David interrupted her. 'Okay, fair enough. But even if it *was* a virus that infected Alex and Charlie – or two different viruses – that doesn't explain the screaming we've heard, does it? Or the weird faces that Lilian and me have seen looking out of the windows, or the men that you said *you've* seen, wandering around the corridors?'

'Well, myself, I'm still inclined to believe that we were suffering from delusions.'

'You honestly think so?'

'As I said before, we may have been seeing things because of mass hysteria among the nursing staff. The atmosphere here was constantly fraught. And when I say "fraught", the whole place felt wound up to the nth degree, day and night. Or maybe our perception was affected by some illness that we'd spread among ourselves without realising it. Malaria can cause psychotic episodes, don't you know, and so can HIV and AIDs, and you can even start hallucinating when your blood sugar levels are low.'

'Whatever Lilian and I saw wasn't caused by low blood sugar. We'd both had a Bakewell slice at lunchtime.'

'*David*,' Lilian admonished him, although she was used to his habit of being flippant when in reality he was seriously worried.

'Sorry,' said David. 'But let's go through to the reception room, shall we, and see what we can see?'

They walked in silence along the corridor that led to the reception room. David went in front with his lantern, while Moses pushed Frank in his wheelchair. The only sound was their footsteps on the gritty linoleum floor, and the wheelchair's one squeaky wheel.

Lilian had taken down the sheets from all the mirrors around the walls, so that when they reached the reception room, the dazzling light from David's lantern flashed left and right. They could see their own reflections on every side, as if thirty people had cautiously entered the room, instead of five.

'Now what?' asked Lilian.

Frank fitted his helmet on to his head, and adjusted his night observation goggles.

'Now we have to switch that lamp off,' he told her. 'My mates won't come down unless it's dark. We'll be able to see them, yes, but they don't like being looked at too clear-like. Some of them have lost half their faces, and they know that too much detail don't show up with the nods. And if you can keep shtum, too. Whispering scares them. Reminds them of snipers.'

Lilian looked around. 'Are we all ready? Then, David, if you can—'

David switched off his lantern, and they were plunged into blackness. As their eyes became accustomed to the dark, however, the faint moonlight from the garden was reflected in the mirrors, and they could see the chandeliers suspended from the ceiling, glistening like giant spiderwebs.

Frank took out his harmonica, gave it a quick single squeak, and then began to play 'If Tomorrow Never Comes' at a high and discordant pitch. He paused every now and then to take a gasping breath, because he had lost one lung as well as half his hip.

He seemed to be playing endlessly, and after nearly five minutes Lilian began to wonder if he, too, had been suffering from delusions. She wanted to ask Brenda if her nurses had seen strange men in the corridors only when it was dark, or near dark. But she kept quiet in case Frank's friends had heard him playing and were close to making an appearance, and she didn't want to frighten them away.

Quite abruptly, in mid-chord, Frank stopped playing. There was a long moment of silence, and then he reached out from his wheelchair, waving his hand around in the darkness until he found Lilian's sleeve. He tugged at it, pulling Lilian towards him and downwards, until she was half crouching beside him. Then he lifted his helmet off his own head and carefully lowered it on to hers. At first it was awkward and uncomfortable and pressed against her forehead, but then she tilted it back a little, and twisted it a fraction to the left. The eyepieces of the goggles lined up with her eyes, and her vision was suddenly flooded with bright green images.

She couldn't help taking a lurching step back, and letting out a squeal of fright. Through the night-vision goggles she could see at least twenty men gathered at the opposite end of the reception room. Their figures were all glowing green, so she couldn't clearly see their faces, but she could tell that some of them had an arm missing or stick-like prosthetic legs.

'*David!*' she screamed. '*I can see them! They're here!*'

'Keep quiet!' Frank hissed at her. 'For Christ's sake! You'll set them off!'

But Lilian could see that the men were already moving towards her. Some were marching forward as if they were determined to seize hold of her, others were hobbling on their prosthetic legs, others were swinging on crutches.

She was terrified. She shivered from head to foot as if she had been drenched in ice-cold water and she let out a scream so high-pitched that she could hardly hear it herself.

The men screamed back at her, the same agonised screams that she had heard from Alex and around the wards. All twenty of them started screaming, like some hellish choir, and even through her night goggles she could see that their mouths were stretched wide open. Their screaming went on and on, and as they came nearer it grew louder, until Lilian was deafened, and the chandeliers started to set up a tingling noise.

Lilian turned, and saw that Frank was frantically backing up his wheelchair.

'You've set them off!' he yelled at her. 'You stupid bitch! You've only fucking set them off!'

She wrenched off the helmet and the night-vision goggles and threw them into the darkness.

'David!' she called out. 'Switch your lamp on!'

Nothing happened. The room stayed pitch dark. The screaming was so overwhelming now that David couldn't have heard her. She groped her way back to where she had last seen him standing, bumping into Moses first.

'What is happening? Who is screaming?' Moses shouted, into her face.

Lilian pushed her way past him and then found David, who was reeling around and around in bewilderment. The screaming was not only terrifying but disorientating, too, so loud that their brains could no longer tell which was left and which was right, where they were or even *who* they were.

'Your lamp!' Lilian yelled, right into his ear.

David switched it on, and the reception room was instantly lit up. At the same moment the screaming stopped, and there was deathly silence. The twenty men had vanished, and the five of them were left looking at each other – all of them in shock except for Frank, who was shaking his head in anger and disappointment.

'You really fucked that up, didn't you, love?' he said to Lilian. 'You really fucking fucked that up! What did I tell you? Keep shtum, that's what I said! Was that too much to ask? Out in Afghanistan, if you didn't keep shtum, the Terences would hear you and pick you off before you could say "why didn't I keep my bleeding yap shut?".'

Lilian ignored him and turned to the others. 'I *saw* them,' she said, and she was still breathing hard. 'I saw them with those night glasses. There were nearly two dozen of them. They were Army casualties all right, from what I could see. Some of them had artificial legs and others looked as if they had arms missing.'

'So we weren't suffering from mass hysteria after all,' said Brenda. She sounded as shaken as Lilian.

'That screaming,' put in Moses, holding his fingertips up to his ears. 'I have never heard screaming like that before. Even that Alex did not scream as loud as that.'

'So what are they, then?' said David, in a trembling voice. 'Are they *ghosts*?'

'It depends what you think a "ghost" actually is,' said Lilian. 'I've never believed in ghosts, or spirits, or anything like that.'

'Then what did you see here tonight? I mean, *what*?'

'I don't know, David. All those green men – I simply don't know. I went to a séance once, in Brighton, and you could tell that the whole thing was fake. It took the medium more than twenty guesses to work out the name of the dead person she was supposed to be talking to. But what I've seen here this evening—'

'If you hadn't fucked it up, they would have told you who they were,' said Frank, pushing his wheelchair forward.

'But *you* know who they are, don't you? They're your old Army friends, or so you say.'

'I can give you name, rank and number for all of them, love. Most of them, anyhow. And I can tell you one thing. They ain't ghosts. They're my old muckers, and they live here.'

'Jesus,' said David. 'I need a drink.'

Lilian turned to Frank. 'Is there any chance that you could call them back? We could be quiet this time, because they wouldn't be taking us so much by surprise.'

'Nah, they won't come back tonight. They're too wary. We could try again tomorrow night, if you want to. But you've seen them now, right? You've seen them, so you know they're for real.'

'It depends what you mean by "real". My God, I can't stop shivering. But I'm still not a hundred per cent sure that this isn't all some kind of elaborate hoax.'

'What do you mean, "hoax"? That's insulting them, that is

– what they went through, what they suffered. I can't believe you even said that. "Hoax"! You want to try having half your bleeding pelvis blown off and then see if you feel like playing tricks on people.'

'Frank,' said Marion, 'I think we should call it a night, don't you? You don't want to get yourself all worked up. You know what it does to your blood pressure.'

'But what do you think, Marion?' Lilian asked her. 'Has Frank ever let *you* take a look through his night goggles?'

'He offered, but I didn't want to. My husband, Ted, was brought here after he was wounded in Helmand Province, and he passed away here. I don't want to find out that his spirit is still here.'

'So you believe that these men I saw – you believe they could be spirits?'

'I don't know what to believe, quite honestly. All I want to do is remember with affection those who died and take care of those who survived.'

Marion wheeled Frank back to her car and stowed his wheelchair in the back. Before she drove him away, she said to Lilian, 'I hope you're not going to tell anybody about this. I mean like the MoD or the media.'

'There's no reason to,' Lilian told her. She didn't say that if a news story got out about screaming apparitions at Philomena Park, it could well lead to the cancellation of Downland's development plans for good, and Roger French could potentially lose millions.

David left, too, because he was supposed to be taking his daughter to McDonald's. He said nothing about this evening's events before he drove off, but Lilian could see that he was seriously shaken and he gave her a look that meant, 'what the hell are we going to do now?'

Lilian locked up the hospital, and then she invited Moses and Brenda to come with her to the Cock Inn along the road, for a drink and a talk. The three of them sat in a booth in silence for a while, nursing their drinks and wondering what to say to each other.

It was Moses who spoke first. 'Lilian, you were the only one of us who actually saw those men, but all of us heard them screaming.'

'That's right. So it wasn't as if those night goggles were fixed in some way so that I could see and hear some men who weren't really there. You know, like those virtual reality headsets. We have some of those in the office to show our customers what their developments are going to look like, and they're uncanny.'

Moses was repeatedly drawing a circle on the tabletop with his fingertip, as if he could conjure up some explanation of what they had witnessed. 'To me, there is definitely some connection between what has been happening at St Philomena's and what happened in Afghanistan.'

'There certainly seems to be. But what, exactly?'

'When he believed that he was Corporal Simons, Alex told me he needed to go back to the moment when he was blown up by an IED. On top of that, neither he nor Charlene had ever met me before, yet both of them recognised me and called me by the nickname that I was given when I was serving in Helmand.'

Moses paused for a moment, thinking. Then he said, 'Tonight, that was so scary. I am still shaking in my shoes, to be truthful. So it is no surprise that we are all wondering if the hospital is haunted. Maybe it *is* haunted, in a way, but not in the way that we usually think about places being haunted. Not by ghosts, how they always appear in ghost stories, transparent, or wearing sheets, you know the kind of thing, but by some other kind of energy.'

'Go on,' said Brenda. 'I think I know what you're trying to say.'

'Are you talking about those spooky white figures that Frank and his friend were telling us about? Those "dah-dahs"?' asked Lilian.

'Well, it would do us no harm to find out more about them. They could have been hallucinations, those "dah-dahs", brought on by drink or drugs. But whatever they were, they might have had some lasting effect on the minds of those men who thought that they saw them. Perhaps what we have here at St Philomena's is a case of collective post-traumatic stress disorder.'

'What do you mean by that?'

'I mean that all the trauma that every casualty suffered while they were in Afghanistan, perhaps it has set up some lasting vibration in the building, and this vibration can sometimes make itself felt as screaming and phantom figures.

'I am only theorising. Maybe this is all nonsense, and your suspicion is right, and we are being played for fools by some very clever pranksters. But maybe what we have here is a sort of echo from the past, when St Philomena's was still a hospital. Perhaps that is what *all* hauntings are: an echo from the past.'

'So how are we going to find out more about these "dah-dahs"?'

'I have been trying, but there is nothing on Google or any other search engine. They only say that "dah" is a word used in Morse code. You know, like "dot-dot-dah". But I used to be friends with a Russian who served in Afghanistan. He knew everything there was to know about Afghani culture and mythology.'

'Can you get in touch with him?'

'I will try. He lived in London because he came to England to work for the Russian Embassy. He ended up marrying an Englishwoman and never went back to Russia. Artyom Gorokhov, his name is. I do not know if he is still living in England because I have not seen him for seven or eight years, but I could try to get in touch with him.'

'Anything to help us understand what's going on here,' said Lilian. 'I don't believe in demons, not for a moment, but if we find out that these screaming men are demons, then at least we could arrange for an exorcism.'

Brenda said, 'I shall never know why the MoD didn't pull the whole hospital down.'

'Perhaps they were afraid it would make no difference,' said Moses. 'Sometimes it is supposed to be places that are haunted, rather than the buildings that stand on them. Or perhaps the minister was concerned that somebody would ask why they were demolishing such a historic building, and he would not know what to say. "Oh, we had to, because it was haunted."'

'Do you want another drink?' asked Lilian. 'Because I'm going to have one.'

17

A few minutes past midnight, although he was still supposed to be sedated, Dr Wells started to scream again.

He was alone in a private room, but as soon as the staff nurse on duty at the end of the corridor heard him she was able to switch to the CCTV camera above his bed. She could see that he was throwing himself violently from side to side, bouncing up and down, and pulling at the restraints that were holding him down.

She called for the junior registrar who was on call that night, and then she hurried along to Dr Wells's room. When she opened his door, his screaming was so loud that she felt almost as if she were walking into a solid wall. She went up to his bedside with her hands over her ears and she had to shout at him to make herself heard.

'Dr Wells! Dr Wells!'

He took no notice of her, but continued to thrash around his bed, his eyes staring and his mouth opening and closing like a landed fish. He seemed to be able to scream continuously, without taking a breath.

Dr Kummunduh, the junior registrar, came bustling into the room with his surgical coat still unbuttoned. He was young, with a sparse black moustache and hair that stuck up vertically like a clothes brush, but he was already qualified in pain management.

'This is insane! He is supposed to be comatose. Look – he is still attached to his IV drip! How can he be awake and making such a noise?'

He leaned over the bed and took hold of Dr Wells's shoulders, struggling to keep him still.

'Dr Wells, try to calm down! Tell me, if you can, how much it hurts, and where! Can you hear what I am saying to you? I will increase your dose of ketamine but I do not want to risk raising your blood pressure or your heart rate! They are already very high!'

Dr Wells kept on screaming, staring at Dr Kummunduh, but blindly.

'I will give him an injection of hydromorphone!' Dr Kummunduh shouted at the staff nurse. 'Hopefully that will relieve his pain for now and then I can see if he needs to be taken off ketamine and put on to something stronger!'

He had only just finished shouting when Dr Wells abruptly stopped screaming and lay stiff and still, with his arms down by his sides.

'Dr Wells?' said Dr Kummunduh cautiously, releasing his grip on his shoulders.

Dr Wells looked up at him and whispered something that sounded like '*strap*'.

'Are you still feeling pain, Dr Wells?'

'*Strap.*'

'I'm sorry, I don't understand what you mean.'

'Will you still be wanting the hydromorphone, doctor?' the staff nurse asked him.

Dr Wells was clenching and unclenching his fists, and breathing deeply, his nostrils flaring with every breath. For some reason, there was a sense of high tension in the room, and the staff nurse cautiously began to back away from Dr Wells's bedside.

'I'm not – I'm not sure,' said Dr Kummunduh. 'I don't know if he's feeling any pain or not. Dr Wells? Can you hear me? Are you still hurting, Dr Wells?'

'*Strap.*'

'I don't know what you're trying to tell me. Are these restraints too tight? Is that it?'

Dr Wells blinked at him, and then reached up and clutched at the sleeve of his coat.

'It's. A. Trap,' he said, in three husky words.

'It's a trap? I still don't understand. What is a trap?'

At that instant, Dr Wells exploded. There was a deafening bang, and he was blown apart in a shower of blood and ribs and torn bed sheets. His head was ripped from his neck and hit the rail at the top of the bed, his face glaring like a demonic mask. His intestines looped into the air and then flopped down again in a slippery jumble. Both bumpers at the sides of the bed were knocked flat, and the walls and carpet were sprayed with red.

Dr Kummunduh was pitched backwards by the blast. His lower jaw was torn off so that his tongue was flailing wildly, and both his eyeballs had burst. The staff nurse had been halfway through the door, but she was sent tumbling into the corridor outside, hitting her head against the skirting board and breaking her neck.

There was a moment of utter silence. Then the fire alarm started to ring and the corridor was filled with the sound of running feet.

* * *

Within less than twenty minutes, the third floor of St Helier Hospital had been evacuated and the corridor outside Dr Wells's room was crowded with half a dozen police in yellow high-vis jackets, three forensic investigators in white Tyvek coveralls and four bomb disposal specialists from the Royal Logistic Corps, all wearing fawn protective blast suits.

A little over an hour later, Detective Inspector Routledge arrived, his hair uncombed and his sweater back to front. He was greeted by Detective Sergeant Woods, who was having a last word with the captain in charge of the bomb team.

'Ah, glad you could make it, guv,' said DS Woods. 'Captain Forbes here has just given us the all-clear.'

'But there was an explosion? And a doctor was killed?'

'That's right – Dr Wells. Apparently, he was up on this floor being treated for chronic pain when it happened. A duty doctor was attending him and he's been seriously injured, and a nurse has had her neck broke, too.'

'What are we talking about? Some kind of terrorist incident?'

Captain Forbes shook his head. 'As far as we can tell, there was no explosive device involved. We can't actually understand how the victim was traumatised so severely. There were none of the usual burn marks you get with a bomb and no shrapnel. There's an oxygen cylinder in the room but that's still intact.'

'The forensics are in there now,' said DS Woods. 'It's a hell of a mess. One of them brought up his supper when he saw it.'

'We've thoroughly searched all the other rooms on this floor, including the toilets,' said Captain Forbes. 'There's no sign of explosive devices in any of them, so I've told the nursing staff that they can bring the patients back up.'

Captain Forbes was joined by the other members of his bomb disposal team, carrying their blastproof helmets under their arms like deep-sea divers.

'Right then,' he said. 'We'll be on our way. But I'll be very interested to know what forensics find out. In the whole of my career I've never witnessed a spontaneous human explosion like this. And that's what it appears to have been – spontaneous.'

When the bomb disposal team had gone waddling off, DS Woods nodded towards the door of Dr Wells's room.

'Do you want to take a butcher's inside?' he asked DI Routledge.

'I will in a minute.'

'Don't blame you, to be honest. It's like a pig's dinner in there.'

'You mentioned something on the phone about this doctor being connected to that weird business we've been looking into at St Philomena's.'

'Well, yes, guv, that's the main reason I called you. I was talking to the sister in charge here tonight, and she told me that Dr Wells had been treating that bloke who was brought in from St Philomena's. It was the same bloke that Mrs Chesterfield mentioned – the one who was screaming out with pain all the time. The bloke snuffed it yesterday, so the sister told me, but almost the second he died, Dr Wells started screaming the same. They had to put him into an induced coma so that he wouldn't feel the pain.'

'Dr Wells started suffering the same pain as this dead bloke? How?'

'The sister told me that none of the doctors could work it out. They were still running tests. But he woke up about an hour ago and started screaming again and when the night duty doctor went to see what was wrong with him, he blew up.'

'How the hell does somebody blow up?'

'I guess forensics will be able to work that out. Or not. To be honest with you, it wouldn't surprise me if they can't. I mean, you've got to admit that this case gets more and more bonkers by the minute. First, them buried bones. Then poor old Quest going all stiff like that and snuffing it. Now a doctor exploding. You couldn't bleeding make it up.'

DI Routledge said nothing for a few moments, but stared at the door of Dr Wells's room, obviously trying to steady himself to take a look inside.

Eventually, he pushed the door open. Inside, the room was brightly illuminated with four LED lamps so that the forensic investigators could take photographs and samples – so blindingly bright that DI Routledge had to hold up his hand to shield his eyes.

He had seen people stabbed and burned and crushed in car accidents. He had once seen a man who had fallen into a printing press and who had been twisted almost out of recognition as a human being. But he had never seen anything so grisly as Dr Wells's exploded body. His ribcage had been blown wide apart, his lungs and his liver and his intestines were all jumbled together in a bloody glistening mess, and his penis and his scrotum were dangling from the clipboard at the very end of the bed like a lost glove that had been hung on a fence.

All four walls had been sprayed to the ceiling with blood and faeces and blobs of sticky flesh.

DI Routledge lifted his hand to the forensic investigators but if they saw him they didn't acknowledge it. He stayed in the room a few seconds more and then he stepped out again and closed the door behind him. DS Woods stared at him but said nothing, waiting for his reaction.

'Fucking hell,' he breathed, and held his hand against his stomach as if he were making sure that last night's dinner was going to stay there.

'See what I mean?' said DS Woods. 'Like Captain Forbes said, if it had been a bomb there would have been loads of evidence. Even a lump of C4 would have needed a blasting cap to set it off. If you light C4 with a match, it only burns like wood.'

'I do know a little about plastic explosives,' said DI Routledge sourly, pressing his fist against his mouth to suppress a burp.

'What's the plan of action now, then?'

'A routine check of CCTV. There might be no material evidence that anybody planted a bomb in Dr Wells's bed, but we still need to check if anybody entered his room apart from authorised hospital staff – or any intruders who might have disguised themselves as hospital staff. Go down to the security office and ask them for their camera recordings for this floor for the past eight hours.'

Outside Dr Wells's door the corridor was still cordoned off, but down at the far end they could see patients being wheeled back to the rooms where they were undergoing intensive care.

'What about that woman who was brought in from St Philomena's?' asked DS Woods. 'The one who was paralysed? Perhaps we should check up on her.'

'I can't really see the logic in it. She's not suffering the same problem as Dr Wells. But I suppose we might as well. This case makes about as much sense as a Chinese jigsaw.'

DS Woods went up to the night sister, who was standing behind the police tape talking to two of the police officers.

She was a short plump woman with bulging cheeks and frizzy ginger hair, and she reminded DS Woods of one of the Munchkins in *The Wizard of Oz*.

'The woman you're treating from St Philomena's, the paralysed one. Is it possible we can take a look and make sure that she's okay?'

'Charlene Thorndyke? No, I'm afraid not. She passed yesterday afternoon.'

'She's *dead*?'

'I'm afraid so. We don't yet know the cause of death. But her paralysis must have been infectious, because the nurse who was taking care of her contracted it.'

'Excuse me? She died and when she died her nurse became paralysed? Is that what you're telling me?'

DI Routledge came over. 'What's the problem?'

'The woman from St Philomena's, she died today, too. And her nurse got paralysed the same as her. It's almost identical to what happened with Dr Wells, In a way, anyway.'

'Nurse O'Grady,' said the night sister. 'Lovely girl, very hard-working. She'd been with us for less than a month. But now she's suffering from spastic tetraplegia. She can't move a muscle. She can't even blink. So far we have no idea if it was transmitted to her from Charlene Thorndyke, or how it could have been, if it was. We were quite certain that Charlene Thorndyke's paralysis wasn't caused by any kind of virus or bacterial infection.'

'Is it possible we could see her?' asked DI Routledge. 'After what's happened to Dr Wells, I think we might well post a police guard on her.'

'You don't think that somebody is going to try to blow her up, too?'

'I've no evidence at all that anybody might want to harm

her. Come to that, I have no evidence that Dr Wells was the victim of anything other than some highly unusual accident. But I'd rather be safe than sorry.'

'Very well,' said the night sister. 'They should be fetching her up from the emergency department now.'

She beckoned DI Routledge and DS Woods to follow her along the corridor. When they turned the corner, they saw that two porters were manoeuvring a trolley out of the lift. As it was pushed past them, they saw that an elderly man was lying on it, his hair like a half-blown dandelion puff. He was fast asleep with his mouth hanging open.

'Hold on,' said the night sister. 'She shouldn't be too long.'

They waited, with DI Routledge still repeatedly swallowing. His mouth kept filling with bile, and he felt as if his evening meal might make at least a token reappearance. But then the lift doors opened again, and another trolley was pushed out.

'Here she is,' said the night sister.

Nurse O'Grady was lying on her back in the same rigid position in which Dr Latimer had found her, covered with a thin white woven blanket. Her face was utterly expressionless, as if she were a shop window mannequin, and her dark hair was spread out on the pillow. The porter who was pushing her said, 'Three-oh-nine, this one?'

'That's right.'

The porter started to wheel her along the corridor, with DI Routledge and DS Woods and the night sister following behind.

'Is that the last of them?' asked the night sister.

'Last but one,' said the porter. 'That old girl they brought in from Bethany Park nursing home, she's had a seizure.'

They had almost reached the end of the corridor when DI

Routledge became aware that wisps of white smoke were curling out from underneath the trolley.

'Here, wait a second! *Stop!*' he said, catching hold of the porter's shoulder. The porter stepped back, and as he did so the smoke began to billow out in clouds, as thick as an autumn bonfire. In a few seconds, the whole corridor was filled with acrid-smelling smoke.

Before any of them could react, or understand what was happening, the trolley with Nurse O'Grady lying on it caught fire. It started to blaze ferociously from end to end, hissing and spitting like a funeral pyre.

'Extinguisher!' shouted DI Routledge, although the porter was already running off down the corridor. He unhooked the red foam extinguisher that was hanging on the wall by the lifts and came running back.

Flames began to dance up so high that they almost touched the ceiling. DS Woods tried to approach the trolley to drag Nurse O'Grady off it, but the heat had already become so intense that it was impossible for him to get anywhere near it. He was forced to retreat, both hands raised to protect his face.

Among the flames, her hair alight, Nurse O'Grady slowly sat up. Although she was paralysed, the heat was bending her body, and her bones were crackling as she was cremated alive. She couldn't scream. All she could do was stare at them through the flames as if she were sitting in hell.

The porter came back down the corridor swinging the fire extinguisher, but by then it was already too late. Nurse O'Grady dropped back on to the blazing trolley, her face blackened and her arms lifted in the monkey-like posture of all burns victims.

The porter sprayed foam all over the trolley, from end to

end, and gradually the flames died down. The corridor was choked with smoke and floating ash and the smell of burning flesh.

DI Routledge turned to look at DS Woods and the night sister. Their cheeks were reddened from the heat and their eyes were watering.

He was about to ask what had happened, and how the trolley could conceivably have caught fire like that, but when he opened his mouth his stomach clenched and he vomited half-digested Irish stew all down the front of his overcoat.

18

When Lilian arrived at St Philomena's the following morning, she found Martin Slater beside the porch, trimming the purple wisteria around it with a pair of shears.

He lowered his shears as she approached, and stepped back, smiling at her with that smile that made her think every time she met him that he had discovered some embarrassing secret about her but wouldn't tell her what it was.

'Oh, you're back, then, Mr Slater.'

'I reckoned the wisteria was overdue for a prune,' he smiled. 'Late summer is when I usually cut it.'

'You disappeared rather quickly the other day.'

'Did I? I must have had some urgent business to attend to. Now and again, I do have urgent business to attend to. Gardening, that's not all I do.'

'You missed seeing what I discovered in the wood.'

'I guessed you might have found something, because I saw that tent down there this morning, and those police tapes all around it.'

Lilian looked at him with narrowed eyes, trying to read his expression, but he was giving nothing away. All she could detect was that secrecy, and that hint of amusement, as if no matter how tragic anything turned out to be, he would see the funny side of it.

'It was bones. Human bones. A whole skeleton in fact, minus the skull.'

'Well, how about that. A skeleton. But no skull, you say?'

'You don't happen to have any idea why they might have been buried there, those bones? The police were interested in talking to you about them, but of course you'd vanished, and I don't have any way of getting in touch with you. You should give me your mobile number.'

Martin Slater continued to smile at her, but he didn't answer her, and after a while he went back to snipping at the wisteria stems.

'Did you know they were there?' Lilian persisted.

'I know something about wisteria, and it's the same with people.'

'What on earth are you talking about?'

'The harder you cut wisteria back, the wilder it spreads. So next time you have to cut it back even harder.'

'I'm not talking about wisteria. I'm talking about that skeleton I found in the woods. The forensic officer told me that it was a man, most likely.'

'I wouldn't know. I couldn't know, could I?'

'What do you mean, you *couldn't* know?'

'When I cut off these here branches, do you think *they* know where they came from?'

Lilian was about to snap back at him, but she realised that he was playing with her, and he was never going to give her a serious answer.

'Write down your mobile number for me, if you would. And there's every chance the police will be back here this morning, so if you know anything about that skeleton you'll be able to tell them yourself.'

Martin Slater continued to smile, and continued to prune the wisteria. *Snip, snip, snip.*

After Lilian had stepped in through the front door, though, and was about to close it behind her, he called out after her, 'Those men you said you saw? Did the cops find any trace of them?'

'No, Mr Slater, they didn't.'

'Hm. Didn't think they would.'

'Why do you think that?'

'Why do I think that? I think that because some things are here and some things are there, and what you can see isn't always what there is.'

'Are you going to want paying for doing this work?' Lilian asked him, deliberately changing the subject. 'If so, how much?'

'Whatever you think fit, ma'am. Whatever you think fit.'

Lilian said nothing, but closed the door as quietly as she could.

First she went through to the drawing room and looked out over the garden. The forensic investigators had arrived, and were lifting up the flap of their tent. To her surprise, she saw Martin Slater walking towards them. It didn't seem possible that in less than half a minute he had managed to make his way all around the side of the hospital, past the tennis courts and the veranda at the back of the reception room, and was already halfway down the grassy slope.

She watched him talking to the two investigators for a while. They raised the flap of the tent a little higher so that he could see inside, but of course the bones had already been taken away. She wondered what they were talking about. Whatever it was, they were all nodding their heads very seriously.

Her phone warbled. When she took it out of her jacket pocket she saw that it was David calling her. His dishwasher had flooded the kitchen floor and so he probably wouldn't be able to come in before lunchtime.

As soon as she had dropped her phone back in her pocket it warbled again, and this time she saw that it was Tim.

'Yes, Tim?' she said impatiently, trying to sound as if he had interrupted her in the middle of something important.

'Look, Lilian, I wanted to say sorry, that's all.'

'You don't have to apologise, Tim. All you need to do is get yourself some help.'

'I know that, and I will. I promise. But I still need to pay my rent.'

Lilian closed her eyes and took a deep breath.

'I swear to you, Lil. I absolutely swear on my honour that as soon as I get a new job I'll pay you back. Every single penny. With interest.'

'How much do you need?'

'Three hundred and fifty. You'll get it all back, on my honour.'

'Honour? What honour?'

'Oh, come on, Lil. I've said I'm sorry.'

'Do you still have the same bank account?'

'Yes, but don't pay the money into my bank. It'll simply get swallowed up by my overdraft. Where did you say you were working? If you can manage it in cash, I'll come over and pick it up sometime this afternoon.'

'All right. I must be mad as a box of frogs, but all right.

Come over about three. I'll get the cash when I take a break at lunchtime. I'm still at St Philomena's.'

'You're a star, Lil, after the way I treated you. You would have been well within your rights to tell me to piss off.'

'You don't know how close I came, Tim, believe me.'

Lilian dropped her phone back in her pocket. When she looked out of the French windows again, there was no sign of Martin Slater and the two forensic investigators had disappeared inside their tent. She had the strangest feeling that she had witnessed more than three people talking to each other but rather a kind of mystery play, with some obscure religious significance. One minute they had all been there, the next minute they had all vanished. Dry leaves were scuttling across the grass.

She walked along the corridor to the reception room. As she approached the heavy oak door she felt her heart beating a little faster, and she realised that she was frightened of what might be waiting for her on the other side of it. The hospital was almost completely silent this morning, except for the intermittent rattling of a window frame somewhere upstairs – and then, as she was about to push the door open, she could hear again the *snip, snip, snip* of Martin Slater's shears.

My God, she thought, had he *run* back from the garden?

The door to the reception room swung back with a long, complaining squeak, as if a rat were trapped underneath it. Lilian stepped into the middle of the room, along with all the other Lilians in the mirrors on either side.

There was nobody else there – only her and her reflections. None of the green screaming men. Yet when she stopped to listen and look around her, she thought she could hear not only the window rattling and the snipping of Martin Slater's shears, but music. It was so faint that she couldn't be sure if it was coming from some car parked in the road outside the hospital grounds, or if she could hear it at all. It came and went. But when she could hear it, she thought it sounded Middle Eastern – that wavering music they played on dombura lutes, with the distinctive bipping of tabla drums.

'Where are you hiding?' she said out loud. 'Come along, I've seen you, I've heard you screaming. Where are you?'

There was no response. Only the snipping of Martin Slater's shears and the window rattling. The music had stopped, or else it was so far away now that she could no longer hear it.

'You might think you can scare me into giving up this project!' she called out, even louder. 'Well, I'm afraid you've got another think coming! Whoever you are, I'm not giving up and I'm not giving in, so you'd better get used to the idea!'

She circled around the reception room, stopping now and again to listen, and to drum her fingertips on the backs of abandoned chairs, like an impatient teacher.

She was thinking: maybe, if those green screaming men are real people, or the holographic images of real people, they're hiding in some cubbyhole or some secret passageway, and they can hear me.

Maybe they'll realise at last that I don't believe in ghosts and that they can't frighten me away.

But what if they *are* ghosts? a sly voice asked, in the back of her head. Why do you think the MoD abandoned this hospital, but gave no explanation for it? If they really *are* ghosts, what are you going to do then?

At that moment, she heard a clattering sound from the direction of the kitchens. She hurried out of the reception room, along the corridor to the hallway, and then through the archway with its marble cherubs. Inside the kitchen she found what she had found before, only this time it wasn't cutlery that was scattered across the floor, it was cooking utensils such as a cheese grater and a whisk and spatulas of different sizes.

Again, the kitchen was empty, and so was the scullery, but Lilian went back and kicked at all the utensils.

'*Where are you?*' she screamed. '*I know you're hiding somewhere! Why don't you have the nerve to come out and face me, instead of playing these stupid childish games?*'

She kicked at the utensils again, and then she stood beside the kitchen table, with both hands pressing down on it as if she were trying to push it right down through the floor, her nostrils flaring with anger and frustration.

She was still breathing hard when she heard a postman's knock at the front door.

'I'll find you!' she said loudly and unsteadily. 'You mark my words, I'll find you! And when I find you, you'll wish you'd never been conceived, let alone *born*!'

With that, she left the kitchen and went to answer the front door.

It was DI Routledge and DS Woods, accompanied by three uniformed officers and a police dog handler with a panting Belgian Malinois. The dog's ears were erect, as if he had already sensed that there was something suspicious inside the hospital.

'Good morning to you, Ms Chesterfield,' said DI Routledge. 'We've been given the go-ahead to undertake another sniffer dog search of the premises.'

'So that poor Quest wasn't poisoned?'

'No, ma'am. He was given a thorough veterinary autopsy at Lambeth Road, but they couldn't find any trace of toxins in his system – none whatsoever. They don't yet know the cause of death for certain. Some kind of stroke, that's what they reckon. I'd asked them as a matter of high priority to check if he'd been poisoned, and they assured me that he hadn't been, no.'

'All right, then. You'd better come in.'

DI Routledge hesitated. 'I'm afraid that before we start searching I've got some rather bad news for you. Both your surveyors passed away yesterday – Alex Fowler and Charlene Thorndyke. I thought I ought to tell you in person.'

'I know already. Moses Akinyemi came by yesterday and told me. It's tragic. He also told me about Dr Wells and the nurse who was taking care of Charlene – how they suddenly started to suffer the same kind of pain.'

'We've no explanation for that. But it makes it all the more critical that we search these premises without delay. I have no idea what we're looking for, to tell you the truth. It's a mystery. But I'm hoping that we'll know what it is when we find it. *If* we find it.'

Lilian saw the bald-headed forensic investigator walking across the forecourt towards his van, and suddenly thought about the bones. She looked around for Martin Slater, but he was no longer here, trimming the wisteria, although the twigs and purple blossoms that he had cut off were still strewn on the ground.

'Our gardener – Martin Slater – the one you wanted to talk to about the skeleton. He was here a few minutes ago. I expect he's round the back somewhere. I'll see if I can find him for you.'

'That would be helpful. We can have a bit of a chat with him when we've completed our search indoors.'

Lilian stepped back and opened the front door wider so

that the police team could come inside. They all entered the hallway, except for the dog handler. He was tugging at his dog's lead and saying, 'Come on, Orion, for Christ's sake. What's the matter with you?'

He tugged and he tugged but the dog refused to move, his ears still pricked up and his legs as rigid as pokers. His handler tried to drag him towards the porch, but his paws simply slid in the shingle. His eyes were bulging as if he were terrified.

DI Routledge went back to the front door and said, 'Let's be having you, Barnett! We don't have all day!'

'It's Orion, guv! He won't fucking budge!'

'What's wrong with him? Tell him if he doesn't shift his arse he won't be getting any Bonios!'

'He's never acted up like this before! Don't know what's wrong with him!'

The dog handler tugged at Orion's lead again, and whistled, and shouted, 'Move, you disobedient mutt!'

But after nearly five more minutes of shouting and cajoling, the dog handler gave up and flung Orion's lead on to the ground.

'It's no use, guv. Something's giving him the willies. I can't think what. He's easily the most macho dog we've got. He's obedient, like, good as gold, but if I tell him to go after some offender, he'll be off like a fucking mad beast.'

'So what's scaring him here?'

'Don't ask me. But he's got a hell of a nose on him, I'll tell you that. If there's a geezer in a room who's all keyed up to do something violent, Orion can actually smell it before he does it, and he'll go all snarly and bristly. So what's putting the shits up him here – well, God only knows.'

DI Routledge thought for a few moments, and then he

turned back to DS Woods. 'We'll have to rethink this, Andy. There's obviously something about this building that sniffer dogs really don't like. It could be the same something that did for Quest. But there's no point in us searching it without a dog. Ms Chesterfield here and her colleagues have been through it top to bottom and they've found nothing.'

'What have you got in mind, guv? Your thermal imaging?'

DI Routledge nodded. 'At least an infrared camera won't drop dead, or refuse to come inside. And if there's any secret passages or hidey-holes, it'll find them. A thermal imaging survey isn't going to be cheap, a building this size, but under the circumstances I think I can get approval for it.'

Lilian said, 'None of this is going to come out, is it? You're not going to tell the press what you're doing here?'

'Normally, yes, we do brief the media on what we're up to,' said DI Routledge.

'But if what you're doing here gets into the news, that could badly affect this whole development. It might have to be abandoned, or postponed at the very least. It could cost Downland a fortune.'

DI Routledge closed his eyes for a moment as if he were searching inside himself for the restraint to reply to her politely.

Eventually he said, 'Ms Chesterfield, something may have occurred here that has directly or indirectly led to a number of people losing their lives. Right now, my most important consideration is to find out what it was and who was responsible. If your employers happen to lose some of their investment, then I'm afraid that I don't give a monkey's.'

'I don't expect you to,' Lilian replied. 'And I don't want you to believe that I don't care about those people who have died, because I do, deeply.'

Lilian was about to explain that if Philomena Park had to be abandoned, it was likely that she would lose her job and her whole life would fall apart, but then she thought how self-serving and hysterical that would sound, and so she stopped herself.

'I'll go and see if I can find Martin Slater,' she told DI Routledge.

'Okay, I'll wait. But don't be too long. I want to get back to Reigate and arrange for a thermal imaging survey.'

Lilian hurried around the side of the hospital building. There was no sign of Martin Slater by the tennis courts, and no sign of him in the gardens either. She went down the grassy slope to see if he had gone back to talk to the forensic investigators, but she was only halfway down before she could see that they were packing up and that Martin Slater wasn't with them.

She turned around, climbed up the slope, and made her way back through the drawing room. She found DI Routledge standing by the open door of his car, waiting for her with obvious impatience. By now she was out of breath.

'I'm sorry, he's gone again. I asked him to leave me his phone number but he hasn't.'

'All right. We're still waiting to find out whose remains they were. But if you can make sure that you ask him for his number the next time you see him, or find out some way that we can contact him. He probably doesn't have anything useful to tell us, but we have to cover all the bases. Oh – and can you let me have a plan of this hospital so that I can forward it to the thermal imaging engineers?'

As if to reply on Lilian's behalf, a crow on top of one of the hospital chimneys let out a harsh *caw! caw!* and two other crows joined in.

19

After the police had left, Lilian went back to the drawing room and looked out of the French windows to see if Martin Slater had reappeared, but the garden was deserted. The wind was rising and more dead leaves were tumbling across the grass.

She went through to the kitchen and bent down to pick up the spatulas and whisks and cheese grater that had been scattered across the floor. She didn't really know why she was bothering to collect them all up, but she was still feeling shocked and off balance from hearing that Alex and Charlie had died, and she needed to focus on a task that was completely mundane.

She dropped the last spatula into the drawer and then she returned the drawing room and sat down by the fireplace. She was shivering, even though the room wasn't cold.

As unsettled as she was, she still felt that she couldn't simply walk away from St Philomena's and never come back. Even before Frank Willard had summoned up those terrifying green men, she had been frightened enough by the screaming and the bloodstained bed and the strange faces that she and David had seen looking out of the windows. Alex and Charlie's deaths had left her feeling even more chilled. But the destructive effect it might have on her career was only part of the reason she was convinced she had to stay.

She still suspected that it could be local activists who had created all these scary occurrences in an effort to put a stop to Downland's development. If it was, then she couldn't let them win and go unpunished – especially if they had been responsible for what had happened to Alex and Charlie, either directly or indirectly.

It would still take much more to convince her that the hospital could be haunted by ghosts or supernatural beings of some kind. If it really *was* haunted, though, how could she leave these spirits here, endlessly screaming in pain? It would be like seeing a dog lying badly injured in the road and simply driving away.

She heard a door slam somewhere upstairs, and so she stood up and went out into the hallway.

'Hallo?' she called out, and stood there listening. There was no answer, but the draught that was softly whistling under the doors made it sound as if the hospital itself were breathing.

She was still standing there when there was a loud *rat-a-tat!* knock at the front door, and she jumped. She hoped that it wasn't Tim, because she hadn't yet been to the bank to draw out the cash he wanted. When she went to open it, though, she found Moses standing in the porch, together with a short grey-haired man in rimless spectacles.

'I found him,' said Moses, with a smile. 'This is my old friend Artyom Gorokhov. As it turns out, he was not living too far away. I reckoned there could only be one Artyom Gorokhov in England and so I looked him up on Google, and there he was. He and his wife run a gift shop in Coulsdon.'

Artyom smiled too, revealing a mouthful of broken teeth, as if he had been trying to chew lumps of concrete.

'*Ochen' priyatno poznakomit'sya*, madam,' he said, tugging off a tight brown leather glove and holding out his hand. 'I am most pleased to meet you.'

Moses said, 'I described to Artyom what Frank and his friend told us about the "dah-dahs". He believes he knows what they were referring to.'

'Why don't you come inside?' said Lilian. 'The police were here only twenty minutes ago.'

'Did they bring another sniffer dog?' Moses asked her, as they went through to the drawing room.

'They did, yes, and they were all ready to search the building again, but would you believe that the dog refused to do it? Absolutely point-blank refused. His handler couldn't even drag him into the porch.'

'Really? I cannot say that I blame the poor beast. I was telling Artyom about the screaming that we heard yesterday when Frank called up those Army friends of his. Well, I say "friends", but who knows what they were. "Scary" is not the word! I would not be so vulgar as to tell you what they nearly made all of us do.'

Lilian said, 'I *saw* them, as well as hearing them, but I have no idea what it was that I actually saw. I still think they could have been some sort of optical illusion – some sort of trick. Listen – I'm sorry I can't offer you anything to drink, but if you like we could go along to the pub for a coffee. I have to go to the bank anyway.'

Artyom circled around the drawing room, sniffing, as if he were a sniffer dog himself.

'This place has such an eerie feeling,' he said. 'In Russian in an unfamiliar house we call this *zhutkoye chuvstvo*. My parents once had a dacha that felt similar to this – very creepy. They found out that years before, in this dacha, a young boy had stabbed his parents to death in their bed, and then thrown his baby sister into the *pechka*, the stove.'

Moses was looking out of the French windows, not only at the garden but at his own transparent reflection, as if a ghost of himself were standing outside looking in.

'It was so strange that both Alex and Charlie knew who I was, even though they had never met me before, and Charlie called me by that nickname I was given in Camp Bastion – Mingus.'

He turned around. 'The last time I saw Alex, I could have sworn for a few seconds that he even *looked* like Corporal Simons. Even his legs appeared to be missing. But I expect that was just a delusion. What I saw in Afghanistan, it affected me more than I realised until I returned home and tried to carry on living a normal life. You cannot live a normal life, after you have witnessed things like that, and it is no use pretending that you can.'

'Yes. I agree with you completely about the psychological effects of combat,' said Artyom. 'But those figures in white robes that your veteran claims to have seen in Musa Qaleh – I seriously have to question if they were hallucinations, caused by stress. It could have been that they were something more.'

Lilian was interested in his accent. He was clearly Russian, yet he had the drawn-out vowels of the English upper class. He pronounced 'yes' as 'ears'.

'You mean these "dah-dahs"?' she asked him.

'That's right. And the reason I question if they were nothing more than hallucinations is that Moses' description of those figures exactly matches the ancient drawings I have seen of the Da Dard Rohonah. In Afghani mythology they are called "Spirits of Pain". The white robes, the red eyes that shine like hot coals, and the black hair that sticks up like a brush.'

'So what are they supposed to do, these Spirits of Pain?'

'The first written mention of them is after the Battle of Peshawar, which was on the twenty-seventh of November, in the year one thousand and one. But there are pictures of them that go back many hundreds of years before that.'

'The Battle of Peshawar? I can't say I've ever heard of it.'

'It was between the Ghaznavid army of Sultan Mahmud bin Sebuktigin and the Hindu Shahi army of Jayapala. It was a massive battle for control of the territory that was then called the Kabul Shahan. Although the Ghaznavid army was outnumbered, they were said to have fought like wolves against a flock of sheep. They won an overwhelming victory and they slaughtered thousands of Jayapala's soldiers. It was a bloodbath.

'According to several historians, the Mahmud of Ghazni not only won the battle on that day... Legend says that after the battle was over, the Da Dard Rohonah appeared, the Spirits of Pain, and they made sure the Hindus would be punished for ever after, and never try to invade those lands again.'

'So how did they do that?'

'The Da Dard Rohonah have always fiercely protected those sacred lands against outside invaders and unbelievers. They make sure that any enemy soldiers who are wounded in battle will never recover from those wounds, ever. In that way, they will never be able to return.

'After the Battle of Peshawar, the casualties from Jayapala's army continued to suffer terrible pain for months, and many of them killed themselves because they could no longer bear the endless agony. Jayapala himself was so humiliated by his defeat that he threw himself on to a funeral pyre and immolated himself.'

'But these Spirits of Pain – they're only a myth, aren't they?' said Lilian. 'I mean, they can't be real. Here in Britain we used to believe that cot deaths were caused by witches, and it was demons that made people go mad, but of course that was only superstition.'

'Maybe they are mythical,' Moses put in. 'But Frank Willard was convinced that he and his fellow soldiers actually saw them. And as Artyom says, he described them exactly as they appear in ancient drawings, with white robes and red eyes and black hair that sticks up. How did he do that?'

'Perhaps Frank had seen pictures of them in a book or on a TV programme,' Lilian suggested. 'And – well – perhaps he was high on something.'

'It is possible, I suppose,' said Moses. 'There was widespread opium use among our troops in Helmand. And of course opium can make you see things that are not really there.'

'Ah, but what interests me is the screaming that you have been hearing in this building,' said Artyom. 'It almost sounds as if you still have soldiers here who were wounded in Afghanistan but who are continuing to feel pain. If not the soldiers themselves, but an echo of them.'

'I suggested myself that it might be some kind of resonance from the past,' said Lilian. 'But I still don't see how that could have caused the pain that Alex was suffering, or Charlie to be paralysed.'

Artyom nodded. 'I have an old friend who works for the Union of Veterans of Afghanistan in Moscow. The Soviet Army withdrew from Afghanistan in 1989, but he told me in strict confidence that almost all of the veterans who were wounded there went on feeling terrible agony from their wounds after the war was over, and are still feeling it, even today.'

'But that was so long ago.'

'Yes. But even now most of them still have to be sedated or take painkillers, and hundreds of them have committed suicide, just like Jayapala's wounded soldiers. And do you know how many Soviet troops were wounded? Sixty thousand. Our withdrawal from Afghanistan was not only a one-time victory for the mujahideen, it was a timeless victory for the Da Dard Rohonah. There is no way that Russia will ever try to invade Afghanistan again.'

'So you think that what's been happening here at St Philomena's – it could all be connected to Afghanistan?'

Artyom pulled a face. 'It's impossible to say for sure. I'm telling you about these legends only because they seem to have such remarkable parallels with what you have been experiencing here in this hospital.'

'I don't want to believe any of this,' said Lilian, sitting down on the window sill. 'You don't know how much.'

Moses said, 'I wonder if American veterans of Afghanistan have been feeling the same way, since *they* pulled out?'

'It is more than likely, Moses,' said Artyom. 'But the Americans made such a mess of their withdrawal that I expect it would be very difficult to verify. I doubt if they will ever be ready to admit that their suffering from that campaign there is going to be never-ending. Not until all of their wounded veterans have committed suicide, anyway, or died of old age.

'In Russia, the official description of the lasting effects of the war is "Afghanskii syndrome".'

They drove together to the Cock Inn and hurried inside from the car park because it had started to rain. They found themselves a corner table and ordered coffee and salt beef sandwiches. The rain pattered against the window as if it were listening to them.

Moses told Lilian how he and Artyom had met in London at the publication party for a book about the fighting in Afghanistan, *Sixty-Nine Degrees East*.

'We had so many stories to share. But we both agreed that neither Russia nor America nor Britain should ever have intervened in Afghanistan. Thousands were killed on both sides for a country that none of us understood.'

'But it is a fascinating country when it comes to its mythology,' said Artyom. 'There are so many legends about giants and trolls and jinns.'

'From the way you were talking about those Spirits of Pain, you seem to believe that those legends are real,' said Lilian. 'Or some of them, anyway.'

'Many millions of people believe that God is real, don't they, with even less evidence? Your veteran – what was his name? Frank? He said that both he and his fellow soldiers actually saw the Da Dard Rohonah. How many people have seen God?'

'Please—' said Moses, with his mouth full. 'Can we not get ourselves involved in a religious argument? Religious arguments give me indigestion.'

'I don't intend to. Yet your Alex suffered horrendous pain that wouldn't go away, didn't he, and that sounds as if it could have been inflicted by the Da Dard Rohonah. And that young woman was paralysed.'

'She didn't seem to be feeling any pain,' said Lilian. 'It was simply that she couldn't move a muscle.'

'So Moses told me. And it so happens that there is a jinn called Al Kaboos, who can totally paralyse you. Mostly he does it when you're asleep, but there have been stories about him paralysing people when they're awake, right in the middle of eating a meal or working in a field picking poppies or even making love. If you have said or done something of which Al Kaboos disapproves, he will freeze you rigid for the rest of your life, or until you beg for his forgiveness.'

Lilian slowly shook her head. 'Even if you could make me believe in spirits and jinns, I still find it hard to believe that they're here in England, making my life miserable.'

'Why do you think it is so far-fetched? Can you imagine what it was like for the Afghani people, to be constantly invaded by foreign forces? Why do you think they would not try to make sure that it never happens again? If there is one thing my experiences have taught me, it is that you cannot force your way of life on to other people, no matter how much you disapprove of their culture or their religion. Sooner or later, what you have done will come back to haunt you.'

'This is getting too deep for me,' said Lilian. 'Besides, I have to go and get some money out.'

When she returned from the bank, Lilian found Tim already waiting for her outside St Philomena's. One side of his coat collar was turned up and his shoelaces were undone. His eyes were tinted yellow, as if he were suffering from jaundice.

'I really appreciate this, Lil. You don't know how much. I was a cat's whisker away from being made homeless.'

'Come inside and I'll give you your cash.'

Tim followed her through the front door and into the hallway. 'I swear you'll get it back as soon as I get my dole money.'

'This is an act of charity, Tim. Not a loan. I'd give it to any man who was forced to sleep in the street.'

She put her handbag down on the hall table, opened it up and took out the envelope full of cash. She had withdrawn £100 for herself, so she counted out £350 for Tim and while she was counting he looked around.

'This is a hell of a place, isn't it? I'm not sure I'd like to live here, though. It's not exactly what you'd call cosy.'

'Well, it was a private house and then a hospital and it still looks and smells like a hospital. But you wait until Downland have finished with it. You won't believe it. This hallway will be somebody's indoor swimming pool.'

She tucked the banknotes back into the envelope and handed them to him.

'You're a princess, Lil. You really are. Can I give you a kiss?'

'I'd rather you didn't, Tim. Like I said, this is an act of charity and our kissing days are over.'

At that moment, she heard a car outside on the gravel and a few seconds later there was a knock at the front door. It was Moses again, and he looked grim-faced.

'Moses! What's happened?' Lilian asked him.

'Some bad news. I was on my way home when I heard it on the radio. There was an explosion at St Helier Hospital and a doctor was killed. Also, a nurse died in a fire. There is no explanation yet for the explosion, or the fire, and it is not known if they are connected. But the doctor who died was Dr Robert Wells, the one who was taking care of Alex Fowler.'

'Oh, my God,' said Lilian. 'That must have been what Detective Inspector Routledge was talking about. He told me that something bad had happened after Alex and Charlie died, but he wouldn't tell me what it was. Oh – this is Tim, by the way. My former husband. Tim, this is Moses Akinyemi.'

'Pleased to meet you,' said Tim, giving Moses a salute.

Moses saluted him back, and then said to Lilian, 'I thought I ought to come back and tell you, in case you had not heard already. What I am trying to say to you is, do you not think that you might be at risk yourself, if you continue to work here at St Philomena's?'

'I don't exactly see how Dr Wells being killed at St Helier can have any connection with what happened here.'

'Well, neither do I, to be frank with you. But I have a feeling that they are like pieces of a jigsaw, do you not think that? First of all there was Alex suffering pain when he was here, then dying, and then Dr Wells being killed. Then there was Charlene becoming paralysed while she was here, and dying. Then you saw those men through Frank's night-glasses, and we all heard them screaming. And now Artyom has told us all about the Da Dard Rohonah, and that jinn that paralyses people in their sleep.'

'I don't know,' said Lilian. 'It all seems so mixed up. Some of it seems real, like Alex and Charlie, and some of it seems like some kind of fairy story, like these "dah-dahs" and jinns.'

While they were talking, Tim went to the window at the far end of the hallway and looked out over the gardens. Then he wandered over to the archway that led to the kitchens, with its broken cherubs.

Moses said, 'If there is some connection between Dr Wells being killed and Alex and Charlene dying, then is it not possible that there could also be a connection with what we have been seeing and hearing here at St Philomena's? Maybe it is not local activists after all.'

'You don't really believe it could be ghosts? Or jinns? Or some kind of spirits, anyway?'

'I am not necessarily saying that. Just because people tell stories about ghosts and jinns and suchlike, that does not mean we are faced with anything like that here in this hospital. As I said before, what we have here may be some completely different form of energy. Albert Einstein pointed out that we are all made up of nothing but energy. And like you suggested yourself, maybe it could be some kind of resonance, like that creepy feeling that Artyom was talking about, in the house where his parents used to live.

'All I am saying is, maybe it would be safer for you to stay away from St Philomena's for a while – at least until the police have carried out this survey. Let us be realistic, Lilian. One of their sniffer dogs died and the other was too frightened to come in here, so who knows what the police might find?'

Lilian looked across at the gloomy portrait of Sir Edmond Carver. Today he looked wearier than ever.

'Of course I've got the heebie-jeebies being here, Moses, especially when I'm on my own. But what's the point of running away? If I run away, I may never find out who's screaming and whispering and I may never know if all these people that we've been seeing are real or not, and if I don't find out I won't be able to put a stop to it all, will I? And if I don't put a stop to it, I'll probably lose my job and get a reputation in the development business for being an hysterical woman who thought that St Philomena's was haunted. Yes, of course something extremely weird's going on here – but I'm not going to rest until I know what it really is.'

'I understand where you are coming from,' said Moses. 'Although I still think it would be wiser for you to wait until the police have given the building a thorough search. And I am speaking as someone who has served in a war zone.'

'Well, thank you. I appreciate your concern. I really do. But now – look – I have a lot to be getting on with. I have to see if my boss can find me yet another surveyor. And I have some really complicated ground plans to work on – how each apartment is going to be connected to the mains.'

'You are a very determined woman.'

'I think "stubborn" is probably a better description.'

'Very well,' Moses told her. 'But you will let me know as soon as the police have conducted their survey? Before I go, I should say goodbye to your former husband.'

'Tim!' called Lilian. 'Moses is going now!'

They waited, but there was no answer from out of the archway.

'Tim!' Lilian called again, but there was still no response.

'He must have left without us noticing,' said Moses.

'That doesn't surprise me in the slightest,' Lilian told him. 'We would go to dinner parties sometimes and if he didn't like the other guests he would simply disappear without telling anybody – even me.'

Moses went to the front door and opened it. Before he stepped out, though, he turned to Lilian and said, 'Please… I mean it. You should be very cautious while you are here at St Philomena's. After hearing that screaming, I certainly would not stay here. I am still shaken by what has happened to Dr Wells. I will see what I can do to discover more about what happened at St Helier and if I learn more I will let you know.'

'Thank you, Moses.'

'You know something – after what I witnessed in my days in the Army Medical Corps, I find it hard to believe that we still seem to take war for granted. Our politicians make foolish decisions that lead to misery and death on a scale that it is almost impossible to imagine, and yet all we do is shrug and say "how terrible".'

'Well, yes, you're right. But do you seriously think the world is ever going to change?'

'It is not only those millions of innocent men, women and children who are killed. I myself am still having endless nightmares, and there are tens of thousands of soldiers who will go on suffering mental and physical torture for the rest of their lives. And, in the end, for what?'

'I don't know, Moses. There's really no answer to that.'

Lilian looked around the forecourt. 'Tim's car's not here, so he must have gone. Mind you, I can't say that I noticed it before.'

Moses raised his hand. 'I must go now. Stay safe. There is a saying we have in Nigeria. *Ìjàpá kì í kúrò ní ilé rè nítorí èrù ní bà á.* It means that the tortoise never leaves his house because he is afraid. But I seriously believe that you should think about doing the opposite. Leaving this house until you are sure that it is safe.'

Lilian went back into the hallway.

'Tim!' she called out. 'Are you still here, Tim?'

There was still no answer, so she went through the archway into the kitchen.

'Tim?'

The kitchen was empty and silent.

Damn that man. Damn him! And he wondered why I left him. I gave him all that money and I know he'll never be able to afford to pay me back, but he didn't even have the decency to say goodbye.

20

Marion Crosby was upstairs changing the beds when there was a ring at the doorbell.

'Michael!' she called down from the landing. 'Could you see who's at the front door, please?'

'On my way,' Michael called back.

He limped into the hall and opened the front door. A tall man with curly brown hair and a brown leather jerkin was standing outside, smiling as if he knew Michael but hadn't seen him for months.

'Yes?' said Michael.

'I'm looking for Frank,' the man told him. 'Frank Willard. Is he in?'

'Well, he might be. What is it you're after?'

'A brief word, that's all. What you might call a bit of a catch-up.'

'You were out there, too? Afghanistan?'

The man smiled again, briefly closing his eyes as if he were remembering some idyllic moment.

'Who is it?' called Marion, from upstairs.

'An old friend of Frank's. He says he's come round for a bit of a chinwag.'

'Oh, all right then. But ask him to take his shoes off, if he doesn't mind.'

The man in the leather jerkin stepped into the hall and prised off his green rubber boots. He was wearing no socks underneath, and his toenails were jagged, as if he picked them with his fingernails rather than trimmed them with clippers.

'Frank's through here,' said Michael, and led him into the living room. 'Frank, boy! You have a visitor, so you do!'

Frank was sitting alone in the living room because the other three veterans had gone down to Epsom Hospital for their weekly physiotherapy. He was drinking a cup of tea and eating a biscuit and watching a repeat of last night's football game, Chelsea versus Everton. He looked up and blinked at the man in the tan leather jerkin but made no attempt to turn down the volume.

The man held out his hand. 'How are you, Frank? How have you been keeping?'

'Do I know you?' Frank asked him.

The man dragged a Parker-Knoll armchair closer to Frank and sat down beside him. 'Know me? I should think so. Maybe I look different than I did when you first saw me. But you've changed too. You look at least twenty years older, if you don't mind me saying so.'

'Oh, thanks for the compliment. But it doesn't do much to improve a bloke's youthful appearance, losing half his fucking hip.'

The man leaned close to Frank and stared at him for over twenty seconds without saying anything. There was an advertising break in the football game and Frank picked up the remote and turned off the sound.

'You don't remember me, do you?' the man said at last.

'There's a song about that,' said Michael.

Frank slowly shook his head. 'No, to be honest, I don't remember you. But then there's a whole lot I can't remember because of being wounded. It buggers up your brainbox, a serious injury like that, as well as your body.'

'I saw you in Musa Qaleh, Frank, and I saw you in Kandahar and I saw you in Kabul.'

'Really? What regiment were you with?'

'Oh, I wasn't with a regiment.'

'Why were you there, then? You weren't press, were you? You don't look like press.'

The man smiled again, almost lovingly, and at the same time he reached across and laid his hand on Frank's arm.

'I was there to make sure that you were punished for your intrusion into my country. Not only then, but for ever more.'

Frank jerked his arm free and stared at the man with his milky eyes, his pupils only two black pinpricks.

'What do you mean, *your* country? You're not a Terence, are you? Or are you?'

'I am a guardian of my lands, mountains and plains, rivers and lakes, and all who live there. I have been protecting it for longer than you could possibly imagine. It is *our* land, not yours, and you must never be allowed to forget that.'

'Do you know something, mate?' Frank retorted. 'I don't have a fucking clue what you're rabbiting on about. What's he rabbiting on about, Michael?'

Michael looked up from scrolling through his iPhone.

'No idea, Frank. I can't say that I was actually listening, to tell you the truth.'

Frank turned back to the man. 'I don't know who you are, mate, or why you've come round here to give me all this guff. But if I was you, I'd put a sock in it and sling my hook. Like, now.'

The man kept on smiling benignly, but for some reason

Frank found that even more threatening than if he had been scowling.

'You've been interfering, Frank. It was one thing for you to come to the hospital to see your old Army friends for yourself. That was no worse than visiting inmates in a prison. No harm done. But then you went and brought those other people along with you, didn't you, and you let them see your old Army friends for themselves.'

'So? What's it got to do with you?'

'Frank – you know as well as I do that those other people will do everything they can to release your friends from their punishment. I can't allow that to happen. Your friends must serve their term, and their term is forever.'

Frank held up the TV remote. 'Listen, mate – I still don't have the faintest fucking clue what you're on about, and I'm trying to watch the football here, if it's all the same to you. If you don't clear off I'll call Ms Crosby down here and if you still won't clear off then Ms Crosby could well be inclined to call for the coppers.'

The man remained seated for a few more moments, as if he were trying to remember something that had slipped his mind. Then he stood up, and held his right hand out flat, about six inches above Frank's head.

'*Khwdey de pa tandar owaha!*' he said in a threatening whisper. '*Khwar au zar shay!*'

Frank irritably tilted his head to one side and gave the man a dismissive flap of his hand. 'Why don't you just shut your cakehole and get out of here! Bloody nutter!'

Without another word, the man turned around, left the living room, and went across the hallway to pick up his rubber boots.

'See him out, Michael, would you?' said Frank, and Michael

followed him, but the man made no attempt to put on his boots. Instead, he opened the front door himself and stepped out on to the porch barefoot, carrying his boots in his hand.

Michael went to the open door and called out after him, 'Don't you be thinking of coming back, like, do you hear me?'

Somehow, though, the man had already disappeared. The five-bar gate was still closed, and there was no sign of him walking away down Tumber Street, but he was gone.

'You were right, Frank,' said Michael, closing the front door and returning to the living room. 'He was a bloody nutter, that feller, and no mistake. I'm sorry I let him in.'

Frank pointed the remote at the television to switch the sound back on. The commentator excitedly said, '*Yes! The Blues are deservedly ahead with a well-crafted goal—*' and at that instant, Frank exploded.

The bang was no louder than a large plastic bag bursting, but Frank's maroon dressing gown was blasted into shreds. His ribcage burst apart like a shuttered window being flung wide open, so that his heart and his lungs and his liver were splattered all over the television screen. His head was blown backwards off his neck and tumbled down behind his chair, while his intestines slithered down between his legs and piled up on the carpet in a glistening heap.

The living-room wallpaper was plastered with blood and lace-like strings of Frank's skin, and the net curtains beside his chair were soaked red.

Michael stood staring at Frank's grisly remains in utter shock, his mouth still half open to ask him what the football score was. He crossed himself and then he sank down on to his knees, unable to call out for help, unable to speak. He felt that he was back in Afghanistan, at the moment when his Jackal had run over an explosive device and his head had been hit so hard against the armour plating that he had been unconscious for almost a month afterwards.

Marion called out from the landing. 'Frank? What was that noise?' Then, after a moment's silence, 'Frank?'

She came hurrying downstairs and into the living room. At first she couldn't understand what she was looking at, but then she laid her hand on Michael's shoulder and said, 'My God, Michael. What's happened?'

Michael could only shake his head and make mute noises in the back of his throat.

Marion approached Frank's body, staring at it in horror. Then she turned around, stalked quickly out of the living room and into the downstairs toilet, where she vomited the kippers that she had eaten for breakfast into the washbasin.

It was growing dark by the time Captain Forbes came out of the front door of Marion Crosby's house, tugging off his vinyl gloves.

Blue police and ambulance lights were flashing all along Tumber Street. The forensic team had just arrived and were setting up LED lights around the front garden, although they would stay out of the house itself until the explosive disposal squad had given them the all-clear.

'Well?' asked DI Routledge, as Captain Forbes walked up to him. 'Don't tell me it's the same MO as that doctor at St Helier's.'

'I'm afraid it looks like it, Barry. He's been blown to smithereens but there's no trace of any explosive residue whatsoever. None. Not even Semtex or C-4, both of which would have contained a detection agent. We can't work it out.'

'You really have no idea how he could have been killed?'

Captain Forbes pulled a face. 'It's a complete bloody mystery. We were even thinking that somebody might have pushed a high-pressure air hose up his what's-its-name, but there's no way that anybody could have done that and removed it without leaving any trace.'

'So you have no idea what we're dealing with here? Lambeth Road still haven't been able to come up with an explanation for how that doctor was done for, neither. Nor how that nurse was killed – the one who was burned to death on that trolley.'

'You think the same perp was responsible for both of them – the doctor and the nurse?'

'It seems like a strong possibility, but there's no way of telling for sure. We still don't have the first idea how the doctor was blown up and we still don't know how the nurse was set on fire. The lab said that no flammable chemicals were used to set her alight. Besides, there's no obvious motive for killing either of them, and there doesn't seem to be any obvious motive for killing this bloke, either. It's all circumstantial.'

Two more explosives experts emerged from the house, looking like giant teddy bears in their fawn blast suits. As they waddled over to DI Routledge and Captain Forbes, one of the forensic investigators came up to them too – a tall mournful man with ears like Roald Dahl's Big Friendly Giant.

'All right to make a start now?' the forensic investigator asked them. He sounded as if he would rather be anywhere than here, at half-past six in the evening, faced with the prospect of examining a crime scene in which a man had been violently blown into hundreds of pieces.

'Yes, you can go in now,' said one of the EODs. 'Tell you

what, though. I'd take a mop and a bucket with me, if I was you.'

Four or five reporters were waiting outside the five-bar gate, along with a television crew from Sky News. Captain Forbes nodded his head towards them and said, 'What are you going to tell that lot?'

'There's not much I can say, is there, except to inform them that one of the patients in a private hospice for wounded Army veterans has unfortunately been found deceased, and so far the cause is death is yet to be determined.'

'They're going to ask what the EOD is doing here, aren't they?'

'God knows how I'm going to explain that. Perhaps I should say we suspected that the deceased might have had some explosives in his possession. You know, souvenirs from his military service – hand grenades or machine-gun bullets or suchlike.'

'You could say that. After all, they called us out last week when that chap in Gloucestershire turned up at his local hospital with an anti-tank shell lodged up his jacksie. He collected munitions, that's what he told us, and he claimed that he'd accidentally sat on one. Jolly good shot, that's all I could say. But fortunately it wasn't live, and fortunately the doctors had removed it before we had to check it over.'

DI Routledge looked towards the front door. 'I suppose I'd better go inside and take a look at him. How much of a mess is he? As bad as the doctor?'

'Slightly more spectacular than that, I'm afraid,' said Captain Forbes. 'I'm going to have a large Scotch as soon as we get back to barracks tonight, I can tell you. Maybe three.'

He was silent for a while, and then he said, 'These two call-outs, they've really worried me, if you want to know the truth.

Both of the victims' bodies have shown all the indications of massive detonations. We're talking about the same explosive pressure as a hand grenade – something in the region of 3 bar or 44 psi. Absolutely lethal, especially in a confined space. And yet not even a sniff of explosive.'

'I've heard of spontaneous human combustion,' said DI Routledge. 'You know, people just bursting into flames for no reason. But spontaneous human explosion – never.'

21

As David hung up his raincoat in the hallway the next morning, he called out, 'Lilian? Have we got visitors?'

'No,' Lilian called back, from the drawing room. 'The police will be round later this morning to do their thermal imaging survey. But there's nobody here yet. I was expecting a new surveyor this afternoon, from Johnson's in Guildford, but he'll probably be coming round on Monday now. Why?'

'There's a car parked beside our back gate, that's all. And it's pissing with rain. So why would anybody park there unless they were coming here?'

'I have no idea. I'm a bit concerned about the sewerage connections from each of the new flats. I've got three possible layouts here, do you want to come and take a look?'

David came into the drawing room, where Lilian was sitting on the window sill with her iPad.

'Almost looked like somebody was living in it,' he remarked, as he sat down next to her.

Lilian blinked at him. 'What did?'

'That car that's parked down by the back gate. Full of old newspapers and KFC boxes.'

'What make is it?'

'Mercedes C-class, dirty green colour. My dad's got one in silver.'

Lilian put down her iPad and stood up.

'What's the matter?' David asked her.

'That sounds awfully like my ex-husband's car. He came here yesterday but he left without saying goodbye. He simply vanished.'

'Maybe he couldn't get it to start and he called an Uber.'

'Let me take a look.'

Lilian went into the hallway for her raincoat and her umbrella. David put his raincoat back on, too. They went out of the French windows and down the grassy slope, making their way round the forensic tent that was still standing over the site where the skeleton had been removed, and then down through the trees to the back gate.

As soon as Lilian caught sight of the Mercedes, she recognised it as Tim's. She went out through the gate, tried the car's door handles, and then peered in through the windows.

'Why would he have parked it here?' asked David. 'He hasn't left a note on it or anything, if he has broken down.'

'Oh, I know exactly why he parked it here. He was afraid that if he rolled up to the front driveway in it I might have changed my mind about lending him his rent money, and pretended that I wasn't in.'

Lilian took her phone out of her raincoat pocket and prodded out Tim's number. It rang and it rang, while David shuffled his feet and the raindrops pattered through the trees. Eventually she gave up, and sent Tim a WhatsApp message, asking him to call her.

'No luck?' asked David.

'I'll try him again later. Knowing him, he's gone down to the newsagent for the *Racing Post* and left his phone at home.'

They trudged back up the slope.

'I wonder if they'll be able to find out who those bones belonged to,' said David, looking back at the forensic tent.

'Who knows? Perhaps it wasn't anybody who belonged to the Carver family at all. Perhaps it was some tramp who died in the woods and the robins covered him with leaves, just like Hansel and Gretel.'

'Huh! Sometimes I feel this whole bloody development is like some kind of Grimms' fairy tale, I can tell you.'

Back indoors, they hung up their coats and returned to the drawing room. Lilian had brought a flask of coffee with her and she poured a mug for each of them.

'I'll have to meet up with South East Water to decide if each apartment can be connected separately to the main sewer, or if we'll have to join them all together on our own property here so that we only have one connection.'

'We have a septic tank at the moment, don't we?'

'Yes, but we have a legal right to be connected to the main drain and I'd prefer that for Philomena Park.'

While David scrolled back and forth through the various sewerage schemes that had been drawn up by their planners, Lilian tried phoning Tim again.

'Here… we could connect all the individual pipes together underneath the tennis court,' David suggested. 'Then we'd need less than a hundred metres of pipe to reach the main drain under the road.'

'Shh!' said Lilian, lifting her hand. 'Can you hear that?'

David looked up, frowning. 'It's a phone. Sounds like it's upstairs somewhere.'

Lilian stood up. 'I'm ringing Tim's mobile. Hang on.'

She prodded her phone to end the call, and the phone upstairs went silent.

'Try it again,' said David.

Lilian dialled Tim's number again, and immediately they could hear the phone ringing upstairs.

'Put that down,' she said, pointing to her iPad. 'Let's go upstairs and see why his phone's up there. He didn't even *go* upstairs, so far as I know. The last time I saw him he was going through the arch towards the kitchens.'

Together, they went out into the hallway and climbed the staircase to the first-floor landing. They stopped there and listened again. The phone was still ringing but it was on the floor above them.

'Montgomery Wing, it sounds like,' said Lilian.

They quickly climbed up the next flight of stairs, and by the time they reached the landing Lilian was out of breath. They hurried along the corridor to the Montgomery Wing and pushed open the doors. The phone stopped ringing the instant they stepped inside, so Lilian called Tim's number for a third time.

'This is giving me the right creeps,' said David, as Tim's phone started ringing again.

They found it lying on the pillow of the very last bed. Lilian picked it up and stared at it until it stopped.

'So where's *he*?' asked David, looking around the ward. 'His car's parked outside, his phone's in here. He must be somewhere around.'

Lilian was quickly flicking through Tim's last few calls. 'The last person he rang was his letting agents, Bartlett and Cooke. Then he rang somebody called Sandra. Then me. Then Sandra again. Then the Thai Cottage Restaurant.'

Lilian had no idea what to do. If Tim had made his way upstairs yesterday while she was talking to Moses, there was no question that she would have seen him. But why would he have wanted to come up here? And why would he have left his phone behind? Tim and his phone had always been inseparable. He would be scrolling through it while he sat on the lavatory, first thing in the morning. He would still be scrolling through it in the evening while he ate his dinner on his lap, even while the television news was on.

David looked around and sniffed, as if Tim might have left some telltale scent. 'The coppers will be here soon, won't they, with their thermal oojamaflips? If he's hiding somewhere here, they're bound to find him, aren't they?'

Lilian said nothing. The hospital was suddenly silent. No plumbing sounds, no creaking. Even the rain trickling down the windows made no sound at all.

She was filled with a dark sense of dread, like no other fear she had ever felt in her life. It took all of her self-control for her not to march quickly out of the ward, hurry down the stairs and run out of the hospital into the rain.

'We could look for him, if you like,' said David, without much conviction.

Lilian thought: yes, we could look for him. But supposing we find him, and he's paralysed, like Charlie, or supposing he's dead?

She was still standing there when a voice very close to her said, '*Lil?*'

Shocked, she spun around.

'Tim?' she said. 'Tim, is that you? David – did you hear that?'

'I heard something,' said David. 'I thought it was maybe that phone.'

Lilian's heart was beating hard. She turned around and around, saying, 'Tim? Where are you? Tim? Speak to me, Tim! Where are you?'

'It could have been anything, Lilian,' said David. 'You know what this place is like.'

'*Lil!*' shrieked a voice, harsh and high and ragged with terror. '*Lil! For Christ's sake, Lil! Save me!*'

This was immediately followed by a scream – a scream of pain that went on and on, rising up and screeching down like some terrible roller-coaster ride through hell. It was coming from Tim's phone, louder than anything that Lilian had heard from a phone, ever. She dropped the phone on to the floor, but the screaming continued, more and more agonised with every second.

Lilian backed away, her hands clamped over her ears, her eyes bursting with tears. No matter how much Tim had hurt her and belittled her, she had loved him once, and here he was, screaming for her to save him, and she didn't know how.

David was clearly as shocked as she was, but he bent down and snatched up the phone as if it were red-hot. He tried to switch it off, but the screen stayed black, with no settings symbols on it, and even when he frantically jabbed at the sleep button with his thumbnail, that only seemed to make the screaming louder and even more tortured.

'Smash it!' Lilian shouted at him.

'What?'

'Smash it! I can't bear it any more!'

David dropped the phone on to the floor and stamped on it. He stamped on it again and again, and still the screaming went on, but at last the screen cracked and there was silence.

Lilian lowered her hands from her ears and stared at David with eyes that were still blurred with tears.

'How could that be?' she asked him. 'That was Tim, and he was crying out for me. How could that possibly be?'

David looked down at the shattered phone.

'Maybe – I don't know. Maybe he was trying to call you from somewhere. I can't think where, though. But this is *his* phone, isn't it? So how was he calling you?'

Lilian paced up and down the ward, opening and closing her fists in bewilderment and frustration.

'He must be here somewhere, here at St Philomena's. I can feel it! Where else could he be?'

David was tempted to say, *Hell, by the sound of it*, but he kept his mouth closed.

Grim-faced, Lilian hurried across the landing to the Wellington Wing. She burst through the double doors and shouted out, 'Tim! Are you in here? Tim?'

There was no answer, so she went along the length of the ward, repeatedly bending down so that she could see if Tim was lying underneath one of the empty beds.

David appeared in the open doorway. 'Not in here? I'll go and take a look in the rooms upstairs.'

While he climbed up to the third floor, Lilian went down to the Wavell Wing. There was no sign of Tim there either.

'Tim!' she shouted, yet again, from the first-floor landing. 'Tim, if you're here in the hospital anywhere, call out and let me know where! If you can't call out, whistle, or make a banging noise, anything!'

She waited, and listened, but there was silence.

'Tim,' she said, almost inaudibly, thinking of all the times he had sworn at her and hit her. Why should she care where he was now, or why he had been screaming for help? But she did care. She couldn't help herself.

David looked over the banisters from the third-floor landing and said, 'He's not up here, Lilian. I can't think where he could be. He could have been phoning from anywhere, couldn't he? He could be miles away, for all we know.'

'But how? And why was he screaming for me to save him? I have a feeling he's still here in the hospital somewhere. We'll just have to search it, room by room.'

She was about to climb the stairs to join David up on the third floor when she heard the crunching of cars on the driveway outside. She looked out of the window and saw three police cars, a van and two other cars.

'They're here for the survey,' she said. 'If Tim's still here, they'll find him, won't they?'

She went downstairs and opened the front door. DI Routledge stepped inside, accompanied by DS Woods and five uniformed officers, as well as three men and a woman carrying cases with thermal imaging cameras.

'You must be Lilian Chesterfield,' said the woman, holding out her hand. 'Sarah Saunders, Surrey Thermal Screening. This is our A-team, all level two certified thermographers. All except for me, that is. I'm level three.'

'I've explained to Ms Saunders what we're looking for,' said DI Routledge. 'Any concealed rooms or passageways, and any indication that we have unwanted visitors hiding themselves somewhere on the premises.'

'I need you to know that it's possible that my former husband may be here somewhere,' Lilian told him, trying to keep her voice from shaking. 'He came here to see me yesterday and I thought he had left, but his car's still parked by the back gate and we found his phone in the Montgomery Wing.'

DI Routledge frowned at her. 'Are you all right, Ms Chesterfield? You're looking somewhat distressed, if I you don't mind my saying so.'

Lilian's eyes filled up with tears again. 'We found his phone and somehow we could hear him screaming out of it. He was begging me to save him. I'm afraid it was too much for me and I asked David to smash it. It's still on the floor upstairs.'

'You heard him screaming out of his own phone?'

Lilian nodded, tugging out her handkerchief and wiping her eyes.

'And the phone's still upstairs but you broke it?'

'If you'd only heard it,' David put in.

'Okay. It may not be damaged so badly that we can't retrieve any data from it. What's your ex-husband's name, Ms Chesterfield?'

'Tim. Tim Chesterfield. I can give you his address and his phone number and his email and everything. He was here one minute and the next he was gone.'

DI Routledge turned round to Sarah Saunders. 'Did you hear that? Ms Chesterfield's ex might be somewhere here on the premises. Do you want to start screening?'

'Yes. We have it all worked out. John – Pete – you'll be starting on the third floor upstairs, won't you? And Gary, you're going to screen that large reception room, aren't you? I'll do the kitchens first, and then the drawing room.'

DI Routledge turned to his officers next. 'Sahni – Johnson – go upstairs with DS Woods and take some pictures of that broken phone, will you? Ms Chesterfield here will tell you exactly where it is. Then pop it in an evidence bag. If we can't locate Ms Chesterfield's ex here in the hospital, we can send it up to Lambeth Road to see if they can track where his message might have come from.

'Harris – Williams – Treadwell – if you can accompany these engineers here. Keep your eyes peeled for anything out of the ordinary. As I briefed you earlier, there's been some strange goings-on here, and I really can't tell you for certain what to expect. Probably nothing, but you know what the Boy Scouts say.'

'Akela, we'll dob-dob-dob?' asked the officer called Harris.

'That's the Cubs, you pillock. Now get on with it.'

Sarah Saunders and her three survey engineers went off to screen St Philomena's floor by floor with their thermographic cameras, while Lilian and David and DI Routledge went through to the drawing room.

'If I could ask you if you're on good terms with your former husband?' asked DI Routledge.

'I don't see what that has to do with anything.'

'It may possibly explain why he seems to have disappeared, and the possibility that he may still be here in the hospital somewhere. There's no accounting for the things that some people get up to. We had one chap in Redhill who hid in his ex-wife's attic and spied on her through a hole in the bedroom ceiling.'

'Well, we were on fairly rocky terms, if you must know. But he came here because he needed to borrow some money for his rent, or else he could have ended up homeless. Three hundred and fifty pounds in cash.'

'If he's still here and his phone's still here then the cash could still be here.'

'I don't care about the money. We may still be at war with each other, but I don't want the same to happen to him as happened to Alex Fowler, or to Charlie Thorndyke.'

DI Routledge went over to the French windows and looked out at the gardens. The rain had eased off now, and a watery sun was beginning to shine.

'Speaking of that, I gather that a one-time patient paid you a visit here recently. A certain Frank Willard.'

'That's right.'

DI Routledge turned away from the window and raised an eyebrow, as if he were expecting her to say more. But she was reluctant to tell him about the ghostly Army friends that Frank had summoned out of thin air, and how she and the others had all heard them screaming. She didn't want it to sound as if they had been suffering from some kind of mass hysteria. A police inspector would want facts, not hallucinations.

'He's being looked after by a woman called Marion Crosby, at a private hospice down the road.'

'Well, he was,' said DI Routledge. 'I'm afraid to tell you that he's gone to higher service.'

'He's *dead*? Oh my God! How did he die?'

'We're not sure yet. But he was the victim of a very nasty accident. The funny thing is, he died in exactly the same way as Dr Wells at St Helier Hospital. So I'd be interested to know if there was anything about his visit here that you thought was unusual in any way.'

'What kind of "nasty accident"?'

'I'm not at liberty to go into details just yet, Ms Chesterfield. Another of Ms Crosby's patients was in the room at the time when it happened, an Irish chap, but he was so seriously traumatised by what he saw that up until now he's been unable to speak about it. Or about anything, as it happens. Struck totally dumb.'

Lilian was about to ask him more when one of the engineers came into the drawing room, along with two uniformed officers. All three of them looked shocked, as if they had just witnessed a serious accident.

'What's the story?' asked DI Routledge. 'Don't tell me you've found something.'

The engineer came up to them and with a trembling hand he held up his thermographic camera, which was like a large black pistol with a screen on the back.

'Take a look at this,' he said. 'This was on the third floor, right down at the north-east end.'

He held the camera up so that both Lilian and DI Routledge could see the screen, and he played back the video he had recorded. It showed the corridor in iridescent purples and greens and reds and yellows, with the image wobbling a little from side to side as the engineer walked along it. As he neared the end of the corridor, a slender figure came out of the last bedroom, and then hesitated, as if it had suddenly caught sight of the engineer and the police officer coming towards him. It was glowing purple, this figure, which indicated that its temperature was lower than the doorway behind it.

A second purple figure appeared, equally attenuated, and this figure also stopped. Because the camera was responsive only to heat, rather than light, both figures were featureless and fluid, as if they had been cut out of purple cellophane.

They remained motionless in the doorway for a few seconds, but as the engineer approached them, they twisted around and disappeared into the darkness of the doorway.

'They weren't visible to the naked eye, only on this screen,' said the engineer, lowering his camera. 'But I told the officers here that I had seen them, and we went straight into that bedroom to see if we could find them.'

'Not a sausage, guv,' the police officer put in. 'Not a sign of nobody. Not beneath the bed, not behind the curtains. Not in the wardrobe, neither.'

The engineer nodded in agreement. 'I scanned the whole room but they didn't show up on the camera again, so God knows how they managed to vanish like that. But you can see them here on this video, so this is the proof that they were actually there.'

'I think we need to go up there and double-check,' said DI Routledge. 'Ms Chesterfield? You want to come with us?'

They all left the drawing room and climbed up the stairs to the third floor. The engineer led the way along the corridor, holding up his thermographic camera in front of him.

'I was right here when I saw them, only three metres away. But by the time I got *here*, they had disappeared back inside the doorway.'

They went into the bedroom and looked around, and the engineer continued to scan the walls and under the bed.

'I can only think that those figures were some sort of projection,' he said. 'How it was done, though, I can't even begin to guess. It's like they were holograms, but created with heat, or refrigeration, rather, instead of light. But where were they projected from? That's what I'd like to know. There was nobody in here, and I can't see any equipment that they could have been projected from.'

'Perhaps they was ghosts,' said one of the police officers.

'Oh, get a life, Harris,' said his colleague.

But they had only just started to walk back along the corridor when they heard screaming from downstairs. This wasn't the agonised screaming that Lilian and David had heard before, the mass screaming of badly wounded men. This was a single woman screaming, and it sounded like Sarah Saunders.

'Oh God! Oh God! We have to get out of here! All of you! We have to get out of here now!'

22

They all hurried down the three flights of stairs and their footsteps sounded like three rolls of thunder.

They found Sarah Saunders standing in the middle of the hallway, flapping her arms in distress.

'Pete, John, Gary, grab your coats! We're going!'

'Here, here, what's up?' DI Routledge asked her. 'Don't tell me you've seen some spooks as well?'

'I'm not staying here a moment longer,' she told him. 'I don't know what's the matter with this place and I don't want to find out!'

'Come on, what's happened?' DI Routledge persisted. 'Your colleague here has just recorded some pretty strange goings-on upstairs. What have you seen?'

Sarah Saunders lifted down her raincoat with its nylon fur collar and buttoned it up wrongly. Then she went straight to the front door and opened it, holding it open while her engineers struggled into their raincoats too.

She waved one hand towards the arch that led to the kitchens. She was so upset that she could barely speak.

'In there – in the kitchen – there was nobody there but I saw somebody on my camera screen. I saw a man on my screen, right in front of me! But there was nobody there!'

'Here, settle down,' said DI Routledge. 'By the sound of it, it sounds similar to what your colleague here saw upstairs. Why don't you show us your video of it?'

'Because I dropped my camera and I'm not going back for it!'

'Don't worry, we can retrieve it for you. Harris – go to the kitchens and fetch it, would you? Williams, go with him, would you, just to make sure there's nobody actually lurking around in there.'

'I don't care about my camera! I don't want it!' said Sarah Saunders hysterically.

Lilian went up to her and put her arm around her shivering shoulders. 'It's all right,' she said. 'We've seen and heard lots of peculiar things here since we started work, but we think that somebody's been playing tricks on us, on purpose, trying to scare us away.'

'This wasn't a trick! There was no way in the world that this was a trick! I went into the kitchen and when I went into the kitchen I heard this man and he was groaning and when I pointed my camera in the direction where the groaning was coming from I could *see* him! But he wasn't there! There was nobody there!'

'Hush,' said Lilian, because Sarah Saunders was shivering so violently that she felt as if she had Covid.

'And then – and then – I saw him pull out one of the drawers – he pulled out one of the drawers from the dresser and all these knives and forks fell out on to the floor. They went *crash!* all over the floor. And on the screen I saw him pick up one of the knives – like a great big carving knife – and he took it over to the table – and I saw the knife floating towards the table – it was floating in the air, I swear it! Oh God, I saw it actually floating!'

'Why don't you come inside and calm down and tell us about it?' said DI Routledge.

'I'm going! I'm going! And I'm never coming back here, ever!'

'All right, you're going and you're never coming back here ever. But before you go, let's take a look at what's recorded on your camera, shall we?'

'He laid his hand flat in the middle of the kitchen table and he stabbed it! He stabbed his own hand! But his hand wasn't there, and neither was he – there was only the knife sticking in the table!'

PC Harris had returned, holding up the Testo thermographic camera.

'It's still there, guv. The knife, sticking in the table. And all the knives and forks all over the floor, like she said.'

DI Routledge took the camera and turned it this way and that.

'How do you work this thing?'

One of the engineers came forward, took the camera from him and switched it on.

'I need to see this,' said Lilian. 'It's happened before, the cutlery falling all over the floor, and a knife sticking in the table. I thought it was probably a prank, but if this is proof that it wasn't—'

The engineer started the video and they all gathered around him and watched it in silence. Just as Sarah Saunders had said, an attenuated figure came shimmering across the kitchen and dragged one of the drawers out of the dresser, so that kitchen cutlery was scattered all over the floor. The figure was mostly purplish, with iridescent blotches of yellow and green.

'It's freezing cold, minus three degrees Celsius, but you

can see that its temperature varies,' the engineer commented. Lilian found it hard to believe how matter-of-fact he sounded, as if he regularly saw phantom figures dancing on his video screen.

They saw the figure carrying a carving knife over to the kitchen table. It spread out the fingers of its left hand, and then it stabbed the knife so forcefully into the back of its hand that the knife remained upright by itself, still quivering. It was then that Sarah Saunders dropped the camera on the floor, so that it abruptly stopped recording.

'But there was nobody there?' asked DI Routledge, turning around to PC Williams.

'No, sir. And I checked the washroom as well, just to make sure.'

'Let's take another look at that,' said DI Routledge.

The engineer held up the camera again, and DI Routledge peered at the screen closely as the purple figure flickered across it, scattering the cutlery and then stabbing its hand.

'What do you reckon that is? I mean, seriously? And those figures you recorded upstairs?'

'Incontrovertible evidence that this hospital is haunted, in my opinion,' said David.

'I'm going,' said Sarah Saunders, and she stepped out on to the porch. 'Come on, the rest of you. If there's knives flying around by themselves, and any of you get hurt, I don't want the company to be liable.'

'We'll need to keep hold of your cameras for now,' DI Routledge told her. 'But forensics will be able to transfer these two video recordings off of them, so we can return them to you in due course.'

'Well, as long as you do,' said one of the engineers. 'Those bad boys cost nearly fifteen hundred pounds each.'

Sarah Saunders and her three engineers crossed the driveway to their cars, climbed in and drove away.

When they had gone, Lilian closed the front door. 'What now?' she asked DI Routledge.

'To be honest with you, Ms Chesterfield, I'm not entirely sure. Your friend here seems to believe these premises are haunted, but I'm afraid that "haunting" isn't included in the list of English criminal offences. Causing alarm and distress, or harassing somebody, that comes under the Public Order Act, nineteen eighty-six, but I'm not at all sure what action I can take if the offender can't be said to exist in the normal definition of "existing".'

'You've seen those videos. Somebody or something exists here, and they've been causing us alarm and distress every day.'

'Well, you've seen them too. What do you think they are? Because I've never seen anything like them in the whole of my career.'

'Perhaps they're some sort of energy, like we've discussed before. Vibrations, perhaps. Echoes. Or else they're what that engineer said they might be, thermal projections. How should I know? I'm a property developer, not a physics professor.'

DI Routledge turned down the corners of his mouth. 'I'm sorry I can't be more positive. But I need to have reasonable suspicions that an offence has an actual perpetrator before I can justify a full-scale investigation. Even with these video recordings, there don't seem to *be* any actual perpetrators. How can I put it to you? It would be like trying to prosecute lightning for striking a man on a golf course.'

'You might find some more evidence on my ex's phone.'

'That's possible. We'll be taking your former husband's

phone with us to be examined, and the knife from the kitchen, and DS Woods here will be dusting the kitchen table before we go for latent fingerprints. Not that I'm confident he'll find any.'

'So what am I supposed to do until you can come up with an answer?' Lilian demanded. 'If you can't find out what's happening here with sniffer dogs, and you can't persuade anyone to carry out a thermal imaging survey, how are we going to stop all this screaming and doors banging and cutlery being thrown around? Most of all, how are we going to make sure that no more people end up like Alex Fowler and Charlie Thorndyke?'

DI Routledge looked weary. 'I don't have the authority to order you to do this, Ms Chesterfield, because these premises aren't technically a crime scene, despite the human remains that were exhumed in the garden and the knife in the kitchen table. However, my personal recommendation would be for you to vacate the building for the time being, making sure that it's secure, at least until we have a clearer idea of what's going on here.'

'You're not the first person who's suggested that. But how are we going to get a clearer idea if it's all locked up? Besides, my company simply can't afford to leave it empty. Every single day that it remains undeveloped costs us a great deal of money.'

David said again, 'Personally, *I* really believe now that it's haunted, whatever "haunted" means.'

'In that case, you'll have to find yourself an exorcist,' said DS Woods. He had returned from his car with a case containing a fingerprint kit, and was taking out the magnetic wand, and peering inside to make sure he had everything he needed.

'An exorcist?' said Lilian. 'There's no evidence that these figures are demons, is there, like in the film? And I can't believe that what's been happening here has anything at all to do with religion.'

'Well, suit yourself,' said DI Routledge. 'I'm up to my ears at the moment. I have Frank Willard's death to look into, as well as that of Dr Wells and Nurse O'Grady. Once I hear from forensics I may be able to make a more informed decision about what steps we can take next. I would advise you, though, to be extremely cautious while you're here in the hospital, and to report immediately any unusual occurrences like those we've witnessed today. Sahni – you've got that broken phone with you, haven't you? And Johnson – you've got that knife?'

Once the police had all left, Lilian and David went back into the drawing room. David picked up Lilian's iPad with the sewage plans on it, but then put it down again.

'Perhaps he's right, Lil, and we *should* stay away for a while. Supposing what happened to Alex and Charlie happens to us? Because there's definitely something here, isn't there, even if it's not ghosts, and even if it's not demons? Those videos proved it.'

'Yes. There's no question about that,' said Lilian. She was silent for a few moments because her brain felt as if it were turning over and over like a tumble dryer full of wet clothes. 'I'm beginning to think that maybe I've been wrong. Maybe this isn't local activists trying to scare us off. Everything that we've seen, everything that we've heard, it's all too sophisticated. Those figures – I don't see how anybody could have created those. And that knife floating through the air and sticking into the kitchen table. Even that spoon-bending chap couldn't have done that.'

'Oh, you mean Uri Geller?'

Lilian could see her reflection in the mirror over the mantelpiece. She thought she looked like a ghost herself.

'You know what I can feel here now? Suffering. I think I should have been more sensitive to it before. This used to be a hospital, after all, and what do people do in hospital? They suffer. Maybe there are some kind of ghosts here, only they're not trying to frighten us. Maybe they're just trying to tell us how much pain they're in.

'It was hearing Tim on his phone. I think that's what changed my mind more than anything else. I *know* it was Tim, I'm sure of it. Nobody else could have pretended to be him. And he was in terrible pain. He burned his hand once really badly when he was trying to light a bonfire in the garden with petrol and he sounded exactly the same.'

'Do you think he's still here somewhere, in the hospital?'

'I don't know, David. I just don't know. But where else could he be? It's almost as if there are *two* hospitals here, side by side, do you understand what I'm getting at, and sometimes they overlap.'

'I still think we should get out of here, at least until the police have come up with some answers. What if we go ahead and develop the place, but it still turns out be haunted, and nobody wants to live here? We'll lose a hell of a lot more money then.'

'I'm going to take another look around,' said Lilian. 'Maybe Tim *is* here somewhere, or maybe I can find something that gives me a clue to where he's gone.'

'On your own?'

'Yes. On my own.'

'Well, all I can say is be careful. And give me a yell if you need me. Meanwhile, I'll… go back to looking through these drainage schemes. Bit of an anticlimax, wouldn't you think? Seeing ghosts one minute and looking at sewers the next.'

Lilian didn't answer. Her mind was still churning over and over and part of the reason she wanted to look around the hospital to see if she could find Tim was so that she could be alone.

She didn't believe in ghosts. Yet these figures that appeared to be ghosts had brought her whole life to a standstill.

Before she went upstairs, she phoned Roger French and told him that there had been a delay in completing the thermographic survey.

'Why's that, then?' he wanted to know.

'Some technical problem with their equipment.'

'Nothing to do with the building, then? We're not going to have to lash out for anything structural? You know, like foundations, or something major like that?'

'No. Nothing like that. I'll keep you updated.'

'Good. Because Shelby and Kellogg are going great guns with the advertising material. They've just sent me some stunning artist's impressions of what Philomena Park is going to look like when it's ready for sale. I'll email them to you.'

'Thank you. I'll get back to you later today.'

'Are you all right, Lil? You sound a bit – I don't know. You sound a bit flat.'

'Everything's good, Roger, thank you.'

'Okay. You know what they say, when life gives you shit, fertilise your field!'

Lilian dropped her phone into her jacket pocket and climbed slowly upstairs to the third floor. Suddenly she felt overwhelmingly tired, and when she reached the third-floor landing she stopped and held on to the banisters, listening to the hospital all around her.

She could hear floorboards softly creaking and the whispering sound of draughts blowing beneath badly fitting doors. She could almost believe that the building was crowded all around her with invisible people, watching her and waiting to see what she would do next.

She thought of the happy times she had enjoyed with Tim, when they were first married. How funny he used to be, and how loving, and how he used to surprise her with flowers and bracelets and boxes of chocolates when she was least expecting them. She thought how much she needed a man in her life now. As strong as she was, she needed a man she could turn to, a man who could protect her and restore her confidence. Somehow, the stress of all of the strange things that had been happening here at St Philomena's was making her feel useless and worthless and unattractive. She simply felt as if she couldn't cope any more.

She walked along the corridor to the last bedroom, where the engineer had seen the glowing figures on his camera screen.

She stopped by the half-open door and listened. Then, very quietly, she said, '*Tim?*'

There was no reply. She pushed the door open wider and went inside. The room had a stale smell to it, because it had been closed up for so long, as well as the smell of oak flooring, and another smell, too, faint but peppery and quite distinctive. Lilian had smelled it before, but couldn't think where or when.

She looked under the bed, but there was nothing there. She had already been seeking estimates to have all the remaining beds in the hospital removed, but so far all of them had been too high, mainly because of the cost of recycling the mattresses.

She left the room and walked slowly back along the corridor, looking into one room after another, and in each room saying, 'Tim? Are you there?'

Eventually, she returned to the head of the staircase. *This is futile*, she thought. *Wherever he went, however he managed to scream for help on his phone, he doesn't seem to be here – or if he is, he's not answering me. Maybe he's dead, and his body's hidden in some cupboard or under the floorboards or behind some wall.*

She started back down the stairs, but then her phone warbled. She stopped and took it out but it didn't show who was calling. She pressed the green button to answer, but all she heard to begin with was a thin hissing noise. She had received scores of cold calls lately, mostly from Vodafone, and she was about to press the red button to end the call when she heard a hoarse, ragged voice say, '*Lil? Lilian?*'

'Who is this?'

'*I'm hurting, Lil, I can't tell you how much. I never hurt like this, not in the whole of my life.*'

'Tim? Is that you, Tim? Where are you?'

'*Help me, Lil, for the love of God.*'

'Where are you, Tim? I can't help you if I don't know where you are!'

'*Oh God, Lil! Save me! Save me, Lil! I'm sorry for everything! I'm sorry for everything I did to you! I'm sorry! I'm sorry! But save me!*'

'Tim – where are you?'

'*I'm here!*' he screamed. '*I'm here! For the love of God, Lil! I'm here!*'

As soon as he had said that, Lilian's phone crackled and

then went silent. She stood halfway down the staircase, feeling utterly numb.

She was still standing there when David called out from the hallway.

'Lilian? You said you wanted to see Martin Slater, didn't you, next time he showed up? Well, he's outside, trimming the hedge.'

23

She was still shaking when she put on her raincoat and went out to talk to Martin Slater. She put up her hood and then wrapped her arms tightly around her, as if she were freezing cold.

Martin Slater was trimming the laurel hedge near the entrance to the driveway. He stopped when he heard her walking across the shingle and lowered his clippers.

'Where did you disappear to?' she asked him. 'The police were here again and they're keen to talk to you about that skeleton.'

'Are they now?'

'Yes, well, they think that since you've been gardening here for so long, you might know something about it. They told me they're having some trouble finding out whose remains they are.'

'Do you think it matters? Once you're nothing but bones, you're nothing but bones.'

'All the same, if you can give me a contact number, or your address. Or if you can get in touch with Detective Inspector Routledge at Reigate police station.'

'A contact number?'

'Yes. You do have a mobile phone, don't you?'

'Got a bit of paper? I'll write it down for you.'

Lilian found a dog-eared business card from Epsom Double Glazing in her raincoat pocket and took the Downland Developments ball pen out of her jacket. She handed them to Martin Slater and watched him as he wrote down his number.

'So where did you vanish to?' she asked him.

'What, earlier? I had a bit of business to attend to, that's all.'

'You do have a way of vanishing.'

Martin Slater gave her back her business card and her ball pen, and smiled in that enigmatic way of his, as if he knew something about her that nobody else knew.

'You'll tidy up all those wisteria clippings, won't you?'

He kept on smiling. 'You know what they say about wisteria, don't you? It's the best demon repellent you can find. Very effective against low-ranking demons, and it can even paralyse high-ranking demons.'

Lilian didn't know what to say to that. She couldn't make up her mind if he were serious or if he were teasing her.

'They also say that wisteria is the symbol of eternal life. If you have wisteria growing around your house, you have every chance of living forever.'

'I don't want to live for ever, thank you.'

'Some people have no choice in the matter.'

'Well, whatever. If you can just make sure you tidy it all up.'

Martin Slater said nothing more, but returned to his hedge-clipping. Lilian waited for a moment, wondering if she ought to ask him if she had his approval to pass his mobile number to DI Routledge, but then she decided she would do it anyway. Martin Slater would probably only give her one of his obscure answers, or disappear.

She went back into the hospital. David was waiting for her in the drawing room, looking worried.

'Everything all right, Lilian? I think I've picked out the best sewage schematic.'

'I don't know, David. When I was upstairs, I thought I heard Tim again, on my phone.'

'Blimey. Are you sure it was him?'

Lilian nodded. 'Yes, it had to be. And he was screaming again, and begging me for help. And he said he was here.'

'Meaning here in the hospital?'

'I suppose so.'

David closed the iPad and put it down on the window sill next to him. 'Well, here's a thought. If he's here in the hospital, but we can't see him with the naked eye, then maybe we could see him with some of those night-vision goggles. It's only a thought. You saw Frank's Army mates, didn't you? Maybe the same thing's happened to your Tim that happened to them.'

'I can't even begin to think where he is. How can I hear him on my phone like that? He kept saying he was "here", but "here" could mean anywhere.'

'You could try the goggles. If the police haven't taken Frank's pair, maybe Marion Crosby would lend us a borrow of them. Then at least you could see if your Tim was here or not.'

'You really believe that St Philomena's is haunted, don't you?'

'After everything we've seen and heard, Lilian, don't you?'

'I don't know what to believe. I think I'm losing my mind, that's all. And that bloody Martin Slater doesn't help, the way he keeps appearing and disappearing like some conjuring trick, and saying the most peculiar things. But at least he gave me his phone number, so that I can give it to DI Routledge.'

'My parents used to have a gardener a bit like that once. He kept disappearing when he was supposed to be weeding. In the end they found him in the shed asleep, with an empty half-bottle of Bell's beside him.'

Lilian took out the business card and looked at the number that Martin Slater had scrawled on the back of it. It didn't look like a regular eleven-digit mobile number, although it started with 07. When she counted the digits, she realised that there were only ten.

'I think he's missed out a number,' she said, and went back through the hallway and opened the front door. The hedge-trimming was only half finished, but Martin Slater was no longer there.

'Damn him,' she breathed. She closed the door, went back into the drawing room and took out her own phone. She prodded the ten numbers and listened.

At first she heard nothing but a soft hissing sound. Then, so faintly that it was barely audible, she heard music, that same wavering music she had heard before in the reception room, with its sporadic tapping of tabla drums, like somebody's fingertips tapping impatiently on a tabletop.

'Listen to this,' she said, and passed her phone to David.

He put the phone to his ear, and listened, and frowned, but after a few seconds he handed her phone back.

'I couldn't hear anything, I'm afraid. What was it?'

'Music. Like Middle-Eastern music. You know, like belly-dancers dance to.'

'Blimey.'

'But I think you're right, David. I think we should search this whole hospital with night-vision goggles. If Marion

Crosby can't lend us Frank's pair, or the police have taken them, then we'll have to buy some. I think Moses should come and help us too. He was a medic out in Afghanistan, he'll have a better idea of what we're looking for. He treated dozens of soldiers for injuries. Who knows – maybe he'll even recognise some of them.'

David looked down at Lilian's iPad. 'Before we do that, do you want to know which sewage schematic I think we ought to plump for?'

They drove along to Tumber Street and parked behind the police car and the forensic van that were still blocking the road outside Marion Crosby's house. A bored-looking officer in a high-vis jacket was standing by the five-bar gate, and when they approached he held up his hand and said, 'Sorry, folks. Restricted area.'

'Is the owner still here, Mrs Crosby?' Lilian asked him. 'She knows me and I need to have a word, quite urgently.'

'Yes, she's still on the premises.'

'Then is it possible that you can ask her to come out and talk to me? Tell her it's Lilian Chesterfield, from St Philomena's.'

'All right, if she agrees. But please remain here, if you don't mind.'

The officer went off and Lilian and David waited by the gate. The living-room window was brightly lit, and inside it they could see two forensic investigators in white suits like giant snowmen, moving backwards and forwards.

After a few minutes, Marion Crosby and the police officer came out together. Marion Crosby was wearing a thick grey sweater and she looked washed out, her face pale and her hair pinned back in a scruffy French pleat.

'*Lilian,*' she said, as if she were deeply relieved to see her, and she nodded to David.

'Marion... Detective Inspector Routledge told us about Frank. I'm so sorry.'

Marion gave her a twitchy shrug. 'I'd tell you what happened but the police said I shouldn't say anything to anybody about it, not yet anyway. But it was ghastly. It was more than ghastly. It was like something out of a horror film.'

'I won't beat about the bush, Marion. We've been seeing and hearing more strange things up at the hospital. We've seen images of people, walking around, and heard screaming. And on top of that, my ex-husband came to visit and he disappeared, and I think he might be – I'm not at all sure. I think he might be trapped there somehow. I can't explain it because I don't understand it myself.'

Marion said, 'The way Frank died... I can't sleep because I can't get the picture of it out of my mind. And poor Michael, he was actually there when it happened, and he hasn't been able to speak. He's literally struck dumb. They're sending a police psychologist to try and coax him into talking again, because he's the only eyewitness they have.'

'What I want to ask you is if Frank's night-vision goggles are still here. I was hoping we might borrow them. If I can see his old Army friends again, maybe I can understand why they still seem to be stuck in the hospital – or their spirits, anyhow, if that's what they are. And maybe I can find out what's happened to my ex.'

'The police searched his room,' said Marion. 'I know they've taken away his phone and some of his diaries, but I don't know if those goggles are still there. I'll go and take a look for you.'

Lilian nodded towards the officer, who was pacing up and down nearby.

'If you can find them, we don't have to tell the police we've borrowed them. I'm sure that Detective Inspector Routledge thinks we've all gone mad. Mind you, I'm beginning to believe that he's right, and we *have* gone mad.'

Marion went back into the house. They waited, while the police officer softly whistled and a few more spots of rain began to fall.

David said, 'I had some bad news this morning. I think my grandma's on the way out. Breast cancer. For some reason, you don't think of breast cancer at that age, do you?'

'I'm sorry.'

'Well, nobody lives for ever, do they? We've all got to die one day, one way or another.'

Lilian thought of what Martin Slater had said, before he went back to his hedge-clipping. '*Some people have no choice in the matter.*' She was still wondering what he had meant by that.

After only a few minutes, Marion returned, carrying a Sainsbury's shopping bag. 'It's in here,' she said, lifting it over the gate. 'Don't ask me how it works, because I don't have the first idea. But you're welcome to borrow it. Keep if, if you like. Poor Frank won't be using it again.'

The police officer looked across at them but he didn't ask them what was in the bag.

'We can look up on Google how to operate it,' said David. 'It can't be that complicated.'

'If you find out anything that explains how Frank could have died… you'll let me know, won't you?' said Marion. 'If I don't have some sort of closure, I think I'll be going mad, too.'

Lilian reached across the top of the gate and held Marion's hand. 'Was it really that terrible?'

Marion nodded, her lips tightly pursed, close to tears.

'I'll come back later and see you anyway,' Lilian told her. 'Whatever's going on here, we can't let it ruin our lives.'

'He was in pieces!' Marion sobbed. 'He was in hundreds of pieces!'

Before they drove back to St Philomena's, Lilian called Moses.

'Moses? It's Lilian Chesterfield. Listen, I have some really bad news. Frank Willard's dead. Yes – Frank Willard who called up all his old Army friends for us.'

'He is dead? How did he die?'

'I don't know exactly. The police are being quite cagey about it. But that Detective Inspector Routledge told me he died in the same way that Dr Wells died at St Helier's.'

'So you think there might be some connection?'

'Again, I don't know. But my former husband came to see me at the hospital and went missing, and I think he may still be somewhere in the building, although I can't think where. Not only that, we had some engineers around earlier to carry out a thermographic survey. They saw some weird figures with their cameras that were quite like the figures Frank Willard conjured up. It scared the life out of them, and they left.'

'That does not surprise me one bit. So what are you planning to do now?'

'I've borrowed Frank's night-vision goggles. I want to see if I can find my former husband, and maybe see some of those other figures too. Last time, I started them all screaming by shouting at them, but I won't do that again. Thinking about it, I probably frightened them as much as they frightened me.'

'What if you do see them?'

'I'm going to try and find out who they are and why they're still haunting the hospital. I don't know if they're really some kind of ghosts, but "haunting" is about the only word I can think of. I was hoping that you might be able to come over and help us, me and David. You were out in Afghanistan, treating them, weren't you? You know better than we do what they've been through, and you'll be able to talk the same language.'

'You want me to come over this evening? Grace is making egusi soup because it is Independence Day.'

'Can you?'

'Hold on for a moment.'

Lilian could hear Moses calling out to his wife. There was a moment's pause and then he came back and said, 'Yes, I can come, so long as I am home by nine. I will see you in about half an hour.'

Lilian and David drove back to St Philomena's. It was beginning to grow dark, and Lilian thought that somehow the hospital seemed to have taken on a gloomy look, as if a building were capable of brooding over its own past.

David took his camping lantern out of his car and they went inside. As they walked through the hallway, their shadows jumped and danced on the walls all around them, and even the oil painting of Sir Edmond Carver seemed to come to life, as if he could climb out of his gilded frame like the girl in *The Ring* came climbing out of the TV.

'I know it was my idea,' said David. In the bright light from his lantern, he suddenly looked boyish and immature. 'I'm just wondering if we really want to go through with this.'

'David – I have to find out what's happened to Tim. And

what are we going to do if we can't find out what all this screaming and all these figures and faces are all about? We'll be finished. I'll be finished.'

'I'll be honest with you, Lilian. Now that we're actually going to do it, I'm shit-scared.'

'And you think I'm not?'

She took the night-vision goggles out of the Sainsbury's bag. David held his lantern close to them, and she could see that they had a simple on-off switch. She lifted them on to her head and adjusted the rubber eyepieces over her eyes. They fitted tightly so that no green light would shine out on to the wearer's face and provide a target for an enemy sniper. When she clicked the switch, the hallway appeared in dazzling bright green, because it was already lit up by David's lantern, but she could also see into the darkness of the arch that led to the kitchens, and into the drawing-room door.

'Right,' she said, switching the goggles off. 'As soon as Moses gets here we can get cracking. I think we should start on the third floor. That's where that thermographic chap saw those two figures, and that's where I heard Tim on my phone saying that he was here.'

'You don't want to try going back to the reception room first? That's where you saw those Army friends of Frank's.'

'Maybe afterwards. Remember that Frank had called them all there, with his harmonica. Even if I had a harmonica, I wouldn't know how to play it. Tim could play, but he always sounded like somebody in prison.'

It was only twenty minutes later that they heard the crunch of car tyres on the forecourt outside, and Moses knocked at the door. He was wearing a round green Fila cap and a scarf in green and white, the Nigerian national colours.

'Still no electric?' he said, as he stepped into the hallway.

'Tomorrow, I hope. Thank you so much for coming over. I have no idea if we're actually going to be able to find any of Frank's friends, or if we'll be able to speak to them, or they'll be able to speak to us, but you'll be such a help if we do, and they can.'

'I had a call from Artyom this morning, believe it or not,' Moses told her. 'He has been digging more deeply into the stories about the Spirits of Pain. He said that a curse of everlasting agony was definitely given to any foreign intruder who was wounded when they tried to take over the sacred lands that are now known as Afghanistan – even after they had left. For the rest of their lives, in fact.'

Lilian held up the night-vision goggles. 'I'll wear these first, in case we see Tim – that's my former husband. But if I see anybody else, Moses, I'll pass them straight over to you. And this time I'll try to be calm, so that I don't set them off screaming.'

They climbed the stairs up to the third floor. Again, Lilian was out of breath by the time she reached the landing.

'The lifts should be working tomorrow, thank God,' she panted. 'Mind you, I think I've managed to lose quite a bit of weight since I've been here.'

She strapped the night-vision goggles on to her head again and switched them on.

'I'll walk right down to the end, and have a look in that last room. That's where the surveyor saw those figures. Then I'll come back, looking into every room one after the other. Moses, do you want to walk close beside me? And David, if you can turn off your lamp, but follow close behind us.'

'What if a whole lot of screaming soldiers come after us, like the ones you saw downstairs?'

'I don't know, David. I really don't. If they're only some kind of energy, then I don't know if they can hurt us or not.'

'Alex and Charlie got hurt badly enough, didn't they? And your Tim's hurting badly, too, by the sound of it.'

'So what do we do? Just walk out of here and never come back, because we're frightened?'

Moses raised one eyebrow, as if he were expecting her to answer that herself, while David looked back at her and pursed his lips but said nothing. Then, after a moment's hesitation, he switched off his lantern. The corridor was not totally black. Faint patterns of light flickered on the ceiling from the street lamps that shone through the trees outside. All the same, Moses laid a hand on her shoulder and said, 'Wait for a moment, please, until my eyes get accustomed to the darkness.'

Eventually, he said, 'Okay, let us go,' and they began to make their way slowly along the corridor, with Lilian leading them.

'Do you see anything?' Moses asked her, as they neared the end.

'Not yet. Don't worry, I'll tell you if I do, you can be certain of that.'

They reached the last bedroom, opened the door and went inside. Lilian scanned it left and right with her night-vision goggles, ducking down to look under the bed, but there was no sign of anybody there. She opened the wardrobe, but there was nobody hiding inside it, either real or illusionary.

'No. Nothing. Perhaps those figures *were* some kind of technological trick. In a way, I'm still hoping they were.'

'Yes, but what about that flying knife?' said David. For Moses' benefit, he described how Sarah Saunders had seen a figure in the kitchen, and how it had pulled out a drawer full of cutlery and stuck a carving knife into the table.

'And you saw that for yourselves, on the video, this knife?' asked Moses. 'How could that have been done?'

'I haven't the faintest idea, Moses. But after this, we can go downstairs and check out the kitchen.'

They went back into the corridor and opened the door to the next bedroom. There was nobody in there, either, but as they came back out, Lilian heard a croaky voice saying, '*Lil?*'

She felt an electric tingling of shock all the way down her back. She turned around and looked back, and there, standing beside the door to the last bedroom, was Tim. Because of the phosphor in the night-vision goggles he was shining green, but he also appeared to be two-dimensional, as if he were an image of Tim cut out of celluloid, wavering in some unfelt draught.

'Lil,' he begged her, and he sounded harsh and agonised. 'Lil, I can't bear this. I can't bear it. Save me, Lil. For Christ's sake, save me.'

Lilian said, 'Tim? Is that really you?'

'Save me, Lil. I don't know what I've done to deserve this but save me.'

'I can hear him!' said Moses. 'Can you see him, too?'

'It hurts so much, Lil! I never knew anything could hurt so much!'

'Lilian – can you see him?' Moses repeated.

'Oh, my God,' said Lilian. She dragged off the night-vision goggles and handed them to Moses, and he quickly tugged off his Fila cap and fitted them over his head.

'Yes! Yes! I can see him too! Is that your Tim?'

'Holy shit,' said David. 'Do you want me to switch the lantern back on?'

'No, no, not yet, David. I need to see if I can help him.'

Although she couldn't see Tim without the goggles, Lilian could still hear him. His voice became rougher and rougher, and then rose into a ragged scream.

'Lil! Save me! Get me out of here! Lil! I can't take it any more! Lil! I'm sorry! I'm sorry for everything I did! I'm sorry I hurt you! But get me out of here!'

'Here—' said Moses, and he handed the goggles back to her.

When she fitted the goggles back on, she could see that Tim was down on his hands and knees in the doorway, screaming and pounding the floor with his fists. Lilian slowly and cautiously approached him, one hand held out in front of her, afraid to touch him in case she could actually feel him, but also afraid that he might not be there at all. Moses stayed close behind her, with one hand raised too, in case she jolted suddenly backwards and lost her balance.

Tim's screaming slowly sank into a low, agonised howling, more like a miserable child or an injured animal than a man in pain. It was then that another green figure appeared in Lilian's goggles. He came out of the darkened doorway and stood next to Tim, resting one hand on his shoulder. It appeared to Lilian that he was wearing battledress, although his image was translucent, too, like Tim's, and it was hard to tell. His face, though, she could make out quite distinctly. He was young, with a pointed chin, a long nose, and quite deep-set eyes. He seemed to be staring at her directly.

'Who are you?' she whispered. She didn't want to alarm him.

The young man opened his mouth, but only a blurry sound came out, like a recording being played at the wrong speed.

'Who – are – you?' she repeated, even though she was so hyperventilated she could barely speak.

'*Mmmmmerrrrr…*' he answered.

'Moses!' she said, pulling off the goggles again and pushing them into his hand. 'Moses, there's somebody there! He looks like a soldier!'

Moses struggled to put the goggles back on. Lilian could tell the young man was still there, because she could hear him speaking in that deep, indistinct voice.

'*Bwwvverrrrrrrr…*'

Moses adjusted the eyepieces and focused on the new figure standing in the doorway.

'*Do mi!* I cannot believe it! I *know* him! Buller, his name is! For some reason, that name stuck in my mind! I treated him for shrapnel wounds at Ghazni!'

He took a step closer to the young man.

'Buller? I remember you. Do you remember me? You were badly injured when that IED went off on highway one. I was the medic who came to help you. Do you remember me? Mingus, they called me.'

Moses waited for the young man to respond. The young man appeared to be looking back at him, but there was no indication that he could actually see him. After a few seconds, he reached down and helped Tim to his feet. The two of them remained motionless for a moment, although their images were beginning to ripple and distort. Then they turned and disappeared into the doorway.

'Tim!' said Lilian. 'Is he still there, Moses?'

Moses went into the bedroom and looked around. 'No. They have gone, both of them. Who can say where?'

David switched on his lantern and they stood blinking at each other in the sudden bright light.

'That soldier,' said Lilian. 'You really recognised him?'

'Yes. Buller. I don't know why I remembered his name. A roadside bomb exploded about a kilometre south of Ghazni. That is on the main road between Kabul and Kandahar. One of his arms was blown off at the shoulder and his insides were all hanging out. Somehow I managed to bandage him up and believe it or not he was still talking, even joking, as if what had happened to him was only a scratch.'

'Do you know what happened to him after that?' asked Lilian. She was still shaking from having seen Tim, or Tim's image, or whatever it had been.

'Yes. He was flown back to England and brought here to St Philomena's to recover, and to be rehabilitated. I came here soon after I returned from Afghanistan to find out what progress he was making – him and several other troops I had treated.'

'And?'

'They told me that only about a week after he had arrived here, he died.'

24

DI Routledge was buttoning up his coat to go home when DS Woods came into his office and said, 'I think we've identified a possible suspect.'

'Where? At Downlea?'

DS Woods held up a large Toshiba USB. 'No, guv, St Helier. We didn't pick him up on the CCTV recordings right away, because he managed to mingle in with members of the nursing staff so that it was difficult to pick him out, and it was some time before Dr Wells – well, before Dr Wells exploded, for want of a better word. But there's one split second when you can see him opening the door of Dr Wells's room and going inside.'

'When was that?'

'When Dr Wells was on his own, unattended. It was about forty minutes before he started screaming and Dr Kummunduh went in to see him. If you can switch on your PC, guv, I'll show you.'

DI Routledge went over to his desk and switched on his computer, and DS Woods plugged in the USB. The first sequence from the security CCTV showed five or six doctors and nurses waiting for the lift in the hospital, along with two women visitors, but DS Woods pointed to another man who was mostly hidden behind one of the doctors. All they could see of him was the back of his head, with tousled hair, as if he never bothered to comb it.

In the next sequence, the doctors and nurses all emerged from the lift on the second floor. The two women visitors had obviously left it already, on the first floor. The man with the tousled hair was keeping close behind two of the doctors, who were talking to each other. It was only when the group passed one security camera and were picked up by the next that they saw him turn to the left and open the door of Dr Wells's room. He ducked quickly inside and closed it behind him.

DS Woods reversed the recording and froze the image of the man as he reached for the door handle. He was tall, and broad-shouldered, and he was wearing a long gilet or sleeveless tunic. The recording was in black and white, so they were unable to see what colour this tunic was, although it appeared to be slightly shiny, as if it were nylon or leather.

'Pity we can't see his face,' said DI Routledge. 'Do we see him coming out again?'

'Well, that's the really strange part about it,' said DS Woods. 'We *don't* see him coming out. We've run it right through until we see the bomb squad turning up, but he doesn't reappear. Not coming out of this door again, anyhow. But this'll make you scratch your head.'

He fast-forwarded the recording until it showed a sequence from the CCTV camera overlooking the car park at the side of the hospital. For a split second, it caught the back view of a man walking quickly up Wrythe Lane towards Rose Hill, before he disappeared behind the large hospital noticeboard. When DS Wood froze that image, DI Routledge could see that the man bore a distinct resemblance to the man in the gilet who had entered Dr Wells's room.

'It certainly *looks* like the same bloke,' said DI Routledge. 'So he couldn't have been hiding in Dr Wells's room until he could sneak out later, and even then the CCTV would have picked him up. But how the hell did he get out there on the street without the CCTV catching him in the corridor, for that matter, or in the lift?'

DS Woods flicked backwards and forwards between the two still images of the man – one opening Dr Wells's door and the other outside on the pavement.

'They *are* the same bloke, guv. They must be. Do you reckon we should post these on Twitter and send them to the local media? You can't see his mush but he's quite distinctive looking. Somebody must know who he is.'

'Yes, let's do that, Andy, and the sooner the better. This whole bloody thing is getting weirder by the minute.'

He looked at his watch and said, 'Look at the bloody time. I didn't get any sleep at all last night and I haven't had a bite to eat since breakfast. I'm off home now but let me know when you've posted those pictures.'

He had almost reached the door of his office when his phone trilled.

'I'm not here,' he said, when he saw that DC Merrick was calling. 'Speak to DS Woods.'

DC Merrick said, 'Sorry, sir. But a body's just been found on Epsom racecourse.'

'Oh, shit. Natural causes, I hope.'

'Might be suicide, but doubtful. It's been cremated, pretty much, burnt to a cinder, so you can't even tell what sex it is. But there's no sign of a petrol can anywhere nearby.'

'You've got to be joking. Where on the racecourse?'

'Right by Tattenham Corner.'

DI Routledge closed his eyes for a moment and took a

deep breath. Then he said, 'All right, Merrick. Give me fifteen minutes, and I'll be there. Alert forensics, would you?'

'Already done, sir.'

DS Woods frowned at DI Routledge as he tucked his phone back into his pocket.

'What's the story, guv?'

'More bloody weirdness, Andy. Only more bloody weirdness.'

DI Routledge parked by the railings at Tattenham Corner, where Epsom racecourse curved around for the final stretch towards the winning post. Brilliant LED lights had already been set up on tripods to illuminate the area where the body had been found, and at least eight police officers were standing around. A second forensics van had just arrived.

The grass was still wet from today's rain, and there was a damp south-west breeze blowing, so that DI Routledge could smell burning as soon as he climbed out of his car.

DC Merrick walked up to him, looking pasty and tired.

'Sorry to pull you in on this one, sir. I did try to call DCI Pomeroy but he was at some Stonecutters dinner and I couldn't get through to him.'

'Never mind, Merrick. I can take early retirement in thirteen years' time. I'll be on a reduced pension but at least I'll be able to get some kip.'

'We have a witness, as it happens. This lady over here. She was walking her dog on the Downs when she saw these flames. She went over to see what it was and as soon as she got close enough she realised it was a body. She called us straight away.'

'She didn't try to stamp the fire out?'

'No, she said it was too hot to get anywhere near it, and the victim must have been dead already. But here's the thing. She caught sight of some fellow crossing the road towards the train station, walking really fast. She called out to him but he didn't turn around.'

'Was she able to give you a description?'

'She's still in a bit of a state, but she can tell you what she saw. PC Hepburn's taking care of her.'

'Let's take a look at the remains first. I want to know exactly what we're dealing with here.'

DC Merrick led DI Routledge across the racecourse to a black scorched area, which was lit unnaturally brightly, like a film set. In the middle of the shrivelled-up grass lay a skeleton, face down. Both its legs had been bent upwards and backwards at the knee, because of the heat. Its internal organs had been reduced to a heap of ashes, and even its shoes had been incinerated, so that it was impossible to tell for certain if it was a man or a woman, although from its size it was probably a man.

'Jesus,' said DI Routledge. 'Do you know what temperature this body must have reached to end up like this? At least a thousand degrees, maybe more, same as a crematorium. But how in the name of God do you burn a body at that kind of temperature out here on a racecourse? Even if someone had soaked it in petrol it wouldn't have burned like this, and a cremation usually takes at least two hours.'

'Like I told you on the phone, sir, there's no sign of a jerry can anywhere, and apart from that there's no smell of petrol or ethanol or paint thinner or any other flammable liquid.'

'This is the same as that nurse at St Helier. She was burned right down to her bones and yet there was nothing around that could have started a fire. I can tell you, Merrick, this is beginning to do my head in.'

Two forensic investigators were kneeling down beside the skeleton in their puffy white protective suits and taking flash photographs, as well as shining infrared lights into its ribcage. DI Routledge went up to them and said, 'What does it look like to you? Ever seen anything like this before?'

One of the investigators pulled down his face mask. 'Only once. There was a woman on Box Hill last year who got struck three times by lightning, but it's very rare to get burned as badly as this. Usually you only get the Lichtenberg pattern, which is like a branchy red tattoo on your skin. But lightning can raise the surrounding air temperature to twenty-seven thousand degrees.'

DI Routledge looked around and sniffed the air. 'There's no lightning around tonight.'

'Well, exactly. So right now we don't have any idea what could have burned this poor bugger. It certainly wasn't petrol, or paint thinner, or any other flammable liquid that we can identify. Not offhand, anyway.'

DI Routledge stood looking down at the skeleton for a while. The fire that had consumed it must have been intense, because its bones were scorched to an amber colour, like spare ribs on a barbecue.

The forensic investigator picked a gold ring out of the ashes between finger and thumb, and held it up so that DI Routledge could see it.

'Definitely man-sized. And a married man, too, by the look of it.'

'Maybe his wife put a curse on him,' put in DC Merrick. 'I know my wife would happily see me cremated sometimes, especially when I want to watch the football.'

DI Routledge left the skeleton and went over to the woman witness, who was standing with PC Hepburn next to the railings. Her black Labrador was lying on the grass at her feet, panting.

'Detective Inspector Barry Routledge,' he introduced himself. 'Thank you for staying around. We shouldn't keep you long this evening, but we may want to be in touch with you again later.'

'Mary Stubbs,' she told him. 'You'll have to forgive me. I'm still very shaken. I've never seen anything like that before. Not a dead body.'

'When did you first see it?'

'I was walking Nero past the grandstand and I caught sight of these flames up here by Tattenham Corner. They were only small flames at first, but suddenly they shot up high into the air and they looked incredibly fierce. I thought that it was a bonfire or something like that, although I couldn't think why anybody would light a bonfire in the middle of the racecourse. I went up to take a closer look and it was then that I saw it was a body on fire. I've never been so shocked in my life.'

'And apparently you saw a man walking away?'

Mary Stubbs nodded, and pointed across the road to Tattenham Corner railway station, where racegoers usually arrived for Derby Day.

'He was walking very fast, as if he was in a hurry to catch a train, or maybe to get away. I shouted out to him, but he didn't even turn around.'

'Can you describe him?'

'Not really, because I didn't see his face. But he was tall, with messy hair, and he was wearing some kind of sleeveless jacket.'

DI Routledge looked round at DC Merrick. 'Sleeveless jacket? Could you see what it was made of?'

'I think it was leather, like soldiers sometimes wear.'

DI Routledge didn't know what to say to her. The street by the station was covered by CCTV, so it was likely that it might have caught this man as he came up the road from the racecourse. But messy hair? And a sleeveless jacket? He sounded so much like the man who had been picked up by the CCTV cameras at St Helier. After all, Nurse O'Grady had been inexplicably burned to a cinder too.

He thanked Mary Stubbs and then walked back to look at the skeleton again.

'They say that an unsolved crime is like a jigsaw, Merrick, don't they? All you have to do is fit all the bits together and *voilà*. But what if the bits come from two different jigsaws, and nobody's told you that? No matter how hard you try to make a picture out of them, you can't, because they don't all belong to the same picture.'

'What jigsaw do you reckon this one is?' asked DC Merrick, although DI Routledge had the impression that he didn't really understand what he had meant.

'Well, it's not *And When Did You Last See Your Father*, is it?' he replied.

They were still standing by the skeleton with its upraised shinbones when one of the forensic investigators appeared like a ghost out of the darkness behind the LED lamps. She was accompanied by a dog handler with a German shepherd that kept looking up at his master as if it were extremely pleased with itself.

'We've come across this, sir,' said the forensic investigator, holding out one of her nitrile-gloved hands. 'I don't know if it's relevant, but I've marked the exact location where we found it. Of course, it might have no bearing at all. It could have been dropped by some random dog walker.'

She handed him a worn brown leather wallet. He opened it up and saw that tucked inside it were a driving licence, an Ocean credit card, an Asda card and a card saying that the holder had been given a Pfizer vaccination against Covid-19. The back of the wallet was crammed with £20 notes and one £10 note, and when DI Routledge quickly thumbed through them, he counted a total of £350.

He took out the driving licence and saw that it was in the name of Timothy Nigel Chesterfield. And what had Lilian Chesterfield told him? That she had lent her ex-husband three hundred and fifty pounds to pay his rent, in cash.

He turned back to the forensic investigator, who was still kneeling by the skeleton. 'Do you want to let me have that gold ring?' he asked him. 'Does it have anything engraved on it?'

The investigator took it out of its polythene bag, held it up to the light and peered at it. 'Yes, it does, on the inside. It says "TCLLC". I thought they might have been trying to engrave it with "TLC" but got the stutters.'

'It could stand for "Timothy Chesterfield Loves Lilian Chesterfield,' said DI Routledge. 'Lilian Chesterfield is the woman in charge of the renovation work they're doing over at St Philomena's Hospital. She's reported her ex-husband missing after he visited her there. I'll bet you anything you like that this is him.'

He looked down at the skeleton. The breeze was still filled with the acrid smell of charred flesh. 'Or what's left of him, any road.'

25

Moses had opened the front door of St Philomena's and was about to leave when DI Routledge drove into the forecourt. He parked, climbed out of his car and walked over with something lifted up in his hand.

'What now?' asked Lilian.

'I'll leave you to it,' said Moses. 'Grace is going to kill me as it is.'

All the same, he stayed in the doorway as DI Routledge came up to them, with his hand still raised.

'What have you got there?' said Lilian.

'I'm sorry to say that it may be some bad news, Ms Chesterfield. Do you want to take a look?'

He handed her a polyethylene evidence bag, with all its details already scrawled on it in felt-tip pen. Inside was a brown leather wallet, and when Lilian stepped back into the hallway so that she could examine it in the light of David's lantern, she recognised it almost immediately.

'This is Tim's,' she said. 'This is my ex-husband's wallet. Where did you find it?'

'A sniffer dog located it on Epsom racecourse, near the finish line,' DI Routledge told her. He pointed to it and said, 'It has three hundred and fifty quid in it. Three hundred and forty in new twenties and one very well-used tenner.'

'Three hundred and fifty pounds? That's what I gave Tim for his rent. So where is he? Don't tell me he's simply dropped it.'

'Well, that's the bad news, I'm afraid. A deceased person has been found on the racecourse, by Tattenham Corner.'

Lilian stared at him. 'Deceased? You mean he's out on the racecourse? *Dead?* But we think we saw him here, in St Philomena's, only about twenty minutes ago.'

'Perhaps this'll confirm it,' said DI Routledge, and gave her a smaller evidence bag.

Lilian took the bag and held it up to the light. It contained a gold wedding ring, mottled from heat, but clearly engraved with the initials TCLLC.

Lilian looked at DI Routledge and the sad expression on her face was almost like a Disney animal that has lost its young. She pressed her hand over her mouth and walked slowly across to the last remaining chair in the hallway, a tall oak throne that stood beside the portrait of Sir Edmond Carver, and sat down. There were no tears in her eyes. She was feeling only pain and regret.

'That's his?' asked DI Routledge, and she nodded mutely.

'Then I'm truly sorry, Ms Chesterfield,' he told her. 'We have yet to make a formal identification, but with that wallet and that ring, the likelihood is that the deceased *is* your former husband, Timothy Nigel Chesterfield. Even though you say you saw him here as recently as twenty minutes ago.'

'But I saw him too,' Moses insisted.

'And I *heard* him,' David put in. 'I didn't see him because I didn't get the chance to wear the night goggles. But I heard him all right. I heard him clear as day.'

'You're sure he wasn't one of these what's-its-names... one of these optical illusions?'

'Maybe you should come upstairs and see him for yourself,' said Moses. 'You know what they say about seeing is believing.'

'Are you serious?'

Lilian held out the night goggles. 'Here... you can wear these. With these, you can see everybody who's hiding in this hospital. These used to belong to Frank Willard. He told us they were the only way he could still meet up with all his old Army friends here. And they certainly work, whatever it is that you can see when you wear them. Here – put them on.'

She held out the night goggles but at first DI Routledge made no move to take them.

'Frank Willard's dead,' he said. 'I'm not so sure about wearing a dead man's goggles.'

'If it makes you feel better, detective inspector, I wiped them with Clinell wipes before I first put them on. They're perfectly sterile.'

'I'm not worried about catching anything, Ms Chesterfield. It's the thought, that's all.'

After hesitating a moment longer, though, he took the goggles and examined them.

'All right,' he said at last. 'Why don't you take me to where you think you saw your ex-husband, and let's find out if I can see him too. If I *can* see him, though, I don't know who the hell that body belongs to, up on the racecourse.'

They all started to climb the stairs. Moses hesitated for a moment and then followed them.

'I thought Grace was going to kill you if you didn't get back home on time,' said Lilian.

'I have an obligation to my wife, yes,' Moses told her. 'But I also have an obligation to those young men that I treated out in Helmand. I made a promise that I would always protect them from harm and ease their pain, and as far as I am concerned "always" means exactly that. My commitment to that promise did not end when we withdrew from Afghanistan and came back home.'

Lilian looked across at DI Routledge and she could see that he was impressed by what Moses had said.

They carried on climbing until they reached the third floor. Lilian took the goggles from DI Routledge and fitted them on to her head.

'If I see anybody – whether it's Tim or not – I'll hand them straight back to you so that you can see them for yourself.'

They started to walk along the corridor towards the last room, as they had before. They had left all the bedroom doors open, and Lilian stopped to look into every one. There was no sign of any figures in any of them.

'Nothing?' asked DI Routledge.

'Not so far.'

At last they reached the end. Lilian took a step into the last room and looked around, but there were no figures in here either. No Tim, no Buller. But she could smell that same distinctive peppery aroma that she had smelled before. Again it reminded her of something, although she still couldn't think what.

'Perhaps that *is* Tim, up on the racecourse,' she said, lifting up the goggles.

'We'll have to do a dental and a DNA, but in all probability it is your ex. He doesn't seem to be here, does he?'

They started to walk back towards the staircase, but they had taken only a few paces before Lilian heard that clogged-up voice behind her say, '*Lil?*'

She turned around at once, fitting the rubber eyepieces back over her eyes. And there he was, Tim, standing by the open doorway of the last bedroom, with both hands held out. The expression on his face was one of agonised pleading.

'Lil? You came back, sweetheart! Save me, Lil, you've got to get me out of here!'

'Tim, can you hear me?'

'I'm hurting, Lil! You can't even imagine how much I'm hurting! It's like I'm burning! It's like I'm on fire! You've got to get me out of here, Lil! I can't take this any more!'

'Can you see him?' asked DI Routledge excitedly. 'I can hear him, clear enough! Can you actually see him?'

Lilian was about to tug the goggles off and pass them over to him when Tim took a deep breath and started to scream, so harsh and high that she could hardly hear herself think. Almost at once, another voice joined him, screaming equally loudly, but twice as shrill – a woman, by the sound of it. Then another screamer, male this time, and another, and another. Within a few seconds, the corridor was filled with a wall of screams.

'Who is it?' shouted DI Routledge, leaning close so that Lilian could hear him. 'Who's doing this screaming? Can you see them?'

She was about to tell him that she could still only see Tim, who was wildly waving his arms around now. But then another green figure came bursting out of the bedroom doorway, its mouth dragged down like the Edvard Munch painting *The Scream*, and then another figure, and another. Within a few seconds, the end of the corridor was crowded with screaming green figures, and they continued to pour out of the bedroom, more and more of them.

DI Routledge had to bellow at the top of his voice so that Lilian could hear him. 'What in the name of *Jesus* is going on?'

The figures began making their way towards them now, pushing and jostling each other. It looked to Lilian as if they were all wearing military fatigues of some kind, and it was clear that all of them were wounded in one way or another. Some of them had no arms, so that they were swaying from side to side. Even more were lacking one or both legs, and were hobbling along on sticklike prosthetics.

The screaming was overwhelming. Even when Frank had summoned up his Army friends downstairs in the reception room, Lilian had never heard anything like this. It sounded like the choir from hell – a hideous cacophony of pain and pleading and rage. And she was terrified by the way in which the figures were all limping and lurching towards her. It looked as if the dead were pouring out of the world beyond to take their revenge on the living.

'We have to get out of here!' she shouted at DI Routledge. 'There's scores of them!'

'Show me! Let me see them!'

Lilian started to pull off the goggles but then she felt somebody snatching at the hem of her jacket. She swung her arm around to knock them away, and even though she couldn't see anybody, she felt a man's hand, as solid as if he were real.

'No time!' she gasped. 'David! Moses! Run! Let's get out of here! *Now!*'

David and Moses couldn't see the figures, either, but Lilian's panic was enough to start both of them running back along the corridor. DI Routledge put his arm around Lilian's shoulders and they ran together. She was panting by the time they reached the staircase, but he was clearly much fitter. She passed him the goggles and he fitted them over his head and looked back.

His reaction was immediate. 'Jesus Christ!' he burst out, and he seized Lilian's arm and pulled her towards the stairs. 'You two! Come on!'

The four of them started to clatter down the first flight of stairs, but they were not even halfway down when they heard another wave of screaming, and this was coming from the floor below. DI Routledge pulled the goggles over his eyes again and looked downwards.

'Oh, shit! There's more of them! And they're coming up!'

The next thing Lilian knew, somebody she couldn't see had seized the lapels of her jacket and pulled at them hard, so that she stumbled forward and lost her balance. She grabbed the banister rail to stop herself from falling, but she also collided with a man who wasn't there. She felt the buttons on his shirt and his belt buckle, and when she reached up to push him away, she could feel the prickly stubble on his jaw. His mouth was wide open and he was screaming, too. His lips were slippery with saliva.

The stairs were now crowded with invisible screaming figures. Lilian and David and Moses and DI Routledge looked as if they were performing some strange karate exercise as they struggled their way down towards the second-floor landing. They were bumped and elbowed and Moses lost his footing and fell down seven or eight stairs on his back.

None of them spoke. They were too caught up in wrestling with the men who were pushing them and pulling them and screaming in their faces, even though they couldn't see them. But although they kept tugging at her sleeves and even snatching at her hair, Lilian was able to force her way down between them until she reached the second-floor landing. She shouldered the invisible men aside and started to make her way down the next flight of stairs.

DI Routledge was close behind her, swinging his arms from side to side to beat off the men who were trying to grab his jacket, and both David and Moses were close behind him.

'They are not – they are not trying to hurt us!' Moses shouted.

'Then *what*?' DI Routledge shouted back, as he started down towards the first-floor landing.

'I have seen – I have seen this behaviour before! I saw it many times in Afghanistan!'

David pushed away an invisible man with both hands. 'For God's sake, who cares, let's just get out of here!'

'Do you not understand? They are hurting! They are in pain! They are desperate for somebody to take away their suffering!'

'Take away their suffering?' DI Routledge retorted. 'If I could, I would! But I don't have the faintest idea how, so all I want to do is get the hell out!'

From below them on the ground floor, they heard scores of people running across the hallway. The hurried tappity-tapping of crutches and prosthetic feet made them sound like pebbles being washed in by the tide.

'God almighty, they're everywhere!' exclaimed DI Routledge. 'The whole building's *teeming* with them!'

'What could you expect?' said Moses. He was twisting his arm around and around like a windmill so that an invisible man had to release his grip on his sweater. 'More than six hundred service personnel were seriously wounded in Afghanistan. Most of them ended up here! And it seems as if they are *still* here, whether they are dead or alive!'

They reached the ground floor. Although there was nobody visible in the hallway, Lilian could feel that it was jammed as tightly as a football crowd with screaming men, all of whom were staggering and lurching and bumping into each other, as well as trying to tug at her clothing. It was surreal, to be pushed and jostled from every side, and to be able to feel these men, as well as to be nearly deafened by their screaming, and yet to see nobody.

Behind her, DI Routledge and David and Moses were desperately fighting their way through the invisible throng, but it was apparent that Moses had been right, and that the men were not trying to hurt them, only clawing at them, begging to be relieved of their pain.

Lilian reached the front door and pulled down the handle, but the door refused to open, like it had before when she had been trapped. She pulled it again and again, but it still wouldn't budge.

'Here,' said DI Routledge, and he took hold of the handle himself. He yanked it as hard as he could, but he couldn't open the door either. At the same time, an invisible man gripped the collar of his jacket and tried to drag him backwards. David realised what was happening and stepped quickly forward to seize this invisible assailant and swing him away. To Lilian it looked as if he were doing nothing more than swinging his arms in a vigorous exercise routine, but she heard the man collide with another invisible man and then fall heavily on to the floor.

'The door's jammed!' she shouted. 'This happened to me before! Let's try the French windows in the drawing room!'

They struggled their way back through the screaming crowd and opened the drawing-room door. From the silence and the stillness inside, it seemed as if there were no invisible men in the drawing room, although they could feel four or five of them trying to force their way in behind them. David and Moses pushed them back and then slammed the door shut.

They could hear furious knocking and screaming that was even louder and even more pitiful, but David held on to the door handle to stop them from pulling it downwards.

'Go on,' he said. 'Go for the windows. I'll follow you as soon as you've opened them.'

Lilian crossed the drawing room and tried to open the French windows. Like before, though, they seemed to be jammed. She shook them and shook them, but they stayed shut.

'We'll have to do what I was going to do before – throw that chair through them.'

She turned around to point to the armchair. When she turned back, though, she was stunned to see Martin Slater standing a few yards away outside, between the rose beds. A gibbous moon had come out from behind the clouds, so she could make him out quite clearly. He had his arms folded and he was looking directly towards the hospital, so that he must have been able to see her behind the French windows.

She beat on the window with her fist and shouted out, 'Mr Slater! Mr Slater! Martin! Come here and open these windows, will you?'

DI Routledge came up close behind her. 'Who's that?' he asked her. 'That's not your gardener, is it? That fellow who keeps pulling a disappearing act every time we want to have a word with him?'

'That's him, yes. Martin Slater. I got locked in here before and somehow he was able to let me out.'

DI Routledge narrowed his eyes. 'I hate to say this, but he matches the description of a suspect we're very keen to interview. A fellow a lot like him was caught on CCTV at St Helier Hospital, and a witness who saw the remains at Tattenham Corner also noticed a man in a leather jerkin leaving the scene as if he was anxious to get away as quick as he could.'

'What? You mean where Tim's wallet was found?'

'Well, we don't know for certain if the deceased actually *was* your former husband, do we? On top of which, I've just seen him and heard him right here in this hospital – or some illusion of him, anyway.'

He stared at Martin Slater for a few more moments, but then he turned to Lilian.

'I'll tell you this much, Ms Chesterfield, after what we've been experiencing here this evening, I'm keeping a very open mind about a lot of things. That includes ghosts, or what might be passing for ghosts.'

Lilian banged on the window again. 'Mr Slater! *Mr Slater!* Come and let us out of here!'

Martin Slater must have heard her, but he gave no indication that he had, and when she banged yet again, he turned his back and walked off between the rose beds. Lilian watched in frustration and disbelief as he reached the end of the hospital building and disappeared.

'Thanks for *nothing*, chum,' said David, with his teeth clenched, because he had seen Martin Slater vanishing too. He was still gripping the door handle with both hands to stop the invisible horde outside from pulling it down. They continued to scream and howl and beat at the door, and they had split one of the lower panels where they had kicked it.

Moses dragged the armchair over to the French windows and said, 'Here, detective inspector, perhaps you can give me a hand. This chair weighs a ton.'

But DI Routledge took out his phone. 'Before we go smashing the windows in a listed building, let me see if I can get in touch with my colleagues at Epsom. We have some experts at breaking into locked properties, with the minimum of collateral damage, and they could be here in five minutes.'

'Well, make it as quick as you can,' said David. 'It's not going to be long before this lot come breaking in here.'

'As I said, I am sure that they are not out to hurt us,' said Moses.

'Maybe they're not, but people get crushed to death at pop concerts, don't they, even if nobody's out to hurt them.'

DI Routledge held up his phone and prodded at it, but then frowned and prodded at it again.

'It's dead,' he said. 'Do you want to try yours, Ms Chesterfield?'

There was an ear-splitting crack from the drawing-room door, which made Lilian jump. The screaming was at such a high pitch now that it sounded more like fifty circular saws all screeching at once. Lilian took out her phone and jabbed at it, but the screen of her phone was black too. She was starting to panic now. Her chest felt tight and she was panting.

'Mine's dead as well!' she shouted to DI Routledge.

Moses reached into his pocket for his phone, but it was the same. 'I know it is charged up, and it is switched on,' he said, shaking it hard. 'But I cannot even switch it off so that I can try to switch it on again.'

DI Routledge rattled the window handles again. The windows still refused to budge, so he barged into them with his shoulder, twice, and then he kicked them next to their lock, so hard that he staggered backwards. He couldn't even shake them.

'Right,' he said. 'I don't see we've got much choice. We'll just have to smash our way out.'

He went across and bent down to pick up one side of the armchair, while Moses bent down to pick up the other.

'All right, you ready? We'll take a short run and hit the windows with its legs, like a battering ram.'

They tilted the chair over backwards and adjusted their grip on it, and they were all ready to run towards the windows with it when Lilian said, '*Look!* Who's that?'

DI Routledge and Moses lowered the chair a little and peered out into the gardens. A man in a black hooded parka was walking quickly between the rose beds towards the windows. He came right up to the glass and pressed the palms of both hands against it, although his hood still obscured most of his face.

'Can you let us out? We're trapped in here!' Lilian shouted, gesturing that the windows wouldn't open from the inside.

The man nodded. He made no attempt to open the windows, but he stood back and roared out some words so loud that Lilian could clearly hear him through the glass. She could even hear him over the screaming of the invisible horde, who had now kicked out an entire door panel and were seconds away from breaking into the drawing room.

26

The hooded man stepped forward again, gripped the handles of both French windows and flung them wide apart.

Lilian immediately stepped out into the garden, followed by Moses and DI Routledge. David stayed by the door until the last possible moment, and then he ran across the drawing room and jumped out through the windows as if it were some kind of Olympic event.

The drawing-room door burst open, and even though they could see nobody at all, the screaming surged into the room in a tidal wave of ear-lacerating sound.

'Is this all of you?' the man shouted. His hood dropped back, and it was then that Lilian saw that it was Moses' Russian friend Artyom.

'Yes, Artyom, that is all,' said Moses, and between them they slammed the French windows shut and twisted the handles.

'What – what are you doing here?' Lilian asked Artyom. 'And how on *earth* did you open those windows? We were going to smash them open with that chair!'

The French windows shook violently as the invisible horde collided with them. Their screaming went on and on.

'Don't worry,' said Artyom. 'As I understand it, these

screamers have to stay inside the hospital building. They are trapped. That is the reason I came looking for you tonight, Moses. I have been doing more research into the Spirits of Pain and I am sure now who the screamers are – or *what* they are, rather than who. Plus I have found out very much more.'

Lilian and the others backed away between the rose beds. The invisible horde kept screaming and knocking against the glass, but it appeared as if Artyom was right, and they were unable to open the French windows and follow them outside into the gardens.

Artyom said, 'I went round to your house first, Moses. You are not the man of the month at home, I can tell you. Grace said that she was going to throw your dinner in the dustbin. I suggest that tomorrow you buy her a very large bunch of roses. She told me that you were here.'

'I'd still like to know how you opened those windows,' said DI Routledge.

'Aha! I have been researching how the Da Dard Rohonah keep the pain of their enemies trapped for all time, so that they will be forever discouraged from returning to Afghanistan.'

'Sorry – the who?'

'The Da Dard Rohonah, the Spirits of Pain. What they do is, they appoint one of their number to be a guardian, like a prison warden, if you like. That guardian can seal off any place where the pain of their enemies is being held captive – this hospital, for instance. Whenever the guardian wishes it, the doors and the windows can be suspended at a moment in time when they could not be opened. Do you understand what I am saying? You cannot open a door if that door is still in yesterday, and yesterday it was locked.'

'What? That sounds completely barmy to me,' said DI Routledge.

'These windows may have been suspended in time as long ago as yesterday, but even if they had only been suspended as they were an hour ago, say, or even less, you would still have been unable to open them.'

'All right, supposing for the sake of argument that really *was* the reason we couldn't get them open. How did *you* manage it?'

'I simply spoke the words that I saw in my research were necessary for breaking the spell. "*Kirkai kulava ka, Q'areen!*" Maybe I spoke them with a British accent, but they worked.'

'What do they mean?'

'They simply mean "open the window, Q'areen!" A Q'areen is what they call the guardian, because it means "double" or "doppelganger". Guardians are Spirits of Pain, but they will always take on the appearance of a human person, so that they can mingle with us and carry out their watch on their enemies without being suspected.'

'So who's the guardian here, at St Philomena's?'

'It could be anybody. It could be one of us.'

'Well, don't look at *me*,' said David.

All of them had been continuing to keep an eye on the French windows, but despite the persistent knocking and screaming, there was still no sign that the windows were going to be opened, and that the invisible horde might come flooding out. Then, quite suddenly, the knocking stopped, and the screaming died away, and there was silence.

They all looked at each other.

'What now?' asked David. 'Do we go back in, or what?'

'Sorry, but there's no way,' said DI Routledge. 'Until we can clear this building of whatever it is that's causing all this screaming and shoving and God knows what, I'm declaring the entire hospital a containment area. It would only need one of you to be pushed downstairs by that invisible mob and break your neck, and I'd be in deep trouble too, for negligence. Remember Hillsborough? Ninety-six football fans got crushed to death and the police got the blame for it.'

'But how are you going to clear them out?' asked Lilian. 'And how long do you think it's going to take? I can't spare you more than a day or two, if that.'

'It depends on what we're dealing with, Ms Chesterfield, doesn't it?'

'It's ghosts,' said David. 'How do you get rid of ghosts?'

'No, no, it isn't ghosts,' put in Artyom. 'We are *not* dealing with ghosts here. Not ghosts in the way that they are usually described, anyhow. Not the spirits of dead people. What we have here in this hospital is *pain*.'

'What exactly do you mean – pain?' asked DI Routledge.

'Anybody who has ever suffered agonising pain will tell you that it feels as if they are possessed by a separate person, a person like themselves but made entirely out of pain. And that is what I believe we have here. Many of the soldiers who were treated here died from their injuries, but their pain remains alive. Even those soldiers who survived and were moved away to the new hospital, they left their pain behind here, trapped in these wards and still screaming for relief. It is the pain from which the Da Dard Rohonah have made sure that they will never be free.'

'You've lost me now – lost me completely,' said DI Routledge. 'Windows that exist in the past and pain that can push you down the stairs? I mean, do me a favour!'

'Well, somebody or something was grabbing hold of us and pushing us down the stairs, wasn't it?' said David. 'And if it wasn't ghosts, what was it?'

Artyom said, 'You are so ready to believe in the miracles

that are described in the Bible – Jesus walking on water and feeding five thousand people with five loaves and two fishes and turning water into wine? It has been scientifically proven that physical objects can be moved by the power of the human mind. Why do you find it so hard to believe that the strongest of all human sensations might have its own independent existence?'

'I believe it,' said Lilian. 'I believe it now that I've seen it and felt it and heard it for myself. And I was the most sceptical person on the planet.'

'I believe it too,' said Moses.

'And me,' David added. 'Something was trying to kick down that drawing-room door, and it wasn't mice, I can tell you.'

DI Routledge looked around at all of them, and then back over to the French windows. 'I don't know,' he said grimly. 'I just don't know. I'll have to go back to the nick and have a serious think about what I'm going to do next. I'm not denying those screaming people exist. I saw them for myself and I felt them for myself and I heard them for myself.'

He lifted the night goggles off his head and handed them back to Lilian. 'Here – you'd better keep these for the moment, although we might well need them again. It's just a question of what these figures really are. Are they really nothing but pain, or are they some sort of technical trick? And if they *are* nothing but pain, how in the name of God do we get rid of them?'

'Maybe you are right, and you do get rid of them in the name of God,' said Moses. 'Maybe you simply pray.'

★ ★ ★

DI Routledge returned to Reigate police station, while Moses went home to face Grace, and David went home to his family too.

Lilian invited Artyom to come back to her house in Epsom so that she could ask him what more he knew about the Spirits of Pain, and if he had discovered any way in which the pain that was haunting St Philomena's could be exorcised.

She was feeling unreal, as if she were acting in a TV soap opera. She found it almost impossible to believe that she had seen that transparent figure of Tim begging her to relieve his agony, and that they had been pushed and jostled down the stairs by a crowd of screaming people who they couldn't see.

She was also finding it difficult to accept that the real Tim might have been found dead on Epsom racecourse. In the last few months of their relationship she had developed such a hatred of him that in one way she felt relieved that he was gone. At the same time, she remembered all the blissful days they had spent together when they had first been married – the holidays and the laughter and the lovemaking. It upset her to think that the Tim she had known in those days was now suffering excruciating pain.

'Would you like a drink?' she asked Artyom, as she switched on the lamps in her living room.

'Maybe a cup of tea, if it's not too much trouble.'

'I have some vodka that a Polish friend gave me, if you fancy something stronger.'

'I never drink when I'm driving. My older brother died because he was driving after drinking at his thirty-first birthday party.'

'Oh. I'm sorry.'

'He was killed instantly when his car went over the bridge

outside Khimki, and into the canal. I suppose I can be thankful that he doesn't have to put up with the same never-ending pain as those poor soldiers at St Philomena's.'

'I still can't get my head round what happened tonight. Thank God you came and opened those windows for us.'

Lilian lit the gas fire and Artyom sat down beside it, leaning forward and chafing his hands. 'Poor circulation,' he explained. 'Not a condition that you need to have if you live in Russia.'

'But you haven't, not for years, from what Moses told me.'

'I am a citizen of the world, that's why. My allegiance is not to one country or another, but to the human race. That is why I have always been so interested in the myths and legends of other cultures.'

Lilian went into her kitchenette, filled the electric kettle and switched it on. She could see herself reflected in the shiny blackness of the window, as if a ghost of Lilian were standing in the small yard outside. It wouldn't have surprised her if she had seen Tim's ghost standing beside her, with his arm around her waist, smiling at her from wherever he was now.

'What these Spirits of Pain do, that seems incredibly cruel,' she said, as she returned to the living room. 'These young soldiers, they didn't *ask* to be sent to Afghanistan, did they? Why should they have to suffer this endless pain, even after they're dead? Surely the ones who should be suffering most of the pain are the politicians and the generals who sent them there.'

'Unfortunately, it doesn't work that way. Before your pain can come to life and take on a separate existence, you have to be badly hurt. It's the young soldiers who had their legs blown off by roadside bombs and were hit by snipers. The politicians and the generals rarely got hurt in any way at all.'

'But my ex-husband, Tim, he's there, and he's in agony, but he was never in the Army and he's never been to Afghanistan.'

'That is what I found out when I was doing more research into the Spirits of Pain and that is what I was going to explain to you. The only way in which those young soldiers can escape from their pain is if they can manage to pass it on to somebody else. I believe that is what happened to your two surveyors. One soldier managed to transfer his pain into the body of your male surveyor—'

'Alex,' Lilian put in.

'—and another soldier who had been paralysed managed to pass his or her paralysis on to your female surveyor.'

'Charlie, as we called her. Charlene.'

'As far as I can understand the ancient texts that I have read about this, the soldiers who were able to pass on their pain and their paralysis to somebody else would have felt as if they were dying. Eternal darkness. But at least they would have been released from their suffering.'

'So the question is, Artyom, how do we release all the rest of them from their suffering without them passing it on to us?'

'It is not entirely clear from the texts that I read. It would seem that there is more than one way. I believe that if the guardian who has been appointed to look after the soldiers can be convinced that they will never try to return to Afghanistan, then he may at his own discretion release them from their pain.'

'But, like I said, my Tim has never been to Afghanistan in the first place. The furthest he's ever been abroad is Marbella, and he didn't like the food. He cut his holiday short and came home early.'

'Then perhaps the guardian can be persuaded to end his pain.'

'But we don't know who the guardian is, do we?'

'No, but we can try asking your Tim himself, to see if he knows. Or if not, we can try taking Tim out of the hospital and see if the guardian makes any attempt to stop us.'

'Detective Inspector Routledge says that we're not allowed to go back in there. Not until this is all sorted out.'

'It cannot be sorted out by policemen, Ms Chesterfield. Policemen deal in evidence and facts and what is generally considered to be reality. You heard that detective inspector. He has witnessed these phenomena for himself – actually *felt* them – and yet he is still prepared to consider that they might have been a clever technological illusion. If we are ever going to be able to relieve those soldiers of their pain, we will have to try and do it ourselves, using the same methodology by which they were trapped.'

'You said that there was more than one way.'

'There is a long incantation that can be recited, which is similar to the words that are spoken in a Roman Catholic exorcism. The problem is that it is all written in Avestan, which is a dead language derived from Pahlavi and Aramaic. It was last used by Zoroastrian priests in the sixth century, and I have absolutely no idea how to pronounce it.'

'And is that it?' asked Lilian, passing him a mug of tea. 'Do you take sugar?'

'There is something mentioned in one of my books about the Spirits of Pain that I didn't really understand at first. It's called The Greater Pain, or The Overwhelming. It is written in very obscure language, so you can interpret it in several different ways. But the essence of it seems to be that the pain that soldiers are still feeling after they have been wounded can be relieved or blotted out if somebody arrives in their vicinity who is suffering a pain that is even more severe than theirs.

'I suppose an analogy would be if a roomful of children were shouting and making an unholy noise, but then an adult came into the room and bellowed at them so loudly that he drowned them all out, and shocked them all into silence.'

Lilian thought for a moment, staring at the fire. 'You're saying that if somebody in St Philomena's was hurt even more than any of those soldiers had been hurt, then all the soldiers' pain would be – what's the word? – redeemed, is that it?'

'That's my understanding of it,' said Artyom. 'To put it another way, it's exactly the same principle as the Crucifixion of Christ, the Redeemer. One person suffers greater pain than everybody else around them, and as a consequence everybody else has their pain relieved.'

'From what you were saying earlier, I thought you didn't believe in the Bible.'

Artyom raised his mug to acknowledge what Lilian had said. 'A great deal of the Bible is absurd, of course. The Garden of Eden. The Ten Commandments. The Ascension. Jesus shot up into the sky like an Apollo rocket? I don't think so! But I accept that some of the stories have parallels in real events. And I'm not only talking about the Crucifixion. There are several mentions in ancient history books and religious texts of martyrs deliberately inflicting pain on themselves in order to relieve the pain of the people around them. And it has happened more recently, too, in Russia.'

'Really?'

'Oh yes, in 2020 a journalist called Irina Slavina burned herself to death, and in the time of the Great Schism of the

Russian Church in the seventeenth century, entire villages of Old Believers killed themselves by self-immolation. It was called "fire baptism" or *soshigateli*. Sometimes they burned only their arms or their hands to imitate the pain that Christ felt on the cross so that they would ease the pain of everybody around them.'

'Do you really think that's possible?'

'I couldn't say. I have to confess I wouldn't have believed that *any* of what you've been experiencing at St Philomena's was possible – not until Moses got in touch with me again and told me about it.'

Lilian said, 'I suppose we could try the first option… seeing if we can find the guardian and persuading him to let them all go. Or at least to let Tim go.'

Artyom finished his tea and put down his mug. 'I agree that would be a good start. You still have the keys to get in, I imagine? And even if we get locked in, in the same way that you did this afternoon, at least I know the words that will let us out.'

Lilian looked over at the clock on the mantelpiece. 'You're not thinking that we should go back there now?'

'The sooner the better, before the police start turning the whole place upside down.'

'But what if we do find the guardian, and he says no, he won't let them go?'

'Then I really don't know. There's no mention of anything like that in any of the texts that I've been reading, or of who or what the guardians actually are. What if we find him, and he turns out to be a she?'

'Then God help us.'

27

When they reached St Philomena's, they found that a tape had been tied across the slope that led up to the driveway, which said *Police Line Do Not Cross*, but that there were no officers on guard. It was only a containment area, after all, not a crime scene. Artyom climbed out of the car and lifted the tape so that Lilian could drive underneath it.

The moon had gone down now behind the trees so St Philomena's was pitch dark, although there was a faint radiance in the sky to the north-east where the forensic lamps were still shining over the racecourse at Tattenham Corner.

Lilian had brought a torch, and she was carrying Frank's night goggles in a plastic carrier bag. Artyom switched on the flashlight on his phone.

'They were supposed to come and reconnect the electricity today, but I don't know if they'll be allowed to now,' said Lilian, as she unlocked the front door. 'It would be a huge help if they could.'

Artyom flicked his flashlight around the hallway. 'Perhaps if we find a way to give all these poor soldiers relief from their pain, we can return this hospital to normal.'

'Do you really believe we can?'

'If Catholic priests can really exorcise demons from people who are supposed to be possessed, I don't see why we can't do something similar here. What has been done to these soldiers comes from a belief system that is far older than Christianity.'

Lilian stopped in the middle of the hallway and listened. She could hear the usual creaking of floorboards and the scuttling of rats or squirrels, as well as the soft persistent knocking of doors that were caught in a draught.

'I've been wracking my brains trying to think who the guardian might be. At first I thought the most likely candidate was Martin Slater, the gardener. He appears and disappears almost like a stage magician and he says the most extraordinary things. But he's been working here since long before we went to war in Afghanistan, so I don't see how he could be.

'Then I thought of Marion Crosby, who runs that hospice for injured veterans. One of the men she was supposed to be looking after has been killed, Frank Willard, although the police haven't yet told us how he died. Frank was the one who showed us all the soldiers who still haunt St Philomena's, using his night goggles. His Army friends, he called them. If Marion Crosby *is* the guardian, perhaps she was angry with him because he did that. You said yourself that the guardian could be a woman.'

'I was only speculating,' said Artyom. 'For all I know, the guardian could be an animal – a dog, or a rabbit, or even a crow.'

Lilian shone her torch up the staircase. 'I saw Tim upstairs, on the third floor. I suppose we should start up there.'

'Moses said that they might have pushed you and pulled you, but they didn't seem to be out to hurt you.'

'It didn't feel as if they were trying to hurt us, but we could have tripped and fallen downstairs, or they could literally have crushed us. They were invisible, but they felt as heavy as real men. They weren't the sort of ghosts you see in films, who can walk through walls.'

Lilian had only just put her foot on the first stair when they heard a high agonised scream. She froze, and turned to Artyom. 'That came from the kitchen, I'm sure of it.'

Before Artyom could say anything, they heard another scream, and another, and another, one staccato scream after another, '*Ah! Ah! Ah! Ah!*'

Artyom headed for the archway, and Lilian followed him. When he threw open the kitchen door, the screaming went on, even though it appeared in the first split second as if there was nobody there, and the kitchen was empty.

But then Lilian saw that two drawers had been pulled out of the dresser and that knives and forks and spatulas had once more been scattered across the floor. Then, to her horror, she saw that a ten-inch carving knife was stabbing itself repeatedly into the pinewood tabletop. Nobody visible was holding it, yet it was stabbing into the table again and again, and each time it stabbed, there was a scream.

'*Who's there?*' she demanded, although she was so frightened she was almost squealing. 'I said, *who's there?*'

She rummaged in her plastic shopping bag and pulled out the night goggles. Artyom was holding his phone up high so that the area around the table was brightly lit, and he was waving it very slowly from side to side. She could see by the red dot on it that he was video-recording.

She fitted the night goggles on her head and switched them on.

'Oh God, Artyom! There's somebody here! He's a soldier and he's stabbing his own hand!'

Through the night goggles she could see a glowing green figure. He had short-cropped bristly hair and he was wearing a flak jacket. She couldn't make out what age he might be, but he was short and solidly built. He had laid his left hand palm upwards on the top of the kitchen table and he was stabbing it again and again with such ferocity that he looked to Lilian like a man determined to kill a large crab.

'Who are you?' she shouted at him. 'I can see you, so there's no point in your thinking that I can't!'

The soldier stopped in mid-stab, with the carving knife upraised. To Artyom, the knife appeared to be floating unsteadily in mid-air.

The soldier looked around at Lilian, and must have been able to see that she was wearing night observation goggles.

'What do you care?' he asked her. His voice sounded muffled, as if he were wearing a mask.

'I'm trying to stop every soldier in this hospital from hurting,' she told him. Then, 'Why are you stabbing yourself like that?'

The soldier held up his left hand. The skin was ragged, where he had stabbed himself ten or eleven times, but there was no visible sign of blood dripping down his wrist or on to the table.

'I was told that I needed to feel more pain than I was feeling already.'

'Who told you that?'

'An old man in a bazaar in Kandahar. He told fortunes as well. He told me I was never going to have children. I mocked him when he said that, because me and the missus we had just got married and we were dead set on a boy and a girl.'

'It's amazing,' said Artyom. 'I can hear him. I can hear every word. But I can't see him at all... only that knife, hanging in the air.'

The soldier laid the carving knife down on the table.

'Oh Christ, I can't tell you how much it hurts,' he said, in that muffled voice, bending forward and cupping both hands around his groin. 'It was a sniper. Once in the shoulder and once between the legs. He shot me only two days after that old man told me that I would never have children. And he warned me that the pain would last forever, and it has.'

'But he told you that if you could hurt yourself even more – then what?' Artyom asked him.

The soldier nodded. 'He said that if I could hurt myself even more than I was hurting already, or if I could hurt somebody else even more than *I* was hurting, then it would all be over. My pain would come to an end. Believe me, I've tried again and again. But I haven't been able to hurt myself enough, and I couldn't bring myself to hurt any of my friends as much as this.'

'What is your name?'

'Kenneth Blackmore. Lieutenant Ken Blackmore, Yorkshire Regiment.'

'Do you understand what has happened to you?' said Artyom. 'Do you know that you are being punished by the spirits who guard Afghanistan from foreign invasions?'

'All I know is that I'm in constant agony, twenty-four hours a day. Even if I stopped hurting I wouldn't go back to Afghanistan, not if you gave me ten million quid. I never want to see that country again as long as I live.'

'Are you aware that there is probably somebody who is watching over you and your fellow soldiers in this hospital? Somebody rather like a prison warden in a way. A guardian. They will appear to be a normal person but they will be possessed by one of the spirits that the Afghans call the Spirits of Pain.'

'All I'm aware of is pain.'

'We are going to try and find this guardian and see if we can get him to agree to put an end to your pain,' said Lilian. 'Him, or her. You have no idea yourself who it might be?'

Lieutenant Blackmore shook his head. 'All I know is pain. You see this hand? You see what I've done to it? But it doesn't hurt half as much as where my balls used to be.'

Lilian took off the night goggles and passed them to Artyom. He fitted them on and stood staring at Lieutenant Blackmore, partly in disbelief and partly in sympathy. It was obvious that he could think of nothing more to say to him, because he took the goggles off again and said, 'We need to go and look for your Tim, Lilian. Perhaps he can help us.'

Lilian held up her hand. 'Lieutenant Blackmore? Can you hear me? We have to leave you now, but I promise you that we're going to be doing everything we can to bring an end to your pain.'

'I tried to kill myself,' said Lieutenant Blackmore's voice out of thin air. 'I tried to cut my throat, and I sliced my Adam's apple in half, but nothing happened. Sometimes I wonder if I'm dead already, but I'm hurting so fucking badly that I must be alive. How could I feel like this if I was dead?'

That was a question that neither Lilian nor Artyom could answer. They left the kitchen, walked out through the archway and crossed over to the staircase.

Before they started to climb the stairs, Lilian stopped and said to Artyom, 'This is insanity, isn't it? Can you really believe that we're doing this? I can't. My ex-husband is supposed to be lying dead on Epsom racecourse and I'm going upstairs in a derelict hospital to talk to him.'

'You don't have to,' said Artyom. 'You could simply walk out of here now and never come back.'

'How can I? How could I ever drive past St Philomena's

again, knowing that he's still here, and that he's in everlasting agony? How could I leave all of these soldiers, all suffering pain that never ends? Apart from that, it would mean the end of my career with Downland and probably the end of my career full stop.'

They started to climb up to the third floor. When she paused on the second landing to catch her breath, Lilian was sure she could feel tension in the air, as if the hospital *knew* that she and Artyom had come here tonight, and why.

'What's wrong?' Artyom asked her.

'I don't know. It's almost as if we were being watched.'

'Perhaps we are. These soldiers are invisible, after all.'

'I always thought that when you were dead, you were dead, and that was the end of it.'

'Energy can neither be created nor destroyed. Perhaps we've discovered what ghosts actually are. Pain is energy, after all, and perhaps that energy has continued to exist, even when the physical body has decayed, or been burned to ashes.'

'I'm just wondering why Tim's here. That's if he is still here.'

'Well, let's go up and find out, shall we?'

They climbed up the last flight. Lilian put on Frank's night goggles again, and they began to walk along the corridor to the doorway where she had last seen Tim. Artyom held her arm to steady her.

'Tim!' she called out, as she neared the end bedroom. 'Tim! Are you there? It's Lilian, Tim! I've come to get you!'

'Any sign of him?' asked Artyom. 'Or anybody?'

'Not so far. If they came out, I'd be able to see them, so they must be hiding. I'm just wondering why. They seem to know that we could help them. They were crowding round us this afternoon before you managed to get us out of here, and it was like they were begging us for help. So where are they now?'

She stopped at the last bedroom door. It was half ajar, so she reached out and pushed it wide open. She shone her torch inside and Artyom raised his phone. There was nobody inside that they could see.

'Tim?' Lilian repeated. 'Tim, are you there? Is anybody there?'

Artyom said loudly, 'If there is any soldier who can hear us, why don't you show yourselves? We are trying to find a way to end your suffering.'

They waited, but all they could hear was the draught that was flowing softly through the wards and along the corridors, as if the whole building were breathing.

'Perhaps we're wasting our time,' said Artyom. 'Perhaps they're sleeping, and we can't see them when they're sleeping. Perhaps they sleep as much as they can, because they can't feel their pain when they're asleep.'

'That Lieutenant Blackmore down in the kitchen, he was awake.'

'Yes, but he told us that he was trying to feel as much pain as possible.'

Lilian took another look inside the bedroom. 'Tim?' she called out, one last time.

Artyom took her arm again. 'Come on,' he said. 'Let's leave it for now. I'll go back to my research material. Perhaps I can find out if there are any other ways to give these poor spirits some peace.'

They started to walk back along the corridor. Lilian was

about to lift off the night goggles when she heard a voice behind her.

'*Lil! Lilian!* Don't leave me, Lil! Where are you going?'

Both she and Artyom turned around, bumping into each other. Standing outside the bedroom door was Tim, or the glowing green image of Tim. Although Lilian couldn't make out the expression on his face, she could see that his shoulders were drooping, like a man who has given up all hope.

'He's there?' said Artyom.

'Yes, he's there!' Lilian told him. She twisted her arm free and walked quickly back to the end of the corridor. 'Tim! You have to come with us! We're going to try and get you out of here!'

She reached out her hand, and the green image of Tim reached out his hand too, and she actually felt it, as if it were his real hand. She could even feel his wedding ring, which he had never taken off, even after they were divorced, and which DI Routledge had shown her as evidence that he was dead.

'This is Artyom,' said Lilian, tugging Tim along the corridor. It felt no different from tugging any real hesitant man to meet a friend, and she could even hear his shoes scuffing on the floor.

Artyom held out his hand too, although Tim to him was invisible. Lilian guided Tim's hand towards Artyom's, and the two of them clasped hands together, firmly, reaching from one dimension into another. Lilian thought that it was like Artyom reaching into a swimming pool to save Tim from drowning.

'Listen to me, Tim,' said Artyom, keeping his grip on Tim's hand. 'Do you know who your guardian is? The person who watches you all?'

'My guardian? I don't know what you mean,' said Tim's disembodied voice.

'Is there somebody who's here at the hospital all the time, keeping an eye on you?'

'No… I don't think so. I haven't seen anybody. But then I haven't seen anything much. I've been in too much pain. I can't even think straight, I've been hurting so much.'

'Where does it hurt, Tim?' Lilian asked him.

'My knees. Both my knees. They feel like all the bones are grinding together.'

'When did it start?'

'When I came here to see you, for the rent money.'

'What happened?'

'I was looking around, that's all. Oh Jesus, Lil, I can't even begin to tell you how much it hurts! There was this soldier… he was standing in the corridor. I said something like hallo to him but I don't remember the rest. All I remember is opening my eyes and I was lying in that bedroom and I felt as if my legs had been chopped off at the knees.'

Artyom looked at Lilian. 'It sounds like that soldier passed his pain on to your Tim somehow. Perhaps that was what happened to your two surveyors, or something similar.'

'But what can we do for him now? I thought you said that none of the people who were haunting St Philomena's could step outside. They didn't follow us, did they, when you opened the drawing-room windows for us?'

'Oh Jesus, Lil,' moaned Tim, and slowly sank to his knees, although Artyom held on to his hand.

'He's in so much pain, Artyom, we have to do something. But if we can't find the guardian to stop him from hurting—?'

'We take him outside.'

'But if we *can't* take him outside?'

'We take him outside,' Artyom repeated. Then he lowered his voice and leaned towards Lilian and said, 'Haven't you heard of mercy killing?'

Lilian looked down at the luminous green image of Tim kneeling on the floor beside her. He was Tim but he wasn't Tim. If DI Routledge was right, and Tim's wallet and wedding ring were almost indisputable evidence that he *was* right, then the real Tim had lost his life on the racecourse. So who or what was this man? Was he Tim's spirit, or his soul, or nothing more than his capacity to feel pain, which had been hijacked by a wounded soldier who wanted to pass his own agony on to somebody else?

If that was all he was, then wouldn't it be kinder to take him outside and end it for him?

For a moment, looking down at him kneeling on the floor, Lilian pictured Tim kneeling next to the tiny white coffin in which their stillborn daughter, Ruth, had been lying, and she thought of the anguish that he must have been feeling then. And now he was going through this.

'I don't know, Artyom. I don't know if I have the nerve to do it. I don't know if I have the moral authority to do it.'

'Then you must leave him here, to suffer for all time, along with all the soldiers who suffer here too. Although I don't know how you're going to be able to develop this hospital into luxury flats, if we can't get rid of them, or give them relief.'

'I won't be able to, will I? I'll just have to walk away from it. But it's not the development that I'm worried about right now. It's how I'm going to be able to abandon all these wounded men. They may be alive or they may be dead. They may be real or they may be nothing but some sort of energy, like you say. But how am I going to live with myself knowing that they're all still here, screaming with pain, for ever?'

Artyom lifted his right fist, which was still holding Tim's fist.

'Then we take him outside? Yes?'

Lilian swallowed, and then nodded. 'Yes. I don't see what else we can do.'

'Tim?' said Artyom, lifting his fist even higher. 'You need to get up on your feet now, Tim. We're going to make you feel better.'

'What – what are you going to do? I don't know how anybody can make me feel better.'

'Get up on your feet and we'll show you.'

Tim looked up at Lilian. 'Lil? Are you really going to save me? I can't take much more of this pain, I swear to God.'

Lilian's night goggles were filled with dancing green tears. 'Yes, Tim, we're really going to save you.'

Between them, Lilian and Artyom helped Tim to stand. He groaned and sucked in his breath with every movement. Once he was upright, Artyom wrapped his arm around him and helped him to shuffle further along the corridor towards the staircase. Lilian took off her night goggles to wipe her eyes, and when she did, the green image of Tim disappeared. All she could see was Artyom making his way carefully downwards, one step at a time, with his right arm held out horizontally.

They had reached the second-floor landing and they were starting to climb down the next flight of stairs when Lilian heard brisk footsteps coming up from the hallway, *chip-chip-chip*, like someone in a hurry. The next thing she knew, Martin Slater appeared below them on the first-floor landing.

He stopped and looked up at them, his fists planted defiantly on his hips.

'What the hell do you think you're doing?' he challenged them.

'I could ask you the same question, Mr Slater,' Lilian retorted. 'You're the gardener. Actually, you're not even the gardener any more. Who gave you permission to come inside?'

'I'm much more than the gardener, madam. I'm the caretaker, too. Employed to take care of this hospital both outside and in.'

'No, you're not. Not by us. And this is no longer a hospital. I thought I'd made that clear enough to you before. I suggest you leave here immediately and don't come back, not for any reason. I'll also have you know that the police are very keen to talk to you, so if you don't go now I'll call them and tell them that you're here.'

'You don't understand, do you? Your company may have the deeds to St Philomena's, but you'll never own it.'

'Oh, I think we do understand, sir,' said Artyom. He was leaning against the banister rail to help him to support Tim's sagging weight. 'Perhaps we don't understand everything. But if you're the guardian here, then it's all beginning to make sense.'

'Where are you going with that man?' Martin Slater demanded.

'How do you know I'm going anywhere with any man?'

'Where are you taking him?'

'You can see him?'

'Of course I can see him. And I know who he is. Or who he *was*, rather.'

'You *are* the guardian, aren't you?' said Artyom. His voice was trembling with emotion, and his Russian accent was even more pronounced. 'You're not the gardener, nor the caretaker. Perhaps you were once. But now you're the one appointed by Da Dard Rohonah, aren't you? You're the one appointed to make sure these poor souls go on feeling the pain that they suffered in Afghanistan, and that they go on feeling it for ever.'

Artyom heaved his hip up sideways. Although Tim was invisible, it was obvious that his legs were buckling and that he was sliding out of Artyom's grasp.

'Look at you,' he said to Martin Slater. 'You know exactly what I'm talking about, don't you? If you really *were* the gardener, you would be baffled. But you're not, are you? You're one of them. One of the Spirits of Pain.'

'Let that man go,' said Martin Slater. 'He deserves to be punished like they all deserve to be punished.'

'This man was not even a soldier.'

'He carries a soldier's pain. That's enough. Now let him go.'

'I come from Russia, my friend. I served in Afghanistan, and I still have nightmares about it. I know how many of my countrymen are still suffering from their service there.'

'So? You shouldn't have tried to take over a sacred land that didn't belong to you. It's as simple as that.'

Artyom turned to Lilian. 'Let's go,' he said, and gave another heave to secure his grip across Tim's shoulders. Then he continued to make his way to the first-floor landing, and Lilian could hear Tim's shoes knocking loosely against the treads as Artyom helped him to stagger downwards.

'I'm warning you, don't bring him down any further,' said Martin Slater.

'Oh yes? Or what will you do? I may not be as young as I was, but I can still pack a punch.'

'I said, don't bring him down any further.'

'You have no authority here, whatever you are, human or spirit. Now, let me past, will you?'

Martin Slater took a step sideways to block off the last flight of stairs that led down to the hall.

'Let go of him,' he said, and his voice was as cold as his eyes.

Still supporting Tim with his right hand, Artyom tried to push Martin Slater out of his way with his left.

'*Artyom*,' Lilian cautioned him, because she sensed that something serious was going to happen – maybe that Martin Slater would push Artyom down the stairs, or produce some gardening tool and stab him with it.

But Martin Slater simply lifted his hands and spoke some words and Artyom exploded. With the loudest bang that Lilian had ever heard, he burst apart. His head was blown off and went spinning through the air, over the banisters and down to the hall, where it bounced again and again before it disappeared through the archway. His arms flew upwards so that his hands clapped together before they tumbled down the stairs. His chest blew open in a blizzard of rags and shattered ribs, and all his internal organs were blasted across the landing in soggy lumps, tangled with spiderwebs of connective tissue.

Even Martin Slater himself didn't escape the explosion. The knees of his trousers were soaked dark red with blood and a glistening coil of small intestine had wrapped itself around one of his boots.

Lilian was so shocked and deafened that for a moment she could do nothing but stand halfway down the stairs with her mouth open, unable to move and unable to speak. At first she thought that Tim must have blown up too, but then she saw what looked like the blood-spattered outline of a man crawling across the landing. It was moaning, and she realised it must be Tim, although it was impossible to tell without putting on her night goggles if he had been badly injured, and if the blood with which he was spattered was his, or Artyom's, or a mixture of both.

All Lilian knew was that she had to get out of there, and as fast as she could. She clattered down to the first-floor landing, dodging around Martin Slater, although he made no attempt to stop her. The soles of her shoes skidded on the blood that coated the floorboards and she almost fell down the stairs that led to the hall, but she managed to seize the banister rail and steady herself.

Once she had reached the hall, she didn't look back to see if Martin Slater was coming after her. She ran towards the front door, praying that it would open, and when it did, and she stumbled out on to the porch, she let out a little scream of relief.

She crossed over to her car, flung open the door and scrambled in. In her panic, she dropped the keys on the floor, and she had to search blindly beneath her seat before she found them. Then she started the engine and drove out of St Philomena's in a slew of shingle. When she reached the police tape, she sped straight through it, snapping it in half.

She drove recklessly fast along the narrow twisting road that led to the racecourse, around the grandstand, and along to Tattenham Corner. The track was still lit up by LED lamps and there were still two police cars parked there, as well as a van from the forensic investigation unit.

Lilian slid her car to a stop beside the railings, climbed out and ran across the track to the blue forensic tent. Two uniformed police officers and a plain-clothes detective were standing outside talking, and the detective was holding open the tent flap so that he could watch what the forensic investigators were doing inside.

'Sorry, ma'am,' said one of the uniformed officers, stepping forward with his hand raised. 'This is a restricted area.'

'There's been a fatality,' Lilian panted. 'A man's just been killed at St Philomena's Hospital – or what used to be St Philomena's Hospital.'

'Killed? How? What's happened?'

'An explosion. Well, like an explosion. The man who died was Artyom Something. I can't remember his surname but he's Russian. I'm in charge of renovating the hospital and he was helping me to check it for safety.'

'So what kind of an explosion are we talking about?' asked the detective. 'Gas, or what?'

'I don't know. I don't know what caused it. I need to speak to Detective Inspector Routledge. He's been investigating some of the trouble we've been having at St Philomena's.'

The detective looked at his watch. 'He'll be off duty by now, ma'am. Can I ask you for your name?'

'Lilian Chesterfield. I work for Downland Developments.'

'Oh, then I know who you are. We've had a briefing about St Philomena's – about the human bones that were found there, and about possible trespassing and vandalism. And I'm afraid to say we have reason to believe that the remains inside this tent are those of your husband.'

'Yes, Detective Inspector Routledge has already told me. He showed me his wallet, and his ring. Actually, he was my former husband. We were divorced.'

'Divorced or not, ma'am, I don't think you want to see what's left of him.'

28

'Here we are, Barry,' said Audrey, opening the oven door with her quilted oven gloves. 'Your favourite! Steak and mushroom pie!'

'Blimey, what's the special occasion?' asked DI Routledge. 'Don't tell me I've forgotten some anniversary!'

'No,' smiled Audrey. 'You've been so wound up these past few days, and you've only been picking at your food, so I thought you deserved a treat. There's a bottle of Malbec in the dining room if you feel like some wine with your pie.'

DI Routledge climbed down from his kitchen stool. 'It's all this how's-your-father at St Philomena's that's been getting to me, love.'

'Come on, darling. You said yourself that it's probably somebody playing some really clever trick.'

'I'm sorry. I promised you I'd never bring my work home. But these particular cases, they're driving me absolutely nuts.'

'I'm not surprised. All those spooky noises and weird figures flitting about and feeling like you were being pushed.'

'It's those five fatalities, too, even the four that happened at St Helier's. They all seem to be connected with St Philomena's in some way, but God knows how. Ever since their bodies were brought in, we've had two of the best forensic pathologists at

East Surrey working on their autopsies but they still can't make head nor tail of how they died.'

He came up to her, laid his hand on her shoulder, and kissed the back of her neck. 'It's at times like these that I really need you and a steak and mushroom pie. Well – I need you much more than the steak and mushroom pie.'

'You don't have to have any if you're not hungry.'

'Are you joking? Let me go and fetch the wine.'

He was returning from the dining room with the bottle of Malbec when his phone chimed the Bell Tower tone.

'Don't answer it,' said Audrey, who had already started to cut the pie. 'Tonight, you're not here. You're – you're entertaining the kids at the Children's Trust, dressed as Coco the Clown. At least, that's what you can tell Leonard tomorrow, if he asks.'

DI Routledge gave her a sad little shake of his head and picked up his phone. 'Routledge,' he said. He listened, expressionless, even when Audrey was silently mouthing, '*Who is it?*'

After a while, he said, 'When? I see. So where is she now? And have you organised the bomb disposal squad? And forensics? Okay. Yes. And you're there now? Okay. I'll see you in ten.'

When he had finished his call, he turned to Audrey. She had already stopped slicing and put down her knife.

'It's another fatality, and this time it's actually taken place at St Philomena's,' he told her. 'You can reheat that pie tomorrow, though, can't you?'

'I'll have to, won't I? There isn't a pie in the world that's anywhere near as important as a murder.'

★★★

He turned into the driveway of St Philomena's and parked behind the three squad cars and two unmarked cars that had already arrived.

Seven uniformed officers in yellow high-vis jackets were gathered around the porch. He found DS Woods, DC Merrick and DC Lakhani sitting in one of the unmarked cars, talking to Lilian. He knocked on the car window and they all climbed out.

'I'm sorry to meet you again in such tragic circumstances, Ms Chesterfield,' he told her.

'I still can't believe it,' said Lilian. 'Look at me! I'm still shaking from head to foot.'

'Do you think you can tell me about it? I imagine you've already spoken to my colleagues here.'

'She's given us a pretty clear idea of what happened,' said DS Woods. 'A male was killed in a serious explosion, almost identical to the explosions that occurred at St Helier's and down the road here at that hospice.'

'And I can tell you who did it, although I have no idea how he did it. It was Martin Slater, the gardener.'

'That fellow in the leather jerkin? The one we saw out in the garden when we got stuck inside?'

'Yes. And the man who was killed, that was Artyom, the Russian man who opened the French windows for us. He and I were looking around the hospital, trying to see if we could find out what's really going on here.'

'Ms Chesterfield has given us a good facial description of this Martin Slater,' said DS Woods. 'We'll be putting out a tweet and an APW.'

DI Routledge turned back to Lilian. 'You heard me say loud and clear, didn't you, that for the time being St Philomena's is a restricted area? You knew that you shouldn't have gone back inside?'

Lilian looked away and didn't answer. She wasn't going to admit to DI Routledge that she had been attempting to save Tim from an eternity of pain. It would have sounded like madness, considering the dead body that had been found on Epsom racecourse was almost certainly Tim.

The forensics van arrived, followed closely by a car. As soon as the driver stepped out of the car, DI Routledge recognised him from his high grey quiff as Dr Richard Horner, one of Surrey's top forensic pathologists.

'Detective Inspector *Routledge*!' he called out in a booming voice as he approached. 'I've been informed that we have something of a mess here!'

'I haven't seen it for myself yet,' DI Routledge told him. 'But apparently it's similar to the two incidents we had at St Helier's and just along the road here at Downlea. An adult male, blown up by some sort of explosion. The bomb squad'll be here in a minute to carry out reconnaissance and check if it's safe to go inside.'

'I don't usually examine bodies *in situ*, as you know,' said Dr Horner. 'But after those last two explosive fatalities I thought it essential that I should be able to see where all the bits ended up. Neither of the last two collections of remains bore any trace of reactive substances, so maybe the splatter pattern of this victim will give me some clue as to how he was killed.

'By the way,' he said, reaching into the inside pocket of his tweed overcoat, 'I'm pleased you're here this evening. I was going to be sending you an email tomorrow morning about the skeleton that was found here at St Philomena's.'

'Oh yes?' said DI Routledge distractedly. Another van had arrived from forensic services, as well as another squad car.

'Yes, we've been able to make a positive identification. It was the trowel that was found along with the bones that gave us the vital clue. It carried DNA that we were able to match with other gardening tools in the shed here, and with the bones themselves.'

Dr Horner took out an envelope and unfolded a sheet of paper. 'Apart from that, the left femur had healed from a complicated and unusual fracture, and when we checked with NHS medical records we were able to find out when and where the operation to repair that fracture had been carried out, and the name of the patient.'

He licked his thumb and unfolded a second sheet of paper. 'His name was Martin Jeremy Slater, and judging by the condition of his bones he was buried approximately seven years ago, at the age of forty-six. He lived at The Old Cottage, Downlea Wood, and he was employed here as a gardener, and had been for eleven years.'

Lilian had been listening to what Dr Horner was saying, and when she heard that she stepped up to him and DI Routledge.

'That can't be right. Martin Slater is still alive, and he's still working here as a gardener, even though we've told him that he's not employed by us, and we haven't been paying him.'

'He's also our prime suspect,' said DI Routledge. 'We have every reason to believe he may be responsible in some way for those two fatalities at St Helier, and the fatality that's occurred here tonight. He was here with Ms Chesterfield when the victim was killed.'

'Perhaps he had a twin,' said Dr Horner, tucking his papers

back in his pocket. 'But I can assure you beyond a shadow of a doubt that the skeleton *was* Martin Jeremy Slater, the same Martin Jeremy Slater who worked as the gardener here.'

'*A doppelganger*,' Lilian whispered. '*A Q'areen.*'

'Sorry, madam, what did you say?' asked Dr Horner, cupping one hand to his ear.

'Let's not jump to any conclusions,' said DI Routledge. 'Not until we've had the chance to look inside.' But then he turned to DS Woods. 'The Old Cottage, Downlea Wood, Andy. Send Merrick and a uniform to check who's living there now, and if they have any idea what happened to Martin Slater, and when he stopped living there.'

Lilian started to shiver again.

'Why don't you take yourself off home?' said DI Routledge. 'You've had enough for one night, I would have thought. Maybe you can drop down to Reigate police station tomorrow morning and we can talk this over some more.'

'No,' Lilian told him. 'I'll stay for a while.' She had the strongest feeling that if she went home now, she would never be able to come back here again. She was already beginning to feel that after Artyom's grisly death, her career in property development was all but over. She also knew that even if she went home, she wouldn't be able to sleep. Artyom's head would be spinning through her nightmares for months to come.

'Well, whatever,' said DI Routledge. 'But why don't you go and sit in your car and warm yourself up? Asma – keep her company, would you?'

Lilian went over and sat in her own car with DC Lakhani, while DI Routledge and the other detectives talked to Dr Horner.

DC Lakhani shook her head and said, 'I have never seen

Inspector Routledge so frustrated. He has such a g[
record for closing cases – better than almost any oth[
senior officer in Surrey. Hercule Routledge, that's what they
call him, because he's always so logical, do you know what
I mean?'

'I don't think there's any logical explanation for what's been
going on here,' said Lilian. She was staring at St Philomena's,
watching in case faces appeared at the upstairs windows,
or flickering lights. But the hospital building remained in
darkness, as if it were refusing to reveal to anybody what had
happened inside.

At last, two white vans from the Royal Logistics Corps
turned up, and four bomb disposal technicians climbed out.
They strapped themselves into their blastproof suits while
DI Routledge and DS Woods briefed the young lieutenant
in charge of the team about what they could expect to find
inside.

'Are you all right?' DC Lakhani asked Lilian. 'I can see that
you're still shivering.'

'All right? I don't think I'm ever going to be all right again.
I can't stop myself from thinking what they're going to find.'

'I didn't see it myself and I hope I don't have to. I saw a dog
run over last week and I couldn't eat for two days after that.'

The EOD technicians went in through the hospital's front
door, leaving it open. Lilian could see their flashlights criss-
crossing the panelled hallway. It was impossible for her not
to picture Artyom's severed head, lying against the skirting
board. He had stared up at her as she ran past it, his eyes
open, but frowning slightly, as if he had been asking her,
*Where are you going in such a hurry? Why are you leaving
me here?*

The technicians had only been inside for two or three

..utes when Lilian heard screaming. It was so loud that she ..uld hear it through her closed car window. She opened her ..oor and climbed out, and as she did so the four technicians came bustling out of the hallway, bumping into each other. They ran out on to the drive as if they were being chased by a bear.

Even though the technicians were all wearing helmets that could absorb acoustics as well as blast, they were pressing their hands to the sides of their heads, and as soon as she stepped out of her car Lilian did the same. The screaming sounded as if a whole chorus of agonised voices was being amplified to stadium level. It reached such a pitch that both windows at the sides of the porch cracked from side to side, and one of them fell out.

DI Routledge came over to Lilian with his fingers in his ears. 'Who the hell is making that noise?' he shouted at her. 'Do you have any idea?'

Lilian shook her head. What was she going to say? *It's all the pain that was suffered in Afghanistan by some soldiers who are either dead or not here any more? And it's my dead ex-husband?*

'Andy!' DI Routledge yelled at DS Woods. 'Do we have any ear defenders?'

The second he said that, the screaming abruptly stopped, and the only sound was the scattered crunching of the officers' feet on the shingle driveway and the distant murmuring of the M25 motorway. Somewhere in the surrounding woods, a fox let out a strangled cry that sounded like a distressed baby. The detectives and the police constables and the EOD technicians all looked at each other in bewilderment.

The lieutenant came stalking over. 'Your sergeant assured me that apart from one deceased male, the building was

completely vacant,' he snapped. 'It certainly doesn't sou
like it, does it?'

'Believe me, lieutenant, we're as baffled as you are. One
of the possibilities is that the premises have been wired for
sound and some other technological trickery. We still have an
open book on it, to be honest.'

Again, Lilian said nothing. But she thought to herself:
*DI Routledge, you've seen those screamers with your own
eyes. You were pushed and shoved downstairs by people
you couldn't see, and then you were trapped behind French
windows that could only be opened by some mystic command.
And you still have an 'open book' on it?*

Then again, she guessed that he might be reluctant to admit
that he was coming close to believing that tonight's screaming
could have been caused by ghosts or phantoms or tortured
spirits. He probably didn't want this young officer to put him
down as some kind of crackpot.

'Well, it's all quiet now,' said the lieutenant. 'If it stays quiet,
we'll try going back inside. If that screaming starts up again,
then I don't know how we're going to proceed. It'll be up to
you what the plan of action is then. I'm not subjecting my
men to some auditory assault that could permanently damage
their hearing.'

DI Routledge couldn't take his eyes off St Philomena's and
Lilian thought she had never seen a man look so much as if
he wanted a building to vanish into thin air.

Another hour passed before the EOD technicians came out of
the front door, lifting off their helmets and tugging off their
gloves. One of them marched briskly over to the side of the
driveway and vomited.

What's happened to your friend, I'm afraid it's pretty
devastating,' said one of the technicians. 'I've seen blast
injuries before, as you can imagine. I've seen what's left of
suicide bombers. But my God, nothing like this.'

Lilian nodded. She was desperately tired and cold now, but
she still couldn't bring herself to leave. She couldn't stop herself
from thinking about Tim, or the agonised spirit that Tim had
become. How can you hate a man and still feel responsible
for him? How can you hate a man and still feel sorry for him?

The lieutenant told DI Routledge that it was all clear now
for his officers and the forensic team to enter the hospital.

'I warn you, though. It's not pretty.'

DI Routledge went in first, followed by Dr Horner. The
hallway was so brightly lit with LED lamps that he had to
shield his eyes with his hand. Artyom's head was still lying
on the floor, although his eyes had become sunken now, and
opaque. The floorboards were spattered with bloodstains in a
pattern like a peacock's tail.

DI Routledge walked over to the staircase in his non-
slip overshoes and looked upwards. Artyom's insides were
hanging from the banisters like washing hung out to dry, and
still dripping.

Dr Horner came over to join him, carrying his aluminium
medical case. They turned to each other, but to begin with
neither of them had words. The rest of the forensic team had
already taken out their cameras and were starting to take
flash photographs, so that both men appeared to be jumping
intermittently in shock.

After a while, Dr Horner said, 'Well... I suppose I'd better
go up and take a closer look.'

DI Routledge knew that he should join him, but when
Dr Horner started to climb the stairs he found himself unable

to move. It reminded him of the day of his father's funeral. A.
the other members of the congregation had been filing up to
the open coffin to say goodbye to him, but Barry Routledge
had stayed kneeling on his hassock, with his eyes tight shut,
pretending that he was in prayer. He hadn't been able to bring
himself to look his dead father in the face.

He was still standing there when he became aware of a
movement up on the first-floor landing. Dr Horner was
still only halfway up the stairs, and had stopped to swap
his medical case from one hand to the other. The first-floor
landing was lit up just as brightly as the hallway, and one of
the lamps was shining directly into DI Routledge's eyes.

He squinted, and it was then that he saw a man standing
directly underneath the lamp. A man with tangled hair and a
leather jerkin, whose shoulders were shining in the lamplight.

It can't be, he thought. *He can't still be here, gloating over
the body, not unless he's an out-and-out psycho.*

The man came right up to the banister rail, next to Artyom's
drooping intestines. He looked down at DI Routledge and
even though it was impossible to see his expression, he pointed
at him, as if he were picking him out in a police line-up.

'Andy!' shouted DI Routledge, and suddenly he was
paralysed no longer. He scrambled towards the staircase and
began to mount the stairs two and three at a time. Dr Horner
turned around in surprise and almost dropped his medical
case.

'Andy! He's still here! The bastard's still here!'

DI Routledge pushed past Dr Horner and stumbled up the
last half-dozen stairs. He reached the landing, breathing hard.
The floorboards were strewn with broken bones and lumps
of liver. Artyom's pelvis was propped up in one corner like a
small child's chair.

The man in the leather jerkin, however, had disappeared. There was no sign of him on the flight of stairs that led up to the second-floor landing, and no sound of running footsteps. DI Routledge danced his way gingerly through the grisly debris on the floor until he reached the corridor that led to the first-floor wards. The corridor was deserted, and the only sound was that of DS Woods and three uniformed officers banging their way up the stairs behind him.

'He was here! That Martin Slater! He was right here! I saw him! Dr Horner? You must have seen him! He was right here!'

Dr Horner was still only halfway up the stairs, fumbling with one of the catches on his medical case. 'Sorry, I didn't see a soul.'

'You must have! He was right here! He came up to the rail here and he pointed at me!'

'Are you sure about that, guv?' asked DS Woods. 'Wasn't just a trick of the light or nothing?'

'Of course I'm sure! He had curly hair and a tan leather sleeveless jacket thing! He came right up to the rail and he pointed at me, just like this!'

DS Woods looked down at the floor. 'I can't see any footprints.'

'You wouldn't, not necessarily. Most of the blood's dried up now.'

DC Merrick looked around. 'If he was here, though, where did he go?'

'How the hell should I know? This whole hospital's full of people coming out of nowhere and then disappearing again! There's probably some secret trapdoor somewhere!'

'Secret trapdoor,' DS Woods repeated, as if they were two words in a foreign language.

DI Routledge was about to snap back at him when screaming started again. This time it sounded even loud although that may have been because they were actually inside the hospital. It was so penetrating that it made DI Routledge's eardrums sing like a circular saw cutting through metal, and gave him an instant blinding headache.

DC Merrick and the uniformed officers backed down the stairs and hurried out of the front door, their hands clamped over their ears. Dr Horner dropped his medical case, which fell clonking down the stairs before its lid sprang open in the hallway, scattering his tools and his sample jars all over the floor. Limping, he followed DC Merrick and the officers outside, while DS Woods and DI Routledge came close behind.

DI Routledge slammed the front door behind them, but it did little to block out the screaming, especially since the windows were already broken.

'What in the *world*?' Dr Horner was almost screaming himself, hoarsely, so that DI Routledge could hear him.

'Don't know!' DI Routledge shouted back. 'But we'll have to give the whole building a thorough search before we can send in forensics again!'

'How are we going to do that?' put in DS Woods. 'The dogs don't want to go near the place, and neither do that thermal imaging lot!'

Lilian had left her car and came up to join them.

'I saw him!' DI Routledge told her. 'I saw that gardener of yours, that Martin Slater! But somehow he gave me the slip!'

Lilian looked at St Philomena's. She could easily believe now that the building was alive, with a malevolent mind of its own, and that it was determined to destroy her life and the lives of anybody else who came near it.

The screaming stopped again, and again there was nothing

the crunching of shingle and the distant sound of the motorway. In a way, Lilian found that more frightening than the screaming had continued. It was like the hospital saying, every time you walk inside, you're going to find it unbearable. So stay out.

'It's cursed,' she said.

'What?' said Dr Horner, cupping his hand to his ear.

'Nothing,' she replied, and walked back to her car.

29

It was past midnight now but Lilian stopped halfway down the long hill next to Epsom cemetery and called Moses. He took a long time to answer and when he did she could tell that she had woken him up.

'Moses? I'm sorry to disturb you so late but I've got some really bad news. I need to talk to you, too. Can I come round and see you?'

'You have bad news? What is it?'

'I'd rather tell you face to face, if you don't mind. I'm still shaking, to tell you the truth.'

'Okay. I live on the Wells estate. Do you know where that is?'

'Yes. Give me five minutes and I'll be with you.'

She drove past the racecourse and along the dark winding roads that led to the Wells. Moses lived in a semi-detached house opposite the Save and Smile shop, with a neatly clipped yew hedge outside. Lilian parked outside and went to ring the doorbell, but Moses opened the door before she could press it. He was wearing a green tartan dressing gown and slippers.

'Please *shh*!' he said, touching his fingertip to his lips. 'Grace had a very hard day at her hospice and she was exhausted. But come on in.'

Lilian followed him into the living room. He had already switched on the three-bar electric fire so it was warm.

'Please, sit down. Is there anything I can get you? I hope you do not mind my saying that you are looking a little pale.'

'It's Artyom,' she told him.

Moses slowly sat down opposite her. He knew that Artyom was dead before she said any more. Her expression and her tone of voice gave it away.

'How?' he asked her. 'How did it happen? My God, I was speaking to him only this morning.'

Lilian described how she and Artyom had gone to St Philomena's to find Tim, or the pain that Tim was still suffering, and how they had been stopped by Martin Slater as they tried to leave. She had to stop now and again and press her hand against her heart.

'It isn't really Martin Slater. It can't be. I think it's what Artyom called his Q'areen. The real Martin Slater has been dead for years, and it wouldn't surprise me if it was this Q'areen who killed him.'

Moses nodded gravely. He had tears in his eyes but he made no attempt to wipe them away, and they slowly slid down his cheeks.

'It was one of the things we were talking about this morning,' he said miserably.

'You mean Martin Slater?'

'Yes. Artyom had a strong suspicion that he might be the Q'areen. It was the way in which he could appear and disappear, as if by magic. Spirits are capable of doing that, because they are volatile energy, unlike human beings, whose energy is stable. He was always dressed the same, too. He probably copied the way the real gardener looked in the last moment that he was alive.'

'But why does he keep on killing people, this Q'areen?'

'Again, this was one of the questions that Artyom and I were asking ourselves this morning. Artyom had come to believe that the Q'areen will kill anybody who threatens to release the figures of pain that he is keeping in his custody, or any figures of pain who manage to escape.'

'I don't understand.'

'One of the figures that was being held at St Philomena's was a corporal that I had treated for his serious injuries in Afghanistan, Corporal Terence Simons. We think that he managed to end his pain by passing it on to your surveyor, Alex. And another soldier who was suffering from paralysis managed to pass his or her immobility on to your woman surveyor.

'After that, Alex transferred *his* pain on to his doctor, and your woman surveyor—'

'Charlie.'

'Yes, that was it, Charlie. She managed to pass her paralysis on to her nurse. But before the doctor and the nurse could pass their pain and their paralysis on to anybody else, the Q'areen caught up with them, and killed them both.'

'And Frank Willard? Do you think the Q'areen killed him, too?'

'I would say that it is almost certain. Frank Willard showed all his Army friends to you and to me and the Q'areen could have seen that as a threat to his guardianship, as if we might help them to escape in some way. I am only speculating, Lilian. This may all be madness. But who else could be screaming in St Philomena's except for the servicemen and women who were injured in Afghanistan? And who else could be trying to keep them imprisoned there, except for a vengeful Afghani spirit?'

Lilian sat back. She was beginning to feel warmer and she had stopped shaking, but her mind was in turmoil, turning over and over like clothes in a tumble dryer.

'What are we going to do?' she asked Moses. 'The police don't seem to be capable of dealing with this, do they? I'm getting to the point where all I can think of is walking away and leaving it. If somebody else wants to develop St Philomena's, good luck to them. But then there's my Tim, who's going to be stuck there forever, and all those soldiers. You should have heard them screaming, Moses. I swear to God you never heard such screaming in your life.'

'We can't leave them,' said Moses. He smeared the tears from his face with both hands, and sniffed. 'At least, *I* can't leave them. I just can't. Can you imagine me turning up at the gates of Heaven and St Peter saying to me, "Excuse me, what about that solemn promise you made to take care of those servicemen and women? What happened to that? I can still hear them screaming down in St Philomena's."'

'You don't really believe in Heaven, do you?'

Moses looked up at the crucifix hanging over the fireplace. 'What else is there to believe in?'

'That still doesn't solve the problem of what we're going to do, if anything. Like you say, we could turn our backs and forget about St Philomena's, but I don't think that's possible for either of us, do you?' She looked up at the crucifix too. 'Maybe we should talk to a priest.'

'Would that do any good? I cannot see how. The power that is holding these figures of pain in that hospital has nothing to do with any religion.'

'Artyom told me that if just one person suffered greater pain than anybody else in that hospital, that would bring everybody's pain to an end. Like Jesus on the cross.'

'Yes,' said Moses. 'Artyom also mentioned to me th had found several stories in his research about martyrs w had willingly sacrificed themselves to save others from pain.

'I don't see how that can be true,' Lilian told him. 'In any case, who's going to volunteer to see if it works? That man that we saw in the kitchen, stabbing himself. He was trying to hurt himself even more than he had been hurt when he was wounded. He said that some old man in Afghanistan had told him he could bring his pain to an end if he suffered even worse pain than he had suffered when he was shot. A bit like shock therapy, I suppose. But he was still in agony, so it hadn't worked for him.'

'Perhaps he was not hurting himself as much as he needed to.'

The two of them sat in silence for a while. The clock on the mantelpiece whirred and chimed two, and Lilian said, 'I'd better get home and try to get some sleep, although I doubt if I will.'

'Perhaps we can meet again tomorrow afternoon,' Moses suggested. 'I have to take my granddaughter to the dentist in the morning. I'll call you.'

He took Lilian to the front door. Outside, it was starting to rain, and the drops were pattering on the concrete path.

'Artyom was such a good man,' he said. 'He bore nobody any ill will, no matter what colour or religion they were. There are some Russians who are like that. Very cultured. Citizens of the world, rather than Russia. I am sure there will be many people who will miss him sorely. I had not seen him in a long time, but I know I will.'

'Do you know, there's one thing that puzzles me,' said Lilian. 'If Martin Slater killed Artyom because he thought Artymon was going to free all the figures of pain that he's

keeping cooped up at St Philomena's, and if he killed
ank Willard for the same reason, why hasn't he done *me*
ny harm?'

'I think the answer to that is simple. You're a woman, and
to the Q'areen, women are less important than insects.'

DI Routledge arrived home almost at the same time that Lilian
was leaving the Wells. He had left three officers guarding St
Philomena's for the rest of the night, with strict instructions
to let nobody inside.

He climbed wearily out of his car and went indoors, being
careful not to make a noise and wake up Audrey. For the first
time in his entire career as a detective, his mind was a blank.
He had absolutely no idea what to do next. It was not only
a question of reporting his progress to his senior officers and
the media, without sounding as if he had completely lost his
marbles. It was a question of how he was going to clear those
screamers out of St Philomena's so that his investigation into
the killing of Artyom Gorokhov could continue.

After he had been jostled down the stairs by what had felt
like invisible people, he was quite convinced that the hospital
was haunted by some inexplicable forces, although he couldn't
even begin to imagine what they were. They certainly weren't
ghosts – at least, not the kind of ghosts who walked around
draped in sheets, or who could walk through closed doors.
They had felt as solid as real people, and he had even been
able to feel their clothes.

He went through to the kitchen, opened the fridge and
took out a carton of milk. He always developed a stomach
ache when he was stressed, and milk helped to soothe it. He
poured himself a glass and stood by the kitchen window to

drink it, staring at his reflection. He saw a flicker of lightnr
in the distance, and heard the grumble of thunder, and spot
of rain started to fall outside.

It was then that he realised there was a man standing
underneath the fir tree at the end of the garden. The man
had his arms folded, as if he had been patiently waiting for
DI Routledge to notice him. His face was hidden by the
shadow from the overhanging branches, but DI Routledge
could make out that he was wearing a shiny sleeveless top. A
leather jerkin. A leather jerkin and wellington boots, just like
a gardener might wear.

DI Routledge unlocked the kitchen door and stepped
outside, on to the patio. It had not yet started to rain in
earnest, although he felt a cold drop on the top of his head,
and another against his cheek.

'Hey, you!' he called out, although not too loudly, because
their bedroom was right above the kitchen.

The man didn't answer, but continued to stand under the
fir tree with his arms folded. DI Routledge crossed the lawn
towards him, taking his phone out of his inside pocket and
switching on the flashlight. The man half turned his face
away when DI Routledge shone the flashlight directly into
his eyes, but stayed where he was. There was no doubt about
it, though. There was no mistaking the tan leather jerkin and
the tangled grey hair. He was Martin Slater, the gardener from
St Philomena's.

'What the hell do you think you're doing in my garden?'
DI Routledge demanded. 'How did you find out where I live?
You know that you're wanted for questioning, don't you?'

'Take that light from out of my eyes,' Martin Slater replied
flatly.

'I'm arresting you on suspicion of murder.'

Oh. You're arresting me on suspicion of murder? And what about all the innocent men, women and children who were murdered by *your* people? Who is going to arrest your murderers, and bring them to trial?'

'I have no idea what you're talking about. I'm talking about Dr Wells and Nurse O'Grady at St Helier Hospital, as well as Frank Willard at Marion Crosby's hospice, Timothy Chesterfield on Epsom racecourse and Artyom Gorokhov at St Philomena's Hospital. That's who I'm talking about.'

'Is that all? The names of my people who have been murdered are far too many to remember. Do you know how many?'

'I don't know who your people are, sunshine, and frankly I don't care how many. I'm arresting you for five homicides and if you know what's good for you, you'll accompany me to the nearest police station without any further argument.'

'More than seventy thousand,' Martin Slater told him. 'Seventy thousand people whose only crime was to have been born.'

'I told you, I'm not interested,' said DI Routledge. 'You can either come along with me quietly or else I'll have to call for some reinforcements. It's up to you. Even if you try to make a run for it we'll catch up with you, you can bet on that.'

'Look at me,' said Martin Slater.

'What?'

'I said, "look at me". You can see me clearly, can't you?'

'Are you coming, or not? Do you want a formal caution, is that it? All right, then. You are under arrest on suspicion of murder. You do not have to say anything, but it may harm your defence if you do not mention when questioned something which you later rely on in court. Anything you do say may be given in evidence. Amen.'

'Look at me.'

'I am looking at you.'

'I've no desire to kill you. You're only doing what you're employed to do.'

'Oh well, that's big of you.'

'One reason I want you to stay alive is so you can warn your colleagues that they need to keep well away from St Philomena's. Not only now, but forever.'

'Really? Then how about you giving me some idea how we can stop all that screaming and bumping around and people getting hurt?'

'Look at me.'

'I am, damn it.'

'Here – arrest me.'

Martin Slater held out his hands, palms uppermost. DI Routledge reached into his jacket pocket and pulled out the black nylon zip ties that he always carried. He tried to take a step towards Martin Slater but he found that he was unable to move. Both his legs were completely numb. He strained and grunted but he couldn't feel them at all.

'What the hell have you done to me?' he demanded.

'Look at me.'

'What the hell have you done to my legs?'

Martin Slater didn't answer. He was staring at DI Routledge but his grey eyes were strangely unfocused, as if he were high on crystal meth. DI Routledge wanted to look away, but he found that his neck muscles were locked, and when he tried to close his own eyes, the lids refused to come down.

'What is this? Some sort of hypnosis?' DI Routledge's eyes were beginning to water, because he couldn't blink.

He attempted to shine his flashlight back into Martin Slater's face, but now his arms stiffened, and his fingers froze.

phone fell to the ground, and it lit up a grinning plaster
ome in the nearby flower bed.

Now DI Routledge felt that his eyes were swelling, and
he was aware of a tugging sensation inside his eye sockets.
He tried to lift his hands to cover his eyes, but his elbows
wouldn't bend.

'What are you doing?' he shouted at Martin Slater. 'What
the fuck are you doing to my eyes?'

The tugging sensation in his eyes grew stronger. He could
actually feel his eyeballs crackle as they were pulled away
from the muscles that surrounded them. He stood in the
middle of the lawn, quivering with pain and fear, but unable
to move. He shouted again, this time incoherently. Upstairs,
behind him, the bedroom light was switched on. The curtains
were drawn back, and Audrey appeared in her nightgown,
peering out into the night.

Both of DI Routledge's eyes popped out of their sockets, so
that for a few seconds he looked almost clownish. His optic
nerves were stretched to the limit like wet string and then they
snapped, so that his eyeballs dropped into the grass.

Blinded, swallowed up by darkness, DI Routledge swayed
and then sank down on to his knees.

'There,' said Martin Slater, stepping out from under the
fir tree. It was raining harder now, but DI Routledge stayed
where he was, bent over the lawn, his fingers held up to the
slippery cavities where his eyes had been. He was in such deep
shock that he was silent.

'I've spared you,' said Martin Slater. 'I could have done to
you what I did to the others, but it's enough that you'll never
be able to see the world again, or what you or anybody else
has done to it.'

The bedroom window opened up. Audrey called out,

'Barry? Barry, is that you down there? What's your ph[...] doing, down on the lawn? Barry?'

DI Routledge started to crawl across the wet grass, with the rain beating down on his back. Martin Slater stood watching him for a while, expressionless, as if he were watching a tortoise. But then Audrey called out, 'Hold on, Barry! I'm coming down!' and closed the bedroom window.

Martin Slater walked to the side of the house, past the dustbins, and out through the gate. He left the gate open, but if Audrey had gone out to the front of the house, and looked down the street, she would have seen nobody.

Lightning flickered again, much closer this time, followed by a loud bellow of thunder.

30

Lilian had been unable to sleep all night but she stayed in bed until half-past nine. When she eventually got up, she took a long shower, washing her hair, and then she dressed in a floppy black turtleneck sweater and jeans. She didn't bother to struggle into her muffin-top Spanx today.

Once she had made herself a mug of coffee, she called David. She asked him to contact the electrical contractors who were booked to reconnect the power supply at St Philomena's and tell them that the job would have to be postponed, and also to get in touch with Johnson's in Guildford and cancel their new surveyor.

'Are you all right, Lilian?' David asked her. 'You sound a bit wobbly, if you don't mind me saying so.'

'What do you think, after what happened yesterday?'

'Well, take it easy today. I'll call you later.'

Lilian took her coffee into the living room and opened her laptop. She scrolled through all the plans and ideas that she had been working on to turn St Philomena's into a luxury residential development. They represented hours and hours of wasted effort, because she was sure now that Philomena Park was never going to happen. She was sure too that her career had been seriously set back, even if it wasn't completely shipwrecked.

ᴐger French texted her again and again, wanting to know
ᴧat was going on at St Philomena's. When she didn't answer
ᴧm, he started to ring her, first on her mobile and then on her
ᴧandline. She let him ring. She knew that if she tried to explain
what had happened yesterday evening, it would sound like
hysterical nonsense; and worse than that, she would start to
shiver again, and probably cry.

It was impossible for her to stop thinking about Artyom
exploding, right in front of her. It was impossible for her to
forget the pain that Tim was continuing to suffer, even though
he was dead. It was impossible not to hear that hideous chorus
of screaming, and to wonder if all those soldiers would have
volunteered if they had known that they were at risk not
only of being wounded, but of suffering the pain from those
wounds for all eternity.

She put on her coat and went out for a walk, just to clear
her mind. She crossed the road to Rosebery Park and sat
on a bench next to the duck pond. She had always felt in
control of her life. That was why she had been able to walk
out on Tim and file for divorce when he had started to drink,
and to hit her. But now she felt completely helpless, swept
away by events and by powers that she couldn't understand.
Despite that helplessness, however, she still felt she was
responsible for those men suffering that endless agony at
St Philomena's, and that she should go on trying to find
some way of saving them. How could she leave them there,
screaming?

Her phone trilled again and she took it out of her coat
pocket. It was Roger French again, and this time she answered
him.

'Roger?'

'Would you kindly explain what the blue blazes is going

on, Lilian? I've been trying to contact you all morning. Whe
have you been?'

'To hell, Roger. And I'm not back yet.'

She walked home and didn't answer him again, even though
he kept on sending her texts and her laptop was pinging
incessantly. It was a grey cloudy day and it began to get dark
early, but she didn't switch on her lights. She made herself a
cheese and tomato sandwich but when she took it into the
sitting room, she couldn't bring herself to eat it. She felt that
even one mouthful would have choked her.

She closed her eyes but all she could see was Artyom's head
spinning through the air, and his bowels flopping over the
banisters like heaps of wet washing.

By five o'clock she was beginning to wonder why Moses
hadn't called her, as he had promised. He was the only person
who really understood what was happening at St Philomena's,
and she badly needed to talk to him about it. Even if he still
had no idea how they could end the suffering of those tortured
souls who were still wandering through the wards, at least he
wouldn't think that she was mad.

She sent him a text message, asking when and where he
wanted to meet. He didn't answer, so after ten minutes she
called him at home.

Grace answered. 'Hallo? Akinyemi household.'

'Is Moses there? This is Lilian Chesterfield.'

'No, Moses has gone out.'

'Do you know what time he's going to be home? He
promised to call me, that's all.'

'As a matter of fact, I am a little worried about him. He
said he would be back by four o'clock but there is no sign of

...n yet. I have called him but he didn't answer. That is unlike ...im.'

'Yes, I've tried calling him too. Well – when he does get back, would you be kind enough to tell him that I rang, and could he ring me back? He has my number.'

'Very well, yes, I will do that. But if you hear from him first, please tell him that his wife is wondering what has happened to him.'

Lilian checked her WhatsApp messages, because her phone had been pinging again and again, but all except two were from Roger French. The other two were from David, confirming that he had spoken to the electrical contractors and to Johnson's.

She checked her emails as well, because she had no alert tone. It was then that she saw that Moses had sent her a message, less than ten minutes ago.

When you find me, you will know that I have kept my pledge to the men I swore to protect. All of them will soon be free of their pain and so will I. I wish you a bright future.

Lilian read the message again, with a growing sense of dread. What did Moses mean by telling her that he had kept his pledge? And even more disturbing, what did he mean when he said that 'All of them will soon be free of their pain and so will I'?

'Oh my God,' she said, out loud.

She picked up her purse and her keys, and then went through to the hall and took down her coat. After she had opened her front door, though, she stopped, and went back into the living room for the plastic bag with Frank Willard's night goggles. Then she hurried outside, climbed into her car, and drove away from the kerb on slithering tyres.

She drove as fast as she dared, past the racecourse, and it

took her less than ten minutes to reach St Philomena's.
police had blocked the main entrance to the hospital w
orange traffic cones and she could see that a squad car wa
parked across the driveway, but she had planned to park
where Tim had left his car, in the muddy lay-by next to the
back gate. When she reached it, she saw that Moses had
parked here too.

Once she had locked her car, she swung open the gate and
climbed the slope towards St Philomena's, carrying the bag
with the night goggles. The hospital building was in total
darkness, and the only sound was the endless tinnitus of
distant motorway traffic and an owl hooting.

She went through the stable yard to the back door that
led to the cloakroom. Ever since the first time she had found
herself locked inside the building, she had made sure she
carried the key to that door and that it remained unbolted,
although she had expected that she would want to open it
from the inside, rather than the outside.

The hospital was quiet. She walked into the hallway and
stood there for a moment, listening. She didn't want to switch
on her flashlight just yet, in case the police officers keeping
watch outside caught sight of it. There was enough light for
her to make out the portrait of Sir Edmond Carver, staring
at her dismally. He looked as if he regretted having ever built
this house, or at least for his portrait to hang here for so long,
and to witness so much pain and suffering.

Lilian went across to the foot of the staircase. 'Moses?' she
called out. 'Moses, are you here?'

There was no reply, although she could hear a door softly
rattling upstairs. Yet Moses' car was parked outside, so he
must be here, even though she couldn't think how he had
managed to get inside. Maybe he had forced open a window.

e was undecided if she ought to go upstairs first, to the
d floor, and see if she could find Tim again. But Moses had
id '*all of them*' and the first time she had seen all of Frank's
Army friends gathered together was in the reception room.
She took two steps up the stairs, but then she hesitated and
came back down.

She walked along the corridor that led to the reception
room, trailing her fingers against the panelled walls to guide
her because it was so dark. The reception room itself was a
little lighter, because of its high windows and the mirrors that
surrounded it on all sides, but she still managed to bump into
one of the chairs that had been left by the door.

'Moses?' she called out again. 'Are you here, Moses?'

There was still no response. She reached into her bag , took
out the night goggles and fitted them on to her head. When
she switched them on and saw the whole reception room in
livid green, she saw at once why Moses hadn't answered her.
He was lying on his back in the middle of the room, next to
a tipped-over chair.

'Moses!' she exclaimed. 'Moses, what's happened?'

She lifted up the night goggles. Moses' eyes were open and
he was staring back at her, but it was plain that he couldn't
see her. He wasn't breathing, either. She knelt down beside
him and pressed her fingertips to his neck, the way she had
been taught at first-aid classes, but she could feel no pulse.

She tried compressing his chest, and kept at it for nearly
three minutes before it became obvious by the way that he
was lolling lifelessly from side to side that he was beyond
revival.

'Oh, Moses,' she said, sitting back and sadly shaking her
head.

She switched on her flashlight. She would have to tell the

police that she had found Moses lying here dead, so t
was no point in trying to hide her presence here any mo
But it was then that she saw why he had come here tonigh
and realised what he had been intending to do. Only a few
feet away, on the seat of one of the chairs, he had placed
a red jerry can, and next to the jerry can there was a box
of matches.

*When you find me, you will know that I have kept my
pledge to the men I swore to protect.*

'Oh, Moses,' she repeated. 'Oh, Moses.'

She stood up, but as she stood up she heard hammering on
the hospital's front door, and shouting.

'Who's in there? Open up!'

Lilian looked down at Moses. He had come here to sacrifice
himself for the men he had promised to care for, but the stress
must have been too much for his heart. He had told her that
he had never been able to forget the horror of his service in
Afghanistan, and now it had caught up with him, almost in
the same way that the soldiers in St Philomena's had never
been allowed to forget their pain.

'Open up! Police!'

She was about to go back to the hallway when she heard a
loud banging, followed by a splintering crack. The police must
have kicked the front door open, or used a door enforcer – a
'bosher' or a 'big red key'.

At the same instant, the screaming started up again. This
time, it sounded like a hundred piercing voices, all screaming
off-key. Lilian pulled up her coat collar to cover her ears, but
the noise was so disorientating that she found herself circling
around and around, barely able to think what she should do
next.

It sounded as if the people who were screaming were all

...nd her. She pulled down the night goggles and fitted them
...er her eyes, and when she switched them on she saw why
...ne screaming was so loud. The reception room was crowded
with soldiers, even more than Frank Willard had summoned
up, two hundred or more. Even though Lilian could only see
them in iridescent green, she could see how badly injured
most of them were. They were missing legs and arms and in
some cases half of their faces had been blown or shot off.

They screamed and screamed in their everlasting agony,
but their screaming was obviously not intended to frighten
her. It was like children screaming – a desperate expression
of their pain, and their realisation that they were going to be
suffering that pain for ever, even after they were dead.

They shuffled towards her, and those who still had arms
were holding them out, begging her to give them release. And
it was then that Tim appeared, pushing his way between them.

'Tim!' she said.

'Forgive me, Lil! Please forgive me!'

Lilian looked down again at Moses lying on the floor and
she knew then with a strange calmness what she had to do.
It was her destiny. It was her fate. She had not been brought
here to St Philomena's for any other reason but this. Not to
develop this one-time hospital into luxury apartments, but
to redeem the pain that had been suffered by these soldiers
fighting a war in a country that wasn't theirs.

Tim watched her as she went over to the chair, picked up
the jerry can and unscrewed its lid. He was the only one out of
the throng who wasn't screaming, although he was clenching
and unclenching his fists in agony, and in anticipation of what
he could see that Lilian was about to do.

She knelt on the floor next to Moses, peeled off the night
goggles and tossed them aside, so that all the soldiers in the

room vanished, and it appeared as if she and Moses we
the only ones there. Their screaming, however, continued, s
shrill now that it was making her eardrums sing, and she was
deafened.

She lifted up the jerry can. The smell of petrol made her
gag, and she had to steady herself for a moment and take two
or three deep breaths, which only made her gag again, and
her mouth fill up with petrol-tasting bile.

'Sorry, God,' she said silently. 'Sorry, Mum. Sorry, Dad.'

With that, she closed her eyes tight shut and poured the
petrol over her head. It was surprisingly cold, and she shivered
as it ran into her coat collar and down her back. When she
had emptied the jerry can, she dropped it on the floor beside
her and reached for the matchbox, squinting against the acrid
fumes with only one eye open.

She took out a match, and was about to strike it when the
door to the billiard room opened up, and Martin Slater came
storming out. He struggled across the reception room floor
towards her, forcing his way through the invisible crowd of
soldiers. His face was distorted in fury.

'*Stop, you bitch!*' he roared at her, and she could hear him
even over the sound of the screaming. '*Don't you dare do
that!*'

Lilian struck the match, and it flared into life.

'*Stop!*' Martin Slater roared again, and suddenly he was
no longer Martin Slater with his tangled grey hair and his
tan leather jerkin. He was a ghostly figure in billowing white
robes, with red eyes like two smouldering coals and black
hair that was standing up on end as if it were being blown by
a hurricane.

Lilian lifted the burning match to her chin, and her face
instantly became a mask of flames. Then the fire engulfed the

st of her petrol-soaked clothing, until she was ablaze from head to foot. For a few seconds, until it all frizzled away, her hair rose up in the air like that of the spirit, except that it was burning.

The Spirit of Pain tried to wrap itself around her and put out the fire, but by now she was blazing too fiercely, and the spirit's robes caught fire too. The two of them were trapped in a fiery embrace, the martyr and the murderer, immolated together.

Lilian had never known that pain as intense as this could even exist. As her skin shrivelled, and before her nerve endings were burned away, she felt an agony that was so far beyond anything she had ever experienced before that she could think of it only as holy.

She was blind by the time the spirit had wrapped its arms around her, so she was unable to see its face, but its mouth was stretched wide open and its eyes were actually smoking.

After a few minutes, Lilian could no longer feel anything at all. She didn't even hear the screaming fade away. By the time two police officers came into the reception room, following the smell of burning, she was nothing but a seated figure made out of charred flesh and bones. The spirit had been reduced to ash, and had blown away in powdery grey streaks across the floor.

The hospital was utterly silent.

Lilian was woken up by the sound of a cuckoo calling.
She opened her eyes and to her surprise she found that
she was lying on a grassy hillock surrounded by wildflowers –
daisies and kingcups and enchanter's nightshade. The sun was
shining and there was a warm breeze blowing.

She sat up. Not far away, Moses was sitting beside a
sparkling pond. He was chewing a grass stem and tossing
pebbles across the pond, so that they bounced, and when they
bounced, the water glittered.

'Moses?' she said.

He turned to her and raised his hand in greeting.

'Lilian, you're awake!'

'Moses, where are we?'

Moses smiled and said, 'Can't you guess?'

About the author

GRAHAM MASTERTON is best known as a writer
of horror and thrillers, but his career as an author
spans many genres, including historical epics and sex-
advice books. His first horror novel, *The Manitou*, became
a bestseller and was made into a film starring Tony Curtis.
In 2019, Graham was given a Lifetime Achievement Award
by the Horror Writers Association. He is also the author of
the Katie Maguire series of crime thrillers, which have
sold more than 1.5 million copies worldwide.